# Lights, Love
# &
# Lip Gloss

**Hollywood High series**

*Hollywood High*
*Get Ready for War*
*Put Your Diamonds Up*
*Lights, Love & Lip Gloss*

**Also by Ni-Ni Simone**
**The Ni-Ni Girl Chronicles**
*Shortie Like Mine*
*If I Was Your Girl*
*A Girl Like Me*
*Teenage Love Affair*
*Upgrade U*
*No Boyz Allowed*
*True Story*

**Also by Amir Abrams**
*Crazy Love*
*The Girl of His Dreams*
*Caught Up*
*Diva Rules*

Published by Kensington Publishing Corp.

# Lights, Love & Lip Gloss

## *Hollywood* HIGH

# Ni-Ni Simone
# Amir Abrams

Dafina KTeen Books
KENSINGTON PUBLISHING CORP.
www.kensingtonbooks.com

DAFINA KTEEN BOOKS are published by

Kensington Publishing Corp.
119 West 40th Street
New York, NY 10018

All Kensington titles, imprints, and distributed lines are available at special quantity discounts for bulk purchases for sales promotion, premiums, fund-raising, and educational or institutional use.

Special book excerpts or customized printings can also be created to fit specific needs. For details, write or phone the office of the Kensington Special Sales Manager: Kensington Publishing Corp., 119 West 40th Street, New York, NY 10018. Attn. Special Sales Department. Phone: 1-800-221-2647.

KTeen logo Reg. U.S. Pat. & TM Off.
Sunburst logo Reg. U.S. Pat. & TM Off.

ISBN-13: 978-0-7582-8854-7
ISBN-10: 0-7582-8854-9
First Kensington Trade Paperback Printing: January 2015

eISBN-13: 978-0-7582-8855-4
eISBN-10: 0-7582-8855-7
First Kensington Electronic Edition: January 2015

10 9 8 7 6 5 4 3 2 1

Printed in the United States of America

*To all the gossip hags, socialite lovers &*
*drama queens…*
*This one's for you!*

## ACKNOWLEDGMENTS

We'd like to thank God for His grace and continued blessings. And to give a special thanks to all the readers and fans for the love.

# Acknowledgments

# 1

# Rich

*2 a.m.*

*I will not be played.*
Or ignored.
And especially by some broke-side jawn.
Never!
I don't care if he is six feet and hey-hey-hollah-back-lil-daddy fine.
Or how much I scribble, doodle, and marry my first name to his last name.
He will *never* be allowed to come at me crazy.
Not Rich Gabrielle Montgomery.
Not this blue-blooded, caramel—thick in the hips, small in the waist, and fly in the face—bust-'em-down princess.
Psst.
Puhlease.
Swerve!

And yeah, once upon a time everything was Care Bear sweet: rainbows, unicorns, and fairy tales. He was feeling me and I was kind enough to let him think we'd be happily ever after.

But. Suddenly.

He turned on me.

Real sucker move.

And so what if I keyed up his car.

Tossed a brick through his windshield.

Kicked a dent in his driver's-side door.

Made a scene at his apartment building and his nosy neighbor called the police on me.

*Still...*

Who did he think he was? Did he forget he was some gutter-rat East Coast transplant?

He better stay in his freakin' lane.

I've been good to him!

I replaced the windshield and had all the brick particles swept from the parking lot.

The next day, I topped myself and replaced the entire car with a brand new black Maserati with a red bow on top.

The ungrateful thot sent the car back. Bow still intact.

I've done it all.

And how does he repay me?

With dead silence.

I don't think so.

I don't have to take that!

And if I have to sit here in my gleaming silver Spyder, in this dusty Manhattan Beach apartment complex, and wait another three hours for Justice Banks to get home, I will.

\* \* \*

*4 a.m.*

I should leave.
Go home.
Call my boyfriend, Knox.
And forget Justice.
If he can't appreciate a mature, sixteen-year-old woman like me, then screw him.
No. I can't leave.
I have to make this right.
No, I don't.
Yes. I do.

*5 a.m.*

Where is he?

*6 a.m.*

There he is.
But where is he coming from?
Was he with some chick?
My eyes followed a black Honda Accord with a dimpled driver's door, as it pulled into the half-empty parking lot and parked in the spot marked 203.
The red sun eased its way into the sky as I pulled in and pushed out three deep breaths, doing all I could to stop the butterflies from racing through my stomach.
*I should go home. Right now.*
After all, he is not my man.
My man is at his campus at San Diego State, thinking about me.

I chewed on the corner of my bottom lip. Swallowed. And eyed the brick two-story, U-shaped, garden-style complex Justice lived in and the small beach across the street where an overdressed homeless woman leaned over the wooden barrier and stared at the surfers riding the rough waves.

"What the —? Are you stalking me?"

I sucked in a breath and held it.

Justice.

I oozed air out the side of my mouth and turned to look out my window. There he was: ice grilling me. Top lip curled up, brown gaze narrowed and burning through me.

*Say something! Do something!*

"Can I, umm...talk to you?" I opened my door and stepped out. "For a minute? Please." I pulled in the left corner of my bottom lip and bit into it.

"Nah. You can't say ish to me, son. What you can do, though, is stop stalkin' me 'n' go get you some help. Thirsty. Loony bird. If I didn't call you, it was for a reason. Deal wit' it. Now get back in ya whip 'n' peel off."

Oh. No. He. Didn't! This scrub is outta control!

"For real? Slow down, low down. When did you become the president? You don't dismiss me. This is a public lot. I ain't leavin'. And you will listen to me. Now, I have *not* been waiting here for seven hours for you to come out the side of your neck and call me a freakin' stalker. You don't get to disrespect me. And loony bird? Really? Seems you've taken your vocabulary to new heights; now maybe we can work on your losin' career. And yeah, maybe I've been waiting here all night. But the last thing I am is some *loony* bird."

Justice arched a brow.

"Or thirsty."

"Whatever." He tossed two fingers in the air, turned his back to me, and walked away.

Unwanted tears beat against the backs of my eyes. But I refused to cry. "Know what, I'm not about to sweat you," I shouted, my trembling voice echoing through the early morning breeze. "I'm out here trying to talk to you. Trying to apologize to you. Trying to tell you that I miss you! That all I do is think about you! But instead of you being understanding, you're being a jerk!"

Justice continued walking. Just as he reached the stairs, I got out of my car and ran behind him. Grabbed his hand. "Why are you doing this?"

He snatched his hand away, spun around, and mushed me in the center of my forehead. "I'm sick of your ish, ma. Word is bond. You don't come runnin' up on me." He took a step closer to me. And we stood breasts to chest, my lips to the base of his neck.

"Justice—"

"Shut up!" His eyes dropped eight inches.

I needed to go. I took a step back and turned to walk away. He reached for my hand and quickly turned me back toward him. Pulled me into his chest.

The scent of his Obsession cologne made love to my nose and I wanted to melt beneath his large hands, which rested on my hips.

He tsked. "Yo, you selfish, you know that, right?" He lifted my chin, taking a soft bite out of it. "Word is bond. What's really good witchu?" He tilted his head and gazed at me. "Just when I start to treat you like no one else matters, you turn around 'n' play me. Leavin' me *yeah boo* letters 'n' money on the nightstand, like I'm some clown mofo. I don't have time for that. And then you get mad 'n' eff up my ride, like that ish is cute. You lucky I ain't knockin' you out for that, for-real-for-real. Yo, you a real savage for that."

I sucked my teeth, feeling the light ocean breeze kiss my face. "I was pissed off!"

He released his hold on my hips. "Oh word? So every time you get pissed you gon' jump off the cliff? Is that it? Yo, you crazy if you think I'ma put up wit' that." He paused and shook his head in disbelief. "Yo, I gotta go. I'm outta here." He took a step to the side of me.

"Wait, don't go!" I stepped into his path. "Justice, please!"

He flicked his right hand as if he were flinging water from his fingertips. "Leave."

I ran back into his path, practically tripping over my feet. "Would you listen to me?!" Tears poured down my cheeks. "Dang, I'm sorry! What else do you want me to do?"

"Nothing."

I threw my hands up in defeat. "I keep calling you and calling you! And calling you!"

"And stalkin' me. Playin' ya'self. Comin' over here bangin' on my door like you crazy, then keyin' up my whip. What kinda ish you on, yo?"

I felt like somebody had taken a blade to my throat.

*Play myself?*

Never.

He had me confused. "I don't deserve—"

"You deserve exactly what ya greasy hand called for. You really tried to play me, yo. You got the game jacked, yo. I ain't no soft dude, real talk. I will take it to ya face." He paused and looked me over. "*Then* you had ya dude roll up on me and sneak me? Word? Are you serious? That ish got me real hot, yo." He paused again. "I shoulda burned a bullet in his chest for that punk move." His dark eyes narrowed. "You lucky I ain't knock ya teeth out."

Was I having an out-of-body experience? No boy had ever spoken to me like this. Ever. I was stunned. Shocked. Confused. Desperate. Scared...

I didn't know if I was quiet because I couldn't think of anything to say or because I felt a tinge of fear that told me I needed to shut up. The bottom of my stomach felt like it had fallen to my feet. I watched him step toward me and I wondered if this was the end.

He yanked me by my right arm. "Let me tell you somethin'. I don't know what you standin' there thinkin' 'bout or what's 'bout to come outta ya mouth, but it better not be nothin' slick." He paused and I swallowed. "Otherwise, you gon' be pickin' ya'self up from this concrete. Or better yet, the evenin' news will be 'bout you floatin' facedown in the ocean."

"I-I-I-I," I stuttered, doing all I could to collect my thoughts. "If you would just listen to me! I didn't have anybody sneak you. I didn't do that!"

His eyes peered into mine. "Well, somebody hit me from behind! Now who was it? Who?!"

Without a second thought. Without concern. Without regard or a moment of hesitation I pushed out, "London!"

That's right. London.

That crazy thot.

My ex-bestie.

Another one who turned on me. Tried to take hate to new heights by inviting me out to Club Tantrum and attacking me. For no rhyme or reason.

"London?" Justice repeated in disbelief. I could tell by the look he gave me that what I'd said took him aback. He frowned. "Are you serious? London?"

"Yes, London! She's the real thirsty loony bird. Real crazy! She even jumped me at the club the other night! I know you had to see the blogs."

"What the . . ." He quickly caught himself. "Do I *look* like the type of dude checkin' blogs?" He pushed his index finger into my right temple, forcing my neck to slant to the left. "Now say somethin' else, stupid."

My kneecaps knocked, my heart pounded, and my throat tightened.

*I should leave.* This was a bad idea. Apparently, he can't appreciate me standing here, trying to woman up and handle our situation.

"Do you hear me talkin' to you, yo?!" he screamed in my face. "I *said*, what you mean it was London?"

I hesitated. "She just came from nowhere. You and I were standing there talking and the next thing I knew, you hit the ground and there was London hovered over you with nunchucks in her hand!"

I searched his eyes to see if he believed me. The truth was it wasn't London. It was Spencer, my real, loyal, ride-or-die bestie. She'd snuck him. Hit him in the back of his head. And when he didn't move, Spencer and I got scared, took off, and left him for dead.

But none of that was the point. London deserved to wear this one. Especially since I was done with her. "I'm telling you it was London! She came from nowhere. You hit the ground and she was there with nunchucks in her hand!"

"London?" he repeated, shaking his head. "I thought she was over in Italy somewhere."

"Lies! She was never in Milan. That lunatic was home all along, curled up in the bed! And I just knew she killed you! I just knew it!" Timely tears poured down my cheeks. "I'm sorry that I left you. I am. I was *sooooo* scared. I didn't know what to do. I called the hospitals! I called the morgues. I was even willing to pay for your funeral. I'm just so sorry. And when you were on that ground, motionless, I tried to shake you and you wouldn't move. London took off! I heard sirens. I got scared and I just ran!"

I boldly took a step toward him and pressed my wet cheeks into his chest. "You gotta believe me, Justice. I just knew you were dead. I really did and I didn't know what to do. I thought the police were coming. And I didn't want them to think it was me who killed you so I ran too! It was stupid." I stammered, "I-I-I left my car. Everything! It was crazy! I just got caught up in the moment! I thought you were hurt. I thought you were dead! You weren't moving! You should've seen the look in her eyes! That girl's crazy!"

I wept into his chest and he wrapped his arms around me and squeezed.

I batted my wet lashes. "Baby, did you do something to that girl?" I asked.

"Oh, so now I'm ya baby?" he asked in disbelief.

"Yes, Justice. Yes. Of course you're my baby."

"Really?"

"Yes. But why does London hate you so much? Did the two of you used to be a couple or something? I thought you were only friends."

"Yeah, we used to be friends. All that's dead now." He

wiped my wet cheeks with his thumbs. "Now, back to you." He lifted my chin and placed a finger against my lips. "The next time you come outta pocket, tryna slick-talk me, I'ma slap ya mouth up." He tapped my lips lightly and I kissed his finger. He snatched his finger away. "Nah, I don't think so. You still in the doghouse wit' me. Now what you gonna do to get outta it?"

"What do you want me to do?" I whined. "I'll do whatever."

"What you *think* I want you to do?"

I slid my arms around his thick neck and whispered against his chin. "I can show you better than I can tell you. Can I come inside?"

"Yeah." He ran his hands over the outline of my body. "Right after you call ya man." He pulled his cell phone out of his back pocket. "And dead it."

My heart dropped. "*Whaaaaaat?* Clutching pearls!" My eyes popped open and I felt my breath being snatched.

"You heard me. Call that punk now." He pushed the phone toward me.

I took a step back and he took a step forward.

"You said you'll do anything, right? So do it. You said I'm ya baby. Then prove it. 'Cause, real ish, yo... I'm second to none."

"You being second to none and me breaking up with Knox, my soul mate, my future husband and future baby daddy, are two different things. He has nothing to do with this."

"Oh word?"

"Word. No. He. Does. Not." I shook my head and placed a hand up on my hip. "You need to learn to play your role as a side piece 'cause you are all out of control. Appreciate the time I'm spending with you instead of standing here and thinking about my man. Like really? Who does that?"

Justice popped me on the mouth, just enough for it to sting but not enough for it to hurt. "Let me be real clear wit' you: You ain't gettin' upstairs. We ain't kickin' it. I ain't effen witchu till you dead it wit' dude. Got it? Now poof. Outta here." He forcefully turned me around, practically yanked me back to my car, snatched open the door, and pushed me inside.

# 2

# London

*Milan, Italy*

The moment had come. It was three thirty p.m., which meant it was six thirty in the morning back in L.A. Back where I wanted to be. Home. Curled up in my bed. Crying my eyes out. But I was here. Caught up in day one of Europe's most prestigious weeklong fashion extravaganza.

I'd stepped on the scale this morning, weighing—to my mother's delight—one hundred fifteen pounds of flesh and bones. Twiglet. That's what I'd become. A tall, thin human hanger. No longer a giant, lumbering water buffalo. I felt like an alien. Wafty and slender. Chiseled cheekbones. Bug-eyed. Elongated neck. Protruding collarbone.

Despite my emotionally fragile state, I'd finally become everything my mother physically hoped for. And in a matter of minutes, the lights would go down, the music would begin, and every model, including myself, would gallop down the catwalk.

All I had to do was survive the next five days, then it'd be over. Finally.

I blinked, staring into the sea of super-thin models who would be gliding down the runway in gorgeous couture and flawless makeup, then peeked out through the opening of our large tent.

Huge posters of famous models for fashion designers DKNY, Gucci, and Cavalli hung outside the cathedral's windows. The cobblestone streets had been literally turned into catwalks. Piazza del Duomo—the heart of Milan's central square surrounded by glamorous boutiques and charming restaurants—was one of the outdoor venues where paparazzi, VIPs, frantic fashionistas and all of the shakers and movers in the industry from around the globe were gathering for the weeklong fashion events.

Out of the seventy-four fashion shows, I'd landed spots in ten of them. And probably would have booked more had my hips been narrower, and my camel humps been steamrolled over and flattened down, and my breasts—which were already duct taped—had been bite-size muffins instead.

Whatever!

The point was, I was here. Right where my mother wanted me to be. She'd won. Even after my bathroom meltdown last week during dinner with Daddy, she still reigned.

"Isn't this exciting?" a shrill voice said, startling me out of my thoughts. I blinked the image before me into view. There stood a strikingly beautiful blond model. She grinned, her blue eyes sparkling. Her skin was as white as porcelain. This was the first time she'd ever opened her mouth to speak, and she'd eyed me and shot daggers enough times in the past weeks to do so. *Why now?* "London, right?"

Her words were thickly coated with a Swedish accent.

I nodded.

"I'm Annika."

I blinked. *Okay, and?* Everyone knew who *she* was. One of the fashion world's most adored teen supermodels who'd been modeling since she was twelve and had graced the covers of hundreds of magazines over the course of her career.

"I wanted to come over and finally introduce myself before the show started. You've been causing quite a stir among some of the other models. Seems like they think you're going to be the next 'it' girl..."

I shrugged my shoulders. Breathing in, deeply. I noticed a few models, a group of white girls, staring over at us, leaning in and whispering. I glared at them, then allowed my eyes to slowly roll back over toward Porcelain Doll.

"Anyway...you *are* very pretty, for a *black* girl." I blinked. "But I don't see what it is everyone else is making such a big fuss over. Well, good luck..."

Before I could recover from the sting of her faux compliment, someone called out my name. "London, darling! London!" A perfectly coiffed redhead was briskly walking over in our direction, waving, her gleaming red lips curled up into a grin as she approached.

Porcelain Doll smiled a wide and phony beauty-pageant smile. "Gisella!" she shrieked excitedly as she air-kissed both of the redhead's cheeks. "I was just wishing London good luck." Her fakeness was sickening. But I refused to be bothered by it. All I needed to do was get through this week. Then the masquerade would all be over, soon...

"Nonsense, darling. London doesn't need luck. She's a natural. This is her moment, darling. She was born for this."

*And it'll be the death of me...*

Porcelain Doll looked over at me sheepishly. *Phony be-yotch!*

My eyes quickly swept around the organized chaos. Toothpick-thin, pouty-lipped, steely-eyed girls fluttered around the dressing area almost robotically as makeup and hair people buzzed around, preparing to transform us.

I was one of five girls who were of color. But that didn't matter. The icy glares, cattiness, and silent hostility were reserved for no one in particular. *Everyone* dished it. *Everyone* got it, some more than others—like *me*. They were all stuck-up and nasty. And I was quickly learning that this trick standing next to me was the worst of them all.

"And today, beautiful London will dazzle us all, *no*?" this Gisella chick continued, eyeing me before cutting her gaze back over at Annika. "She will make her mark. And become the fashion world's most talked about. Now run along. I have things to discuss."

Before walking off, Annika air-kissed Gisella, then turned to me, doing the unthinkable while catching me totally by surprise—she hugged me, and whispered, "You don't belong here. I hope you break your ankles down the runway and they send you back to the jungle where you belong."

She stepped back as Gisella looked from her to me, then back at her. And at that very moment, I realized that I was really no different from any of the other models who were here when I reached for Annika's arm—all the while smiling tightly—pulling her back in, ever so close, then whispering through clenched teeth, "Trick, I will punch *both* of your eye sockets in, then give you a *jungle* beat-down you'll never forget, you coke-snorting pasty-face." I quickly let her arm go. Then added loud enough for everyone in earshot to hear, "I'm not here to be liked by any of you stuck-up skanks. So let this be your warning: *Don't* eff with me. And I *won't* eff with you. Or I will take my *jungle* fists and beat your face in."

Her eyes widened. I tilted my head. Then flashed her a phony smile. She got the hint and scurried off. The Gisella chick clapped her hands. "Love it! So Naomi Campbell, darling! Good for you! Don't *ever* let any of these little snots walk all over you. This industry is full of haters." She introduced herself, firmly shaking my hand. "I'm Gisella Grace with Grace Modeling Agency. And *you,* darling, are absolutely gorgeous. Breathtaking. Stunning. We would love to represent you. I saw the Pink Heat ad that starts running next week. Love it! And with Jade Obi as your mother, my darling, the sky is truly the limit. *Everyone* will want a piece of you."

I cringed. I wanted desperately to tell her I'd already reached my limit. That my mother, whom everyone seemed to adore, had already stretched and pulled and dragged me as far as I could go. I wanted to tell her that I was already at the end.

My end.

There was nowhere else for me to go.

My mother's voice clanked in my head.

\*   \*   \*

"London?" she'd started as she stepped across the threshold of my suite and walked into my sitting area. She'd found me sitting listlessly, blindly staring at my favorite Swarovski butterfly. I'd been sobbing off and on ever since Daddy and I'd finally made it home the night of my break-down. He'd carried me all the way out of the restaurant and held me in his arms until the valet returned with his Bentley. Then he literally slid me into the backseat and strapped me in. Daddy was shaken. He'd never seen me so...broken. I could see his anguish for me. He felt my sorrow. I heard it in his voice. Saw it in his face. And I'd felt it in the way he'd held me in the same way he used to when I was a little girl and would have a scary dream. I was that little girl again.

His frightened, shivering, baby girl. Daddy's little angel.

But I wasn't his little baby girl anymore. I had grown up and told a bunch of lies and broken a ton of rules. Daddy's little angel had long disappeared. My wings had been clipped. And my halo had been replaced by a set of sharp, pointed horns.

My tear-flooded confession—about how I'd been see-ing Justice behind his and my mother's backs, sneaking him in and out of our estate, along with my plot to fix him up with Rich in hopes of scamming her into falling in love with him and helping him get a music deal with her fa-ther's record company—was proof of that.

Daddy said nothing. He listened. Whatever he thought or felt, he'd kept to himself. And as he solemnly drove off from the restaurant that evening, he'd glance up in his rearview mirror every so often, struggling to find some-thing, anything, to say that would soothe me. And each

time, he'd come up blank. He looked as defeated as I felt.
We both knew there was nothing he could say or do to
take away what I was going through. What I had put myself through. My pain would have to run its course. Until
then . . .

"London? I'm speaking to you," my mother continued,
her hand planted deep into the bone of her hip. Her tone
was indifferent, yet laced with a silent edge. She was livid.
I glanced over at her, then shifted my eyes. I braced myself
for a tirade I was certain would follow. I half expected her
to slap my face, then drag her nails into my flesh and rip
my skin off. But this was one of those rare moments when
she and Daddy were home, under the same roof—*together*, so she'd keep her anger in check. Still, I kept my
head down, not wanting to see the fury burning on her
face. I kept my eyes trained on my hands in my lap, staring
at the balled-up tissue I'd been clinging to.

"I'm not *exactly* sure what happened this evening
while you were out with your father," she'd continued.
"But he's very distressed. He tells me you had some kind
of meltdown during dinner. And that he doesn't think it's
best for you to fly back to Milan next week. Is that what
you want? To quit because of some emotional crisis?"

I shrugged.

"Look at me," she'd demanded, impatiently waiting. I
turned my head back toward my crystal butterfly. I dared
not look at her in fear I'd lunge out of my seat and . . . God
forbid. "Well, that's not acceptable. So no matter what
you're going through, the show *still* must go on. Pulling
out now is in poor taste. You have an obligation. People
are counting on you. *I* am counting on you. You made a
commitment. One *you* need to honor up until the very

last flash. Once we've returned to the States, if you wish to no longer model, then fine. We'll discuss your options then. But for now, whatever dark hole you've gotten yourself into, figure out a way to get out of it by the time our plane takes off. *You* will *not* embarrass me. Do I make myself clear, London?"

I slowly turned my head and glared at her. "Very." I turned back away. There was nothing more to say to her. I hated her. I waited until she'd left, then sobbed all over again. Even though I was angry with her, I half hoped she'd put her disappointment and her anger aside for once and console me. I needed, wanted, her to pull me into her arms. I wanted compassion. Something. Not some gestapo! Not some crazed woman wildly wielding a coat hanger at me! I wanted a mother!

I felt the tears coming.

"Well, my darling," Gisella chirped, silencing my thoughts as a short, thin woman in flip-flops and a long black skirt, wearing oversized oval glasses and burnt orange hair summoned me, "it's almost showtime. Do us proud, my love. All eyes will be on you." She pulled me in by the shoulders and air-kissed me, then sauntered off, leaving me feeling flustered.

I spotted Annika sitting in front of a lighted mirror while several makeup and hair people fussed over her. I rolled my eyes, walking over toward my dressing screen. *It's almost over. Just have to push through it. Give 'em what they want.*

"Hi. London, right?" Burnt Orange asked, smiling as she slid a row of pins between her lips. I nodded. "Good. I'm Amber. Now let's get you ready." She reached for my first outfit, pulling it off the rack as I started to undress. Within minutes the dress—black snakeskin with a V-shaped neckline—was being pulled down over my hips, then zipped. The dress wrapped around my body like gauze. "DeAndre, makeup!" she yelled, and then, just like that, she was gone. And a tall, brown-skinned guy rocking a blond Mohawk and multiple tattoos and a lip piercing stood in front of me.

"London Phillips," he said, whisking me into a chair in front of a mirror. "I've heard about you. Yes, yes, yes! Do me, baby! You are giving me *face*. And *body* for days." He raised a big manly hand in the air, stamping a booted foot. "Honey, you are giving me *life*!"

In spite of myself, I couldn't help but smile at his flamboyance as he whipped brushes and powders and tubes out of his black apron. He talked a mile a minute, going on and on and on about the show and the designers and what celebrities might be in the audience, along with the slew of magazine editors. He gossiped and chatted about which models snorted coke, did Mollies, popped pills, and slept around. I half listened, my mind drifting in and out.

"Jade, what were *you* thinking, telling London she needed to have plastic surgery?!" I'd overheard Daddy yelling in his study—something he'd rarely done—late in the evening when I'd crept downstairs toward the kitchen. The yelling is what stopped me in my tracks. The thick double doors were cracked open slightly. "Are you out of your mind? There is *nothing* wrong with the way she is. The only thing your berating and belittling has done is damage her self-esteem."

"I have done no such thing!" my mother snapped. "And I resent you for saying that! I have done *nothing* but the very best for our daughter."

I heard Daddy snort. "Yeah, and look where that's gotten her! London needs a *mother*, not some obsessed woman who's neurotic about her weight, body, and looks."

"I am *not* neurotic! There is nothing wrong with me wanting our daughter to always be and look her very best."

Daddy grunted. "At what cost, huh, Jade? You've done nothing but browbeat her and make her feel worthless. You've broken her spirit. *You* did that. When's the last time you hugged our daughter, huh? Or told her you loved her?"

"London knows I love her! I tell her all the time!"

"Is that *before* or *after* you've put her down?"

"Turner, you will *not* stand there and put how London's turned out all on *me*! She's just as much *your* child as she is mine."

"Yeah, a child *you* couldn't be bothered to carry for nine months…"

"I gave you a child, Turner! I gave you what you wanted! What more did you want from me?!"

"I wanted you, Jade! You! Not some *surrogate* because you were too goddamn concerned about gaining weight!"

I choked back a scream. *A surrogate?* My own mother didn't even carry me in her own womb. No wonder I'd never seen any pictures of her during *her* pregnancy with me. I'd asked her about it and she'd always found a way to be elusive. Always found a way to be evasive. Now I knew why. I was a test-tube baby!

As I stood by the door, eavesdropping on my parents

arguing—about me, over me—I felt my stomach churn. I felt guilty for prying. But it was about me. I had a right to know. Didn't I?

"You've done nothing but put your modeling career before me, our daughter, *and* this marriage!"

"Oh, don't you dare even go there with me, Turner Phillips! Like you haven't put your law practice *before* this marriage! I was modeling way *before* I met you. You knew it was my life!"

"And wanting to be a *mother* and *wife*, instead of galloping up and down runways, should have *also* been your life, Jade! It's what you signed up for when you married me! But it wasn't your life. And now look at us! Look at our daughter! I've always stepped back and let you raise London the way you saw fit, but I see now that that was one of the biggest mistakes I made. I should have been more involved."

"*Yes*, Turner, you're right! Maybe *you* should have been, instead of running off to your *filthy mistress* every chance you got!"

I covered a hand over my mouth. Felt my knees buckle. So the rumors had been true all along. My perfect father wasn't so perfect. His shining armor wasn't so shiny anymore. It was tarnished. It had chinks. Daddy was a cheater! And now I knew my mother's perfect little world wasn't so perfect.

"You better *serve* them, diva!" DeAndre snapped, spinning me out of my daze as the chair turned back toward the mirror. I blinked. "Oh no, oh no! No tears, Miss Superstar! Snap outta that funk!" He spun me back around and yanked out a white napkin, dabbing under my eyes, then retouched my eyeliner. He spun me back around. "Behold! Now *this* is what beautiful is!"

I blinked again. He'd given my eyes a dark, sultry look and painted my lips in dark plum. My hair was gelled down tight to my head with a straight side part, then gave way to an explosion of big bouncy curls. I almost didn't recognize the girl staring back at me. She looked bold and daring. She was beautiful and sophisticated. She was everything I wanted to be, all the time. But couldn't be. Didn't know how to be.

I felt myself slowly unraveling. But it was different this time. I didn't feel lost and vulnerable. I felt...I felt...I don't know. Okay with it. Strangely at peace with it if that made any sense.

*"You're pathetic, yo..."*

"Honey, you got these little skanks shakin' in their heels." DeAndre snapped his fingers. *"Okay?* I don't care what the haters say..." He spun me around again, then again, stopping the chair in front of him. He lifted my chin and stared into my eyes. "You are hot like *fiyah*, boo! Now go out there, pop them hips, and burn that catwalk *down* to the *ground*!"

That being said, it was showtime. Everyone started scrambling, shoulder-bumping anyone in the way, out of the way. This was the moment everyone'd been waiting for. Now I waited too. Everything would be all over soon. The show began. And the first thirteen outfits down the runway were a flurry of flounces, frills, and puffy sleeves and cinched-waist silhouettes. It was all happening so fast. Models stumbled off the stage one after the other, quickly rushing back to get into their second outfits. And now...I was up next.

I inhaled deeply as I waited my turn to walk. Back straight. Chin lifted. Eyes open and focused ahead of the cameras, I stepped out into the blinding lights and pretended to be someone I wasn't.

A famous runway model.

# 3

# Spencer

My phone tolled. *Oh no, oh no!* Then it rang again and again.

I slowly lifted my mask, glancing at the time. It was six a.m. SIX o'clock in the frick-frackin' MORNING! But I couldn't get loosey-goosey and go cluck-cluck cuckoo over the caller disrupting my beauty sleep this time, because the ringtone—"Hakuna Matata" from *The Lion King*—told me who it was.

"Hello?" I answered groggily.

"Cleola, baby?" the gruff voice on the other end whispered.

I blinked. "Huh?" I pulled the phone away from my ear to check the caller ID. It *was* Daddy. It *sounded* like Daddy. But the man on the other end of the phone wasn't *acting* like Daddy. "Daddy? Why are you whispering?"

"You better hide, Cleola Mae. They coming for you, baby."

I shot up in bed, frowning. *What the flimflamfluckery*

*is he talking about now?* "Daddy, who are you talking about? Who's *Cleola*? And who is coming for her?"

"Them boys down in Mississippi. It isn't safe, Cleola. You know I been keeping your secret."

I blinked.

*What secret?*

"Daddy. You're not making any sense. *Who* is Cleola?" I paused, taking a deep breath and swinging my legs over the side of the bed, then shoving my feet into my fluffy slippers. I padded across the room toward my private terrace, swinging the glass doors open. "Please don't tell me this *Cleola* is some secret love child you had with some striped jungle bunny you've kept hidden in some mountain cave, and now you're confusing me with her. I'm not trying to be a sister to anyone unless it's to Sister Mary Louise Francis."

"Sssh, Cleola. Hurry up. They're coming. Did you hide the gun?"

I gasped, almost dropping my phone. Either Daddy was going cuckoo, or he needed to find the nearest confession booth and get his sin book stamped because he was really, really acting like he had something scandalous going on, something deliciously smarmy and shady, and I needed to get to the nit and grit of it.

"Cleola? Cleola?"

I bit down on my bottom lip. Resisted the urge to go off. This is what most of my conversations with Daddy were starting to be like—crazy and foolish. And lately they were becoming more consistent. And I didn't do crazy and foolish well. And I wasn't sure if I'd be able to do it now. But Daddy was the only person, aside from Vera, whom I'd never turned the fire up on. And I didn't want to start now.

However, Daddy's phone calls were starting to test my nerves. And every time we'd hang up, or he'd hang up on me, or I'd *accidentally*—which I'd been telling myself lately so that I wouldn't feel bad for being messy—hang up on him, I'd toss and turn for most of the night. Or would start crying.

And I don't even know why I'd be crying. It wasn't like Daddy had been home spending quality time with me since I'd been back from Le Rosey—the Swiss boarding school where I'd spent three-and-a-half years of my life up until this summer, when I returned home from studies abroad. No. The Himalayas and Kenya had gotten all of his attention since I'd been back.

The last holiday I'd actually spent with Daddy was last year, one of those rare occasions when I'd returned to the States. He'd come home to surprise me for Thanksgiving and ended up staying through Christmas. That was one of the best times of my life, ever. I had Daddy for a whole month, all to myself.

But, of course Kitty had to be a real rattlesnake and start with her hissing and tail rattling when I'd asked her to take some time off from her precious TV networks so that we could be—okay, dang it, *act* like—a family for *once*. "*Spencer, dear. Get your pretty little head out of those billowy clouds of yours and stop living in fantasy, darling. You can sit around inhaling old-man fumes and counting the wrinkles in your father's forehead if you'd like, but I'm not interested in acting like a family. Now come give your mother a kiss. I have a plane to catch. Now be a doll. Call me when your father's gone.*"

And with that said, she was out the door. She didn't step her heeled feet back through these doors until *two* weeks later! So what if she didn't want to play nice with Daddy? It's what *I* wanted.

This was about Daddy. Not that low-down treacherous lizard.

Mmph.

"Cleola, talk to me, dammit!" Daddy barked into the phone as I stepped out onto my terrace, trying to decompress my stewing temper. I inhaled, breathing in the faint scent of jasmine.

"Daddy, for the hundredth time, this is *not* Cleola, *got-dangit*! And what kind of woman would name her child some mess like that, anyway? Either you tell me who you're talking about, or I'm going to need to greet you with the dial tone. And you know I'll do it, Daddy. So don't have me press the rooter to the tooter on you. Please and thank you."

"Here they come! Run, Cleola, run!" It sounded like Daddy was running. "Don't let 'em get you, Cleola." I could hear scuffling. "Get off of me! Run, Cleola, run! Get your hands off of me!"

My heart dropped. "Daddy? Daddy? What is going on?"

After several moments of muffled scuffling, it sounded like Daddy's phone dropped. "Hello? Hello?" I waited a few seconds more then decided to hang up.

Some woman with a British-sounding accent spoke into the phone. "Hello? Is this Spencer Ellington?"

"Uhhh, yeah. Now what the hot *fawk* are you scavengers, you, you gypsy-pirates, doing to my father, huh?! Are you *Cleola*?"

"No, no. This is Vivian Lee. I'm part of Doctor Ellington's traveling medical team."

My lashes fluttered. "Uh, ohhhkay, Miss Tour Guide. Why are you Village People down there roughhousing with my father? Do I need to call the embassy? Have you brought up on charges?"

"No, no. Not at all. If you'd just let me explain." She wheezed, sounding as if the air was being wrung out of her lungs.

I sighed, tapping my foot. "Okay, I'm listening. Make it quick. Now how can I help you?"

She took several deep breaths, then slowly said, "Well, um ... there's no easy way to say this ..."

I huffed. "Then say it, please and thank you."

"It's your father's condition. I'm afraid it's gotten worse ..."

*His condition?* I blinked. "Well, you just ought to be afraid, Miss Lady In The Safari, because I have no daggone idea what you are talking about."

"Oh. I'm sorry." She cleared her throat. "I thought you knew. Your father's been diagnosed with Alzheimer's ..."

*"Alztimer* what?"

"No, no. Alz. Hei. Mer's," she corrected as she enunciated the word like I was some special-needs dumbo who rode a tricycle on three flats. "The doctors here say the disease ..."

My heart dropped. *Disease?* Ohsweetheavens. I plopped down on my chaise lounge, reaching for a pack of electronic cigarettes I'd left out on the mini–round table. I pulled one out of its pack, then turned on the LED light. This was too much for my nerves so early in the dang morning. I inhaled. Jeezus! I couldn't even enjoy watching the sunrise. Or watching the L.A. smog roll over the hills. Oh, these barbarians had no shame. They couldn't even be decent enough to wait until around noontime to trick my vibe up with this sort of news.

I exhaled. "What kind of disease, Sara Lee?"

"It's *Vivian* Lee."

"Okay," I said dismissively. "Thank you for the update. But, right now, it's too early and I'm too grief stricken to care. Now did something wild and nasty bite him out in the jungle? Is there something eating the inside of his brain up? Is that why he has this Alzy-palsy?" My lips quivered as I fired off a round of questions. "Is my daddy going to die? Can't you give him a shot of penicillin or some nerve gas? Anything to fix him?"

I felt myself getting choked up as she assured me Daddy hadn't gotten bitten by anything with wings, legs, teeth, or fangs. But he had been bitten by some kind of oldies-but-not-so-goodie brain disease that couldn't be cured. Everything around me started to spin and I could feel the blood draining from my face as she told me how Daddy's old-folks condition, this Alzhiney disease, was the sixth leading cause of death.

I gasped, my eyes filled with tears. "So my father's g-gonna die," I said in almost a whisper. She tried to give me hope by telling me there were medications that could help Daddy's quality of life, but it didn't matter because all I heard was that there was *nothing* that anyone could do to stop this nasty thing that had gotten ahold of Daddy and would eventually suck the life out of him.

She was talking but her words swirled around in my head, making her sound like a wounded chipmunk. The only things I heard coming out of her mouth that made any sense were: "He's in stage three...he's forgetting things... he's repeating himself...misplacing personal effects..."

*Stage three?* "H-h-how many stages are there?" I asked.

Seven, she told me. I breathed a sigh of relief. So he wasn't slipping on his banana peel just yet. He was going to die a slow death. He still had time.

I blinked. Wait one dingdong minute! If he's only in stage three, why in heaven's grace was I on the phone talking to *her*? I frowned, then pushed out in a rush of agitation, "Why are you getting me all upset and worried about all of this *now*? At *this* hour, huh? You have ruined my whole morning. You must not know about me, sweetness! I will Rollerblade up and down your face for try—"

She cut me off. "Miss Ellington, *please*. I can understand your concern and frustration. But I assure you we've done everything we can on this end. We've tried to manage Dr. Ellington, but your father's illness is becoming progressively worse."

My nose flared. "Listen, Miss Dora the Explorer, I don't know what type of helter-skelter shenanigans your swamp operation is running down there, but I want to know *right* now why you'd wait until my father's practically broke down to call here with this mess. Explain yourself."

What she told me next knocked the wind from beneath my dang wings. Kitty had known. And Daddy had been refusing medications for over a year, and they'd been speaking to Kitty about his condition. All this time, she *knew* Daddy's mind was playing peek-a-boo with reality. And not once did she open her dang litter box to tell me about it.

"We last spoke to Mrs.—well, *now* Ms.—Ellington, about seven months ago, advising her then that we thought it best your father return home…"

I blinked.

"At that time she made it very clear she wasn't interested. That we should find Dr. Ellington a nursing home with an ocean view somewhere here in the hills, but for us to keep him here. And we haven't heard from her since."

I was hotter than a volcano. That no-good, dirty litter box! How dare she do that! *Ooh, you just wait until I lay my hands—I mean, my eyes—on her! I'm going to give it to her good!*

"He's already wandered off twice, causing us to send out search parties to look for him. And this is his third incident. We can't keep doing this. The last time he wandered off we found him four days later down in a watering hole. Thankfully, it was dried up. And this time, we found your father about twenty minutes ago, after a two-day search, in one of the Kenyan villages three hours away, dancing naked."

I almost threw up in the back of my mouth at the visual of Daddy flapping around in his loincloth doing a jungle striptease. I took two frantic puffs from my cigarette, then put it out and flicked it over the terrace as if it were a real cigarette.

I fought back a batch of fresh tears. If Daddy could no longer ride the blue skies in hot-air balloons, wrestle alligators in mud-slick rivers, dance with buffalo and count wildebeests and mate with Mother Nature...If he had to stop tongue-lapping in the Fountain of Youth and doing what he loved most because of some ole raggedy illness, then she was right. Daddy needed to come home. I swallowed, willing myself to stay calm and focused despite my insides shaking like a salt shaker.

My lips quivered. "I'll have our private jet come get him." I asked for her number and wrote it down. Then told her I'd have the house manager call back with the rest of the details. I overheard Daddy screaming in the background, "Run, Cleola Mae. They're coming for you!"

Then the call ended. I tried calling back but kept getting a busy signal. I wiped my eyes with the back of my sleeve. Scrolled through my cell and quickly dialed our pilot, Stanley. I told him that it was time for him to spread his wings and swoop down on the Masai Mara in Kenya to get Daddy. He was coming home.

*Daddy is coming home*, I repeated in my head, closing my eyes as I ended the call. *Sweetpeachlickers!* I took several deep breaths. I didn't know anything about this *All-timers* disease, but it sounded mean and nasty. And if it was causing Daddy to lose his mind, dancing around naked in villages and calling me some dang *Cleola*, then it had to be something terribly awful.

I opened my eyes and tried to remember if I'd ever really known Daddy. I didn't have to think long. I didn't. Not really. I knew more about Kitty than I did him. That she was messy and hateful and ruthless. That she was an ole nasty cougar that stalked boy-toys in schoolyards, then mauled at their man parts. That she was a nasty hot-box, gold-digging tramp who threw her kitty up in the lap of a desperate man who was forty-two years older than her, spawned an heir to his fortunes, then screwed her way to success. I knew all this about Kitty. But Kitty didn't know a thing about me.

But Daddy did. At least he used to. Now, he could barely remember who the heck he was talking to. Something inside of me snapped and I started hyperventilating and crying all over again. Because, aside from last year's holiday visit, my interaction with Daddy—over the last three years—had been limited to phone calls, postcards, the occasional one-page letter, at times Skype, and tons of gifts.

Now, after almost three dang years of being footloose and fancy-free, chanting and yodeling through the tropics, he was finally coming home. But I wasn't all that excited about it. How could I be? He wasn't coming home because *he* wanted to. *Noooo. He* was coming back here because he *had* to. And he wasn't even coming back here for *me*. *Nooo*. He was coming back here because he was being forced to. And *that* had my nerves fried and scrambled hard. I didn't know what to expect when Daddy arrived. But one diggity-dingdong thing I knew for certain. I was frightened out of my lace panties of what I would see when he walked through the door. And I was even more petrified of what I'd do when he did.

I had less than forty-eight hours to get Daddy's wing of the house in order. But, first things first, the minute Kitty walked through these doors, I was going to butter her biscuits real good, then drag her through the muggahfuggin' gotdangit gutter!

# 4

# Heather

"Cuuuuuut!" Philippe Pinelle, famed reality TV director, screamed like a beyotch as he stormed through my room and pushed the cameraman who stood over my bed.

I looked him over and instead of serving him with a dropkick to his throat, I snuggled back into my pillow and closed my eyes.

This dude was trippin'. Hard.

*First of all*: It was eleven a.m.

Eleven. a.m. in the crunked-up, mothersuckin' mornin'! Monday mornin'!

Like, word?

Really?

What did he think this was? *Run's House*?

Second of all: I had enough of people telling me what to do. I once had my own television show—the *Wu-Wu Tanner Show*, one of the hottest teen shows there'd ever been—that was stolen from up underneath me thanks to

Spencer not minding her business and turning state's evidence against me by having me arrested for throwing myself a fabulous get-right, get-tight Skittles celebration with the rest of my pill-popping buddies. So what if the drugs were illegal? So what if my people had rummaged through their grannies heart medication? We were having fun. That was what life was all about! I was a good time party girl. I was sick of these mud rats tryna snatch my vibe and sabotage me. These hoes ain't never been loyal. And don't know how to be.

Anyway, now I'm stuck doing this ridiculous reality show because tricks stayed hating on me. Like it was my fault that I was a star.

And prettier than the rest of them. My chocolate eyes were shaped like an ancient Egyptian's. My hair was Sicilian thick and full of sandy brown coils. My skin was deep bronze, or more like a white girl baked by the Caribbean sun. So what if I didn't look black or white? Why they hating on me? It's not my fault they can't be me.

"No! No! No!" Phillipe carried on, pacing from one end of the room to the other, as sweat dripped down his temples and melted his foundation, turning his white linen scarf dull peach. "What *don't* you all understand?! Did you *not* get the script?" He paused and his eyes scanned the room for an answer.

He must have been on drugs.

Philippe clapped his hands. "Get it together, people! Camille cannot be the only professional around here!"

*Camille?*

"She's already rehearsed her part!"

*Rehearsed? Part? What part?*

He carried on. "And though it was a struggle for her, she's agreed to play the role of the control freak."

*Play the role? That's who my mother* is. I opened one eye and arched a brow.

"And for added measure, she's even agreed to stroll in here in a white gown and matted mink slippers, with a drink in her hand."

*Added measure? That's her morning glory!*

He squealed, flinging peach sweat from his forehead. "Classic! Magnificent! Do you know what that will mean for ratings?"

*What the . . .*

Was he serious with this? Camille always waltzed in here in her raggedy uniform with her sunup round of scotch in her hand. This mofo was stupid. He had to be. And obviously he didn't read the blogs or research Hollywood's wayward drunk.

Whatever! This was supposed to be a reality show, not a flippin' sitcom! And I wasn't agreeing to be scripted. So for-real-for-real, this creep, his scripts, and his cameramen could all line up and each take turns kissing the new crack of my . . .

Wait.

I sat up and looked at the clock again: eleven fifteen a.m.

Monday.

A school day.

I haven't been at Hollywood High yet. Drop a few squats and show the Pampered Trolls how boss I'd become.

And yeah, I'm sure they'd watched Co-Co and me rip 'em on that YouTube video. After all, "Put Your Diamonds

Up" was the craze I'd forecast it to be. But the Pampered Princesses had yet to experience the new me...live and in concert.

I hopped out of bed and Philippe lost his mind. "What are you doing? Where are you going?! Camille is supposed to drag you out of bed! Camille is supposed to snatch the covers off of you! And you're supposed to jump in her face and try and knock her to the floor! Get back in that bed now!"

I didn't even respond to him; instead I raced into my en suite bathroom.

Showered.

Dressed in leopard skinny jeans, a white tank top, a denim midriff vest, and black leather, peep-toe, four-inch shoe boots.

I grabbed my exclusive Louis Valtone Korean hobo bag, slid on my aviators, and sauntered past Camille. Brushed by the director of my reality TV show, who was red and screaming Kitty's—the creator and producer of the show and owner of the Kitty-Kitty network—name into his cell phone, and past the cameramen who were clearly confused about whether they should follow me or not.

I hopped in my '57 Chevy and left 'em all in a puff of my tailpipe's smoke.

"Well, well, what alleyway are you crawling out of?" Headmaster Westwick frowned as I walked into his office at Hollywood High Academy, and he looked me over. "What, you just wake up from your Brazilian stupor, got yourself a new booty lift and finally realized that you needed to be at school? You were due back here three weeks ago. We don't have any chairs to seat you and that monstrous behind of yours. And here I was prepared to send the truant officers to Sleazy Eight." He picked up a manila file from his desk with my name and picture on it and tossed it into another pile marked "Derelicts."

I rolled my eyes to the ceiling and then dropped my gaze back over at him. "First of all. I'm not at Sleazy Eight and never was. Get your facts straight, *Wes. Wick.*"

He tooted his lips and mocked me. "Get your facts straight, *Wes. Wick.*" He smirked. "And it's Mr. *Wes Wick* to you, Missy Used-To-Be Wu-Wu."

I sighed. "Look. It's lunchtime and I need a pass. I don't feel like the hassle from security."

"Passes are a grand." He held out his pink palm. "Black Card. Oops, bad credit. That'll be cash or money order from you."

I blinked, and placed a hand up on my hip. My purse slid down my arm and hung around my wrist. "What?"

"A grand. Or get sent home."

"If I pay you a grand"—I pressed my palms on his desk and leaned into his oval face—"then that means all bets are off. And your dancing on K-town bar tables in a mask, fishnets, and lipstick will no longer be a secret. And your wife will know all about it." I stood up straight and his eyes burned into my gaze. "Now," I said to him, "I need a pass."

He pulled out his brown leather notebook and slammed it on his desk. "This is it for you. No more chances and no more passes." He scribbled *Pass to Déjeuner Café* on the thick ecru paper, stamped it, ripped it from his book, and handed it to me. "Now get out, Cummings."

I smiled and gave him a small wave. "Have a great day, Mr. Westwick!" I blew him a kiss.

By the time I stepped through the sliding glass doors it was obvious that word of me being in the building had spread. The Stalkers and the Gawkers were all lined up, and the moment I stepped onto the red carpet most of them bowed down, throwing flowers at my feet. A few of them had even passed out.

"Oh, bless you." I smiled at my beauties as I stood back and took it all in. I'd been gone for a minute, but absolutely nothing had changed.

Déjeuner Café could easily pass for any top-notch club in the city. White couches, white leather reclining chairs, lava-lamp-topped tables, and plasma TVs.

Lunch was served via white-gloved waiters and everyone in here looked as if they'd been on pause since the day I'd left; all seated in the same exact place they'd always been.

The Jocks table was next to the Cheerleaders, who sat to the left of the Glees. The Wannabes sat behind the Newbies, who sat across from their rivals the Fogies—better known as old money.

The Foodies, who complained about their weight all day, and the Super Skinnies, who complained about their weight all day, both sat next to the hibachi and the dessert bar.

The Preppies, who wouldn't be caught dead not wearing Polo, and the Hip-Hop crew, who wouldn't be caught dead wearing Polo, sat across from one another.

The Rock Star Goth kids, whose parents hoped that one day they would appreciate the sun, and the half-dead Twilight kids who wore pale white makeup on purpose and whose secret code words for cuties were *team Edward* and *team Jacob*, opted to share a table.

The Stalkers and the Gawkers sat near the door so they could welcome me in.

And in the center of the room was the clique of all cliques: the It clique. The Hollywood Trolls and the Pampered Hoes. I frowned, and before I could decide if I wanted to go over there or not, I spotted Rich Montgomery ice grilling me.

I swallowed and for a moment I felt myself shrinking.

*Stop it.*

I cleared my throat and flipped my hair over my shoulders. Besides, she was sitting alone. London and Spencer were nowhere to be seen. And I had a crew of at least fifty following behind me. Eyes fixed on my new booty, of course.

I walked over to the It table and stood behind the chair where I would usually sit.

"Rich." I greeted her.

She crossed her legs and for the first time I noticed that we had the same warm brown almonds for eyes.

*Richard Montgomery is your . . .*

*Stop it!*

"And why are you eye-effen' me, Heather?!" Rich spat. "I know you didn't come over here tryna serve me. You better get your eye-swag together and stop looking at me all crazy. And after the stunts you pulled, you shouldn't be over here." She took half a breath. "And what the eff are you speaking to me for anyway? You need to keep my name outcha mouth and stop trying to revive your career off of me, Wu-Wu! You already know that I don't do you. Never have. Never will. You out making broke-down BlackBerry videos talking about pampered trolls and pampered slores! Mmph, you must've been talking about your pet unicorn Co-Co and your drunk mother."

Oh. No. She. Didn't! Tryna drag my two-faced bestie Co-Co Ming. I turned around and looked at the Stalkers and Gawkers, who stood in a semicircle behind me, glaring at Rich and waiting on my cue to bury this chick. But I didn't need them to bring it for me. I could serve my own death sentence.

I curled my lips and leaned into Rich's face. "You Jenny Craig, gastric bypass, chubby trick! I will drag you up in this beyotch and have you crying for that slore mother of yours! You, your mama, and that whack clique you claim, are all a buncha lame label slores." I snapped my fingers and the Stalkers and the Gawkers completely surrounded the table.

Rich's eyes swiftly looked from left to right.

I pointed into her face. "And if you come for me again, I'ma take it to the streets on you. You might think you're hood, Rich, but before I have you marked and murked, I will have you stomped down into the ground. Don't play me, you chubby Smurf! What you better do is grab your Glock and call the cops when you see me. And all my girls circled around you that you've been bullying and disrespecting like you're the only one around here with money.

"Ya daddy's a convict. Ya mama's one too. You're nothing but the offspring of a jailhouse. If you ever ice grill me again, I'ma take it straight to your double chin. Get smoked up! Eff around and have a heart attack messing wit' me! And if your crew wanna come and see about me, then let them know that my new address is 555 West Lawson Boulevard." I paused, made sure she was absorbing the thought of me busting her in the throat, and then I continued. "But until one of you slores gets the courage to come to my door, I advise you to shut the eff up and keep away from me!"

And in the midst of cameras flashing and thunderous giggles, I spun off on my heels and left that crazy-lookin' tramp sitting there with her face cracked.

*Boom!*

Guess who's back!

# 5

# Spencer

I sat.
Waited.
And waited.
And waited.

I'd been sitting in this same chair, in this same spot, for the last four hours, waiting. Squeezing the valves to my kidneys and urethra shut to keep from spraying a golden shower all over myself. No. I was not moving until Kitty walked through the door and we got down and dirty once and for all.

I was going to serve her, feet and hands.

We were going to roll around on this floor and tear through this house like we used to when I was five and six, for old times' sake. Yes, indeedy. I didn't believe in giving to the greedy. But I believed in attacking the seedy. Now, now...that didn't mean I enjoyed being a potty mouth or getting all happy-handed with Kitty. No. It gave me no real pleasure the way slipping my feet into a plush new pair of heels did. But, once again, Kitty dragged her cat claws into the wrong sandbox and crossed the wrong dang line. Now that trash-can tramp had to pay the sandman.

*"... She made it very clear she wasn't interested. That we should find Dr. Ellington a nursing home with an ocean view somewhere here in the hills, but for us to keep him here..."*

She had no muthasuckin' business telling anyone to put my father away in some old folks factory. None. Who the yabba-dabba-Scooby-Doo did she think she was? The only one who should be put away anywhere was *her*. How dare that gas-pipe sucker! That hookah!

Daddy was the same man who'd taken that little tramp stamp in and given her a home when she was streetwalking the pig feet circuit. Wait, wait...I mean the pigtail...no, no. Not that. When she was crawling through pig guts trying to find a come-up. Daddy was the one who cleaned her up and got her out of whatever life she'd come from. Mmph.

Not that I knew much about the secret life of Kitty-Kitty Smut-Smut since she was so ziplock tight about her past. Other than her being from some small town in North Carolina—Muffinsboro or some silly mess like that—and being raised by her grandparents because her parents were killed in a house fire, that's all I really knew about the elusive woman who was supposed to be my mother instead of trying to be an enemy of mine.

Bottom line, Daddy was dang good to her. Even after he found her hanging upside down performing tongue tricks on our pool boy's man-hose when I was seven, and even after he caught her doing a Russian split over our chef's face when I was nine, Daddy *still* remained loving and kind when in fact he should have tossed her out in nothing but her birthday thong. But he didn't! And this was how she wanted to repay him! Abandon him! Toss him aside like some used tissue, like she'd done me for most of my life!

*"Oh, by the way, your father and I are getting divorced. And you're going to South Africa to live with him..."*

*"What? South Africa? Oh no, I'm not..."*

*"You heard what I said. You're going to live with your father. It's time he started acting like a parent instead of running off into the wilderness. He's the one who wanted you in the first place. I've done my part. I gave birth to you. Now it's time for me to start living my life..."*

I blinked. So that's why that heartless witch divorced Daddy. She didn't want to play Daddy's nursemaid, or deal with his illness. Instead of being his wife and standing by her vows, she pulled open her booty cheeks and told him to kiss where the fresh air didn't blow. Just like that. Kitty had gotten too gotdang fancy!

Well, I was sick of it!

I don't know what kind of *Wizard of Oz* games my mother *thought* she was playing with me. But I was not the one, the two, or the gotdang three. My name was not Dorothy, Tin Man, or Cowardly Lion, or one of the got-dang Munchkins.

No.

My name was Spencer Ellington.

And this girl was on fire!

So my mother had better click her heels three times and get it right. Or get burned down in the flames. Either way, she was going to learn today. Well, tonight, since I'd

been sitting and sitting on my numb booty cheeks for almost forever. Waiting and thinking. Thinking and waiting.

Waiting.

Thinking.

Ever since she'd parted her red sea and gave birth to
me, I'd been nothing but loving and kind to that woman.
Coo-cooing and drooling and smiling, pretending to be
her bouncing bundle of joy when all I'd ever been to her
was a means to building her billion-dollar media empire.

What a trickster! A scammer!

All she'd ever done was do whatever she could to hurt
me. To see me broken. It seemed like, felt like, her life's
mission was to see me miserable.

Well, guess what?

It was working.

First, she snatched Esmeralda and Solenne—my care-
takers the first three years of my life, the only women I
knew as mothers—away from me. They nursed me from
their breasts. They loved me. And what did she do when
I'd cry out for either one of them? She fired them.

Then from ages six to nine, after Constantina, my third
nanny, worked her way into my heart and I grew to love
her like a mother, she got rid of her. Then age nine, came
Vera. My auntie Vera. The woman with the thick Trinida-
dian accent who loved me, and catered to me, and made
me feel as if I were one of her very own.

Then, as punishment for my loyalty to Vera, the minute
I turned twelve that evil hooch shipped me off to Switzerland under some flimsy guise that living and going to
school abroad was the best thing for me. Hogwash! It was
best for her. She wanted me out of her life.

Every- and anything that woman has ever done has been best for her. Not anyone else.

My nose flared.

Every time I tried to forgive Kitty for abandoning me, for dumping me on everyone else, the despicable woman did something else. Like stalk the schoolyard and sleep with my ex-boyfriend Curtis on his eighteenth birthday. Like crawling her way into my ex-boyfriend Joey's tent and hiking up her skirt and letting him dig in her cat box with his man tools.

Like her trying to feed Anderson Ford her ratchet roadside scallops, knowing good dang well I was trying to sink my own clampers into his man meat. So what if he was London's cover-up? Kitty still knew my mouth watered for a taste of his custard. And he should have been off-limits to her. But, *noooo.* She had to try to seduce him on the sly. Kitty was a relentless vulture, always somewhere trying to swoop down on someone else's prey.

And now this...

The news of my father having some Alzy-palsy old timer's disease was still gnawing away at me. *"I'm sorry. I thought you knew...Your father has Alzheimer's..."*

Then to learn that Kitty had known for at least a year that Daddy's mind was slowly rotting away like some raggedy basket of old fruit had my burners on high. And the more I replayed the call from early this morning in my head, the longer I had to wait for Kitty to meander her scandalous, messy self home, the more agitated I felt myself becoming.

I was molten hot lava.

And it didn't help matters any that my stomach was

packed with gas from holding everything in. I'd been calling Kitty all dang day, leaving her message after message to
get her mind together because we were going to have it
out the minute she stepped her jeweled heels through the
door.

Ugh! That selfish woman didn't even have the decency
to return any of my calls. No. The only thing she did was
send me some drab text message: SPENCER! MAKE YOURSELF USEFUL
& STOP ACTING LIKE DAMAGED GOODS! SMOOCHES!

*Oh, I'll show her damaged goods all right!*

I was on the verge of hurling out red-hot ash, rocks,
and a slew of dirty words.

The nerve of her!

Kitty was the worst kind of heathen there was in this
world. She knew nothing about worshipping in the House
of Good Deeds. No. My mother was low-down and dirty. She
was down-low and shady. She was a swing low, hateful bat.

I crossed my legs at the knees and bounced a heeled
foot up and down. It was all I could do to keep from leap-
ing up and slinging syrup all over the kitchen and smear-
ing cream cheese from this morning's breakfast all over
the windows.

I'd let the house manager and the rest of the house staff
leave hours ago. The movers who'd helped me get Daddy's
rooms ready had already come and gone about two hours
ago. I wanted everyone gone when Kitty and I got footloose and fancy and danced this dance.

My pulse quickened the minute I heard the alarm chirp.

Yessss, gotdiggitydangit, ring the alarms!

Turn up the flames!

It's getting hot in here!

Turn it up! Turn it up!

Kitty was home.

And I was about to tear the roof off the mothersucker!

I reached for my crystal flute, guzzled back the rest of my bubbly mineral water, then wiped my wet mouth with the back of my left hand. I rubbed my palms together, then shook the nerves out of my fingertips.

It was time to skin Kitty's fur back.

# 6

# Heather

"Okay, that's a wrap!" a thick-muscled, dark-skinned guy said into the intercom from the mixing board on the other side of the glass. "Wu-Wu, baby. You killed it! This that fire, ma!"

I stepped back from the mic, blinking out of my lyrical zone. For the last four hours, I'd been floating on a musical cloud with a little slice of *get right* to keep my mind in full gear—nothing too serious, though, because I didn't want to be up in the booth tweaking, like this bish, Co-Co. His eyeballs were about the size of golf balls. Now he was standing here grinding his teeth. This geisha boy had his crunk-meter turned all the way up from doing lines of Murder. I passed on that craziness. I wasn't messing with that ish. One, I didn't like how it made me feel the one time I tried it. And, two, I wasn't even about to let myself get turned out and end up some street-corner junkie turning tricks for a few crushed lines of powdered treat. No, ma'am. Being some junkie was not in my future. So I wasn't interested in becoming one. But I did get my spirits lifted off a few hits of that Suicide that Miss Co-Co brought along in his satchel. I needed to be in control, so I wasn't about to do anything else. Besides, I just needed a little *pinch* of goodness so I could rip through my verses for the single I was dropping on iTunes.

I was trying to get this money up. I wasn't about to let nothing stop my hustle and flow. I was back. And I planned on claiming my spot on top where I belonged; especially after Kitty had the audacity to tell me I was going to eventually end up being a washed-up actress like my mother, when I'd stopped by her estate yesterday to discuss my issues with doing this reality TV crap. I was sick of it. As far as I was concerned, it was a step down from my real worth. Reality TV was for losers. It was cute for someone who wanted a start, someone who wanted to break into show business. Or looking for a comeback.

That wasn't me. I'd already made my mark. I didn't need a break. I was a star. And this reality TV mess was beneath me. It was cramping my style. And I wasn't having it. And I told her so, demanding she release me from my contract.

"*What?!* A star?" She laughed in my face. "Little girl, stop being a silly trick and think! You either work and keep money coming in or hit the welfare line. Hollywood is not just about getting in the spotlight by being splashed all up in the media. It's about staying relevant. So what you have—no, correction, *had*—a little stardom. At the end of the day—when you find yourself tossed out of your dressing room with your nameplate thrown in your face, all of your belongings stuffed in some raggedy box, and that little twinkling silver star gets yanked out of your hands, do you really think anyone is going to care about who you *used* to be in Hollywood?

"You think they care about *you* being some bozo named Wu-Wu? No, dear, you are sadly mistaken if you think they do! Wu-Wu is dead, silly girl! Yeah, everyone with a clue knows who starred as Wu-Wu. *You.* But you are dumber and more delusional than I thought if you actually believe that *you* are Wu-Wu. Little girl, wake up! Go somewhere and have a seat! You didn't write the script for Wu-Wu. Or pitch the idea. You *auditioned* for the role." She laughed again. "You don't even own the rights to the name *Wu-Wu*. The network does!

"So don't you *ever* stand in front of me and call yourself Wu-Wu again. What you better do is figure out who Heather Cummings is. Because right now, from where I'm sitting, Heather Cummings is broke! Heather Cummings is irrelevant! And Heather Cummings is getting on my last nerve! And that's exactly how everyone in Hollywood is going to view you.

"You want fame? Then be smart about it! Amass you a fortune! Because fame *without* fortune doesn't mean a thing when you're sleeping in a tent under a bridge, which is where you're going to find yourself, little girl— smelling and looking like the inside of a third-world sewer, if you don't stay focused. Being a star, having star power, is about *getting* on top and knowing how to *stay* on top. Branding, dear! That's how you do it. Now, what I'm offering you, little girl, is an opportunity to get it right. So until you do, you'll do reality TV. And for the next thirteen episodes, I'm your pimp. Now get out of my house and get out there and get me my money!" *Bam!* She slammed the door behind me as I walked out, feeling like I'd been beaten worse by Kitty's words than I'd been with Camille's fists and feet.

"*Bish*, you did that!" Co-Co said, bringing me out of my thoughts as we stepped out of the sound booth. We were at Thug Hitz, a recording studio over on Martin Luther King Jr. Boulevard in Baldwin Village—or as it was once known, the Jungle—finishing up the track for my first single: "Put Your Diamonds Up"!

Ever since someone had posted a video of me and Co-Co ripping the stage at Club Noir Kiss on YouTube, I'd been getting crazy requests from Wu-Wu fans to drop a single. Co-Co said he knew a spot where we could go to make it happen. And so here we were. In the hood, at a studio packed wall-to-wall with thugs and thick clouds of weed smoke, getting ready to drop fire on the streets.

"*You did. That!*" Co-Co repeated as he punctuated each word with a finger snap. "*Yes gawd,* honey! That ish right there . . . is hotness!" He pulled out his cell and started texting real quick, then after a few minutes slid his phone down into the front pocket of his pink fishnet jumper. "These tricks not gonna know what hit 'em when that ish drops tomorrow . . ."

We high-fived.

"You know that's right," I said as I shimmied my shoulders. "I'm about to drop hot turds on them Hollywood slores and trolls."

"Yes! Yes!" Co-Co threw a hand up in the air. "Droppin' turds on all them silly birds!" He pulled out his compact and powdered his nose, then snapped it shut. I eyed him as he pulled out his phone and started texting again. When he was done, he shoved it back down into his pocket then stepped out of his heels and slid his size elevens into a pair of black Timbs that he had stuffed in his oversized bag.

He'd been acting extra jumpy most of the night, kept stepping out of the room to "use the bathroom," so he said. But all his strolling back and forth looked to me like he was trying to score himself some chocolate boy-joy for the night.

Whatever! I wasn't interested in none of them. Yeah, most of 'em kept eyeballing me and licking their lips at me most of the day. And, yeah, a few were real cute. Still, I was. Not. Interested. We gathered our things, I said my good-byes to everyone in the studio, then headed out into the lobby with Co-Co behind me. I gave him the side eye as he—with his page-boy cut and sweeping bang, full beard, glossed lips, and his long slender fingers with each pinky painted pink—let the straps of his handbag drop into the crook of his arm. I had to bite the inside of my cheek to keep from laughing as Camille's voice floated in my head. *"Trans-Confusion, don't come for Norma Marie...That rainbow cookie..."*

He tossed his bang from out of his left eye. "What? Why you looking at me like that?"

"Like what?"

He popped his lips. "Um. Like you sizing me up for a late night snack or something. I know you see all this sweet Asian lusciousness, boo. But you know Miss Co-Co don't do the lesbian thing. My special duck sauce is for one thing and one thing only, honey."

I blinked. *And what makes you think I do?* Please, like

I'd want to do him. I flicked a dismissive wave at him, ignoring his *lesbian* remark. "Chile, *cheese.* Don't let your delusions get your feelings hurt. Now let's get out of here. The limo should already be out front."

He stopped in his tracks, snapping a finger. "Oh, shoot. I got something I need to handle right quick. I'll holla at you a little later."

I shot Miss Girl Wannabe a look, placing a hand up on my waist. "Something like *what*? We made plans. I *thought* we were stopping through Club Kix for a quick nightcap."

"We were," he quickly said. He was acting real strange all of a sudden. "I have to meet someone real quick." His phone started buzzing. He ignored it. "I gotta collect these coins so we can do it up, boo."

I eyed him suspiciously. "And you're sure you don't want a ride?"

"No, no. I'll get one of the little thug daddies in the studio to give me a lift." He smacked his lips together. "You know how I do it, boo."

I threw a hand up in the air, waving him on. Told him to call me later and walked off. I thought I heard him giggle and looked over my shoulder, catching him putting his phone up to his ear. I rolled my eyes and headed down the hall toward the glass doors, the cameraman from the TV show in tow. The minute we stepped out of the building, a haze of flashbulbs blinded me.

"Here she is now!"

"Heather! Heather!"

My eyes rapidly blinked then popped open. It was a herd of paparazzi charging at me. I turned to get back into the building, but the glass doors had already locked behind me. I saw the back of Co-Co's black thong and flat booty cheeks peeking through the netting of his jumper as he quickly turned off down a corridor while I frantically banged on the door, having flashbacks of being back in Brazil, being dragged and disrespected by that reporter. So what if I'd called him myself? He still had no right to come there and play me. "Co-Co! Co-Co!" *No, I know he wouldn't do me like that.*

"Heather! Heather!"

*Don't let them do you, girl!*

*Think, Heather, think!*

*Yes. Let these tricksters know what time it is.*

I took two deep breaths, then slowly turned to face the mob circling me like a pack of starved wolves. Cameras and recorders from every direction were being shoved in my face.

"Hey, Heather Cummings. What happened with you and the rest of the Pampered Princesses at Hollywood High? We've heard it's gotten real messy between the four of you."

I smiled my sweetest smile. "I have no use for back-stabbing slores. No shade, boo. I'm doing *me*. And hopefully they're somewhere off doing them. End of discussion."

A camera clicked.

"Heather. Over here," a brown-faced blogger for Dirty Deeds called out, waving a hand in the air. "Is it true you told the Pampered Princesses to put their diamonds up? What did you mean by that? Was that some kind of hidden threat?"

I flashed another smile. "I don't make threats. I make tracks. So what do *you* think it meant?" I took a step forward to leave but got stopped in my tracks. I glanced over and spotted the cameraman zooming in on the crowd, then me. I was furious.

"Hey, Heather Cummings. How does it feel to be Hollywood's fallen teen star?" a tall, dark-haired reporter asked.

I turned to him. "*Fallen?* Ha! Never that. You better check your facts. I'm a star, baby!" I smacked my lips, tossing my hair and gliding a hand along my hip while turning slightly to the side and allowing my hand to travel over my ten-thousand-dollar clapper. I shook and popped my hips a few times and twerked for the cameras. "I'm the crème de la crème. The best of the best."

"Yeah, with a fake rump!" I heard someone in the crowd shout. "Fake trick went from booty pads to butt plugs!"

Then came a roar of laughter.

I blinked. I wasn't sure if I had heard right. I had to be hearing things. But I know I wasn't that deep into my high that I'd be hallucinating. Not off of a *pinch*, anyway.

Someone asked, "So how does it feel going from having your own sitcom to now being forced to do reality TV because none of the other major networks want to hire you? Do you see it as a kick in the face?"

I blinked. "No. I see it as an *opportunity*." *Yeah, an opportunity to stay in the limelight until something better comes along.* "And for the record, I wasn't *forced* to do anything." *Okay, it was a lie. I hated it! And I felt trapped!*

"Whatever happened to your role as Luda Tutor in that new comedy series airing on the Kitty-Kitty network? We heard it was yours until you went on a drug and booze binge again."

I could feel the effects of my get-right completely draining out of my body, leaving me feeling naked and vulnerable. My hands started sweating. My insides began to tremble. Not one soul out here was screaming out for Wu-Wu. No one was cheering me on or chanting my name. No one was asking for my autograph. No. These vultures swooped down on me to peck me apart. This was an execution! A setup! I'd been ambushed. I couldn't believe I was being cornered and put under attack like this! *How did these media leeches know I was here? And who is this crowd out here? These are not my Wu-Wu fans!*

"Hey, Heather," a reporter for *Ni-Ni Girlz Glamalicious* called out. "Is it true Spencer Ellington had to loan you three million dollars because you and your mother are flat broke?"

*Whaaat?! Who told this trick that?* I wanted to scream out, *I'ma kill that effen beyotch, Spencer!* Instead, I batted my long, purple-tinted mink lashes. "Wrong answer, boo. I wasn't *loaned* anything. It was a gift."

"So you're denying the fact that you're *broke* . . .?" a red-haired journalist for *J-14* questioned.

I felt the ground shake beneath my purple, six-inch gladiator boots. I quickly glanced at all the eyes staring back at me, waiting for the chance to slaughter me. Yeah, I ran through most—*okay, okay*, practically all—of the money Spencer had given me. Still, that didn't give *any-one* the right to pry into my personal affairs! I had to live! I needed things! And what I did with *my* money was no one's business!

"Yeah, she's broke!" Someone shouted way in the back of the mob. *Dear God! I must be hallucinating. Surely no one would be trying to serve me fever.* "Look at her! Cheap, cheesy trick in that hooker suit! Skidrow trash!"

More laughter.

I felt my heart stop. *My Wu-Wu fans would never do me like this!* There was nothing *cheesy* or *cheap* about the outfit I was wearing, a skintight pink leopard-print Lycra catsuit with a plunging V-neckline to give my 34DDs breathing room. I was doing it. Serving it. Eff them!

I craned my neck to see who was trying to toss shade all up over me. Clearly, it had to be someone who couldn't stand all this divaliciousness I was serving up. They had it in for me. *But who?* Rich? Yeah, it had to be that miserable slore. I'd read her for gutter *filth* my first day back at school. So what? I'd finally given her what she'd been giving me behind my back *and* to my face—a taste of her own medicine. *If you can't stand the heat, then stay out the fire!*

I pushed my way through the crowd, flinging my arms as I tried to stomp off with the cameraman trailing behind me. All of this was being captured on film. *These effen cameras! This effen reality show! I gotta get outta here! Away from everyone! I didn't ask for this kind of media attention!*

I signaled for the cameraman to cut off his camera. But the no-good dirty ninja kept on rolling. "Get outta my way!" I shouted, almost knocking someone down trying to get through the crowd.

The media hounds and bloggers rushed behind me. "A source says that in less than a month you've, quote-unquote, *tricked up* all your money on drugs, Korean knockoffs and—"

I whipped my head in the bloggers' direction, slapping

a few of them in the face with my long ponytail. "Lies. Lies. And more lies. I've done no such thing! I haven't touched drugs since I've been home. And if you think I have, show me the receipts!"

"Heather. Is it true that your mother tried to kill you after you'd gone missing for almost three weeks?"

No comment. I kept on fighting my way through the crowd.

"Yeah, the ole drunk tried to kill her!" someone else yelled in back of me. "If you had a daughter who looked like *that* wouldn't you try to kill her too?"

*If you had a daughter who looked like that?* No one laughed. Still, the heckler's words slashed right through me. I felt the stinging in my eyes as I fought back tears. What I looked like was a sore spot for me. No one knew how much I *hated* looking in the mirror at times, seeing the reflection staring back at me.

*Hold it together! Don't you dare let them see you shed one tear!*

"Hey, Heather. A source says you finally know who your father is. Is that true?"

A gasp caught in the back of my throat.

"It's about time someone wanted to claim her!" some-one else jeered, then started yelping like a wounded animal. "Someone call the SPCA! Lost mutt in heels on the loose."

I felt my knees buckle. Then I heard the screaming in my head. Felt the tightening in my chest as the cameraman finally decided to shut off his equipment and help usher me through the swelling crowd, pushing our way through at the same time the limo pulled up to the curb.

The minute the door opened, I slid into the back of the limo and sank dejectedly into my seat, just as a ran-over pump, packed with dog poop, came soaring into the cabin of the limo, splattering all over.

Its message loud and clear: *You ain't nothing, Heather!*

# 7

# Heather

"Get me outta here!" My voice cracked as I tried to hold back my tears. I couldn't believe someone had tossed dog poop into my limo. I was never so humiliated, embarrassed, in my entire life. I shouted at my driver, "Drive, idiot! Run them all down! And what took you so effen long?! You were supposed to already be out here! Waiting on me! Not the other way around! I will have your job for this! You bungling moron! Because of your incompetence I had to suffer public humiliation! You worthless piece of scum!"

He tried to pull off but couldn't. We were blocked in. The crowd had swarmed around us, banging on the windows, throwing eggs and tomatoes at us. I'd never experienced this kind of horror. I was mortified, as it was all being caught on film. I screamed at the cameraman for standing there and letting them animals attack me like that.

He shrugged. I glared at him as he scrunched up his

nose and reached for a stack of napkins, then picked up the heel dripping with brown funk, inched the window down just enough to push the shoe out, then quickly rolled it back up.

He shut the camera off and callously said, "Get over it. It's business. It's all about the ratings. Besides, I'm not your bodyguard." He turned the camera back on as the driver pressed down on the accelerator and was finally able to pull off from the sea of media serpents and haters. "Now tell us. How did all of that craziness make you feel?"

I blinked. *How do you think any of this makes me feel?!* I felt like the ground had opened up and I was being sucked down into the bowels of hell. And effen Spencer was there standing in the middle of the fire with her pitchfork, stabbing me in the center of my big bouncy Brazilian, deflating each of my implants.

I stared into the camera. "I'm pissed! I feel betrayed! That's how the eff I feel! Turned on by some jealous trick who doesn't have a life! I can't believe she tried to drag me like this. Why? Because I traded her raggedy Lamborghini in for something *I* wanted? *Bish,* please! Drink Drano. And die a slow death!"

I was done. And I wasn't in the mood for this goddamn camera either! All I wanted to do was escape. Be left alone. Disappear. Drop off the face of the earth. Find me a dark hole and get lost. All I wanted was a little grace and mercy. That's it. Was that too much to ask for?

I wanted to live. Just not like this. Not under someone else's rules. Not under someone else's microscope, or through someone else's cloudy, rose-colored lenses. No. I wanted to live *my* life, *my* way. But I couldn't!

"So, why do you think people in the crowd were taunting you like that?"

"Eff them haters!" I spat. I felt sick from the lingering smell of poop everywhere. I reached over and rolled my window down. "They don't know me!"

"Then why don't you tell us," the cameraman said, zooming his lens on me. "Tell us who you are. Let the viewers know."

I blinked. Tossed the question around in my pounding head. I was still shaken from being ambushed and demeaned. I couldn't think straight.

*Who am I?*

*A broke nobody who just got dog poo thrown at her!*

A tear rolled down my face. My insecurities kicked in. Next came the avalanche, a rushing well of tears pouring out of my eyes. Then came the screaming for the cameraman to get his goddamn camera out of my face! Followed by the banging on the partition for the driver to stop the limo. I yelled and screamed and cursed and carried on to no end until the driver pulled over. I swung open the door.

"Get out! Get out, NOW!" I kicked and screamed until he finally hopped out. I slammed the door, rolling down the window, sticking my head all the way out. "And STAY outta MY life!"

The driver drove off as I pulled my head back in and laid it on the headrest, pulling in a deep breath, allowing my tears to fall unchecked. This had to be some kind of dirty, vicious trick someone was playing on me. But there wasn't any punch line. No. This was a bad dream. I kept squeezing my eyes shut, then opening them, hoping that the image and the stench of that raggedy pump being thrown at me with crap splattering everywhere would just go away. But it wouldn't.

*Stupid cameraman! Eff reality TV!*

I tsked. *Psst. Who does he think he is? Asking me who I am? What kinda question is that?*

I shook my head. "I'm *Heather Suzanne Cummings*!" I muttered to myself, mocking Camille's voice.

*Okay? And who is she?*

*Who is she?*

I blinked.

I felt the pounding in my chest as soon as I heard the answer in my head. *She's not the girl who gets asked to go to proms, or out on dates, by some wealthy rich kid! No! She's the girl who gets told to pull down her pants and bend over a goddamn desk! She's the wounded little girl who gets a hand placed over her mouth while told to spread her legs so some perverted, sick woman can slide down her body and tamper in her forbidden zones. That's who she is! Scarred! Confused! Hurt!*

I heard myself screaming, *"But that's not who I wanna be!"*

No! I was Wu-Wu, *beyotches*! The pop-lock-and-droppin'-it, fun-loving, exciting, animal-print wearing, good-time party girl! I was Wu-Wu the suburban teenager with a little sister who worked my nerves and an old dog that did nothing but eat, sleep, and pass gas. I was Wu-Wu with two parents who loved *me* and adored and accepted all of my flaws and crazy antics. That's who I was! That's who I'd always be!

Wu-Wu effen Tanner!

A star!

And I didn't care what Kitty, Camille, Spencer, the paparazzi, or anybody else had to say about it. Wu-Wu was not dead! Wu-Wu would never be dead! Because being anything other than Wu-Wu meant being a nobody! It meant I'd have to be stuck in my nightmare of a world as the biracial misfit with a white, angry drunk for a mother and a pathetic black father who knew I existed but didn't care about me.

*God! I need a Black Beauty!*

*Nothing too crazy; just a pinch to take the edge off...*

I slid my hand down inside my handbag, felt around for the little silver case Co-Co had given me earlier, and pushed out a sigh of relief. My guaranteed escape! *"This is them Pink Panties, honey."* He'd told me the pink powder base was speed that was mixed with Adderall and pinch of Molly. *"Honey, this will have you soaring on twenties. Trust."*

I repositioned myself, sliding back the privacy partition. Then opened the case, admiring the pretty pink powder. My mouth watered. *Ole junky!*

*I'm not a junkie!*

*Prove it!*

I swallowed. Stared at the substance one last time before snapping the lid shut and tossing the pill case back into my purse. "Girl, psst. Screw them haters! You don't need anyone! It's you and me against the world, boo! You got this."

*Then why do I feel so lonely?*

They had it all wrong! I *needed* to be Wu-Wu! Not being Wu-Wu meant being that lonely, pathetic girl who ached for acceptance; who hungered for love and attention and affection from someone that she could be herself around;

someone she could share her fears, her secrets, and her first real kiss with.

I pulled out my cell. I needed a friend. I needed someone to talk to. Wanted someone to listen to me rant and ramble, or say nothing at all. And in their silence, I'd know that I mattered. That what I had to say, and what I felt, mattered.

I opened my call log and dialed Co-Co. The only pseudo-friend I had. I tried him three times and each time the call went straight to voice mail. I frowned. *Any other time this trick is Johnny Gung Ho on the spot. Now he doesn't pick up.* I kept scrolling through my call log. *What a loser!* Co-Co was the only so-called friend I had. And the only things he was good for were gossip, parties, and pills.

My breath caught in my chest and I felt those same unexplainable feelings I'd felt the night she'd introduced herself to me. *"Girl, you are beautiful."* I felt my face flush and my body heat as I stared at the contact with the picture of the two of us, remembering everything about that night. I touched the side of my face, remembering the way her hand caressed my cheek. I felt the butterflies fluttering in my stomach just thinking about it; felt warm excitement coursing through my veins.

*"My name is Nikki..."*

*Ohmygod! This is craziness!*

Before I could stop myself, I pressed CALL, holding my breath. *Heather, what are you doing? Are you insane? Hang up! Hang up the phone!* I hung up on the third ring, tossing my phone back in my bag. *Oh, you're really tripping, girl.*

I took a deep breath. I could hear Camille's mouth now.

*"Heather Suzanne! You're spending too much time with Trans-Confusion. I don't know what you're doing, but I ain't having no shortbread sugar cookies up in here..."*

I shook her voice out of my head, turning toward the window and staring out into the darkness. Camille was my Achilles heel.

I hated that *she* used me. Hated that *she* needed me. Hated that no matter how many times *she* treated me like dirt—no matter how many times *she* tossed back a drink and I'd find her passed out drunk; no matter how many times *she* blackmailed me or threatened to have me put away—I couldn't hate her. I tried to. Wanted to. But somehow I'd always come up stuck somewhere in between disdain and disgust. Most times my feelings stayed miserably matted, like Camille's raggedy mink slippers, somewhere between helpless and hopeless. Because, the truth was, that's what I was—helpless and goddamn hopeless!

I was miserably helpless without Camille. And I was miserably hopeless *with* her. Yet, I effen needed her! She was all I effen had! Because no one else wanted me!

I was all she effen had!

Because no one else wanted her, either!

I was my mother.

And my mother was I...

And here was another goddamn truth: No matter how many awards I'd won, no matter how many red carpets I'd strutted down, no matter how many Wu-Wu fans I had, there'd always be some *hater* somewhere, lurking, quietly waiting to toss eggs and goddamn tomatoes at me! Or throw a shoe full of doo-doo at me!

There'd always be some dirty trick somewhere in the

crowd, reminding me that no matter how high I climbed, no matter how high I was perched up on my throne, I was still nothing but country-hick, trailer-park trash!

No matter what I did, I was still the bastard daughter of Norma Marie Schumacker (daughter of Ellie Lou and Gomer aka Big Daddy) of West Virginia, by way of some dirty back-woods town in Mississippi.

*"I swear you're just like—"*

*"Like who?! My father...? Well, who is he?!"*

*"Heather, I know who your father is..."*

*"Who is he, Camille? Say his name! Tell me! I'm tired of not knowing!"*

*"He doesn't want you! He's never wanted anything to do with you..."*

*"I wanna know who MY FATHER IS!"*

*"He's Richard—"*

*"I was supposed to have an abortion..."*

*"He's Richard—"*

*"He already has a daughter...he doesn't want you..."*

*"He's Richard—"*

*"He's never wanted anything to do with you...!"*

The minute the limo pulled up into my Beverly Hills driveway, I swung open the door and jumped out, leaving it wide open as I raced up the walkway, storming through the door. There she stood, in her latest nightwear getup—a white chiffon two-piece nightgown and crystal-studded pencil-heels—at the bar, dropping ice cubes into a crystal tumbler, then filling it with scotch.

She turned toward me, shooting me an annoyed look. "Well, it's about time you—"

I cut her off, hand on hip. Face wild and crazed. "Is

RICHARD MONTGOMERY my *FATHER*?! And don't you DARE lie!"

The drink in her hand dropped to the floor, the glass shattering everywhere.

"I'll take that as a *yes*!"

# 8

# Spencer

"Strike me down, thunder, and hear me roar!" Daddy bellowed, as he stood in the middle of the hall, barefoot, wearing some god-awful Tarzan wrap made from a bedsheet, a safari hat atop his head while he beat his bare chest like an ape. "Oooh-ooh-ooh-aah-aah." He mimicked the primate by sticking his hands under his armpits and hopping from one foot to the other. "Oooh-ooh-ooh-aah-aah..."

I blinked. Sweetnutcrackersandbuttwhackers! Daddy had always been a bit eccentric, but this was going way overboard, even for me. He was acting like a real live jungle creature. And I didn't find one dang thing humorous about his rainforest shenanigans.

"Daddy, how about you put crazy back in the jar for a while, and let me have your assistants help get you out of that diaper you have on." I walked over to the wall intercom and pressed a button. "Consuela," I said to the house manager, "where are Daddy's nursing assistants?" She told

me they were both on break. My eyes widened. Then I
went off. "Break? And Daddy's up here running wild? Ring
the alarm, gotdangit, because I'm about to turn the gas up
in here! You tell that mountain trash they have ten seconds to get up here and put my father back together
again, or find themselves working at the local zoo sifting
through elephant dung with their front teeth."

Daddy took off running down the corridor. "You'll have
to catch me first, tootsie roll!"

I glanced at my watch. It was almost noon. I didn't have
time for Daddy's foolery. I had somewhere to be. And I
wasn't about to be late, pitty-pattying with him. Not today.

Daddy had been home *only* four days, and had already
managed to tear my nerves down to the seams. Dealing
with him was like having a wayward puppy. If he wasn't
running up and down the halls, making all kinds of tribal
chants and calls, he was on repeat nonstop, saying the
same things over and over or singing verses of the same
song over and over and over, loudly.

It was becoming nerve-racking.

Last night, he sang a verse from "Ain't No Mountain High
Enough" literally a hundred and twelve times as he paced
up and down the corridor. I know because I counted.

If he wasn't taking off his clothes and walking through
the house naked, he was picking in his butt crack or playing with his hairy meatballs. There was nothing more disgusting than seeing Daddy naked. Oh, or walking in on
him playing with his limp noodle. Gross!

And it doesn't help that yesterday someone jimmied
the lock to the liquor cabinet and stole bottles of liquor.
When I asked Daddy about it he said, "I haven't been

downstairs all day. You keep me chained and locked in my room, gal. How am I supposed to go anywhere under these horrid conditions? By the way, did I tell you I saved millions of dollars divorcing your...your, um, uh...your mother today?"

Blank stare.

Daddy must have forgotten that Kitty divorced him— months ago.

Anyway, seven o'clock this morning I caught him red-handed with a bottle of Johnnie Walker Black and a shot glass up to his lips. When I asked him where he'd gotten it from, he simply stated, "You must have snuck in my room and put it here."

"Daddy, hush with these tales," I said, grabbing the bottle from him. "I did no such thing."

I started looking around his room, opening up his drawers and closets. He jumped up from his chair. "You can't go in my things! What is the nature of this breach of privacy? You are in violation of my Fourth Amendment rights."

"Daddy, you can't go around breaking into the liquor cabinets stealing booze. If you have this bottle, then I'm sure you've hidden other bottles somewhere around here."

He huffed. "Nonsense. I've done no such thing. You're pathologically obsessed like that Kitty gal I married."

"Daddy, that *gal* is my mother."

"Then that explains it," he said, giving me a pitiful look. "Both of you are scandalous thieves. And we all know there's no honor among hoes and thieves."

My jaw dropped. *"Daddy!"* I shrieked. "How could you

say such a thing? I'm not a ho! I can't speak for Kitty, though. I've never taken anything from you. But I'm going to leave you before I say or do something that you will regret."

"You better not take my money with you! I'll have you put away with the rest of the crooks!" Daddy snapped. Then he started yelling at me for no ding-dang reason. "Thief! Thief! Thief! Liar, liar, liar!" He'd never done that before. Yelling. Accusing me. Calling me a thief and a liar.

How dare he! I'd never *stolen* anything. And I wasn't a *liar*. No. I was the chickie who said what she meant, and meant what she said. And I told you to your face. So him saying that to me stung worse than when I'd gotten zapped on the tip of my nose by a wasp last summer, and my nose swelled up like a pickle. I was never so hurt in my life. I had to walk around for weeks wrapping silk scarves around my mouth and nose and wearing head wraps to keep from being spotted with that hideous bulbous lump on my face.

And now this!

I stormed out of his sitting room, then took off for the garage like a bat out of hell. When I hit the switch on my remote, the car chirped and the doors unlocked, the sounds echoing throughout the heated six-car space. I eased open the car door, tossed my handbag over into the passenger seat, then slid behind the steering wheel of my navy blue Rolls-Royce Phantom Drophead Coupé. It was Kitty's latest gift to me to calm my roaring sea. A peace offering she called it, since she'd come to her senses and realized she was dirt wrong and gotdang cesspool messy for keeping Daddy's condition from me. So, now, ever since our little knock-down, drag-out brawl, she'd been trying to play Miss Nice-Nasty. Still, no matter how little she tried, she couldn't undo the damage she'd already done or take back the hurtful things she'd already said to me after I'd told her that Daddy was on his way back from Africa.

"For the love of God!" she shrieked when I confronted her in our kitchen. "You have got to be kidding me! Why in God's name would you do that?"

"Because Daddy's not well. And he needs to be home."

"Oh, spare me the pity party. Crying over some man who barely remembers his own name, let alone yours. Mmph. I'd probably have done better with a junkie for a daughter than you. At least she'd have an excuse. But you, you ingrate, you get attached to the servants. You pine over some old man who doesn't know you. Never even taken the time to get to know you. But you want to play Florence Nightingale. I don't want him here. Do you hear me?"

"Well, I don't care what you want, Kitty. This is his home too. And he'll be here in less than sixteen hours, so you had better get used to it!"

"I tell you what. If you bring that man here you had better keep him in your wing of the house because I don't want to see him, smell him, or hear him. Because, make no mistake, my darling daughter, if I do I will open up the terrace doors and usher him toward the railing, then show him the way to the promised land. I'll open the doors and let him wander out and get lost. And there's a steep hill out there. It's a hell of a cliff we live on, and he'll be found at the bottom of it if I even see him anywhere on my side of the house. Do you understand me?"

"He's my father. And I want him here. Period, Kitty!"

"Oh, now I'm *Kitty*. Is that it, little girl? Are you that desperate for attention, Spencer, that you'd drag some infirm old fart into this house? Really? Nothing is ever good enough for you? Heather would love to have access to unlimited money. But you..." She shook her head. Then tsked me. "Pathetic. All you want to do is complain and moan. And now you want to walk this sick man into my life again. I divorced him for a reason. You must really want your father falling over that cliff outside. Well, test me if you want. I'm going to tell you what I told them when they called and said he needed to come home: You had better find him a nice little nursing home with an ocean view, feed him intravenously, and throw away the key."

My head jerked back. I batted my lashes. My heart began to pound a little faster. Before I could bring it to Kitty real good, she let out a cruel laugh that made my insides knot. I blinked.

I bit my bottom lip. My head felt like it would explode any second. Kitty had gone too far this time! All the other times she'd been messy and hurtful, I'd excuse it. I'd lock myself away in my room and cry my eyes out. But this time...oh no! Oh no! This time that ole dirty skunk had to get skinned and torched. This time Kitty had to feel every gotdiggitydang inch of my pain. And I didn't give a hot damn what happened afterward. My mind was made up! Kitty was getting rolled out in a trash cart!

Tears sprouted from my eyes, blinding me. I clenched

my fists, feeling the blood boil through me as I screamed at the top of my lungs. I felt myself getting drunk with craziness. "You evil witch! You hateful, soulless wench! You have run your clap-mouth one time too many, Kitty! And you are going to feel my wrath! And by the time I'm done with you, you're going to wish you were born a man and had never spread your legs to have me!"

"Save yourself the trouble, Spencer, dear. I already do! Now do me a favor, little girl. Get out of my sight! I have a new boy-toy I picked up today and I want to break him in. So I need you to make yourself scarce so I can have full use of the house."

She spun on her heel to walk away, tossing her hair. I jumped up from my seat and ran across the floor into the foyer, my heels clicking loudly, and grabbed the crystal flower vase off the large entryway table, and hurled it at her back, knocking her to the floor. She was lucky I'd stepped over her body and left her lying on the floor instead of going wild and bashing her skull in. All I could do was give praise and thanks for being a changed woman.

I sighed, lowering the roof of my new car. I pressed the button to lift the garage door, pulling out a pair of expensive sunglasses and putting them on. I was so over Kitty. But I'd let her think we were all coochie-coochie-crunch-crunch... for now, that is. It was only a matter of time before I'd drag her to the doors of damnation, then push her into the bowels of hell, where she belonged. And if I was feeling generous enough, I'd send her off with me pissing a little gasoline on her first, before I pushed her into the flames.

I threw the stick shift in first gear, jerked forward a few times before getting it together. I sped out of the garage. Swerved around the circular drive, then waited for the gates to slide open. I was making a quick escape from Senior Day Care to San Diego to see Midnight: Rich's future ex-boo Knox's roommate and fraternity brother.

I looked at myself in the rearview mirror. "Woof, woof! Knick-knack paddy whack, give that dog a bone! Yes, goshdangit!" I shook my head. "If that show dog holds his bone right, I might let him get a few tongue laps around momma's milk bowl."

Midnight and I'd been talking on the phone almost every night for the last few weeks. And he'd been sending me "good morning" texts every day since the day Rich and I fled to his and Knox's apartment, where we stayed for almost two days after I whopped and popped her bum dog in Timbs, aka Justice, upside his nugget with my nunchucks. Mmph. But that's another tale, for another time. This was about Micah Rufus Johnson... and *me*.

And as for us, we'd been going real hot and heavy, panting and moaning into the phone at wee hours of the night, talking all kinds of sweet and nasty goodness. We'd even sat up in bed on Skype and played a little game of "I'll Show You Mine If You Show Me Yours" as we told each other dirty bedtime stories. Ooh, he was some kind of freaky.

Anyway, today was going to be our first time seeing each other in flesh and bone. And I was excited. But I was nervous too. And I didn't know why. Well, I did. The truth was, I'd never really been on an official date with anyone before. Not out in public, anyway. Most of my so-called dates were more like "snack outs," which usually ended in the backseat of a car, in one of the locked student lounges at Hollywood High, or down in a dark alley with my face buried in some boy's treasure chest, or his buried in mine.

Although Midnight wasn't officially my boo-boo, I liked him. A lot. But I wasn't sure if I wanted him for a boyfriend. I was scared. I'd only had three boyfriends my entire life. RJ—Rich's older brother, whom I'd given my heart and my gushy-gushy to. In fact, he was my first everything. My first crush. My first kiss. My first love. But that ended in heartache once he was shipped off to England for school.

Then there was Curtis, who I was with for four months and eighteen days before it ended in tragedy with Kitty screwing him sideways and silly on his eighteenth birthday. And let me not even mention Joey. My cardboard-box lover who'd haphazardly gotten himself stuck inside of Kitty's sticky thong juice one late summer night. Being suspicious of Kitty's sudden interest in Joey was what led me to follow her to a secluded location where I watched Joey slide into the passenger seat of her Bentley, then lean over and kiss her. I followed them down to Laguna Beach. And waited. Using a telephoto lens, I captured every dirty deed.

It ended with me slicing all four of Kitty's tires down to the ground, then sneaking down to the beach and wrapping my hands into Kitty's hair and dragging her half-naked body through the sand, macing Joey, then clawing up his face.

Mmph.

The gate slid open, and I was on my way. I shifted the gears and sped off. The sun was shining. The wind was whipping through my hair, blowing it every which way as I worked the stick like a crazed woman, shifting gears up and down, braking then speeding up again. I switched lanes, blowing my horn at any vehicle trying to block my wheel roll. Yes, gotdiggitydangit... I was driving the I-5 at racing-car speeds while I sang at the top of my lungs, sucking in the air that whipped inside of the cabin, every track of K. Michelle's album *Rebellious Soul*, which is exactly what I was.

When I finally arrived at my destination, I peered over the rim of my designer shades and eyed daddy long legs as Midnight stepped out of his building and swaggered his way over to the car, stylishly dressed in a pair of slightly baggy designer jeans, a black long-sleeved Gucci T-shirt, and a pair of very expensive slip-ons. The front of his shirt was tucked in just so, to show off the Gucci symbols on his belt buckle.

I could already hear the sound it would make as it hit the floor. I squirmed and bounced in my seat. I felt my hello kitty starting to purr and come alive. Oooh, sookie-sookie-meow-meow! Spankmybiscuitsraw! Umph-mmph. He was a tall, lanky glass of dark, smoldering sexiness!

I licked my MAC-painted, glossed lips. *Come to momma, my little boo-daddy!* I pressed the button to unlock the door, then watched as he opened it and slid in real smooth. I caught a whiff of his cologne. *Mmmm, he smells delish*, I mused as I played the guessing game of what scent he had on. He smelled like Kenneth Cole Black.

He leaned over and kissed my cheek, then flicked his long tongue along the side of my neck, causing me to shiver as a jolt of electricity zapped to the tip of my good 'n' plenty.

"What's good, sweet potato? You looking so tasty I could crawl up under your skirt, eat up ya crumbs, and get lost forever."

"Oooh, you dirty dog!" I couldn't help but grin as I playfully swatted his hand off of my thigh. I reached into my console and pulled out a spiked dog collar and studded dog chain. "You must want momma to strap you up and yank you by the chain."

"Woof, woof! Strap me. Drag me. Yank me. Do me up right, baby. I don't care what you do as long as you just get to it. And I like it real nasty."

He puckered his lips up to get a kiss. And I happily smooched it up with him. I reached in his lap and grabbed his goody bag a few times. Midnight growled when I pulled away. "Hey, hey, don't stop. You got my dog bone stretching. You got me ready to get up in them yams, sweet cheeks. I think I'ma fall hard for you, girl. You like a twelve-piece, extra-crispy, with a side order of slaw, rolls, 'n' mac 'n' cheese, baby." He smacked his lips like he was sucking barbecue sauce from his fingers. "Yeah, you the full-course meal, boo."

I giggled, pressing down on the accelerator and speeding off.

"Whoa! Whoa!" Midnight scrambled trying to put on his seat belt. "Wait! Wait! Please, don't kill me! Please!" He wrapped his arms around himself. "I don't wanna die!"

He started praying and chanting and rocking.

I snickered. "Oh, I'm not going to kill you, dark daddy. But I am going to tie you up, then introduce you to my weapons of mass destruction."

Ooh, yes. I was the bone handler, baby. And when I was done nibbling on Midnight, he was going to be in the fetal position, sucking his thumb, drool slowly sliding out the corner of his mouth, his eyes rolling around in their sockets, and in need of a wheelchair.

Heeheehee.

# 9

# Rich

I gripped the cool edges of my lava vanity, barely inching my throbbing head past my shoulders and up to the mirror to scan my reflection. My eyelids were creased and hung like crescent moons, making my irises look half their size.

I couldn't believe this was happening to me again...

*Not again*...

Just when I had made up my mind that I was going to put my boom-bop-make-it-hot-and-make-it-drop on pause for a minute and collect my thoughts...

Just when I swore I was going to stop trippin' over my latest bouts with whiny testosterone and the major shade it had thrown my way...

Just.

When.

I.

Decided.

To get my ish together, in stepped this...

I was pregnant.

Again.

I had to be.

I knew all the signs.

I'd been there too many times before.

Besides, I hadn't seen my period in two months.

My breasts ached.

My stomach hurt.

And I threw up every morning. Sometimes at night.

I needed my mother.

I needed her to show me a way out of this.

She was the only one who could help me.

But.

She hadn't spoken to me in weeks. And she'd stopped making her morning rounds—coming to my room to wake me up for breakfast. And at breakfast, when I sat at the table, she got up.

*Get it together.*

I walked back into my room and as I sat in my day area, I could see my mother sunbathing by the pool while the dancing flames from the outdoor fireplace reflected in the round eyes of her bumblebee Chanels.

She leafed through the pages of a book, the cover shielded by her hands.

Her life looked storybook perfect and for a moment I was pissed. How dare she ignore me? Not speak to me! Her own child. Who does that? Like really? Who did she think she was to treat me like this?

This had to end!

Today!

I pulled the drawstring in my black Richard Chai sweats tight around my waist, threw on a baggy hoodie, and walked outside. Poolside. Stood before my mother and said, "So you're never going to speak to me again? Is this what your silent temper tantrums are about? You're cutting me off? Who does that to their own child?"

I could tell by the lines around her mouth that she'd swallowed at least three or four things that she wanted to say to me, and it was obvious by the way her left hand clutched the reclining lounge chair she sat in, that it took everything in her not to jump out of her seat and drown me.

Instead she fluttered her mink lashes up at me and said, "Would you like Shakeesha to answer that? Or Logan?"

See, this is the bull-ish I'm talking about! Shakeesha Logan Gatling was gutter rat trash, but Logan Montgomery had class. And that's who I need to speak to. "I want *my mother, Logan.*"

"Oh really." She gave a half laugh, half grunt, and topped it off with a snort. "Since when?"

I sucked in a breath and shoved out a deep sigh. "I don't like the way you're treating me." I placed my hands up on my hips and when I saw her eyes land on my stomach, I quickly took my hands down.

I sat in the chair next to her and crossed my arms over my breasts. She was sure to inspect those next.

"Ma," I continued. "What you're doing isn't right. I'm only sixteen and every sixteen-year-old needs a mother in their life! One who speaks to them!"

"Well, I'm tired of being your mother," she said with ease, returning to leafing through the pages of her book.

Tears rushed to my eyes.

She glanced over at me and frowned. "Please, not today."

I wiped my wet cheeks with the backs of my hands. "Why would you say something like that to me?! Why? Don't you know I have feelings? RJ is not the only child you have!"

She snapped her neck toward me. I knew that would get her attention. "Oh, now you'd like to be my child?" She was as calm as a brewing storm. "Is that so? Really? Last I checked you were tired of my bitchazzness."

"I never—"

"Be. Quiet." She slid her Chanels down the bridge of her nose and arched her brow with every word. She curled her lips in disgust. "All my hopes. Dreams. And teachings. Wasted on you! Laid up every week on some boy's bed-sheets."

"Ma—!"

"Did I tell you to speak? You and little girlfriend tag-teaming some twins."

*Twins?* My eyes scanned her face. *How does she know that?*

"Then there was Damon." She ripped a page out of her book. "Jonathan." She ripped another page. "Corey. Knox. The freak you picked up in the bar. Justice." She paused and I watched the pages flutter like feathers. "*Yes, Justice.* And the umpteen other names I didn't rattle off!"

My eyes landed on the pages as they floated to the pavers and suddenly the ground felt like it had opened up and was pulling me into the pits of hell.

She had my diary! *My diary!* In her hands! My whole world! Ripping pages out of it and taking my innermost thoughts and secrets and tossing them into the air like confetti.

I couldn't believe it. My head was spinning and I could feel the bile rising at the back of my throat, bubbling its way onto my tongue.

She continued, "You're up in lounges drinking. Walking around with fake IDs. Lying about being twenty-one. Stressing out and eating platters and platters of buffalo wings. All the money I spent on that bypass surgery. I should've let you stay fat. I would've had a better chance of you not turning into a whore!"

"How dare you!" I jumped up and she shot me a look that made me pause midair.

"If you take another step, Shakeesha will beat you like a woman in the street." She waited and I sat down, humiliated, and surrendered to dying.

*Dear God…*

She continued on. "You've been pregnant so many times that I've lost count. And God knows you can't have any more abortions because no doctor will touch you."

I couldn't breathe.

I couldn't.

I stood up to leave and my legs were like willow branches.

But I had to get out of there some kind of way. Even if I had to crawl my way out.

"Sit. Down," my mother said calmly. "Now. You wanted me to speak. Well, I'm speaking."

Completely lost to the moment, I did as she said.

"You think being out here in these streets is something big." She rattled off, "You think it makes you relevant. You think because they write articles about you on all the blogs, the gossip sites, and because little girls dream of being like you that you have made it. Ha! Well, honey, let me inform you, because obviously you've been misguided. At the rate you're going, those same sites, blogs, and little girls, will be mourning you soon."

"I can't believe you said that!"

"Believe it. You don't use condoms. You don't use discretion. Who would've ever thought that Knox—your father's accountant's son—would be the best decision you've ever made? All of these wealthy families with sons who have promising futures, and your best choice is the help. *And then Justice.* Some R & B, dime-a-dozen wannabe. All he'll ever do is smoke-filled lounges and child-support courtrooms. That's about it."

She drowned me in more ripped pages of my diary.

"You do horrible in school. You're a C and D student on your best days. Countless checks we've written so you would have decent grades. Countless teachers we've paid off and still nothing works. No child left behind except Rich.

"And you called *me* stupid? You actually wrote in here that you thought I was stupid." She stabbed an index finger into my diary. "Isn't that amusing. You think I don't know anything about your father's five and six mistresses? His whores? Little girl, they are not even worthy enough for me to speak their names. But guess what? I'm number one. I don't compromise. And any man who has ever hit this, knows that he received a prize, not some everyday, common good-time-number-on-the-bathroom-wall slore! So no, there's nothing stupid about me, honey." She tossed her hair over a shoulder. "But you're entitled to your opinion." She ripped more pages out of my diary and tossed them at me.

I swear, I could feel the heat from the hellfire engulfing me and the sinking Earth pulling me down into it.

"And now"—she closed my diary—"you're pregnant again. And I bet you don't even know who the father is."

I felt a round of bullets splash open my chest and every particle of air left my body. I wanted to speak but I couldn't. My tongue was frozen, heavy, and I couldn't move.

The truth was: I didn't know who the father was. And I'd been trying to figure it out. Pinpoint a day. A time. A minute. A moment. But I couldn't. All I knew for sure was that the baby could've been Knox's, Justice's, or . . .

Tears escaped down my cheeks.

After a long and deafening pause my mother eased out of her chair, grabbed her outdoor chiffon robe, slipped it on, and tied the belt around her waist. She slid her Chanels back up the bridge of her nose. And as she tossed my diary into my lap she spat, "Put it on Knox."

# 10

# London

*Milan, Italy*

This was it. The Fashion Week finale was finally here. It was over. I kept my eyes focused on the photographers at the end of the runway as I glided, one foot in front of the other. Flashbulbs went off and I got lost in the moment until I got to the end of the catwalk.

Justice's face flashed in front of me, his lips curled into a sneer.

*"Ain't nobody checkin' for ya... you worthless... Ain't nobody gonna ever love you like me... stupid trick... you make me sick, yo..."*

I didn't know who I was without him. He'd been all I'd ever been. All I'd ever known. Everything I was had been wrapped up in him. But it was over now.

I blinked. Turned and posed for the cameras.

*"Look at you, six-foot-tall, giraffe-neck self... big-foot Amazon... I was the best thing you'll ever have..."*

I was becoming overwhelmed with emotion. I stood in a defiant pose, hand on hip, and realized as the photographers took shots of my dress that I was just as soulless as the industry my mother had forced me to be in. Sadly, in the end, when each model's mask was removed and all the layers were pulled back, we were all the same.

Insanely insecure.

We all wanted the same.

To be beautiful.

To be wanted.

To be loved.

To be seen.

And, yes, whether I openly admitted it or not, I wanted what every one of these attention-starved girls wanted... to be in the spotlight.

But fame came with a price.

Being beautiful came with unwanted attention.

Being wanted came with rejection.

Being loved came with heartache and no guarantees.

Out of nowhere, Rich, Spencer, and Heather zoomed into view. Frenemies turned enemies. Like it or not, in the end, we were still all the same...

Fame whores.

Fighting, fighting, fighting. Fighting for love. Fighting for acceptance. Fighting for happiness. Fighting to outdo, outwit, and outshine the other. Fighting to stay hot. Fighting to stay on top. The only difference was, I was tired of fighting. I was turning in my crown and bowing out gracefully. I was done.

I swallowed, willing back tears. And just as I spun on

my toe to turn, I caught a glimpse of my mother, beaming. I felt my eyes rolling in my head. Seated to the right of her was Alek Wek, the Sudanese supermodel. And to the left of her was Daddy. *Ohmygodno! Daddy's here! To see me!* I caught his wink as he smiled at me, and felt what was left of my broken heart crack into a thousand more pieces as flashes of that night my parents argued resurfaced.

*"You pushed me into someone else's bed when you stopped wanting to handle your wifely duties in and out of our bedroom..."*

*"Oh, Turner, stop! You were screwing that* ghetto *tramp long before I stopped letting you crawl up on top of me. So don't you dare even go there with me! You and I both know the real reason you wanted to relocate here! And it had* nothing *to do with getting London out of New York or being closer to your firm in Beverly Hills and* everything *to do with you wanting to be near that gold-digging home wrecker!"*

I'd never heard them fight before. *Never.* But they argued, and yelled, and pointed fingers. All because of me! I'd caused that! Me! Everything was a mess because of *me!*

Feeling light-headed, I quickly strutted back up the runway and almost toppled over as I made my way backstage to change into my next outfit. I heard a few models sniggle. I shot them nasty looks, hurriedly changing into my next outfit. I made it just in time as models edged up to take the stage again.

*"I want a divorce."*

*"Fine! Go be with your mistress, Turner! London and I will move to Milan..."*

I felt myself starting to hyperventilate. Again, I stepped out into the blinding lights. This time in a red coatdress, draped off the shoulders, and knee-high boots. I worked the runway. Trying to block out the voices in my head. Daddy, my mother, Justice, Rich, Anderson...Anderson!

*"That dude's a bum...he doesn't deserve you...why do you keep letting him hurt you...?*

*"At least ya girl Chunky Monkey was ready to show me some love...at least she knows what a real man is all about...Stop sweatin' me...I'm done with you..."*

*"Yeah, it's obvious you like him...What, are you a reject? Or am I standing in the way? I gave him a lil taste of goodness..."*

A scream caught in the back of my throat as the image of Justice's hand in those photos that had been overnighted to me by some anonymous sender back in the States came into view. *The butterfly. The two R's on the antennas! It was Rich in those photos!*

I cringed inwardly, pushing through one showing after the other, floating through each one until the final hour. The masquerade was finally going to be over. There was so much commotion. It was frantic. Models were scurrying around to line up. It was ten minutes to the runway finale. Yet, I was surprisingly calm.

It all became surreal. I was here. But I wasn't. I felt like I was having an out-of-body experience. A wave of relief washed over me as I stepped in line amongst a sea of flowing satins, quivering feathers, plunging necklines, and fishnet.

I was positioned second to last, wearing a snow-white one-shoulder shift dress with a sheer train and matching satin heels and ankle cuffs. A jeweled crown was set atop my head. My face was covered by a white veil.

I no longer felt wretched and broken.

I felt...beautiful.

Two more models were ahead of me, then I'd be next to go. It was almost over. Everything around me started moving in slow motion as I eased up closer toward the stage.

*"It's not my fault that you have to wallow in self-pity knowing you weren't missed..."*

The voices inside my head banged around each other, but I was numb to them. I slid my hand into the sliver of a side pocket, pulling out my shiny farewell trinket. I never took my eyes off of the stage ahead of me as I sliced a perfect straight line into the center of my flesh, then slashed across my wrist. The blade bit in deep, causing me to swoon. Heat flashed through me as I stepped into the flashing lights.

Effortlessly, I owned the runway with a signature strong-legged bounce; with each step demonstrating an effervescent power I'd thought long gone. A straight line of blood bloomed, burned, and burst into a lush crimson pool. It dripped heavy and unchecked as I *worked* the runway one last time.

It was almost over—*finally!*

*"Just look at you. Pig. Hog...You straight up worthless...I wish you dropped dead..."*

I was metamorphosing.

I was no longer a moth drawn to a flame.

*"When I am done with you, Turner, you'll be penniless! Let's see how devoted your mistress is when you're rotting in a jail cell..."*

Cameras flashed. Anderson's voice replayed in my head. *"You don't even realize what you have in front of you... I'm taking off the red cape, hanging up my Captain Save A Dumb Ho hat and moving on. I'm in love with you, London...."*

I was a colorful butterfly.

I was floating.

I no longer hurt.

I heard the gasps and shrieks.

My heart beat violently at first, echoing in my ears. Then slowed to a deafening pace. I felt myself fading. I blinked. A newborn baby wailed somewhere across the stage. Then it was being violently snatched out of its mother's fragile arms. *But there wouldn't be babies here...* Her little brown face seeped into my consciousness. I had to be dreaming. I blinked. More flashing lights were blinding me. People were scrambling. There was my great-grandmother in a white gown, waiting on the other side of a white gate trimmed in gold, her arms stretched open, smiling at me.

*"Come on home to Nana, baby..."*

My eyes fluttered.

I was getting weaker.

*"I know who your mistress is..."*

*"You aren't taking London with you..."*

*"I most certainly am. Try to stop me, Turner!"*

I was slipping. I was almost there. It was almost over.

Tears streamed down my face as I stepped farther into the white lights. I felt large vibrant wings spreading in back of me. My eyes flickered as thousands of butterflies covered me, slowly lifting me.

*"And the next call I'll be making will be to Richard Montgomery, letting him know you've been screwing his wife...!"*

I was flying. Fluttering away. And the world around me faded to black...

# 11

# Spencer

*Click-click*...

"Hey, aren't you Spencer Ellington?"

I tilted my head. "Who wants to know?"

"Kenya Irvington. With TMZ."

I blinked as the reporter's camera flashed brightly in my face, disorienting me and trying to burn out my retinas.

"Who's your new hottie?"

"I'm Midnight Rufus Johnson," he offered before I had a chance to recover from my flashbulb trauma. "That's M-I-D-N-I-G-H-T..."

*Click-click*...

"So, Spencer...what brings you way out to San Diego? Are you on the creep with someone else's boo?"

I rolled my eyes with annoyance. It took all of my self-control not to get gutter mouth on her. But she was pressing the right button to see what kind of shade I was going to toss up on her. I shifted in my seat.

"Ummm, do you mind, sweetie? As you see, I'm here

minding my business. Hint, hint: I'm not interested in chitchat. So run along. Please and thank you."

"Just one question. So are you *sharing* your new beau with one of the Pampered Princesses? It's no secret you like borrowing everyone else's man."

The camera flashed in my face again.

I lost my cookies right there on the spot.

"Ohmygod, Helen Keller! What the *fawk*! You're trying to blind me!" I screamed. "You intruder! You ratchet skank! Get that camera out of my dang face before I beat you down to the white meat with it." I reached for my goblet and slung water on her. Then hopped up from my seat like a wild woman and wrestled her camera out of her hand. "You want photo ops then you will need to call my publicist." I threw her camera across the room. "Security! Security! Help! I'm being stalked!"

I snatched rolls and cornbread from out of the woven breadbasket on the table and started throwing them at her, hitting her upside the head. She tried to cover her head with her hands. But I was baseball-pitcher ready.

Midnight tried to intervene, but I let him know I had this under control. I yanked a butter knife from off the table.

"I will line your face with slash marks if you don't pop your fanny away from this table and out of my gotdang face!"

Management quickly rushed over and ushered her out of the establishment, apologizing profusely for any inconvenience. Five minutes later, we were being seated in a private dining room.

We placed our orders. The waitress took the menus and headed off. I eyed Ole Mister MacNasty to see if his eyeballs were going to bounce and roll along to the shake in her rump-a-dump. They didn't. Because had they bounced to her shake, that would have been a deal-killer. And then Mr. Dream Date would have had to die a slow, torturous death.

"Now, this is more like it," I said, snapping open the linen napkin and placing it across my lap. I was at Fashion Valley Mall in San Diego with Midnight, having lunch at the Neiman Marcus Zodiac restaurant, then going to the AMC theater to see that ole goofy Madea in her new movie.

"Yo, baby. You went green eggs 'n' ham on that reporter. Straight hood fists with it. My pet rock got real hard watching you get turnt up. You like hot popping fish grease when you go in."

"Well, she should know when to scrape the wax out of her own bees instead of trying to pluck her fingers all in mine."

"Baby, when you mad, you sexier than a bowl of cheese 'n' grits."

I tooted my lips up, dismissing the compliment. "Soooo, Midniiiiiight...I've been meaning to ask you, how was Vegas?" I asked, tilting my head and twirling the end of a curl around my finger. I tended to do that when I was either really, really nervous, about to set it off, or just being coy. Today, I was none of the aforementioned. Heehee. As a matter of fact, I was feeling a little way-too-comfy for my own good. I was relaxed enough to turn my iPhone off and toss it into my purse. And thanks to my raging hormones and purring kitty, I was relaxed enough to slip a foot out of my heels and ease it up into Midnight's lap and start toe-massaging his almond joy.

"Oh, real love. We got it in real right. Sin City was all that."

"Uh-huh. And who all went, again?" I leaned forward, regarding Midnight with genuine interest. I really, really liked him.

"It was me 'n' six of my frat bros 'n' a few other fellas from the yard."

"Oh, that's nice." I took a sip of my pomegranate lemonade. "And I'm sure you nasty hound dogs had a stash of hookers sniffing around you."

Midnight shook his head. "Nah, nah. It wasn't even that kinda party. Not for me anyway. I already got my eye, my nose, my taste buds, my tongue on someone."

I grinned. "Oh. Let the dogs out, Daddy. Do tell."

"Nikki was the only female with us."

I blinked. "*Nikki?* Nikki as in the same Nikki that's always gooey-goo-goo popping it up in Knox's face? Nikki as in the hooker? The Nikki that Rich can't stand?"

He chuckled. "Yeah. But it isn't about nothing, 'cause she's like one of the fellas."

I raised a brow. "Oh really? And how's that? Is *she* really a *he*? A he-she? 'Cause last I saw, she looked like a real girl to me with real boobs and real bouncy booty cheeks. Well, not as bouncy as mine. But they still bounced. And so did her boobs. So how is she one of the *fellas*? Is she wearing a pair of boxers over her pink-laced thong or something?"

Midnight shifted in his seat. "Nikki's cool peeps. That's all I'ma say on that. Trust me, dumpling. She ain't checking for *none* of us. But, yoooooo, that's crazy 'bout BJ's homegirl..."

*"BJ's homegirl,"* I repeated, frowning. "Since when does

a blow job have a homegirl? Where they teaching that at? Mmph."

Midnight laughed. "Nah, nah, cherry pie. BJ stands for big jawn, baby cakes. It's what I call ya girl, Rich."

"*Rich?!*" I shrieked. "Hold up, wait a minute...You're dark-chocolate cute and all, but you're not even about to disrespect my bestie. No, no, no. It's not even going down like that. You have Rich confused. Her big jaws only open for hot wings and beer. Not man parts. Get it right. Or get left with my handprint across your fine face, and my nails clawed into your beautiful cheeks. I will crack your face. You not gonna do my friend. Don't do me. Don't get turnt up for what? I promise you I will gut your eye sockets up in here."

"Yeah, that's it, baby. Talk dirty to me. Gut. Me. Trick me up, lil mama. Take my sight. I don't need to see what I can feel."

I swallowed. Drool gathered at the corners of my mouth. I licked my lips in heated excitement. Ooh, this boy had me tempted to say, *Let's skip dessert and head straight for the nightcap*. But first I had to know..."Why did you feel the need to bring up Rich and her jaws at the dinner table? How disrespectful. Now who is this *BJ* you're talking about? And don't even think about playing riddles with me. Give it to me chopped raw."

Midnight licked his lips. "Marry me, boo. You sure know how to pull at my heart. And my friend likes you too." He glanced down at his lap and smirked. "You got him achin' for you. But, a'ight. Here's the deal. But I need for you to keep this on the low-low, you feel me? You can't flap them pretty lips on this one. This is some *LA Confidential*–type ish."

I blinked. "*Flap* my lips on it? Boy, I don't flap my lips or my tongue up on just any-ole-thing. I got to like you, first." I yanked my napkin from out of my lap and tossed it up on my plate, covering my half-eaten meal.

Midnight shook his head. "Yo, chill, chill, buttermilk. I'm not talking 'bout puttin' in that lip service. I'm sayin' what I'm about to tell you gotta stay on the hush-hush. Between you and me, boo."

"Oh. Well, why didn't you just say that? Geesh, Midnight. Didn't your parents teach you how to communicate? I mean, really. I'm going to need you to work a little harder on your communication skills. All of this deciphering is hectic on my brain cells."

"I got you, muffin. But, uh, anyway...dig this. Rich's girl. What's her name?" He scratched his temple. "That extra-tall one, like seven feet tall..."

"Does she have a long neck?"

"Yeah, yeah. Her," he said excitedly. "Real golden-brown glamazon-type. Prettier than a batch of chicken deep-fried in fresh grease."

I narrowed my eyes. "So you twirled your dipstick in her sourdough?"

"Nah, nah. Not even. But you know who I'm talking 'bout, right?"

I played along, pretending to be dumber than a doorknob. "Ummm, does she have like a supersize head and big feet that look like flippers?"

"I don't know about her feet, babe. All I know is, she was one of them big, sweet, juicy jawns. Keeping it straight gulley with you, that night all I saw was those big fluffy breasts and those two big buttery biscuits she had stuffed in them jeans she had on.

"She was skyscraper tall. Smooth brown skin. I ain't gonna hold you, boo. I almost gave up on the Statue of Liberty and wifed her that night, but she walked like she was holding a potato chip wedged between her booty cheeks. Ole uppity tight-drawls jawn."

I felt my pressure cooker about to whistle. I banged my hand on the table. "How dare you disrespect me, talking about some other girl like that? Right here to my face! Where they teaching that at? Have you no shame?"

He reached over the table and grabbed my hand. "Aww, daaaaayum, sweet potato. Don't be like that. She didn't mean anything to me. I mean. Yeah, she looked good. But hands down she doesn't have a thing on you. Word to mother, you the sweetest, juiciest, freshest..."

"And don't forget the finest," I said, eyeing him with raised brow.

"True indeed. The finest of them all."

I twisted my lips, pulled my hand away. "Uh-huh. Now tell me something I don't already know. Why are you all jolly green giant ho-ho over some big-faced trick?"

"It's not even like that, honey dip."

"Then what is it like? Because from where I'm sitting that's exactly what it's looking like. Now, I'm going to count to twenty, then count backwards to give you a chance to free your mind before I go stunt-girl crazy up in this eatery. One, two, three, four..."

"C'mon, now. You don't even gotta go all urban on me."

"Five, six, seven..."

"All I'm tryna do is remember that jawn's name so I can tell you about how foul she is. Do you know who I'm talking about?"

"Nope," I said spitefully. But of course I did. London. Mmph. "Eight, nine, ten..."

"See, now you're mad. Forget it then. I probably shouldn't put her out there like that anyway."

"Oh no. Put the *bish* out there. Eleven, twelve, thirteen..."

"Are you really gonna keep counting?"

"Umm, yes, I am. I am trying to stay loving and kind, but you are really trying to take me to the dark side. You've really pushed the bullet, Midnight. Now you're going to have to deal with the smoking gun. I feel my other side about to show her derrière, and I'm telling you now it's about to get real funky up in here if I don't cool down my jets. Now go ahead. Keep talking."

"Nah, I'm done, honey-boo. The only beef I like to have is on a plate slathered in steak sauce, not with my boo-thang."

I smirked. "Oh, so now I'm your boo-thang?"

He leaned in, lowered his voice. "Yeah, you my boo-thang, babe. You already know what it is. You my eight-piece chicken 'n' rib combo. You my jumbo shrimp basket, babe. You my king crab legs soaked in beer suds. My lobster soufflé. My Philly cheesesteak smothered with onions, green peppers, lots of ketchup, and a little mayo. It doesn't get any deeper than that."

I shifted in my seat. My frown slowly eased into a slight smile. "Well, act like it, then. Now enough of all this nicey-nicey. Get down to business, Midnight. Tell momma all about this foul creature you were talking about. And don't be giving out compliments or talking all sideways and crazy. Give it to me straight."

He tells me Rich brought London down to San Diego

State for one of his frat parties during the beginning of last semester. I frowned. I knew what party he was talking about. The one snagglepuss Rich failed to invite me to. The one she dragged her hyena to. I was on the verge of saying something but decided to keep my trap shut and sit back to see exactly where he was going with this.

I tapped my fingernails on the table, waiting. One more wrong thing, and I was going to split his eyeballs open and pluck 'em out of his sockets. I slid my hand down into my purse, felt around for my diamond-encrusted nail file. I clutched it in my hand.

"Uh-huh. Go 'head, freak daddy," I said calmly. "I'm listening."

He snapped his fingers. "London. Yeah, that's that seven-foot jawn's name . . ."

Mmph. London, London, London! Hearing that spineless woman's name made my cat hairs sprout. The news of her bloody disaster on the Italian runway disgusted me. Okay, okay, and for an itsy-bitsy second it had me saddened. I wanted her gone. Not like that, though.

FROM THE CATWALK TO THE CRASH CART read one news headline about the tragic ordeal. Another headline read: SWITCHBLADE CUCKOO! TEEN SOCIALITE AND MODELING SENSATION GOES SLICEY DICEY.

Ooh, the minute I heard the news, my heart sank. I was so distressed by the thought of her being . . . of her not (deep sigh) . . . Dear high heavens. I couldn't bear to think it. Her passed on! Perished! Never to be seen again! It was all too much of a diamond cross for me to wear. Wait. Or was I supposed to bear it? The cross, that is.

Whatever! Wear it or bare it. The point was, I kept no secrets hidden about it. I wanted London ruined and destroyed. But I didn't want her dying on me. Oh noooo. I needed her alive. I needed her to suffer in her misery standing on her two ginormous hooves; long enough for me to expose her for the fraudulent three-dollar trick she was. I needed to annihilate her. Strip her down to her granny panties and air out her trickery. I was so, so close to uncovering something juicy. I knew it.

Mmph. Trying to steal my joy with her murderous antics. I think not! That moo-moo brown cow had no dang regard for anyone else's needs but her own. Just gotdang selfish and rotten to the core! I tell you. They didn't breed good fighters anymore. No, ma'am. These little girls today were a bunch of cotton eaters. Pussy willows dangling from rotted branches. That's all they were. And London Phillips was the biggest dang bucket of barnyard cow crap I'd ever laid eyes on.

She had the gossip hounds yelping and wagging their tails and tongues at the horrid details of her epic fail. London might have been trying to make her way to the promised land, but instead she landed on her back on the soil of grits and piss.

Dear baby Jeezus. Spin the wheel and snatch the tail on the donkey! With all that was going on with Daddy at the house and Kitty being the miserable witch she was, all I wanted was to be spared the indignities of London's thoughtlessness and have me a bite to eat with stud daddy. And here he was, bringing her name up, sucking the sap juice out of my nectarine. God, what a pound dog!

The sound of Midnight's dreamy voice pulled me out of the abyss of my thoughts. "Yo, that jawn is a savage. Straight like that."

I blinked. My ears perked up. This was the big break I'd

been looking for. I could feel it in my loins. The pang. I pressed my legs shut tight. And licked my lips with anticipation. "Oh really?"

"Yeah, she s'posed to be BJ's homegirl 'n' she straight-up played her behind her back. Had my man all effed up like spoiled cabbage too."

I clung to the edge of my seat. Held on to every nail-biting second as he reached for his iced tea and took three slow sips. Ooh, he was going to make me beg for it. "Goshdangit, Midnight. Give it to me, daddy. What did that savage beast do?"

He eyed me over the rim of his glass. "She told Knox that Rich had an abortion . . ."

# 12

# London

*Milan, Italy*

*Noooooo! No, no, no, nooooooooooo!*
*This can't be!*

The first thing I heard was the beeping sound. Next came the muffled voices. Then I felt the squeezing on my hand.

Then I knew...

I was still alive!!

*Noooooooo!*

*Why, God, why?*

I couldn't even end my own life right.

*You're so effen pathetic, London...*

My head pounded.

This had to be some cruel joke God was playing on me.

"She's lucky to be alive," I overheard someone say. It was a man's voice. His English was broken and thick with the accent of his native tongue. Italian. From what I gathered from his conversation, I'd been in the hospital for two days already. I'd severed a tendon and damaged nerves in my arm. And as a result, I might never regain full use of my left hand again.

"No, Doc, we're the lucky ones." *Daddy's still here, with me!*

He was sooo wrong. This wasn't luck. There was no blessing in my botched suicide attempt. This was unfortunate. It was a travesty. What had I done to suffer like this?

In a flash, I heard the Italian lilt. I cringed at the sound of her voice. It was my mother. Speaking to the doctor in Italian. About me! Wanting to know how long it'd take for my scars to heal, before a plastic surgeon could be called in. She didn't sound pleased with his response.

"Let's not focus on the scarring, and concentrate more on the healing for now. Let's take one day at a time, shall we? I'll be back in a minute to check in on her."

"Maybe I should have listened to you, Turner..." This was the same woman who didn't even have the desire to carry me inside of her womb, to give birth to me. Half admitting fault. That *maybe* she'd done something wrong, for once in her life. "Maybe none of this would have happened had I simply not pushed her so hard..."

Her words were met with silence.

In my mind's eye, I imagined Daddy's eyes boring a hole through her. I could almost see his handsome face etched in worry for me; disgust for her.

She did this to me.

Justice did this to me.

I did this to me.

I felt the tears swelling behind my closed eyelids.

The fact that I was still here was all my fault.

All of it.

Why hadn't I cut deeper?

Why hadn't I bled out faster?

"Oh, dear God, what has happened to our daughter, Turner? Maybe we both should have been more involved." Her voice cracked. Then I heard sniffling. "Look at her. Our daughter. She looks so...so wounded."

I heard myself screaming, "I *am* wounded!"

Emotionally, mentally...physically!

*Why, God? Why would you punish me by keeping me alive?*

Daddy finally spoke. "She's had a...very trying few weeks, Jade." I could hear the tight, clipped edge in his tone. I could tell he was trying to keep it together, the way he'd do with me whenever I'd defy him. Or when a difficult client of his was working his last nerve. He was trying to choose his words carefully. It was a lawyer thing, I always presumed. "I told you to let her be, but this is what you wanted, Jade."

"So you do blame me? I knew it. You really do think I'm to blame for this, don't you? Say it, Turner. You think I pushed our daughter to do...to do this? Attempt suicide? Never mind, you don't have to say a word. I can see it in your face."

"Listen, Jade. We are going to have to figure out a way to put our differences aside, for London's sake."

*"Our differences?"* I heard my mother say, her voice dipping to a hushed whisper. "Meaning your little *hooker*?"

"Jade, what is wrong with you? We're not doing this. Not now, Jade. And definitely not here. This is about our daughter. So let's focus on that."

"You've hurt me so deeply, Turner. I've only wanted

what was best for our daughter. Why can't you believe that?"

If my own eyes were open, I'd be rolling them at her. It was so typical of her to want to play the martyr. She was not the victim in this. I was. And this horror tale, this calamity, had no happy ending for me.

Something had gone terribly awry. But what? The plan was simple. End it all right there on the runway. I did everything right. Slid the razor up through my skin, ripping open tendons and flesh. Glided down the catwalk. All I needed to do was bleed out.

I thought it was a peaceful and surefire way to end it all.

I remembered floating. Remembered feeling the happiest I'd felt in a long time. The runway seemed to roll under my heels. I was going to finally be free. Free from Justice. Free from his lies and obsessive mind games. Free from my mother and her constant ridicule. Free from prying eyes and gossipy, two-faced bitches like Rich Montgomery.

I remembered the warm, prickly sensation coursing through my arm. Then collapsing. Remembered feeling the life slowly draining out of my body as I was being lifted. Thousands of butterflies covered me. It wasn't a dream. No. No.

I was leaving this Earth.

I remembered the sharp pain shooting up my arm. I remembered seeing lots of white light. Blinding light. Then I started getting dizzy. Started fading in and out. I remembered the image of a beautiful brown baby's face flash in front of my eyes. Then the aching in my heart ripped through me.

I choked back a scream.

I was on my deathbed. But I wasn't dead!

I'd been robbed of the afterlife.

I heard Daddy say, "Seeing London through this is all that matters right now. I don't want to point fingers, or blame. And I don't want to discuss anything other than the two of us being by our daughter's side. That's all I want to focus on."

*But you're leaving us?*

*"I know who your mistress is . . ."*

"That's right, let's pretend. Let's act like you're not screwing your client's wife and want to abandon your family."

All of a sudden I felt dizzy. The air around me thickened. I struggled to take a few deep breaths, but it was useless. *Maybe I'll suffocate to death*, I thought as I slowly clawed at the sheets.

"Enough, Jade." Daddy sounded irritated. "I've already warned you." I heard movement. "I'm going out to make a call. I'll be back in a few."

"Whom are you running out to call now, Turner, huh? That *home-wrecker* of yours?"

"This isn't the time for that, Jade. I already told you I'm not doing this with you. Not here."

And then he was gone.

Even Daddy wanted an escape. At least he already *had* an escape. Logan Montgomery. Rich's mother. He'd run off into her arms when it was all said and done. And I'd still be here.

With my mother.

Stuck.

Doomed to a life of misery.

Abandoned.

I pushed out a groan. Slowly opened my eyes against

the blinding brightness in the room, a stark contrast to the darkness that took up space in every part of my body.

"London, darling. Oh, dear God. You're finally awake." My mother leapt up from her seat. Then she was at my bedside, touching the side of my face, choking back a sob. "You've had your father and me sick with worry." I blinked her into view. Her eyes were red and swollen. She looked as if she'd been crying. "Why would you do this, London, huh? Why?"

I blinked.

"Dear Lord. Do you hate me that much to want to..." Her voice trailed off. She sniffled. "How could you do this to *me*, to us? Have you no shame? Do you realize the embarrassment you've caused me? Why couldn't you wait... one more day. That's all you had to do. That's all I asked of you. To wait to have whatever emotional meltdown you were having until we were back home. You did this to spite me. To ruin my good name."

I blinked again.

"You have a fabulous life, London... you're just ungrateful. Spoiled rotten and selfish. That you would scar yourself, knowing your modeling opportunities will now be limited to doing Sears catalogues for gaudy long-sleeved blouses. Why would you want to do something so unthinkable, like... like this? Why? Your father and I have given you everything."

A sob gurgled out of me. I knew it was too good to be true. That she'd care more about me, for once, than she cared about her precious image, of what others were saying and thinking.

I swallowed back the bile that bubbled up in the back of my throat. I wanted to scream, but couldn't.

Hot tears crept out from the corners of my closed lids. *What did I have to live for?*

"Jade, stop!" Daddy stalked back into the room toward her, yanking her by the arm. "Have you lost your goddamn mind?! What is wrong with you, huh? This is our daughter you're talking to like that. Not some unruly model you chastise for clumsily missing a step or making a wrong turn. I will not have you interrogating her, or browbeating her. Now get your things and get out!" He snatched up her purse, shoving it at her as he dragged her to the door. He pushed her out, then shut the door behind him.

I was beside myself. Literally on the verge of losing it all over again.

Daddy looked at me. Studied me. He looked stricken. Sickened by the turn of events, I mused. There were dark circles under his eyes, and his hair was uncombed. He had a five o'clock shadow. Even in his disheveled, scruffy state, I could faintly smell his six-hundred-and-ten-dollar cologne, Ambre Topkapi, still clinging to his pores. The way I was clinging to the idea of dying. Of being dead.

I was disappointed that I was here. Strapped in a hospital bed. Breathing. Eyes open. Bandaged. Tubed up. Daddy was probably disappointed too, that he was here. Instead of being...I don't know, somewhere, anywhere but here.

This drastic setback probably put a slight kink in his escape plan. Might have derailed his freedom train for a moment. But he'd be on his way soon enough.

Then where would that leave me?

Alone.

I was feeling somewhat conflicted: The way Daddy was looking at me, stroking my hair, being attentive and protective of me, had me confused. I was thankful, but...

My heart ached. I knew this wasn't where he wanted to be. He wanted to be with her. His ghetto lover.

*I know who your mistress is . . .*

His mouth made words I couldn't hear. I freeze-framed this moment in my mind, before turning away. I couldn't bear to look at him. But I didn't want it to end. I needed to store it in my memory. His love for me.

Beneath my bandaged limb, I felt the searing heat as it shot through my arm. I wanted to grasp my wrist, but my right hand was restrained to the bed railing. As Daddy spoke—as he assured me that no matter what was happening between him and my mother, he'd always be there for me—I half listened. Half believed.

All I knew was, I had nothing to live for and nothing to fight for.

Justice had stolen my heart.

My mother had stolen my spirit.

Rich's mother had stolen my father.

And God had robbed me of death.

# 13

# Heather

"You're boring. The world is no longer checking for you. Anymore. We tested the pilot and your ratings broke a world record. They are the worst anyone's ever seen. Something's gotta give or you gotta go!" My producer, Philippe, had barged into my room this morning, interrupting my on-camera confessional. "You may as well drop the mic and exit stage left. Again. The critics were crystal clear. No one wants to see a has-been Wu-Wu, the ex-junkie. And her washed-up drunk of a mother."

"I resent that! I have an audience!"

"You're right, you do. But it's one, two, maybe three of your redneck West Virginian relatives sitting around at your family barbecue, bashing you and your mother! Not enough to get you any sponsors or a prime-time slot. You want to be a where-are-they-now special? I can get you on at three in the morning. You want to be a star, then you get your behind up and go and get the Pampered Princesses!"

"*Never!*" *I jumped off the edge of my bed.*

"*Then you will never be a hit.*" *He paced.* "*You will always be a has-been. And it's not that we didn't try. Oh, we tried. But your mother is some sloppy drunk who only wakes up once a week to refresh her drink! And to think we not only bought her act, but that dear, sweet Kitty believed she'd stopped drinking! We've all been duped!*"

"*That's not my problem!*"

"*It is your problem!*"

"*The world wants to see my life!*"

"*The world wants to see you, Spencer, Rich, and London, together! The insides of the crazy antics of the Pampered Princesses! I can see it now!*" *He gave a tight smile and then turned back to me.* "*Now, if you want to continue your career on TV then you get us in the palace or get shut down.*"

"*My show will be a hit! I will be a hit!*"

"*At the rate you're going, you will be no more than the new millennium's Dana Plato married to a recycled Todd Bridges!*"

*I gave Philippe a blank look and he returned my stare.* "*Do your history, Miss Actress!*" *He shoved his beet-red face into mine.* "*The kids from* Diff'rent Strokes! *Now the choice is yours. You either do what you gotta do to get back into the good graces of the Pampered Princesses*"— *he dusted his hands*—"*or our work here is done...*"

"A moment of silence, please." Mr. Westwick's voice boomed through the café's intercom system, jolting me out of my thoughts. "Students, we need to pray for and reach out to our dearly beloved London Phillips, our little runaway supermodel who has succumbed to tragedy. As you all know, she is now home recovering, and I want to make sure each of you acknowledge her. Show her the Hollywood High spirit. I believe her knowing that we are all here thinking of her and wishing her a speedy recovery will make quite a difference. That'll be all. Oh, one more thing. There will be a one-hundred-dollar fee billed to all the upperclassmen for the arrangement of flowers that will be sent from the school and all the students at Hollywood High. Thank you and good day."

"Oh. My. God." Rich smacked her gums and banged a fist on the edge of our lunch table. "Really, though. London tries to kill herself and Westwick rolls out a national holiday?" She flicked a wrist. "Psst, please. Chile, cheese. Baby, boom! Attention whores stay doing the most." She tossed a hard look over at me.

Spencer tsked and shifted in her seat. "I guess at any moment we'll be bowing our heads and singing 'Kumbaya'!"

"First Miley Cyrus," Rich said.

"And now London," Spencer added.

"Dear God...who's next?"

I couldn't believe it! These two slores were incredible. All I could do was stare at these insensitive tricks in disbelief. Did they really think this was something to laugh at?

And no, I didn't like London. Actually, I hated her. She was phony. Stuck-up. Turned up her nose at people, especially me.

Still.

She didn't deserve these cruel comments and snide remarks from the same chicks who I knew for sure would be smiling in her face and sending flowers. These hookers were out of control.

I leaned forward and frowned at the two of them as they sat across from me. "Obviously," I sneered, eyeballing the two of them, "she was going through something. Something that pained her enough to make her feel like her life wasn't worth living. But you two wouldn't know anything about that since both of your worlds are so perfect."

"Slow down, low-down." Rich popped her glossy lips.

"No, you slow down! I don't like the comments you made!"

Spencer batted her lashes. "Who died and made you London's bestie? Since when did you become the spokesperson for the lonely?"

"I'm not her bestie! And I'm not her spokesperson. I just know what it's like to take one too many pills on purpose. But clearly you two Gucci queens don't. No, you're too busy being mean and nasty and self-absorbed to know anything about that!"

"Well, dear God, Spencer." Rich snickered. "I think we've just been read."

"Mmph, sounded like a sermon to me!"

Rich said, "Hand me the collection plate."

Spencer yanked her oversized bag open and pulled out a tambourine. She slapped it rhythmically against the palm of her right hand and Rich sprang out of her seat, hopped up and down, and sang, "The dead has arisen 'cause we've been read, honey! Yaaaaaas! We've been read! Give it to me, baby. Chile, cheese! Baby, boom!"

All I could do was shake my head. This was exactly why I was anti–dumb broads. They were soooo detached from

reality. God, I hated them! And to think I'd actually enter-
tained the thought of asking them to be on my show.

Not!

I was done with these two, especially Rich. The last
time we were together she tried to read me for filth. But
not this time! Mmph. Never again! No more high road. No
more white towel. I don't care if the producers don't want
to see me solo or they're pissed off because Camille's
been discovered for who she really is. Whatever!

I looked over at Spencer and she was tossing twenties
into the air while Rich popped a booty dance. "You two
are a disgrace!" I shouted.

Immediately, Spencer stopped making it rain and Rich
stopped dancing. *"Screech!"* Rich spat, as she placed a hand
up on her hip and held an index finger in the air. "Who
could be more of a disgrace than you, Ms. Baby Tylenol?
And first of all and forever more, when I come to school I
come to have a good time. Not be stressed over the woes
of the young, the dumb, and the selfish. Okay, London did
what she did. Boo-hoo. We've all shed our tears. Everybody's sad for a second. But my world goes on. The
school gave her a national holiday. What more do you
want?!"

"Exactly." Spencer tossed her curls. "And since you're
trying to come for people, Miss Fortune Reader without
the cookie, let's get you together. Now where is that Lamborghini?"

I drew in a breath. I'd forgotten about that expensive
trash she'd given me.

She continued. "Yeah. You thought I'd forgotten, didn't
you? But I've seen you driving that old, souped-up, kitted-

down whoremobile! Now where is that Lamborghini? And don't lie."

"Pause. *Reeeeeewind*," Rich interjected, slamming a fist on the table and flopping down in her chair. "You bought this trickazoid a what? A what? A *Lamborghini*? Really, Spencer? A Ford Escort, okay. I can see that. I can even see you trying to upgrade her to an Acura. But a Lambo? Girl, you dead wrong for that. All you've ever given me is a chocolate diamond tennis bracelet with a BFF charm!"

"Rich, stop being so selfish! And be happy you received that bracelet. And besides, you're not poor. Heather was homeless, living in a motel. In squalor. No transportation. And was seconds away from Camille tricking her out!"

"You mean renting her out!"

Spencer screamed in laughter. "Rent to own a ho!" She laughed so hard tears poured from her eyes. Then abruptly she stopped, looked back over to me and spat, "Now. Where. Is. That. Lamborghini?"

The veins in my neck felt like they were due to pop out at any moment. "You know what? I don't have to take this!" I rose from my seat. "You two *bishes* are stupid. Ignorant. And I'm sick of y'all! Yeah, I was homeless. Broke. And I didn't have a ride. But I'm not any of that anymore. And to think I wanted to invite you two to be on my reality show! Screw that and screw you! I'm tired of trying to play nice. Extending the olive branch and tolerating your foolishness.

"You are two of the messiest ballguzzlers I've ever seen in my life! And I don't know what people see in you, but I'm over it! You're overrated and so is your fake friendship! And when you get to fallin' out, don't come and see me, 'cause I'm not gon' be checkin' for you. And as for your Lamborghini, I sold it. It's scrap metal! Now let me get out of here before I hook off on a *beyotch*!"

I twirled around, slung my twenty-four-inch ponytail, then patted my behind and said, "Now kiss what you paid for! I'm done with the Gucci clique! Click! Click!"

# 14

# London

"You selfish trash..."

At first I thought I was dreaming. But then I heard the voice again.

"You despicable slore..."

No. This wasn't a dream. Someone was in my room. Hovering over me. I slowly opened my eyes, and screamed. My worst nightmare was standing inches away from my face, sneering. She was the last person I expected (or wanted) to see. This was the second time she'd ever been inside my house. The first time being a few months back, at the beginning of the school year, when we were trying to patch up our tarnished media images by forging a faux alliance, while Heather was in rehab. Of course, nothing ever went according to plan when we were all forced to be in the same room for any length of time. She ended up whipping out a blade and wielding it at Rich, threatening to rock, sock, and slice her to sleep. Her words, not mine.

"Sp-Sp-Spencer...ohmygod! What are you doing here? Who let you in?"

She blew out a blast of watermelon-scented breath. "God, you're so ugly. And, ohmygod, bring in the cavalry! Send in the fat gods! Where is the rest of your body? You're a sickly sack of stones. No, twigs! You're a skeletal disaster. Dear Lord! Have mercy on my eyes!"

I clutched the covers up to my neck, feeling ridiculously more unnerved, more self-conscious than I already was about the fact that I now weighed a hundred and two pounds. I'd been home for almost a week and had managed to gain two pounds. Still, it wasn't enough. My doctor was concerned. I overheard him telling my parents I was deteriorating. That I would end up back in the hospital again if I wasn't able or willing to consume food. And it has been the only time my mother has ever begged me to eat. I didn't have much of an appetite. And what little I did attempt to eat I'd throw up. So now I was on a liquid diet. An IV drip. Followed by horrible protein shakes.

"What are you trying to do now? Slicing your wrists didn't work so now you want to starve yourself to death? Is that it, Twiggy-used-to-be Miss Piggy?"

I blinked.

"You want to run free and wild? You gotdang joy killer! How dare you try to steal my thunder! You, you, inconsiderate tramp-dog! Is this how you low-money, East Side, troll-dolls do it back across the dirty-dirty? In *New Yawrk, New Yawrk*?" She mocked, trying to imitate my New York accent. "Slicing and dicing yourselves up when life gets you down? Someone tosses you a bucket of lemons and you want to turn around and squeeze out prune juice. You want to hang up your big panties, then throw your hands up in defeat! You gotdiggitydang tramp! You sore loser! I should slap your dang sunken face, you snot ball! You quitter!"

*Quitter? How is giving in to my truths—that I am unhappy; that I'm tired; that I am lonely; that I don't want to live anymore—being a quitter?*

I frowned. I didn't have the strength or the energy to engage in a battle of words with this trick. All I wanted to do was sleep. My life away! Close my eyes and hope to God that when I opened them again it'd be full of bright white light, colorful butterflies, and angels playing harps. Seeing this devil incarnate, standing here in all of her fine jewels and a pair of exquisite heels, shooting fire at me, was more than I could bear.

"Spencer, get out of my room now. And out of my house before I have you tossed off the premises. How dare you come in here and try to judge me." My voice cracked. "You don't know me! You don't know what my life has been like to come up in here and tell me anything! So don't stand there and try to throw stones at me! Now get out!" I reached for the house line to call down to security. However, Spencer was quick on her feet, slapping my hand down and snatching the phone from off my nightstand, then yanking its cord out of the outlet. She then snatched my iPhone out of my hand.

"Oh no. Oh no. You are not having me escorted out of here. I'll leave when I'm good and gotdiggitydang ready. And not a minute sooner. I'm here to see you through whatever it is you're going through."

"I'm touched," I said sarcastically. "I didn't think you cared." I folded my arms across my chest. "Now get out!"

She smirked. "Oh no...oh no, Little Miss Murder War-rant. I am not here to host your pity party. I would love nothing more than to lay you out and roast you on an open barbecue pit and watch your skin snap, crackle, and pop. But that's not how I do mine. I don't ever break bones or throw stones at hookers who are already stretched out on their backs. No, ma'am. I build you up to tear you down. I'm here to nurse you back to health, Miss Death On A Stick. Then—"

I gave her an incredulous look, cutting her off. "Nurse *me* back to health? Are you frickin' serious? I don't need your help. I *need* you to find your way to the door and out of my house."

Her thick diamond bangles clinked as she clapped her hands. "Heeheehee. Instead of wasting good seconds and minutes and hours of the day trying to slice yourself up, you need to be trying to get your neck game up. Maybe you wouldn't be in this pathetic mess you're in, Miss Lonely."

"Miss me with your fake concern and your twisted anec-dote for my recovery. I'm not interested."

"Well, you just ought to be. Look at you. You're a mess. What a waste of good space."

"Why do you care? What does my mess have to do with you, huh? Riddle me that. My life and what I do with it, or in it, is none of your concern. So get a life and have several seats."

I evil-eyed her as she sauntered around my suite, slid-ing her fingers over the furniture as if she were checking for dust particles. She turned toward me, cocked her fin-gers like a gun, pulled an imaginary trigger, then blew on her fingertips.

"Boom, swamp thing, boom! Do you *think* I want to be here? You think I want to be standing up in this makeshift mortuary with you, scarecrow? I have better things to do."

I rolled my eyes, letting out a disgusted sigh. "Then go do you. I didn't ask you here. I don't even want you here. And I definitely don't need you or your phony concern."

"Umm, look around you, ditsy doodle, and tell me what you see." She swept her eyes around the room, then landed them back on me. "That's right, you guessed it. Nothing. No one. That's what you see. And you want to know why? Because you have no friends, London. No one likes you, boo. And the one half of a friend you did have, you backstabbed and gutted. And now she's somewhere doing your thug daddy." She covered her mouth. "Oopsie... was I supposed to say that? Oh well."

She chuckled.

I choked back a sob. This girl was so hateful and hurtful. And for her to stand here and confirm what I already knew in my heart—that Rich was sleeping with Justice—was unconscionable. Spencer was a ruthless snake. And Rich was just dirty!

They all deserved each other!

I quickly turned my head from her so that she wouldn't be able to see the tears building up in my eyes.

"Oh yes, honey. I'm here to deliver the gospel truth. And the truth is, you're an epic fail! Trying to hurt yourself like that! How could you, London? And please tell me this isn't over that bum. That Mister Thug Delight who can croon his way into a girl's sheets and leave his stain marks behind. Ooh, he's the pimp daddy of destruction. I mean, really. You might not want me here, London. But you better thank the high heavens somebody's here right up until the bittersweet end."

I blinked back tears. Her words were like a thousand razor blades slicing into my flesh. "What do you want, Spencer?"

"Oh dear. Isn't it obvious what I want? Haven't I made myself clear?" She opened her large Bottega Veneta and pulled out a black flyswatter. *Whap!* She swatted the foot of my bed, hard. "Let's try this again. Shall we? I want you to get it together, London. Get up and fight! I want you back at Hollywood High so I can annihilate you. So whatever demons you got eating up your insides, go get you a flush, a deep-rinse cleanse, or whatever, and let it go. Move on. *Capisci?*"

*No!* Did she *understand*? No matter what anyone said about moving on and letting go, I still didn't think I could live without Justice. I knew I wasn't ready to accept the fact that he'd moved on—from *me*—to Rich. That he'd let go—of *me*—for Rich. I didn't know who or what I was if I wasn't his girlfriend. Didn't anyone see that's all I was now, all I had been? Justice's girl.

I gave up everything for him. I picked him over my parents. And what did it get me? Spat on! Kicked in the gut! Punched in the throat! Stabbed in the back! Disrespected!

Didn't that boy know everything I had been, everything I did, was for him?

And that was a big part of the problem. I existed for him.

What hurt the most was knowing that after everything we'd shared, he hadn't even tried reaching out to me. I'm sure he'd heard what happened. The media and blogs had been buzzing for the last week or so over my suicide attempt.

He could have sent a text. He could have called. He could have in-boxed me on Facebook, or hit me up on Kik.

All it would have taken was two seconds, if that. But it didn't matter to him. I didn't matter to him. And I needed to find a way to accept that and push through it.

But how?

I felt the sting of tears. I turned away slightly so that she wouldn't see me on the verge of crying. I willed myself to keep it together. Having another crying spell, another meltdown, right here, right now, in front of this messy troll was not an option. I'd rather slice my arm off and eat a pile of army ants than allow her the privilege of seeing me any more broke down than I already was.

God, I couldn't stand looking at her. Miss Flawless. She was effortlessly beautiful and didn't even know it. I hated to admit this, but there had been times when I wished to be Spencer *and* Rich, in the worst way. I didn't want their lives, or any of their despicable ways. And I didn't want to trade places or parents with them; just wanted to trade in my imprisonment for their freedoms. I wanted to swap out my size nines for their dainty size five feet. Wanted to be their normal height in heels, instead of always feeling like a giraffe on stilts.

Where Rich was short and thick, Spencer was built like a dancer. But they were both, *God help me*, beautiful—on the outside, anyway. Still, they had the kind of carefree, I-don't-care-about-the-world-or-anybody-in-it attitude that I envied, admired, and despised all at the same time. Still, parts of me craved the kind of reckless abandon they had. They didn't care about pretenses. Or how they carried themselves in public. They didn't care about social graces, or being refined. *Sit up. Back straight. Chin up. Legs together when sitting. Feet crossed at the ankles. A young lady never belches or poots out loud in mixed company. A young lady is never loud, obnoxious, or crude in her behavior. A young lady never uses profanity.*

No. Rich, in particular, didn't care about social etiquette or proper decorum. She simply lived in the moment. Enjoyed life. Ate with her hands when it required it; licked sauce off her fingers without regard; belched and passed gas loud and proud. All of them, Rich, Spencer, and (eyes rolled up in my head) Heather, did whatever they wanted without restrictions, or someone hovering over them, or ambushing and bullying them into doing what they didn't want to do.

In that regard, they were so lucky! And I wanted that. A mother who just didn't care what I did, or who I did it with!

"Well, I think my charity work here is done for the day," Spencer said, bringing me out of my reverie. She glanced at her jeweled timepiece. "If I hurry, I might be able to catch the second half of my physics class."

"Thank God for small favors," I muttered under my breath, relieved to see this trick finally leaving. She gathered her coat, then reached inside her handbag and pulled out a beautifully wrapped gift. She handed it to me. I frowned. "What's that?"

She rolled her eyes, sucking her teeth. "It's not a bomb, London. Sweetholyjeezus! Somebody come take the wheel! If I wanted to blow you up I would have done it already. Don't have me mace you up in here. Take the dang gift. Or have your eyes set on fire. The choice is yours."

Reluctantly, I took it. Shook it. Then set it beside me on the bed. "Thanks, I guess."

She pursed her lips. "I want you out of this bed, London. And back at school. I mean it. I'll be back tomorrow, and the day after and the day after until. So if you want me out of your face, then you had better get your life back. And stop all this tomfoolery! Trying to like you and be nice to you is too much hotdang work!"

I blinked. Glanced over at the large gift basket she'd brought with her, which was sitting on my chaise. Then stared at her in disbelief.

"Oh, and buckle up. I'm bringing Rich with me tomorrow," she said over her shoulder as she walked toward the door. "Let's hope she plays nice. But if not...heeheeehee... you brought it on yourself. Good day, ma'am."

With that, Spencer was out the door, leaving me in a cloud of bewilderment as I slid my hand along the creases of my comforter, plucking up a piece of candy and quickly slipping it into my mouth.

*This was a day from hell!*

# 15

# Rich

*Dear Diary,*
   *I'm turning over a new leaf today.*
   *I'm done with dream killers.*
   *Cuttin' 'em from my life and moving on.*
   *Scratch that.*
   *'Cause when I die, I want my biographer to serve my Richoids with my forgiving spirit.*
   *So, let me change it up a bit and add forgiveness.*
   *Yeah.*
   *I'ma forgive 'em for tryna do me in.*
   *Right after I greet half-dead London in her hospital bed, take it to her face, and yank the stitches out of her newly sewn-up wrist, I'ma forgive her for sneaking me and tryna bring me down to her level.*
   *Thennnn . . . right after I meat-grind Justice's*

*pubic lifeline, I'ma forgive him too for tryna play me.*

I smiled as I placed my blue Tiffany pen alongside my new pink leather-bound diary, and locked it. Logan will *never* get her grimy hands on this. And if she does, she'd never guess that the verbal password was *My mother is a beyotch.*

Boom!

"Miss Rich, brunch is served," my chef announced as he walked through my room and onto my terrace, setting a large silver tray on the café table. He lifted the dome and revealed crispy bacon, strawberry crêpes, piping hot, extra-creamy and -buttery blueberry muffins, and a gouda cheese and eggwhite omelet garnished with chives, sour cream, and cubed tomatoes.

I swear I love this man. "You're the best, Chef Jean!"

"My pleasure." He smiled and poured me a cup of peppermint tea, dropping in two sugar cubes and a splash of cream.

As my mouth watered, I took a moment and got my proper lady on; flicked my pink linen napkin into the air and placed it carefully onto my lap.

"Have a great day!" Chef Jean tossed over his shoulder as he turned to leave.

I didn't answer. I was too busy closing my eyes and savoring every bite of my muffin. The butter deliciously sank into my taste buds and glazed my tongue. All I could do was squeeze my thighs and shake my head. It should be illegal for food to taste this freakin' good. I was officially gettin' my inner fat girl on! Nothing was better than eating alone, with my eyes closed and head held back.

Blindly, I placed my fork onto my tray, lifted a forkful of something, and slid it into my mouth.

Mmm. Cheese omelet.

Wait. Let me pause and say grace. "Dear God, thank You for the chicken coop where chickens laid their eggs. Thank You for the cow who made the milk. And the farmer who milked the cow! Thank You God for blessing me with this tongue to lap up this bangin' food! Thank You for the nooks and the crannies of my blueberry muffin. Amen."

I opened my eyes and just as I reached for a slice of bacon I spotted my mother standing in my terrace's doorway, gaze all screwed into me.

Next time I write in my diary I'll have to add *forgiving this dream killer* to the list. Although I really don't want to. And to think that all week I've managed to stay out of her way and avoid her breakfast ritual, where she likes to play Clair Huxtable and her husband sits there like a thugged-out Heathcliff.

Chile, cheese.

Bugger boo.

Boy, bye!

'Cause one thing's for sure and two things for certain. Logan and Richard, the ghetto-hood ex-convicts turned trophy husband and wife are anything but. Which would be exactly why I've cut them off. I don't do fakes, flakes, and I stopped letting phonies kill my vibe.

I picked up my muffin, took a bite, let the butter gloss my lips, chewed, and swallowed.

My mother continued to stare.

I sipped my tea, rolled my eyes, and then said, "Yes." I swerved my neck to the left and paused it. "May I help. You?"

She curled her top lip. "Every time I look at you. You disgust me."

I blinked.

*Relax. Ignore her. She wants a reaction. Besides, haters never prosper.*

I swallowed the sting of her words and tossed a look over at her that clearly said, *Whatever*. Then I smiled and took another bite of my muffin.

She carried on. "I am so sick and tired of you."

Unimpressed, unfazed, and unmoved, I lifted a forkful of my omelet, twirled the dripping cheese, placed it into my mouth, chewed slowly, and did my all not to let this thot get to me. 'Cause for-real-for-real I just wanted to be left alone to pursue my dream of eating Chinese food, watching Netflix, and sipping on something bubbly.

As my mother tapped her foot, I slid a piece of bacon into my mouth and sucked the salt out of it before chewing and swallowing.

Her tapping became more intense and my eyes dropped down to her feet.

Flats?

Where were her heels?

I looked back up and into her face. For a moment I wondered why she was so project greasy, and then it hit me that she had slapped Vaseline onto her skin. Dear God, she wanted to fight.

She was so ghetto.

Like really, did she come in here to boom, bop, and drop me? Her own child?

I lifted a forkful of my crêpes, and just as I planned to suck the juice out of the strawberry, my mother snatched my tray and slung it over the balcony. I could've sworn I heard the pool boy drop. I'ma just pray it landed somewhere in the mountains. She then turned to me, snatched my fork out of my hand, and sent it flying behind the tray.

My heart dropped and my eyes bulged open while hers became narrow slits, her jaw clenched, and she shoved her face into mine. "I am three minutes past the time I should've bashed your skull in and tore your throat out!"

*Stay calm.*

*You already know she's nuts.*

*Just try and talk her off the cliff.* "Umm, Mother. Did you forget to chase your happy pill with Cîroc today?"

She tightly gripped my cheeks and I could feel her fingertips pressed into my gums, while her fingernails slightly stabbed my skin. "I will bust you dead in the mouth. Now. The next time you open your lips it better be to tell me how I'm supposed to tell your father that the family ho is knocked up again!"

*What did she say? What did she just call me? Family ho...?*

She continued, "All week long I've been tossing and turning and pacing the floor. And all you've been doing is eating and getting all of your meals sent and served to you on your terrace like you're Princess Kate! I don't know what's with you and this new bullshit you're on, but I have not forgotten that you're pregnant. And I have not forgotten that I told you to put it on Knox. Now, did you do that?!" She flung her hands from my cheeks, causing my head to jerk back and pop forward. She locked onto my gaze and waited for an answer.

I bit the right side of my cheek and did everything I could not to fly-kick her off the cliff for putting her hands on me! I can't believe she just came at me all crazy! Put it on Knox? Like word? Really?

First of all and forever more, I didn't *have to* put it on Knox.

This baby was his.

Point blank.

Period.

I don't know what time my mother thought it was, but Knox was the *only* one I let heat it and hit it raw. And the *only* one I laid and cuddled with, soaking up all his erotic juice.

Justice never had the privilege or the pleasure to spread his mayonnaise around. I would never let some sidepiece blast up in me.

Never.

After Justice and I bit the pillows, clutched the sheets and called God, he always pulled out. And I always jumped up and ran to the bathroom. Peed. And flushed any little sneaky erotic bubble guts that may have crept up in me.

Therefore I was not about to let my mother—of all people—play me like Maury. Swerve. My baby had a daddy. And Christian Knox was his name.

I'm sick of her always coming out the side of her face with something slick. Calling me the family ho? How about we talk about the original ho. Her azz. And since we're on the subject of babies, let's talk about the one she gave away at fourteen.

You know what. I'm not gon' even take it there. I'ma do her a favor and save her life.

I eased up out of my chair and slowly backed into my room, securing my safety.

Then I turned to her, placed a hand up on my hip, wiggled my neck from left to right and said, "Don't do me. 'Cause you wouldn't want me to do you. Trust. And furthermore, I resent what you're trying to imply."

She snickered, like something here was funny.

*This trick is loony.*

"On your best day you couldn't bring it to me," she spat. "And *furthermore*, I don't do implications. The proof is in your stomach. I don't have to imply anything when you're carrying around your sixth child. By the sixth baby daddy. Whoever he shall be."

"See, there you go again being messy. You too old for that. For your information, I've only had five pregnancies and four baby daddies because I've been pregnant by Knox twice and—"

"Shut your stupid mouth! You reckless floozy! Loose hussy! I didn't raise no gutter trash. Nevertheless that's exactly what you're acting like. Every time you spread your legs open to some boy! And here I have to be the one to put my life on hold. Mess up my household because you can't keep your legs shut long enough to get out of the eleventh grade! You have had umpteen abortions! Your uterus is paper-thin and can't be scraped ever again!"

"That's not true and you know it!"

"It may not be true, but you know what is true? I'm not paying for or giving consent for any more freakin' abortions! You're bringing down the Montgomery name—"

"What? Relax. Fall back. I got this. There you go being extra. Why are you bringing up the past? You're supposed to be able to move on. I changed my ways and you need to work on your grudges! Forgiveness goes a long way. Yes, I made a few mistakes. But nobody's perfect! You up in here sweatin' me. Calling me names and just being plain hurtful and disrespectful to your only daughter while RJ is over there in England infiltrating the British race! It's probably a whole lot of beige Montgomerys! But you don't care because it's RJ! So you know what—"

*WHAP! SMACK! DROP!*

"Maaaaa!"

She backhanded me so hard that I fell onto the bed. She pressed her knees on the sides of my arms and pinned me down onto the mattress. "I will effen kill you!" Her spittle covered my face. "Do you understand that I brought you into this world and I will stomp you out of it! I'm not the one. And yeah, I called you the family ho because that's what you are. Everybody knows it! It's no secret. Even the gossip rags that you love and adore have named you one of the top ten hottest hos. Thanks to you, Kim Kardashian stopped trickin'!

"You have always been a problem. When you were five I was dragging you from beneath tables. When you were nine and ten years old you were pinning boys up at their lockers. I swear I should've kept you fat and your teeth bucked. And you always talking slick at the wrong time! This is not a game and no baby should have an irresponsible mother like you, and now I have to raise it! I can only hope and pray it turns out to be a boy and not some fast girl! Hot in the box like you! Now for the last time—get yourself together. Go to San Diego and tell Knox that he is about to be a daddy."

Silence.

"Do you hear me?"

"Yeah."

"Do you need me to go with you?"

I swallowed, "No."

"Good. Now get up. And the next time I see you, you better be saying something that makes some sense!"

# 16

# Rich

I'm *soooo* tired of Logan telling me what the eff to do. Sick. Of. It!

I got this.

This is *my* life.

*My* freakin' body.

*My* freakin' baby.

*My* goddamn decisions!

How can Logan even look at me with a straight face and blame *me* for abortion after abortion?

I never made one appointment.

I never chartered one plane.

And the last two babies I wanted to have.

She knew that.

She knows that.

But what has she always done? Dragged me to the middle of Nowhere, Arizona, and forced me to abandon my secrets on a steel gurney.

And *now* she wants to act like this is all my fault? My fault? Really?

I'm ruining her life?

Excuse me?

The nerve.

Her life.

Eff her stupid life!

Last I checked this was *my* life, and if I was going to have a baby it would bust out of *my* socket. Not hers. So why is she so desperate and concerned?

Fall. Back.

Shyt!

I'm the one driving up here to Knox and forcing myself to look him in the face and tell him I'm pregnant.

And having it.

And now my mother, who never liked him but is willing to put up with him, has to please my father and expects shotguns and wedding bells.

Never once did she ask me if I was *still* feeling Knox.

If I thought he was *still* the one for me.

If I *still* wanted to be with him.

Not *once* did she ever ask me what I thought or what I wanted.

Instead, she had the nerve to threaten to kill me if I didn't do what she told me to. And now the command of the day was for me to have this baby, put my boom, bop, pop on pause, and be stuck with Knox.

I need Jesus.

This was the longest ride of my life. And as I passed the Manhattan Beach exit it took everything in me not to turn off. But. The last thing I needed was Justice trying to diss me again. I couldn't stand the thought of him telling me to step, or get out, or anything else mean and nasty. I understood he was hurt. He'd become like everybody else trying to tell me what to do. I wanted the old Justice back. My ride-or-die. Who I could tell anything to. Do anything with.

That's who I needed.

I needed my quick fix.

My stress reliever.

But after one night too many gripping the sheets, he was turned out, and now, like they all do, he had lost focus . . .

I sucked in a deep breath and pushed it out as I parked in Knox's parking lot and walked up the purple brick steps of his campus apartment building.

*Should I flat out tell him that we're having a baby? Or should I hang around for a minute and then tell him?*

*Maybe I should cry.*

*No.*

*Maybe I should . . . umm . . .*

*What the eff am I supposed to do?*

*I haven't spoken to him in a week.*

*He works every one of my nerves.*

*I know he's good for me and he's the type of boy every girl should marry. But. I'm tired of him. He bores me. He's not fun. He's not funny. He's whack. And I'm sick of being Mrs. Whack. Really, what I need to do is be a woman about mine and end this charade. Stop the games. Stop the acting and be like, "Knox, it was good while it lasted but I gotta go. I'll see you in ten years when I'm ready to get ball-and-chained. But until then . . . deuces."*

*No.*

*Wait.*

*I can't do that.*

*Suppose I change my mind; then he may not take me back. He'll be all in his feelings. All sensitive. And then when I'm ready to be old lady cuffed he'll be holding on to the past.*

*I can't play my hand like that.*

*Just chill, ride this wave. Behave. And just take it one minute at a time.*

I knocked on the door to his apartment and I could smell Midnight's cooking. I hadn't had any morning sickness all week, but the sweet aroma of his homemade barbecue sauce, which I usually loved to lick off my fingertips, suddenly smelled like hot piss and made me feel sick. I sucked in a breath and banged on the door harder.

"Dang, big jawn!" Midnight snatched the door open. "Er' time I cook, here you come drooling."

I couldn't say a word. Instead I rushed to the bathroom, slammed the door behind me, turned on the water to drown out the sound, and lost my breakfast in the toilet.

After a moment of washing out my mouth and pulling myself together, I walked out of the bathroom toward Knox's room. I placed my hand on the knob and Midnight said, "Did you call first?"

"What?" I spun on my heels and faced him. "This is my man. I don't have to call."

"Er' man needs a call. You can't just run up on him."

"Watch me." I flung the door open a little harder than I expected to. Knox jumped up from the edge of his bed and looked over at me, while Nikki, who was sprawled across his bed with a PS4 remote in her hand, blinked and forced a phony and suspicious smile across her lips.

My heart thundered. And I paused for a moment. My eyes scanned the room and everything in me told me that this was nothing. Absolutely nothing. They were truly playing the game. Nothing more. Nothing less. But. At the same time everything in me forced me to lose it. This was just the mothersuckin' excuse I needed to bounce-baby-bounce in peace and not have the ish be about me or anything I've done. Finally. Mr. Perfect had effed up.

"Freeze. Pause. Rewind! Am I seeing things? Am I?" I snapped.

Knox stood up. "Chill. There you go. Calm down. We were just playing a game."

"Calm down?! I'm sick of this trick being all up in your face. Every time I turn around, here this tramp is!"

"Slow down on the tramps, boo," Nikki interjected. "Your problem is with your man, not me."

"Don't call her names, Rich." Knox frowned, his eyes shooting daggers at me.

"Maybe I should go," Nikki said, rising off the bed.

"No, you don't have to leave," Knox said.

My heart knocked and something in my head exploded. "No, you don't have to go 'cause I won't be long. I'm done with you, Knox! You let some funny-lookin' Burger King bird step to me?! Are you crazy? Now I know you're tricking up on this thot! Here I've been trying to reach you for two days—"

He tsked. "Where you been calling, 'cause you sure haven't been calling my number! Don't play me, Rich. You know *I've been the one* calling you for two days and *you've been* sending me straight to voice mail!"

"I've been stressed!"

"So you avoid your man!"

"Yeah, especially if my man is laid up with some reckless broad!" I eyed Nikki and dared her to say something. She didn't open her mouth. Instead Knox stepped in.

"Don't call her another name!" He clenched his jaw.

I placed my hands up on my hips. "Slore!" I couldn't believe this. Part of me wanted to stop the argument, but the other part of me wanted this ish to be over with so I could be about my day and go about my way. "You steppin' to me behind some losin' creep! You're a real pussy-azz douche bag, Knox! Eff you and this whole whack setup you got going over here. This is why I don't deal with corny asses, anyway. You're boring. Your life is boring. Your whole existence is boring. The only thing you good for is sweatin' me! Thank you for showing me the light. I can now see the yellow brick road to freedom. I see a real man coming my way!"

He frowned. "Oh, so is that what this is really about? You want a so-called *real* man, or you already got one? Is that why every time I turn around you're missing?"

I popped my eyes open. Tilted my head. And said, "Blank stare. Duh, idiot. I go missing 'cause I'm stressed! Up here pregnant with your whack baby. I'm about to give birth to boredom. Yeah, that's what I'll name it, Boredom Knox. After its no-good daddy who wants to play video games with some trollop. Both of you—"

*"Pregnant?!"* He paused. Frowned. Looked me over and then spat, "It ain't pregnant by me. And if you are, it ain't

mine! You better go and find your real man who's the real baby daddy. Don't come over here trying to trap me. I don't do insecure."

"Insecure! You stoop to calling me names now. Is that how you doing me now after all we've been through?"

"That's your mind playing tricks on you just so you can have a reason to pick a fight and break up. You wanna go, Rich, you wanna dead it? Done. All of this extra you doing is stupid. I woulda had more respect for you had you just told me you wanted to take a break. I—"

"It is you, Knox!" I stamped my foot, jabbing a finger over at Nikki. "You're the one laid up in the bed getting your foreplay on."

He sighed heavily, shaking his head. "Rich, you're being ridiculous."

"Eff you, Knox! You're lucky I don't take it to your throat, coming at me all crazy. And you know what? Don't you worry about this baby! I got this! And besides, I pissed out all of your lifelines, so you're right! It ain't yours! In my Maury voice, You are not the father! Drops mic..." I snapped my fingers in his face. "Dismissed!"

"Yo, it's time for you to bounce. For real..." He paused, pulling another deep breath. "Get. Out. Now."

"Yeah, I'ma bounce! As a matter of fact you can watch my booty bounce, 'cause you will never bounce up on it again!" I turned and stormed out, expecting him to come behind me, begging and pleading for my forgiveness. But he didn't. Instead, as the door slammed behind me, I heard Midnight laughing.

I rode around for hours. Thinking and thinking. And thinking. Wondering what I was going to do now. I wanted to...for once...make my own decisions. Do what I wanted to do. And right now...right now...at this moment...

I wanted Justice.

I turned off the exit and made a left toward Manhattan Beach. And before I let doubt sink in or any thought that told me this was crazy...I pulled into the parking lot, slammed my car into park, and rushed up the stairs to Justice's door.

*Don't...*

*Stop it. No doubts...no doubts...*

*I should...*

*No...*

I pounded on Justice's door and I could hear footsteps approaching. I pounded again and I could see the peephole's cover slide back.

"Justice," I said in a panic. "I know you're mad at me. I get it. I messed up. One too many times. But. I can't stay away from you. I miss you. I want you back. I need you in my life. I can't lie to myself anymore. I can't lie to you anymore." I paused and he didn't say a word.

I continued. "I ended it. I broke up with Knox. And I'm here because this is where I belong."

Silence.

Nothing.

My heart dropped through my stomach and I felt soooo stupid. Tears filled my eyes and I was doing everything in my power not to cry.

*Just leave.*

I glanced at the door one last time before turning to walk away and just as I approached the stairs I heard, "You came all this way to give up that easy."

Justice.

Tears covered my face as I turned around and walked over toward him. He met me halfway and I broke, clutching onto him. "Now," he said, wrapping his strong arms around me, "you can come inside."

# 17

# London

"**Oh** no! Oh no!" Spencer snapped, sweeping into my bedroom suite unannounced, uninvited, and definitely unwelcome in all of her finery. "You're *still* in bed in that same nasty nightgown I left you in yesterday, wallowing in your pathetic-ness? Dear baby Jeezus, snatch the wheel! I'm about to slide into a ditch! Enough is enough, you selfish slore! Can't you see death doesn't want you? So stop lying around waiting on the grim reaper to come save the day, hon. He isn't coming. And heaven isn't waiting for you either. So you might as well accept your fate here on Earth."

I sighed. "Spencer, I don't need you darkening my doorway with all of these unnecessary visits. Aren't there any cliffs you can go jump off?"

"Oh, you better cool your fanny pack, ma'am. There's no need for that confrontational tone." She tossed me the latest issue of *Juicy*. I blinked. My mouth gaped open. There I was. On the cover, in my father's arms, clutching onto him for dear life, being carried out of the Japanese restaurant, Nobu, after my meltdown in the women's bathroom. The heading read: MED CHECK! PAMPERED PRINCESS KNOCKED OFF THRONE AND FLIES OVER HER CUCKOO'S NEST!

I winced, turning the magazine facedown on the bed. I didn't need to see more, or read the gossip spewed inside. I already knew the story's outcome.

"And then there was this," Spencer said, tossing the latest issue of *Teen Vogue* at me. On the back cover there I was. In a full-page ad for the perfume Pink Heat. I cringed, felt myself tearing up. I stared down at the girl in the ad. She looked beautiful. Confident. Self-assured. Flawless. She was clearly an imposter. That wasn't me.

"I liked hating you better when you were an uppity snot ball. At least you were halfway *cute* in an *Animal Kingdom* kind of way. But this mess you've become, London—weak, helpless—is disgusting."

*Oh, really? You think?*

I'd been home for over a week and this had become my life: therapy twice a week with some flat-faced woman who probed and prodded, trying to get inside my head. It wouldn't be so bad, talking to someone, if it didn't hurt my eyes to look at her. She looked like a Pekingese. Anyway, her ugliness was the least of my concerns. Popping pills—for my mood, they claimed—was. But all the medication did was make me sleepy, and had me feeling like a zombie. Then there was this chick here. Spencer. Being harassed and tormented by her every day.

She wasn't just effen crazy. She was psycho certified. She was put-her-away-and-throw-away-the-key, nut-nut crazy. And she was also extremely cunning, extremely loaded, and extremely vindictive. And she had the queen of media as her mother. *That* alone made this girl extremely dangerous. I had to really stay three steps ahead of her. After the stunt she pulled the last time I was at school, ambushing me in the bathroom stall, I was convinced more than ever that I'd have to keep my frenemies close and this *beyotch* even closer.

I still didn't know how in the world she was able to get into the girls' lounge when I'd locked the door. Or at least I thought I had. My stomach was so tore up and on fire that day from a late-night sugar binge that I was practically delirious. So I can't be for certain if I did or didn't lock it.

All I knew was, I was never more mortified than I was when the stall door practically flew off its hinges and a camera flashed, catching me with my bare essentials exposed. This chick had no shame! No couth! No home training. She was living proof that money—and this little trust fund brat had access to plenty of it—definitely didn't (and couldn't) buy class.

*Snap, snap . . .*

"Umm, hello? Hello? Earth to she-dog! Have you heard a word I've said the last five minutes?"

I blinked Spencer back into view. And there she was, hand on her hip, an arm extended and her fingers snapping in my face. She was wearing a short plaid skirt and white blouse and a pair of killer heels. Her faux Catholic-schoolgirl look was eerily almost believable save the fact that she had horns and carried a pitchfork.

I took a deep breath.

"Oh no. Oh no. Please do not tell me you're about to turn on the waterworks and start that pitiful sniveling over your torrid scandal. There's no need for pissing out of the eyes. So snap out of it! You've wasted enough tissues on tears. Let's face it, London. You're a failure. We all know you're an emotional shipwreck. We get it. The whole world knows what a pathetic loser you are. But if you think I'm going to sit around and wait for you to get fitted for a pair of cement heels so you can stomp the bottom of the Pacific Ocean with the rest of the sea monkeys in your family, you have another gotdiggitydang think coming."

I pushed out an exasperated breath. "Spencer, why are you here again?"

She shot me a nasty look. "London, don't do me. You know I'm here to nurse you back to health and help you free your cluttered mind. Apparently, you're still hooked on crazy. So whatever loony-tune meds your doctor has you on are obviously not working. But no worries..." I eyed her as she rummaged through her oversized YSL bag. "I have just what you need to jumpstart your caboose and get your rump-a-dump from out of those filthy sheets."

I stared at her with a frown, realizing she was holding a manila envelope in one hand and a water gun in the other. She fanned herself with the envelope.

"Whew, I'm about to turn up the flames. I hope you can stand the heat."

I rolled my eyes. "What are you crazy-talking about now, Spencer?" With lightning-quick speed, she was attacking me with a heavy stream of water, soaking my face and hair. I screamed, hopping out of bed.

Spencer giggled. "That's right, you sleazeball otter, get up outta that death trap and face your demons. Get it up! Get it up! Get it uuuuuup!"

"Ohmygod! What do you think you're doing?"

She kept her plastic gun pointed at me. "I'm doing

what your parents can't seem to do. Put the heat to your seat and get you out of that bed."

"Okay, okay. I'm up! Satisfied?"

"Nope." She squirted another stream of water at me. "I want your ugly face washed and that knotty hair smoothed out and that funky nightgown trashed. You're making my eyeballs ache."

"Then get out. I didn't invite you here."

"And I'm not leaving either." She planted herself in my sitting room, crossing her legs. "So go fumigate. You smell like street trash."

I stormed into my bathroom, slamming the door. Pissed that Spencer had come and, once again, disrupted my day of isolation. I removed my clothes. Stared at myself in the mirror, then quickly shifted my eyes from the reflection staring back at me. I showered and washed my hair. Twenty minutes later, I stepped back into my bedroom to find Spencer stretched out on my chaise, her heeled feet crossed at the ankles, flipping through my black portfolio book.

"Mmph," she grunted, tossing the book to the floor as I crawled back into my bed. At that very moment, Rich whisked into the room in grand, over-the-top fashion, the scent of her perfume sweeping through the air around her.

"Mmm ... surprise!" She strutted toward the center of the suite, then paused, taking in the room. Her designer blouse dipped dangerously low, practically flashing her boobs. Her eyes landed on me. There was a glint of something sparkling on her left hand, ring finger. I blinked, my gaze zooming in on her glistening finger, then back up at her, then down to her hand again.

"I'm getting married!" she announced gleefully. No

*hello*. No *so sorry to hear what happened to you*. No *I apologize for saying hurtful things to you and about you*. Nothing.

My mouth dropped.

Spencer's eyes popped.

"You're getting *what*?" Spencer asked, shock registering in her tone and on her face. "*Married?* To whom? *Knox?*"

I held my breath in anticipation—wishful, hopeful thinking rearing its way into my heart and mind. Maybe her and Justice's little fling was officially over.

Rich scowled. "*Knox?* Girl, no! Miss me with that. I dumped him this morning. I have no time for some little boy who wants me to play the backseat to his fraternity and his little silly fan club. No, thank you. Been there, done that. I've moved on to a real man—a man who loves me for me, a man who wants to *honor* and *obey* me. A man who knows how to come home and appreciates a good woman like me."

"You mean a *freak* like you, don't you?" Spencer questioned smugly, narrowing her eyes at Rich. "Is he fine, quick drawz?"

"Yasss, honey! And has the body of a Greek god." She fanned herself. "Sexy. Rugged."

"Ooh, ooh," Spencer said excitedly, clapping her hands. "Milk chocolate skin sliding over thick muscles, huh? Finger-lickin', melting-all-over-your-tongue gooey goodness, I bet."

Rich bounced her shoulders and shook. "Yasss! And his swag's on ten. No, twenty. And he's holding a double-barrel in his CKs, boo."

Spencer bounced in her seat. "Oooh, do it, boo! Bang-bang beat it down, momma!"

"Yasss, yasss. Down to the ground!" Rich popped her collar. "You know how I do it. Big dawg artillery, honey!"

I couldn't believe how the two of them carried on as if I weren't even in the room. I cleared my throat, meeting Rich's gaze with annoyance. Her dark stare bordered somewhere between amusement and challenge. It was clear. Rich wanted a battle. She'd come prepared to duel it out.

But why?

Spencer eased back into her seat, rolling her eyes. "You selfish, inconsiderate stank-a-dank, trick-a-lot! How dare you flounce your rump shaker in here announcing this kind of news in front of the enemy?"

*Enemy?*

I blinked. Surprised at how quickly she'd flipped on Rich. Then again, it didn't take much for Spencer to go bat-crazy.

"Why was I not told about this so-called *engagement* when you were all up in my house snot-nosed and crazy, huh? You wait to do me in front of Big Foot!"

Rich rolled her eyes. "*Screech!* Clutching pearls! Lies! Spencer, *don't*. Do. Me. You've *never* seen me snot-nosed and crazy! I don't do that! I don't drop tears over a man. And I definitely don't try to kill myself over one." She shot an icy glare over at me. "Is that what you tried to do, London? Kill yourself over some boy who didn't want you? Poor thing."

I cringed. Shifted my body weight in bed. It felt like Rich had jabbed a blade to my neck and twisted it. Before I could respond to her cutting remark, Spencer butted in. "Rich, I told you to play nice. Not come over here and be messy."

"Oh no." Rich swiveled her neck in dramatic fashion, pointing a finger over at Spencer. "What is this, save-a-thot day? Is London your new charity? Since when you start taking up for her?"

Spencer twirled the end of a curl around her finger, pursing her lips. "Oh, you really want me to squirt fire in your mouth, don't you? You know I don't like this trick. But I'm not going to drag her when she's already down. And if you had any compassion, you wouldn't do it either, Rich. Now stop being so odious. And have some decency for once."

"*Odious?*" Rich stamped her foot. "*Bish,* you got me confused. You don't smell any odors on me. That's your breath. Nothing stinks on me. I bathe *every* day."

Spencer and I gave her a blank stare.

"I didn't say odiferous," Spencer lamented, rolling her eyes. "I said *odious*. Big difference."

Rich sucked in a breath. "Spare me the details, Spencer. Jealousy is so not cute on you. I mean, really. It's not my fault you can't get a man, unless he's someone else's; or unless he's really, really desperate for a pipe cleaner. Don't hate my fabulousness, sweetie. Hate the fact that *you* can't be, won't ever be—*me*. So stop being selfish! For once, stay in your lane and just be happy for me."

Spencer blinked. "Uh-huh. Oh, I'll be happy for you all right."

"Good. Now fall back and let me have my shine. If you act right, I'll let you be my maid of honor. Otherwise you'll be banned to the back of the church, passing out programs." Rich shot a look over at me. "Mmph. It smells like death in here. So you're just gonna sit in that bed like a zombie with that pitiful, stupid look and not even say hello?

Or *congratulate* me? Or *apologize* to me for that mess you pulled down at Club Tantrum?"

"Last I checked, this was my house. And I didn't pull any mess down at the club. *You* did. Just like now. Everything is always about you, Rich."

"Yes, it is." She tossed her bangs from out of her eye. "Glad you finally realize that."

"Correction. The only thing I realize is, you're effen delusional. You walked into my space. You've insulted and disrespected me, so if anyone should be speaking to anyone, it's *you*. If anyone should be apologizing to anyone, it's *you*!"

Spencer giggled. "Ooh, this is starting to look like old times already."

Rich and I ignored her, staring each other down with burning glares.

"Oh no. Oh no. We are not doing this stare-down contest." Spencer clapped her hands. "Not up in here. Not today."

I refused to back down from Rich. She was a loud-mouthed bully, two-faced troublemaker. A man stealer!

"Why are you here, Rich?" I finally asked. My eyes remained locked on hers in a defiant stare-down. To think I used to really like this girl. Now I couldn't stand the sight of her.

She sneered. "I came to see what misery looked like. Why else would I come to the lowlands? To trash central?"

My heart sank, my bubble of hope burst. It was painfully clear she'd only come to gloat.

"Then it should have been staring back at you this morning in the mirror," I spat, propping another pillow behind me, then folding my arms over my chest.

"Be glad I'm here, London. It's not like anyone else cares about you. You don't even care about you. Who tries to slice their own wrists? I mean, really? How deep is the scar?"

She stalked over to my bed and tried to grab my arm. "What, did you use cheap blades? Admit it, London. All you wanted was attention, making superficial cuts. What, you wanted your neglectful mommy to spend more time at home with you? You wanted your daddy to give you hugs?"

"Screw you, Rich!" I snapped, feeling my cheeks heat with anger as I yanked my arm from her grasp. I fisted my hands at my sides and did my best to restrain my rage. Beating the skin off this hooker would be the highlight of my day, but I needed to keep my temper reined in. "You're always so quick to talk about someone else's parents, but you need to take a look at your own. At least I have a father who acknowledges me instead of one who ignores me. And the only reason your mother pays you as much attention as she does is because her real pride and joy is in England."

"Whatever, London. Unlike you, at least I have a life worth living. I'm not trying to kill myself because I'm worthless. What a waste of a good hospital bed. And my tax dollars! If you really wanted to check out, you shoulda called me. I woulda gladly spared you the ambulance ride."

The hurt in my voice sliced through the silence in the room. I fought conflicting urges to clutch her to me in a big embrace because a part of me missed her and to snap her neck because I now hated her. Rich and I *had*—operative word—been friends. Maybe not the best of friends

where we'd both shared our dirty little secrets and con-
fided our fears and giggled over boy crushes. No. We'd—
okay, okay, *I'd*—kept some things secret from her. I'd
drawn the line in the sand long before our family jet ever
landed in the City of Angels, where hellfire was burning
hotter than ever the day I'd schemed along with Justice to
introduce the two of them so that he could manipulate his
way into her heart, then into her father's record label for
his own recording deal.

Shamefully, it all backfired on me.

My friendship with Rich was ruined.

My relationship with Justice was over.

And now this...

Justice. Just the thought of them together, the image of
them entangled in heat and desire and dirty deeds, had
my heart pounding and my blood pressure rising.

Spencer flicked imaginary dirt from beneath her fingernails. "So, if Knox wasn't dumb enough to marry you, then
exactly *who* is this heinous barbarian who holds your devotion?" Spencer eased back in her seat, crossed her legs,
and tightly pressed her lips together. She clasped her
hands over her knee, waiting.

Rich craned her neck over at Spencer. "And why do you
care? I mean, really? Why you so worried about my hot
pocket?"

"Oh, trust me, girlie. I'm not concerned about that cor-
roded septic tank of yours."

"Oh really? I can't tell."

"Well, I'm telling you, sewer rat." Spencer edged up on
her seat, tilting her head combatively. "So don't try me. Try
keeping your legs shut, instead."

"Maybe you should try keeping your mouth shut instead of hatin' on me. Do I do that to you, Spencer? Do I hate on you and Midnight? No. I don't. Why? Because I'm a grown woman, doing grown things. Not playing kiddie games. I'm royalty, honey. Now both of you, bow down"— she held out her hand—"and kiss the ring."

Spencer huffed. "Rich, kiss my dang duck sauce. I'm waiting for you to tell me who asked you to marry him."

I blinked, blinked again. The answer to Spencer's question was boldly staring back at me on Rich's ring finger. *Dear God! Nooooooo!* I choked back a scream. *Not my diamond! This trick is standing here flaunting, flossing! Wearing my ring! Justice gave her my engagement ring!*

I barely heard anything else being said in the room. My heartbeat pounded in my ears. Hurt and anger and resentment swirled and swelled to dangerous levels, twisting inside of me like a roaring wildfire. I felt my body convulsing as I leapt up from my bed. Darkness danced at the edges of my vision as I swung my fists with all my might and everything around me faded to black...

# 18

# Spencer

How dare Rich try to do me!
And she didn't just do me raw and dirty. She did me
right here in front of this bubblehead, London! She didn't
even have the decency to do me in private, in the comfort
of my own home, or hers. No. She did it right here at the
Wastelands.

Ooh, I was hotter than a rattlesnake.

*Ole ratchet snatch patch!*

But I kept it classy and ladylike as always. And smiled
and played along real nice.

But inside, I felt like burning the balls of Rich's feet for
prancing up in here and announcing some dang engagement like that. Rich. Muddafrickin'. Man-eater. Montgomery.
Officially made me sick!

I'd been nothing but loving and kind to that ole crotch-
rotted heathen. And that's how she showed her appreciation. By sideswiping me with some news like this.

*"I'm getting married…"*

Really? Where they teaching that at?

I couldn't believe my ears.

Then that three-faced, cotton-pickin', two-bit floozy had the audacity to try to bring the noise, talking all lickety-slick to me in front of London like that, looking at me all crazy. Like I was a meatless bone. Oh, when Miss Sophia was locked in her padded room overseas it was all coochie-oochie-yah-yah-crunch-crunch. But now that Miss Sophia was home, back in La-La Land, rocking and wringing her hands, Rich wanted to show me fever.

Well, guess what, goshdangit?

Spencer Ellington was not checking temperatures. Not today. And I wasn't checking the inside of panty liners, either.

No. I had to take a stand. I had to stop the spread of hoetry and slutism.

The revolution had to be televised.

And that's why—while London went happy-fist-and-feet on Rich—I sat here and recorded Rich getting her scallops tossed. Then I slowly eased on up out of my seat and slid over to London's panic button, heehee—and rang the alarm.

I sure did!

That'll learn that trick to do me.

*Whoop! Whoop! That's the sound of the police, goshdiggitydangit! Whatchu gonna do when they come for you?*

*Now marry that, you Judas in a skirt*, I thought as three muscled Mandingos stormed into London's suite and dragged Rich across the carpet by her ankles, then hoisted her up by her wrists and feet, then carried her down the stairs and tossed her out onto the lawn, like the sewer trash she was.

I giggled, imagining that I'd whipped out my cell, placing it to my ear, feigning panic. "Umm, nine-one-one. There's a whopper with a weave on the wild at Low Money's Estate. She's five-six. Half-cute chick with big thighs, big boobs, and a whole lot of junk in her caboose, and she has a permanent fat pocket where I think she's hiding a baby kangaroo. Yes, yes, yes...Holmby Hills. Yes, yes...she's the world's first fat Barbie. Get here quickly."

Heeheeheehee.

Ooh, that loose-lipped louse was lucky I didn't make that call for real and have her served a pair of shiny steel handcuffs. It would have served her right for what she'd done.

I'd never felt more hurt in my life by Trampette. Well, wait. That's not completely true. She'd hurt me deeply when she snuck off and slept with that man-boy, Xavier— the tall, strapping, sexy caramel tenth-grader who dated one of those god-awful Beanie Baby tricklets. *Oh heavens, what the heck are those Nine West slores calling themselves?*

*Strumpets?*

*No, no. That's not it.*

*Payless Bandits?*

*No, that's not it, either.*

Fortheluvofgoodmanmeat...Lawd have mercy! I couldn't think. That mess with Rich had my noodles soggy. I couldn't believe her! The gotdang nerve of her!

Anyway, ole Miss Jane Pittman snuck Xavier down into the underground railroad and had her way with him, knowing I wanted to sit down on his face and ride him straight to freedom. Mmph.

Ooh, nookie-nookie now...the Starlets!

Yeah, that's the clique! The one with the big, oversized forehead, the one I had to fly-swat in the mouth, then greet her in the girls' lounge with duct tape and Nair. Her boyfriend. That's the one Rich snuck off with. Leaving him slumped with his pants wrapped around his ankles.

Stankin' thot!

And that's not the only time Rich hurt me. She'd cut me deep when she traded me in for this ole pumpkin-head troll doll sitting over there in the center of her bed with an ice pack to her face.

Public Enemy Number One, Two, Three, and Four!

"Ohmygod!" London groaned, snapping me out of the monologue in my head. "I can't believe Rich came up in here and treated me like crap! Couldn't she just once think about someone other than herself?"

I shot her a dirty look, rolling my eyeballs fast and hard around in my head. I had to talk myself out of hopping up from my seat and tearing this trick's face off.

*Oh no, oh no...breathe in, breathe out...Don't do it, boo. Stay loving and kind...*

I regarded her for a hot second in silence. Then got up from my seat and sat on the bed alongside her, sandwiching her big left paw between my two dainty hands.

London gave me a stunned look.

"Oh, relax," I said, slapping the top of her paw with my hand. "I'm not going to gut you or anything like that. Not yet, anyway. Heeheehee." I stroked her paw, locking my hazel eyes onto her swollen red eyes. "Rich failed you as a friend. She knew you were lost and alone and that no one

liked you, so the least she could have done was been a little more sympathetic to your poor, pathetic soul..."

London blinked.

"London, I'm sad to say, Rich failed you as a friend. She
should have been a shoulder for you to lean on, a hand for
you to hold, an ear for you to bend. She let you down. And
she let me down. But, oh well. You got what you asked for."

*"Excuuuuuse you?"* She yanked her paw back. "What exactly are you trying to say here, Spencer? That I deserved her
rude, nasty treatment?"

I snatched her paw back and gripped it. "Yes. You did
deserve it. But I told Rich to not bring it to you while you
were afflicted and pitiful. At least I have the good grace to
pretend to like you while you're going through this griev-
ous time. You should be thanking me. But, Rich..." I
shook my head, clutching my chest. "She has no couth. No
social etiquette. What kind of friend does that? Turn on
you in a time of need? Rich was dead wrong for that. But,
oh well. I told her to check her attitude at the door before
she got here. But obviously she didn't take heed to the
memo. Now if you'd pull the ants from out of your mole-
hill and sit still, I'll tell you exactly why." I popped her paw
again. "Stop trying to pull your hoof back from me and let
me finish."

She blinked again.

"See. Once upon a time, not long ago, there was this
cute little chunky princess who thought she was the flyest
of them all. Yeah, she gave you face. And she gave you
booty and a busload of boobs, but she didn't have much
of a brain. But she had a best friend who knew all of her
dirty little secrets. They fought no-good slores together.
Tag-teamed boys together. And traveled and shopped until

they dropped together. But then came along a snaggle-toothed witch whom I'm going to call Dogzilla..."

I paused, narrowing my eyes. "Are you paying attention, DogKeesha, I mean, London? Are you listening? The story gets real juicy, I promise you."

She huffed. "Will you hurry up and get to the point, please and thank you!"

"Oh no! Oh no! You will *not* rush me. And you will *not* disrespect me or use that filthy tone with me. I'm the only one who has cared enough to come and sit with you during this horrific time. So don't you dare go getting all snot-box messy with me."

She yanked her beefy mitt from out of my grasp, folding her arms across her chest.

"Fine. Tell your story. Just get on with it already."

I started from the top again.

"See. Once upon a time..."

Then I told her how the princess and her bestie were inseparable. How they shared everything. Well, everything except for wearing each other's garter belts and panty and bra sets. Heehee. Still...there wasn't anything that this bestie wouldn't do for her little Teletubby friend who once had teeth so big she looked like a chipmunk, even knocking a boy upside the head with nunchucks and leaving him for dead if he put his hands on her.

London's mocha-brown face blanched.

"Then came along Dogzilla with the big globe head and rhino hoofs from the East Coast, who traveled three thousand miles across the dirty Hudson River to the West Coast in pursuit of sugar and spice and everything nice..."

London rolled her eyes. Squirmed in her seat.

"See. But the princess was gullible and she easily fell

into Dogzilla's trap of lies. But her bestie wasn't buying what the tramp was selling and *knew* she was a scam. The princess's bestie knew that Dogzilla was a conniving troll with more secrets and lies than a nun posing for a center-fold. But the bestie couldn't get her fingers on the pulse of it. Until said bestie met *Buff Daddy* . . ."

London gave me a blank stare.

"Oh, don't play coy with me, Queen Kong, I mean, Lon-don. You know *exactly* whom I'm referring to. I'm talking about Mister Big Daddy In Heels. Mister Toot 'Em Up Bang Bang. Mister Cooter Teaser. Mister Trisexual himself, the crumb snatcher. I'm talking about Anderson Ford, your cover-up."

She blinked.

"Yes. Anderson. Ford. The drag-sexual in training. See. He told me after a night of me stretching his goodie bag out that you didn't want him. That you were only with him out of convenience, to keep your secret lover-boy hidden from your parents. That your secret boy-toy was driving you crazy."

London blinked again.

"Yes, ma'am. I know all about your delicious thug daddy! The bum who you kept locked in a closet. Anderson didn't say his name, but I put two and two together and came up with six. I mean, four. Then I started watching you."

I walked over to her chaise and snatched up the large manila envelope I'd had in my hand earlier before I shot her up with my water gun. I walked back over to her bed and slung the envelope at her.

"What is this?"

"Open it and see for yourself."

I eyed London and smirked as she tore open the sealed

packet. She slid her hand inside and withdrew an eight-by-ten glossy photo of her standing outside in the wee hours of the morning in the parking lot of the Kit Kat Lounge. The night I sent her those anonymous text messages and sent her on a wild-goose hunt for her thug boo. The one Miss Freaks R Us, I mean Rich, was up on the twenty-first floor with, putting it on him like her one-legged grandmother Rovina SueDeeka Gatling aka Momma Deeka had shown her in that homemade porn video she'd made of her and Poppa Long Tongue Gatling.

She pulled out another picture and frowned. It was of her speeding out of the parking lot, tailing behind Justice. Another was of her pulled over on the side of the highway, crying. "W-w-what, w-w-where did you get these pictures?"

"Oh, don't you worry about that. I warned you, you ole moose face, that one day I was going to unearth the dirty trick you are. You lucky I don't split your sockets and saw down your ankles for how you played Rich and manipulated her into believing you were her friend."

"I *was* her friend," she shot back.

"Oh really? Were you her friend before or *after* you whispered in Knox's ear and told him Rich had an abortion?"

Her mouth dropped open.

"I-I-I . . ."

I put a hand up. "Save it. You waited for the right moment, until you could get Knox alone at that frat party, then turned on Rich for your own sleazy gain. Now you done ran her crazy. She's crazier than she's ever been. I know all about it. And now so does Rich, so no need to try to spin another web of lies. The gig is up, chickie. You're lucky I don't claw out your guts and peel back your rocket. You had Hot Drawz slap me over something *you* did. *You* set it up to make it look like *I* was the traitor, like *I* was the one who betrayed Rich's trust. When all along it was *you*."

I clapped my hands. "Bravo. Yes, Miss Girlie. Bravo. Standing ovation to you for *almost* getting away with it. Almost."

I slid my hand down into my bag and pulled out a tube of what looked like hand cream. But she was none the wiser that it was really fast-acting gel cream hair-remover. I discreetly smeared some into the palm of my hand, then swiped a dollop up onto my fingertips. I closed the tube and tossed it into my bag.

"You thought you were so clever, huh? Thought you were two-pennies slick, didn't you? You got greedy, heifer. You got sloppy. You betrayed your only friend all over a piece of man trash?"

My eyes narrowed with wicked glee watching the breath leave her body in a single rush. I finally had Miss Tramp-A-Lot right where I wanted her. Over the barrel of a loaded cannon. Now all I had to do was stuff her inside, then strike a match to it and watch her blast off.

"Now look at you. Clawing at death's door over some bum garbage that left you for a man-eater."

"Get out of my house!" London growled. "Before I have you thrown—"

Before she was able to finish the rest of her sentence, I leapt on her with the lightning speed of a panther, pinning her down on the bed and swiping her across her right eyebrow, then running my hand through the top of her head and the roots of her hair.

"Aaaaaah!" she screamed, trying to wrestle me off of

her. "What is that? What are you trying to do? *Aaaaaah! Help! Security!*"

I laughed hysterically as the same Mandingos who'd dragged Rich out just twenty minutes earlier now barged in and manhandled me.

I didn't give a horse's ding-dong about being tossed out of Low Money's home.

Screw with me if you want.

For the next few weeks, Miss Hair Loss would be wearing wigs and using crayon to draw on her eyebrows.

# 19

# Heather

*...By the time my eyes drifted to her thighs I realized what I was doing. I quickly glanced away and turned back toward the bar, sipping my drink again.*

*"Heather, what are you drinking? Let me buy you another one."*

*I did my best to resist the blush I felt creeping back onto my face. "No. Thank you. But no." Why am I nervous?*

*"Okay." She smiled, her beautiful teeth gleaming. "I won't hold you." She unexpectedly swept and twirled the end of a lone curl before winking and sashaying away.*

*I refused to let my eyes follow her and instead, as unwanted butterflies danced in my stomach, I sank my smile into my drink.*

*This was crazy. I knew she wasn't a guy, but I still couldn't stop my throat—which should've been moist—from being dry, or my knees from feeling too weak to stand up. Or my heart from rushing through its beats...*

*Stop it!*

*"I just thought about something." Her words poured over my shoulder. I knew it was her and I didn't have to turn around to confirm it. She reached for my phone, which was next to my drink, clicked on my camera, and surprised me by taking a picture of us. Then she punched in a few numbers and placed my phone back on the bar.*

*She leaned into my ear and whispered, her heated breath making a trail of goose bumps along the side of my neck. "I programmed my number in your phone and the picture is so you won't forget me." She turned to leave and then quickly turned back. "And by the way, I'm Nikki."*

"Hey, cutie, what are you over there thinking about?" Nikki said, her voice pulling me out of the memory of the night we'd met at Club Noir Kiss.

I looked over at Nikki as we sat on the floor in my room, flipping through CDs and listening to music. Her dimpled smile lit up the room and I wondered if she thought I was insane, or silly, or strange...

*This is stupid.*

*Why did I invite this girl here?*

*You wanted to see her.*

*But why?*

*You like her...*

*But why do I like her?*

*How do I like her?*

*You know why you like her.*

*Yeah...*

She was funny. Smart. A sophomore at San Diego State. Nineteen. Pledged Greek. Loved giving back to the community. Was big on loyalty. Had two sisters and a brother.

Was the baby of her family. Had three nieces—triplets. Had a mother. A father. A dog...

*She was perfect.*

*Like I wanted to be...*

I glanced over at the clock and realized that she'd been here for three hours. Three hours of us laughing and talking about everything, and anything, and nothing at all, all at the same time.

Time flies.

"Okay now, Miss Heather. You are being a little too quiet over there for me."

"Am I?" I did my best not to blush.

"Yes. You. Are. And my guess is you're avoiding my question." She waved the rapper Game's CD before me. "I said whatchu know about Game?" She popped her fingers and playfully cocked her neck to the side.

"What do *I* know about Game?" I giggled and my curls bounced into my eyes and over my shoulders. "The question should be, what do *you* know about him?"

Nikki scooted over closer to me and gently brushed my hair out of my eyes, her index finger twirling the same coil she'd snaked around her finger before. "Don't switch this around on me." She eased the curl from her fingertip and it sprang back in place. "I know everything about Jayceon Taylor, boo." She tossed two fingers into the air. "Westside."

I hated that I couldn't help but fall out laughing.

*Why am I laughing so hard?*

*This is so dumb. All she asked me about was a freakin' rapper, who I love. Nothing to laugh at. Nothing to smile about. Just a simple question. That required a simple answer... but I can't even get that right!*

*Shyt!*

*Why am I so nervous?*

*Stop it, girl.*

"Come on now," Nikki insisted. "Don't hold back. As a matter of fact, here's what I think you should do. I think you should bust a rhyme for me."

"A what?" My eyes bulged in surprise.

"You know you turned it out at Club Noir Kiss, girl!" She snapped her fingers. "Don't play all bashful now. Not the way I saw you poppin' them hips and big ole bouncy booty. You were doing it, girl. I still got that night on the brain."

I giggled. "How'd we get from you asking me what do I know about Game to you wanting me to rap?"

"Come on now." She softly hunched her shoulder against mine. "I'm listening. Just pretend you're on stage." She hopped up from the floor. "And the crowd is going wild!"

"And where are you in this scenario?" I did my best not to smile too wide. I failed.

"I'm your hype man!" She extended her hand and pulled me from the floor. "Now come on!" I leapt to my feet and she said, "Wait, wait. We need to Instagram this." She turned on her phone and pressed RECORD.

"Okay, okay!" Nikki announced. "Wu-Wu's here bringing you another freestyle hit!"

I gave in to the silliness of the moment, and said, "Wu-Wu's in the house!" I introduced my rap with a beat box and then I spat:

"I met a girl named Nikki at the club mmmph..."

Nikki looked into her phone screen and said, "That's me..."

I sang, "I thought my drink was the reason she was so pretty."

"I'm always pretty," Nikki sang back.

"Had me feeling giddy."

"Butterflies," Nikki chimed in.

"But I was so used to lies that I knew this couldn't be real."

"It's all real," Nikki sounded back.

I did another beat box and continued, "I met a girl named Nikki..."

"Pretty and fly," Nikki sang, clapping her hands to the beat "That's me..."

"And I find myself asking why—"

"Why what, Heather?" Camille's voice sliced its way into my room, causing Nikki and me to jump. I paused and Nikki quickly turned her phone off.

Just that quick I felt myself shift from ease to intensity. I looked back over at Nikki and she was smiling at Camille. "Hi, Ms. Cummings!" she said a little too excitedly, as if Camille was some kind of celebrity, or mother of the year. "It's such a pleasure to meet you." She extended her hand for a handshake. Camille offered Nikki a limp wrist and shake of her fingertips. That's when I noticed there was no drink in her hand.

"I'm such a fan of yours, Ms. Cummings!"

"A fan?" Camille snorted, looking Nikki over from her pink Jordans to her tie-dye skinny jeans, to her white tank top that showed highlights of her pink lace bra. Camille slowly dragged shade all up and down for no apparent reason.

*Dear God...please...please...please...don't let this woman embarrass me.*

Camille tapped a foot, causing the heel of her mink slippers to sink further into the carpet. "You said a *fan*? Of mine? Really? Shut the front door. And do tell. When I ain't been in a movie in over fifteen years? Little girl, please. Spare me your lies. Now what is your name? And what social circle do you belong to? Who are your parents?"

Nikki blinked not once but three times.

"Camille," I snapped, struggling not to drop-kick her in the throat. "This is my friend Nikki. Now can you leave? Just get out. Go. I know you can see that we're doing something."

"Yeah, I saw you doing something. And I heard singing something. Now you wanna explain exactly what this *something* was about? 'Cause it looks to me like there's a whole lot of sweetness in the room. Now I'm standing here waiting for the fruit flies to appear." She crossed her arms across her white gown and tapped her foot again.

*Deep breath in.*

*Deep breath out.*

*Don't turn it up yet.*

*Check yourself.*

*This is the first time Nikki's been here.*

*You don't want her to see you like this.*

*First time I might have a genuine friend and I don't want to scare her away by her seeing me tearing Camille apart.*

I tossed a hard stare at Camille, scrunched my lips, and narrowed my gaze. "Would you *please*. Leave." I held my breath and then quickly pushed it out. *"Please."*

Camille looked me over from head to toe and back again, the creases in her forehead revealing a million thoughts running through her head. "Um-hmm," she grunted. "I'll leave.

I'll leave from where I'm standing to sit right over here."
She walked over to the edge of my bed and crossed her
legs. "Yep. I'm going to sit right here and chaperone you
and your new friend. Eyeball this questionable party."

*I can't believe this. I swear Camille has stock in ruin-*
*ing my life.*

The room fell completely silent and the air around us
was thick.

Nikki laughed. A fake laugh. An uncomfortable laugh.
"Your mother is so funny and cool."

"Um-hmm." I pressed my lips tightly together. "Real co-
median. A supernatural. A real superhero."

Another round of silence invaded the room.

"Well, umm..." Nikki said. "I'm going to get ready to go.
My nieces are going to be at my parents' and I promised
my mom that I'd show up for more than doing laundry."

My heart sank as I watched Nikki reach for her purse
and push the strap onto her shoulder. I wasn't ready to
see her go. Not yet. Not when we were having so much
fun. Not while I was feeling so carefree.

*I hate Camille!*

"Thanks for inviting me over, Heather," Nikki said as
she walked out of my bedroom and I walked her to the
front door.

I was doing all I could to stay cool and calm. I wanted
to beat Camille's face off and tear her mouth out. Instead,
I forced myself to smile at Nikki. "Thank you for coming."

She smiled. "Hopefully, I can see you again soon."

"Yeah, I'd like that."

Nikki pulled me into her warm, soft embrace, lightly
kissing me on my cheek. "Take care."

"You too," I said as she turned from the door and glided

down the limestone pathway to her car. I leaned against the door frame and as I placed a hand onto the spot she'd kissed, Camille's veiny white arm reached over my shoulder and slammed the door.

"I don't know where you found that one," she spat as I turned around to face her. "But *it* cannot come back here! That little thing is a little too cute and a whole lot of *friendly*. Too friendly for my liking. Where'd you meet her at, Club Rehab?" She snorted and then said mockingly, "I'm your biggest fan. Even though I was only two and still pissing on myself when your last movie came out. Yeah, right. Bull. Sheeeeit. I might have been born at night. But it wasn't last night."

I frowned. "What are you talking about, Camille?" I slammed a hand on my hip and tilted my head, positioning myself in combat mode.

"I'm talking about you and Little Miss Queen Latifah."

"Oh, whatever, Camille! You ought to be happy that you have one fan left in the freakin' world who recognized who you were. Going forward, do not call her a *thing* anymore. She's a girl. A person! And *don't* call her names. As a matter of fact, why do you care how friendly she is?"

"I don't care," Camille snorted. "But what I do care about is my daughter poppin' her collar and two steppin' it. Twisting her thirsty hips and doing a remake of R. Kelly's *Black Panties*!"

"Whatever!" I said, attempting to storm off.

Camille snatched my arm and I snatched it back. "I don't know what kind of sugar games and rainbow dreams you got going on, but you're not hosting your RuPaul parties up in here! So you had better drag race it over to her momma's house with the nieces and the laundry. Or over to Miss Co-Co Chanel's because I know that Miss Trans Confusion is behind all of these carpet games."

I blinked. I was convinced this woman was craaaazy! With a capital C. "Last I checked," I snapped, "this was my house. I pay the rent up in here and I will have who I wanna have up in here! And you will not disrespect my company. Fan or no fan. For once I have a friend who I like, who I want to spend time with and get to know, and you want to ruin it."

She huffed. "You pay rent? You're supposed to pay rent. You're the one who's working! Ingrate! I tell you what, if you want friends, you can have friends. But if you bring Miss Ruff Rider back up in here again, she better be parked in the living room and *not* in your bedroom. I want her out in the open where I can watch *you* in peace! I don't need nobody up in here that I can't have my drinks around. My throat's all parched, but can I have a glass of scotch? *Nooo!* Because I have to play babysitter and watch *you* and keep an eye on your party. I don't know what you think you're doing, but I understand this: It's not going down on my watch. Now stop being a follower, running behind Queen Boxer Shorts and Co-Co, and stick with your own kind. I don't care if he's black, white, or Mexican, but he better not be somebody's sister, or somebody's *auntie* doing laundry. Now go to your room and read your Bible. Thou shall not sin up in here."

I took a deep breath and looked Camille over. She had me twisted. Completely. "You know what, Camille? I don't have to answer to you! Don't question me. Ever! Not when I've been trying to get you to tell me about my father for the last two weeks and you've done nothing but avoid me! Now you wanna play interrogation. Twenty-twenty questions. Then let's start with you and Richard Montgomery! *Why* did you lie to me all of these years about him?!"

Camille's eyes popped open. "I told you before, and I'm telling you again, it's not important. He's not important. He wanted you aborted. I said no. I had you. And when I did, my life went to hell! I lost my man and my career! End of story. So forgive me if I'm not in the mood to talk about Richard-couldn't-appreciate-that-I loved-him-that-I-was-good-to-him-that-I-would've-given-my-life-for-him-Montgomery." She sauntered over to the bar. Poured herself a glass of scotch and then lit a cigarette.

"I'm up in here doing the best that I can and all you'd like to discuss is *Richard.*" She flopped down on the sofa, shaking her head. She flicked her ashes to the floor. "I tell you what." She patted the cushion next to her. "You wanna talk about *Richard?* Your long lost, invisible daddy? You really wanna talk about that? You really wanna know the truth? Then let's chat."

Finally I was going to get some answers. To fill in the blanks, the missing pieces of my life. Reluctantly, I sat on the far end of the sofa. My stomach twirled into knots as she said calmly, "Your father is a no-good bastard. Period." She looked at me and waited for a response. And when I didn't give her one she took a sip of her drink then took a long, deliberate pull from her cigarette, blowing smoke up into the air.

She continued, "I was madly in love with him." She flicked her ashes. Then clutched her heart. "We were engaged to be married. I had done everything except go down the aisle. Invitations were sent out. The cake was ordered. The dress was custom-made. And this old raggedy white slip I always wear was supposed to be worn under my gown. Something new, something borrowed, and something blue."

I blinked. *Dear God...*

"I wanted to marry him and I would've married him had Logan—the groupie she was—not come along and stalked the backstage of every show, throwing her panties up in my man's face every chance she got. I was working. I was on set, making movies and money. I couldn't be with my man on the road at every show. He was just starting out his rap career. I was already a star. I couldn't babysit no man. And guess what? That cost me my man. Logan did everything in her power to break us up, and she succeeded. And he let her. Everyone wanted a piece of MC Wickedness. And Logan got herself a taste along with everyone else. She got pregnant. Had the baby, and gave Richard a son. After that he was done with me. Tossed me to the side. And yes, I took sloppy seconds. Because I loved him that much."

She got up from her seat and walked back over to the bar and instead of refreshing her glass she picked up the bottle and brought it back over to the couch. She sat and took the bottle to the head. "Richard was all I had. All I wanted to have. But did he care? No. Which is exactly why it was so easy for him to tell me to have an abortion. That his wife was having their second baby and that if I wanted him to still be in my life, I had to get rid of mine."

She shook her head. Paused as if she were trying to collect herself.

"My baby, Heather. Imagine that. I should have nothing, while Logan had everything. Well, I told him no. And that was the last time I saw him. So there you have it. Your answers. You wanted to know about Richard Montgomery. Well, mystery solved."

She gulped down the rest of the bottle.

Tears filled my eyes and slowly streamed down my cheeks.

"Oh dear God. Save the theatrics for when the reality TV cameras get here. And what are you crying for, anyway? Stop with the tears, please. I've cried enough for the both of us. Just suck it up and deal with the fact that *you* don't exist to him. He's not interested in you. Never has been, never will be. He has a family. And yeah, you may have his DNA, but he will never be your daddy. And you will never collect his checks. So let it go. Move on. Don't go looking for a fairy-tale ending because you are not going to get it. You will never be a Montgomery. You are a Cummings. And I chose to have you, which is why you will not disrespect me. You will do what I tell you to and we will not discuss that man again!"

She blinked away the water in her eyes.

I swallowed. Wiped more tears. And just as I was prepared to tell Camille that she may have had her experience with Richard Montgomery but that had nothing to do with me, he was my father, and I would be taking my chances and confronting him, the doorbell rang and I heard someone yelling my name.

*"Heather!!!!"*

Oh. No.

I know freakin' well . . .

"Here you go again, Heather!" Camille snapped. "Someone else coming over here unannounced. I need to have my drinks in peace and a moment to reflect on my sorrows, thanks to you dredging up old wounds. And I don't want nobody up in here!"

I rolled my eyes and ignored Camille's rant. Rose from my chair and walked over to the door and opened it. To my surprise, Rich Montgomery was standing in the doorway.

"Heather!" She pushed her way inside in true rude fashion. "You were right! Once again, they turned on me. And before you tell me to get out of your house, that's real cute by the way, I need you to know that I'm done with them whores! It's gonna be me and you on the fame of thrones. Now where are the cameras?!"

# 20

# Spencer

"*Cleola Mae, you in here...?*"

I groaned and tossed in my bed, sinking my head deeper into the comforts of my pillow.

I knew I shouldn't have tossed back those shots of Jack Daniel's with Midnight, then chased it with his tongue. Jack was nothing but a low-down dirty drink.

Nothing but the devil juice.

And Midnight's long tongue was his heated pitchfork.

"*They comin' for you...*"

I hissed between clenched teeth, tossing under the silk sheets.

I knew I wasn't drunk. And I wasn't drunk in love.

No, no. This had to be a horrible nightmare.

Wait. Something wasn't right. Little hairs stood up on my arms. I couldn't hear anyone moving or breathing.

I knew my eyes were shut tight behind my silk eyeshade. And I knew my door was shut, so there was no diggitydang way someone would be in my room. Wait! But I forgot to lock it. Wait, wait... I've never had to lock the door to my suite.

So what was happening here?

I heard the whispering again. *"Cleola? Cleola? Them boys from Mississippi got the dogs out on you..."*

Yes, I was having a bad dream.

*But wait... you can't dream and be aware of your surroundings too, can you? No, no, of course not. Oh, Spencer, stop being silly, girl. It's just the wind hooting and howling outside.*

*"Cleola, wake up... we gotta hide..."*

*Dear God...*

What da flimflamfluck was going on?

I snapped open my eyes behind the mask, soaked in the darkness of the fabric resting over my sockets, and lay perfectly still. I held my breath. Waited. I didn't hear anything stirring about. Nothing rustled. But I felt someone... *something*. It was in my room. I could smell the sweet stink of dank, hot muskiness, of tooth decay and mothballs and Bengay.

Oh no, oh no... sweetdungeonsanddragons! There was a ghost in my room, *again*.

I frowned with frustration. All that good money I'd spent on that priestess last year to come through here ringing bells in every corner of my suite, tossing garlic around the room, burning bundles of sage, and sprinkling sea salt on the windowsills for nothing. All a dingdang waste of my hard-earned trust dollars.

And to think I even had Rich smoking cigars packed with sage with me, just to be on the safe side. Now I was right back where I started last year. In need of another dang ghost buster to come up in here and beat the socks off of this rude, disrespectful spirit.

I huffed. How hard was it for a priestess to do her got-dang job right?

"I swear," I muttered under my breath, "I should report her to the priestess board and have her license revoked. Shiftless dang hussy."

I heard the whispered voice again. *"Cleola, where are you? You in here?"*

Had these ghosts no dang shame? Showing up here all times of the night! Disrupting my beauty sleep! Disrupting my life! Jeezus! We were in the last days. Even ghosts had no dang decency!

Who on earth would be selfish enough to swoop into someone's room at this ungodly hour? I didn't know for sure what time it was, but I knew it had to be smack in the wee hours of the night; a far cry from my usual wake-up time.

Wait. Waaaaaait!

I was losing my cookies.

Old Mister Jack Daniel's was playing nasty tricks on me. Yes, yes. That was it.

I was just imagining things. There wasn't a ghost in my room. Ghosts only boo-hoo'd or moved things around the room without permission.

*Yeah, that's it.*

Heehee.

I sighed, relief washing over me as I finally closed my eyes in hopes of getting lost in sleepy land. I said a silent prayer just in case. "Ole dirty spirits from the wicked underworld world, I rebuke you in the name of the immortals. Get thy invisible self back. I call on the spirit of the ghost slayer to butcher your energy. Call on the fire gods to burn the invisible drawers off your ghostly fanny. Now, poof! Begone, you wretched spirit!"

I started chanting in my head, "What is dark, be filled with light! This is the sanctuary of the loving and kind, not the dead! This is the sanctuary of the loving and kind, not the dead! You are disrupting my vibe, now scram! Boohoo! Shoo! Shoo! You ole ugly ghost. I am not seeing you. I am not hearing you . . ."

My breathing stopped. Fear bit into my gut. I heard another sound. A *thump*. Sounded like something dropped.

Oh no! Oh no! There was a burglar on the loose. A rapist. A cookie monster.

I shot up in bed. "Who's there? Announce yourself this instant. If you've come to rob me, you've got the wrong one. I keep all of my money and valuables over at Rich Montgomery's. That's where you need to go to rob me. And if you're here to kill me, you've got the wrong one there too. Kitty's room is over on the other side of the estate. She's itching for a graveside service. Now get on up out of here. I'm warning you. You have sixty seconds to disappear. You hear me? I'm going to start counting now. Fifty-nine, fifty-eight, fifty-seven, fifty-six . . ."

I stopped counting and listened. It was dead silent. "Thank you, God!" I said, relieved. "Whoever it was is now gone." I slowly lifted my mask, and screamed. "Aaaaaaah!"

There was Daddy hovered over me with a flashlight shining in my face, practically blinding me.

"*Get that out of my face*," I bellowed, slapping his hands away then hopping up with the speed and grace of a gazelle. "What in the heck are you doing in here?"

"Are you okay, pumpkin?"

"Daddy, of course I am. Now why are you prowling around in my room at this time of the night?"

"I gotta find Cleola."

I rolled my eyes. "Daddy, I don't know what kind of conversations you have going on in your head, but there is no Cleola here. Now, please. Let it go."

"Sssh." He placed a finger to his lips. "Gotta go, pumpkin."

He turned on his heel and sailed out of the room.

"Daddy, get back here!"

He broke into a mad sprint down the hall. Time to seal up my doors. The Mad Hatter was on the loose. I called for security and had them chase him down and escort him back to his room, where I found his attendant stretched out in the chaise with drool spooling out of the corners of his mouth, snoring.

I couldn't believe the agency would send me such incompetent help. I went back into my room, rummaged through my trick bag and pulled out what I was looking for, then headed back to Daddy's room.

I swatted Mr. Sleepy Attendant in the mouth with my flyswatter. "Wake your lazy butt-hole up! Or I will have you fired!"

I stormed back to my room, slamming my door shut and locking it. Then for safe measures I jammed a chair up under the handles.

At eight a.m. I found Kitty sitting at the kitchen table sipping from a steaming mug of coffee.

"Gooooooood morning," I all but sang out, walking over to the center aisle and plucking a strawberry from the fruit platter.

Kitty huffed. "Must you be so vociferous? Turn down the volume, and use your inside voice."

I shot her a nasty look. "Don't do me, Mother. It's too early in the dang morning." I tossed my hair. "I'll use whatever voice I see fit. Now be thankful I don't start yelling and screaming at you for being the miserable witch you are."

I took a deep breath to calm myself. I wasn't about to let Kitty drag me into her tunnel of crazy. Not today. Not tomorrow. Not the day after that. No. Crazy could wait. And so would Kitty.

Kitty sniffed. Sniffed again. Then her eyes fluttered up from the pages of her magazine, landing on the piece of jewelry hanging from my neck.

I bit into a strawberry, catching its juice with a swipe of my tongue.

Kitty frowned. "Spencer, dear, what on earth are you doing with that humongous clove of garlic hanging around your neck?"

I huffed, irritation nipping at the back of my last good nerve that she'd ask me such a ridiculous question so early in the morning. Like really? Why else would someone wear garlic? Or eat it, for that matter.

I folded my hands in front of me. Tilted my head. Then stared at her, long and hard. I kept my lips zipped. Thought before I spoke.

*If you don't have anything loving and kind to say, then say nothing at all!* That was the mantra I chose to live by for the next forty-eight hours.

"You know what? I'm not even going to dignify that question with an ounce of my energy. Obviously it's to stave off ghosts and evil spirits."

She shook her head, going back to the pages of the latest edition of her magazine, *Dish the Dirt*.

"So, why are you here, Mother?" I pulled a chair out from the table, sitting across from her. "Didn't you get the notice I tacked on your door yesterday that I wanted you out of my house by sundown?"

"Little Miss Sunshine," she said, slamming her mug down on the table. A few drops of her kopi luwak sloshed over the mug rim. "I knew I should have had the neuropediatricians perform that lobotomy on you like I wanted them to when you were six months old in fear that something like this would come back to haunt me one day."

I blinked. "Excuse *you*, lady?"

She shook her head. "Sadly, there is *no* excuse for you. Dumbness is at an all-time high, thanks to you."

I sighed and rolled my eyes to the ceiling.

"You are becoming more of an embarrassment by the second, Spencer. And I won't stand for it. Do you hear me? I won't." She took another sip of her chocolate poop drink, coffee beans plucked from the turd of some Asian wildlife. "I kick myself every day for being such a fool, thinking you could handle womanhood. Dear God! The problem is, I've given you too much freedom. I've spoiled you rotten. And I've kept you sheltered from the real world. You don't know a thing about reality. But that's about to change."

I blinked. "Oh no! Oh no! You don't change me, sweetie. I change designers. I change my panties. I change cars. And now I'm about to change this conversation. And, if my fairy godmother ever acts right and gets her mind right, hopefully I'll be changing mothers too. Wait. Oops. Scratch that. Wrong person. You've never been a mother. All you've ever been is some loose-goose floozy, swinging upside down from chandeliers. Stalking schoolyards for your next boy toy and lying naked in the sand, spreading your legs open. Don't. Do. Me, *Kitty*."

She smirked. "Ooh, yes, darling. I love it when you give it to me raunchy. Now stop all this foolery and tell your mother all about this secret man muffin you've been sneaking off to San Diego to see."

I frowned, slamming my fork down onto my plate. "Oh no! Oh no! Don't you worry about who he is! He's off-limits to you! You even think about coming anywhere near my man and I will gut out your woman parts and grind them in the meat grinder then stuff them down your throat, Kitty! I mean it! Stay. Out. Of. My. Business. If I think you're day-dreaming about even sniffing my man's boxers, I'm going to slice your nose off your face."

Kitty set her mug back down on the table and clapped. "Wonderful performance, darling. I almost believed it. Now stop being so nasty."

I clenched my fists. "Oh, sweet googly moogly! Some-one peel the liner back. Like you're being Miss Congenial. The first-place prize for nastiness goes to *you*. So don't get it crunked. 'Cause I know you don't want me to sling the funk on you. Now, for once, try to show a little compassion. I didn't get a lick of sleep. Daddy snuck in my room talking craziness."

She rolled her eyes up in her head. "Okay, I'll bite. What has the good doctor done now? Smear his feces on the walls? Put his clothes on backwards? Hide all the silverware? What, Spencer? Tell me all about the wondrous world of the insane."

My lip trembled a bit. Kitty knew how much Daddy

meant to me, but as always she just had to throw darts at my forehead.

"I told you I didn't want that man here anyway. But you defied me. Went behind my back and moved him up in here anyway. No regard for me. So he's your headache. Not mine. Remember, I divorced him."

"Well, he's my father, like it or not. And this is where he'll stay. You do anything to disrupt that and it won't be a crystal vase I'll be hurling at you the next time. It'll be something that sticks into your back."

"Spencer, would you like me to have you committed? Keep up this kind of talk and you'll find yourself strapped to a gurney in a padded room." She glanced at her timepiece. "Now, I have five minutes. Tell me what he's done in a minute and a half."

"He keeps calling me some dang Cleola," I blurted out. "And he's constantly talking about some boys coming to get me—well, not me, this Cleola—from Mississippi. I think maybe I need to call my PI and have him track this hooker down so I can give her a good piece of my mind."

Kitty blinked. Then snickered, shaking her head. "Oh, dear heavens. Spencer, darling, you're about as silly as a rabbit in a hat listening to the ramblings of some old senile man. The man's mind is mush, darling. I swear, one of the nannies had to have dropped you on your head as an infant."

"Whatever!" I glared at Kitty with icy eyes. "I don't see anything funny about Daddy's horrid condition. Something's eating the inside of his brain and some trashy woman named Cleola has him hallucinating. And you want to sit there and make jokes about it."

She shrugged, lifting her mug to her puckered lips. "Like I said, I don't want him here."

"Well, I do." My voice bobbled. "And the least you can do is *act* like you care about my feelings for once!"

She gave me an expressionless stare. "Is this where you turn on the waterworks and fall out sobbing? Because, if so, let me know now so I can get PET out here to cart you up out of here."

*PET?* Oh, she wanted to get messy. She wanted to call the Psychiatric Emergency Team and try to have me put away. I gritted my teeth. I blinked once, twice. Stared at her, stunned. There was nothing crazy about me! Sometimes I hated this woman more days than not. And today was one of those days that I felt like slinging her over the railing and watching her drop over the cliff.

I sprang to my feet. "Don't you dare stand there and play me for some dizzy Lizzy lost in the woods, Mother! I'm *not* some brain-dead bimbo! Follow the winding dirt road, witch, or I'm going to yank you by the hairs of your chinny-chin-chin, then pluck out your gotdangit eye sockets! Don't try me! So we can either do this the messy way, or we can do it my way."

I removed my diamond studs, then my diamond bangles, placing them ever so lightly on the marble table.

"Spencer, what in the world do you think you're doing?" Kitty asked. Oh, little Miss Porgy managed to keep her voice calm. But her eyeballs were spinning around in her head like slot machines, trying to decide if she should make a mad dash out the door or get ready to tackle me.

"Oh, I'm getting ready to tear your face off."

"*Whaaat?*" Her voice shrieked like a dog whistle. "You

will do no such thing. I will have you arrested and hauled off to jail."

I snorted. "Here Kitty, Kitty...call the po-po, repo man if you want. And I will have you hauled off in a trash bag."

She gasped. "Spencer! What has gotten into you?"

"All my life you've dissed me, pissed on me, and never once kissed me." I pulled my hair up into a ponytail, then stretched my neck from left to right, cracking bones.

"Now before I wobble up and down on your face, I'm going to give you a chance to make nice, apologize for being such a miserable, worthless, pathetic mother, and promise to never, ever, talk bad about Daddy..."

She sucked her teeth. "Oh, for Christ's sake, Spencer! Are you *really* going to let your laced panties get all up in a bunch over a man who doesn't even know who you are half the time? You owe him nothing, darling. He—"

"Witch!" I pounded my fist onto the table. "That's *beside* the gotdangit point! *I* know who *he* is!" I felt myself shaking from the inside out. Felt a tidal wave of emotions rushing up against my chest. "And he *knows* who I am! Even when he doesn't always remember my name, he remembers everything else about me! He is the one person on this Earth who I *know* loves me."

Kitty laughed. "Spencer, you little pea brain. Get it together. The only thing that man can ever love now is someone changing his Depends and helping him find his dentures. The man needs to be put down. Sent up the river somewhere. Let your father live out the rest of his life in peace. You already have all of his fortune. You're worth billions. What more do you want?"

"I want my father! And I want you to *stop* being malicious and hateful."

She guffawed. "You silly girl. It most certainly is about money. It's *always* about money. And I will not have you speaking to me this way or acting in this fashion. I'm calling security if you don't settle down!"

*"No! You* settle down before you get knocked down! Daddy loves *me.* Vera loved *me.* Esmeralda and Solenne loved *me!* You're nothing but a hateful, bitter ole snot, Kitty. All my life, anything—or *anyone*—that has ever mattered to me, you've managed to always find some kind of way to snatch them away from me."

This *beeeeeeyotch* had killed my vibe one time too many. And I was sick of her flimflamfluckery! I narrowed my eyes, beaming red lasers of hot gas and steam at her. I was *rrrrready* to torch her tootie-toot-toot booty up. I wanted to scorch her three ways from Sunday, Monday, and Tuesday. But I didn't want to turn the flames all the way up to ten, just yet. Kitty had always said to never play your whole hand of messy all in one shot. So I took several deep breaths to soothe my raging guts. But the longer she stood there with her eyes all bugged out, looking like she'd sucked in lemons and a pint of hairspray, the more I wanted to set it off on her face.

I was done with being nice and sweet to Kitty. She'd done nothing but write me off like some bad debt more times than I could count. And I was sick of her snatching my life from me!

From passing me off from one nanny to another, only to rip them out of my life whenever she felt I'd gotten too close to them, to shipping me off to a boarding school for three years, wanting nothing to do with me. From sleeping with two of my boyfriends once they turned eighteen, to ... to *this*—disrespecting Daddy's memory.

Adrenaline rocketed through my body as I reached over and slung the rest of her coffee on her. I jumped at Kitty, catching her by surprise.

"Aaah! What the —!" she shouted. "Spencer, have you lost your goddamn mind?!"

"No, but I'm about to help you lose yours!"

We tussled until we both toppled over and hit the floor, rolling around.

"Stop this nonsense, Spencer! I have to be at the airport in an hour! I don't have time for this horseplay with you!"

*Whap!*

I screamed. Kitty's hand went hard and swift across my face. I lunged at her and seized her wrists. "You will not put your hands on me! I'm sick of you, Kitty! I want you out of my house!"

The kitchen staff tried to pull us apart, but Kitty and I had our horns locked and were in a full-fledged rodeo beef brawl.

"Spencer, stop this!"

She screamed as I jabbed the heel of my six-inch pump into her shin. "Aaaah! I'm going to have you put away along with your nutty father! You'll both be institutionalized!"

"Oh no! And you'll be eulogized before that ever happens! I've been nothing but loving and kind to you, Kitty! And all you do is mistreat me! And hurt me! And belittle me! You have torn your panties with me, Kitty! Now I'm going to give you a burn from the fires of hell!"

Oh, we wrestled and tussled and clawed at each other just like the good ole days when I was eight and nine years old.

Out of nowhere, gunshots rang out, stopping Kitty and me from our rock-'em-sock-'em party. We both screamed.

My heart dropped to my feet as plaster from the ceiling rained down on Kitty's head and mine.

"*Daddy!*" I shrieked.

"*Ellington!*" Kitty screeched, calling him by his last name. Something she'd always done when she was pretending to be happy and in love.

Daddy was standing there in the middle of the kitchen in a pair of skintight overalls and lizard-skin cowboy boots with a cigar dangling from the corner of his mouth, pointing a shotgun at us.

"Both of you gals stay where you are," he growled in warning. "Now, c'mon, Cleola, I gotta get you out of here before them Mississippi boys come and get you..."

"Daddy, I'm not Cleola! I'm Spencer, your daughter! Now put that gun down right this instant!"

"I know who you are, pumpkin," he shot back, lowering the rifle. "My mind hasn't gone completely bye-bye, yet." He shot a look over at Kitty. "I'm talking about that fine, sexy gal right over there beside you."

I laughed. "Daddy, you're so silly. Hahaha. That's soo cute. That's *not* Cleola. That's Kitty. My mother. Your ex-wife."

He shook his head. "No, no. That gal right there"—he tossed a knowing glare over at Kitty— "is Cleola Mae from Leflore County, Mississippi. Wanted for murder. Ain't that right, *Cleola*?"

# 21

# Rich

Itapped my heels and popped my newly Juvadermed lips, clearly annoyed. Here I'd been in heaven, laid up with my baby boo, Justice, for two days when I appeared on World Star and the Vine in slow motion, being tossed out on London's lawn.

"I can't believe that dirty, half-dead corpse London leaked that video of me," I'd said to Spencer as we sat on my balcony having brunch and sipping mimosas. "That trolloping tramp attacked me! Tried to take it to my face all because she's hatin' on my get-right. Mad because I got the man and the ring. And to think I was anti-hate, -tea, and -shade. Kind enough to go over there to grace her coffin with my love and light, and she attacks me! Hatin' on me. Sending that security footage of me getting dragged out of her suite, manhandled down the stairs, then tossed out on the lawn like last week's trash."

"Well, you are trash," Spencer had interrupted while flicking her white linen napkin onto her lap. Then she took a sip of her smoothie, tilted her head, and locked eyes with me. "And for the record, London didn't leak that video of you. I did."

Of all the dirty things to do! She didn't even have the decency to let me think London did it. No! She tells me she did it! Who does that? And to think I'd been nothing but a good friend to that trick. And what did she do for me in return? Stab me in the front, back, and the sides. Stooping gutter-rat low and spreading lies about my man! Saying Justice drove London crazy. Ummm...helloooooooo... knock, knock! Anybody home? London was born crazy! My man had minus-zero to do with that. She better check her gene pool, and see if her mama was rockin' Baby Phat.

*Annnd thennn* she leaked the video footage of London attacking me to World Star and the Vine! World Star? Really? And the Vine? How insulting! Scandalous! Low-grade!

Spencer is a low-down, dirty snake! Which is why I had no problem sitting here looking into this raggedy and over-tanned face, like a leather handbag, TMZ thot.

I was at Club Lip Gloss having a secret squirrel meeting. The TMZ reporter was waiting for me to spill all of the Pampered Princesses' secrets...Mm-hm. The nitty-gritty of the pampered and the pretty. And, since I invited him here, I needed to drop the goods and I needed to do it quick.

Heck, they weren't my friends. Spencer was a slorish Benedict Arnold who had the nerve to call me last night, crying and babbling in true Spencer fashion about some dumb Cleola Mae and somebody being murdered. And her senile father pulling out a shotgun and shooting up the house.

But, umm, do you think I cared? She needed to apologize to me before she could come crying on my shoulder. No apologies, then she got no sympathy. I didn't give a rat's piss about her rickety old daddy or him trying to shoot up the whole house. And I dang sure didn't care about his bald-headed mistress Cleola Mae, who was wanted for murder. I deserved an apology for being played like some broke trick. World Star? Really? And the Vine? Rich Montgomery would never do it for the Vine! Never!

And as far as Heather was concerned, it would be a hot, steamy day in the desert before I ever had any loyalty to her. Especially after that skid-row trash tried to drag me in the cafeteria and threatened to beat my face in. Yeah, right? And here she'd run through three million dollars on Korean handbags and powdered nose-candy.

And that two-faced London...mmph. By the time I was done with that unstable slore, she was gonna wish they'd kept her locked in a padded room.

"Excuse me, Rich, are you ready to begin?"

I batted my lashes, bringing my attention back to the reporter as I nicely crossed my legs and said, "Revenge is much sweeter with a pitcher of beer and a platter of hot wings. 'Cause the pretty white gloves are off and it is no longer about lights, love, and lip gloss. So Spencer, London, and Heather had better buckle up. Now, it's time to serve them all heels, heartache, and headlines..."

# LIGHTS, LOVE & LIP GLOSS

## Ni-Ni Simone
## Amir Abrams

## ABOUT THIS GUIDE

The following questions are intended to
enhance your group's reading of
LIGHTS, LOVE & LIP GLOSS.

# Discussion Questions

1. What were your thoughts/feelings about London's suicide attempt? Do you know anyone who has attempted suicide? If so, how did their actions make you feel? Do you believe London's self-esteem and the way she sees and feels about herself will ever change?

2. Heather seems to be getting back on top. How far do you think she will go before she hits rock bottom again? Do you think she will ever learn to take responsibility for her actions? What do you think she should do now that she knows that Richard Montgomery is her father, but wants nothing to do with her?

3. Rich believes she's madly in love with Justice Banks. Problem is, she doesn't know the truth about him. What do you think Rich will do when she discovers who he really is? Do you believe she is strong enough to walk away? Or will she make excuses to stay?

4. Once again, Rich is expecting, but she doesn't know who the father of her future baby is. What do you think she will do? Will she put it on Knox? Or Justice? Or will she do the right thing, and tell both of them the truth? Is she even capable of telling the truth?

5. Spencer continues to meddle in everyone's business. The one thing that seems constant is her loyalty to Rich even when she turns on her. Why do you

think she is always jumping to save Rich? Do you think Spencer is a true friend to Rich? Or simply being her scheming, conniving self?

6. Now that Spencer's father is home, how do you think her life will change? Will she ever get over not being Daddy's little girl again? How do you think his Alzheimer's will affect her life? Or her relationship with her mother?

Explosive rumors and a mega-media frenzy almost ended the Pampered Princesses' reign as Hollywood High royalty. Now only one diva can win the ultimate fame of thrones...

Put Your Diamonds Up
Volume 3 of the Hollywood High Series

Turn the page for an excerpt from
*Put Your Diamonds Up* ...

# 1

# London

"*Your body, beauty, and youth are your tickets to fame and fortune...*"

"Look into the camera, London," Luke Luppalozzi, a renowned photographer, cajoled as his camera clicked to life. I blinked my mother's voice out of my head. "Less stiff, more sass, London! Thrust your left hip...Give me seductress, darling!"

*You nasty perv! Sounds to me like you want slutty!*

I was at a photo shoot for a new fragrance—Pink Heat—for some new Italian designer, standing on a seamless swoop of heavy white paper that stretched along the floor for what seemed like miles, from a roll anchored to a beam. I was wearing a pair of six-inch pink spike heels and a slinky pink dress. My sculpted, milk-chocolate shoulders were exposed, shimmering from the glow of the lights. My long, shapely legs were bare. Around my slender, elongated neck hung a five-carat pink diamond necklace, a gift from my mother. Hair and makeup people had been at the ready from the moment I'd stepped through the doors four hours ago.

My shoulder-length hair was curled into cascading ringlets. Long, thick lashes wrapped around my large brown eyes. My sumptuous lips glowed and pulsed, coated in hot pink lipstick and glossed to perfection.

On the outside, I was *fiiiierce*.

On the inside, I felt everything but. I felt like someone had rolled me in a whole bottle of Pepto-Bismol. And I'd become the big pink Amazon. Ugh.

God, I wanted to love my life. Wanted to love the excitement. Wanted to love that I was in Milan . . . Italy, that is; among some of the world's elite fashion editors, being captured on film by renowned photographers for campaign and print ads—doing something most girls my age only dreamed of.

I wanted to love the fact that I was finally becoming the daughter that my well-coiffed, well-heeled, well-bred mother had always desired me to be. Flawless. Hair pinned, face painted, poised, and ready to take the fashion world by storm.

But right at the moment, I was too exhausted to care about any of that. My feet ached from wearing heels all day, standing in uncomfortable positions, being twisted and prodded to hold poses for the camera while gigantic industrial fans blew my hair this way and that.

Yes. I was a trendsetter.

Yes. I was a fashionista extraordinaire.

Yes. I was a lover of heels, handbags, and high fashion.

But on my terms. Not someone else's.

And, right now, at this very minute, this precise second,

my mother defined everything about who I was. I wanted this for her. I wanted this for me, because *she* wanted this for me...for herself. This was her life, her world. And she insisted...no, demanded, expected, that I be a part of it. That I embrace my orchestrated destiny with grace and fervor and be forever swept into the glitz and glamour of it all.

But who I was was all back in California—six thousand forty-five-point-four miles; twelve hours and thirty-three minutes away. In La-La Land. At Hollywood High Academy, my elite private school, where I hadn't been for the last week or so in order to appease my mother's need to have me on the runway. God strike me for parting my lips and admitting this part, but...I'd rather be back at school *with* the Pampered Princesses—the "It Girls" of Hollywood High than be here with a bunch of snotty models.

*Jeezus, the world must really be coming to an end for me to openly admit to missing the likes of Heather and Spencer! It must be the flashing lights! Yeah, that has to be it.*

Yeah, we didn't always get along. And yeah, we fought. And yeah, most times I disliked Heather Cummings, the teen-star junkie; even looked down on her. She was the queen of trashy. Leopard prints and pounds of slut paint on her face. But, minus the fortune, she had fame. Everyone knew who Wu-Wu Tanner was. The fun-loving, animal-print wearing suburban teenager Heather had once played on the number one hit television show in America. But thanks to her druggie behavior and showing up strung out on the set, her show was canceled. And it's been downhill for Heather ever since. Still, like it or not, she had star power. What was left of it, that is. But I digress.

Anhoo yeah, I despised that dizzy-dumb, scatterbrain chick Spencer, the spoiled bratty daughter of the messy media mogul, Kitty Ellington. But she had heart. She had guts. And she was crazier than bat shit. And thanks to me, she'd gotten her face smacked off right in the middle of finance class when I convinced Rich that it was Spencer who'd stabbed her in the back and told her boo Knox that she'd had an abortion when she'd already lied and told him that she'd miscarried. It didn't take much coercion. Rich wasn't the sharpest knife in the cutlery drawer either. And she was as slutty as Spencer. No, no . . . she was sluttier. Still, she was my bestie. And sharing her with that floor-mop Spencer was *not* an option.

And what my mother failed to understand was, I *needed* to get back to my life at Hollywood High to ensure Rich and Spencer stayed enemies. Before Rich, who had the attention span of a bobblehead, went back to cavorting with my nemesis.

And speaking of Rich, why the hell hadn't I heard from her in two days? I called her four times. Sent her six text messages. And nothing! That was soooooo not good! It was an omen. I knew she'd wait until I got thousands of miles across the Atlantic Ocean to show her true two-faced ways. And her lack of regard for *me* and our friendship said one of three things: She was either somewhere chained to some boy's bed with her legs up in her famous V-split, or hiding out at some seedy ranch for sexaholics, or she was back in the manicured clutches of Spencer.

God, I couldn't stand that trampola. Everyone knew her mouth was a used condom, thanks to the viral video of her sucking down watermelon shots in the girls' lounge at school with one of Rich's many boyfriends. But being here, away from my life in Hollywood, was more torturous than being friends with Spencer and Heather. So I'd take being around those two over the likes of the majority of the models I was surrounded by. And that really spoke volumes, considering my contempt for the two of them.

I was besieged by the likes of the living dead, pony-stepping the runways. A gaggle of models who recklessly eyeballed me and mumbled snide remarks under their collagen-plumped lips every chance they got about me receiving preferential treatment because I was the daughter of Jade Obi, one of the world's beloved international supermodels. Whatever!

They had no clue as to what life was like living with their role model, their adored idol. My mother.

Sure, being the daughter of a famous supermodel came with the advantages of a lavish lifestyle. I lived a privileged life. And being young, beautiful, and rich always made me a target. For the paparazzi. For the haters. And for my mother's ridicule.

She was imperious. She was controlling. She was rigid. She was—when I wasn't who she expected me to be—my worst nightmare. *"You're definitely not ugly. And you're far from old-looking, yet. Thank God you have my genes. But, fat... mmmph. You're well on your way...*

*Diet is everything in this industry, London..."*

And dieting I have done. For the last two-and-a-half years, she'd been monitoring my weight, measuring my inches, weighing my food portions, counting my caloric intake, keeping it all in a leather-bound journal, browbeating me to no end until I'd finally lost the fifteen extra pounds she required of me to be runway ready. Now weighing in at one-hundred-and-ten pounds, I had arrived. I'd made it back in front of the flashbulbs popping all around me. It didn't matter to her how I lost the weight as long as it was gone. Buried. To never return for as long as we both shall live. Amen. Amen. Amen.

*"The sooner you can get this god-awful weight off and we can get you back on the runway and onto the covers of all the fashion magazines where you belong... You were born to be in front of the camera..."*

Still, some of the models I'd seen since being here looked like crack whores in couture. Many of them stood over six feet tall. They were needle thin with sunken cheeks and protruding collarbones, speed racing off of caffeine and nicotine. Most of them, ice queens, shot daggers of icicles at me as I was led through the sea of miserable haters to my next photo shoot. From what I've overheard while waiting for casting calls among models vying for the same shoot, campaign, etc., many of them were snorting lines of coke and popping uppers to stay wafer-thin and to keep up with the grueling hours that went along with being a high-fashion print-ad model.

"Oh, my darling London. I am so proud of you!" My mother had bubbled over with joy in the backseat of the stretch Benz during the ride over here at six o'clock this morning. "You are going to be the next hottest thing. *Sei bella, mia cara Londra!*" She beamed as she stroked the side of my face, telling me how beautiful I was. "You are absolutely perfect."

I almost wanted to laugh at the absurdity of that word. *Perfect.* The *perfect* oxymoron, if I'd ever heard one. There was nothing *perfect* about me. Nothing perfect about this world I'd been thrust into.

No. There was definitely nothing perfect about this life.

If it were, I'd be pencil thin instead of curvy like a dangerously winding hillside. I'd have ant-size breasts instead of the melon-sized jugs that fit perfectly in a 34 C-cup. I'd have the derrière of a wood plank instead of a bouncy booty that snapped necks and had a mind of its own, commanding attention without much effort.

*"For the love of God, London, why did you have to ruin your body...You just had to go and screw up everything I've worked for...No one wants a fat, ugly, old-looking girl on their runway..."*

While most models craved bee-stung lips, mine were already naturally plump, ripe, and kissable. Although they hadn't been kissed in two weeks. Still, my beauty was a blessing and a curse. A double-edged sword.

I'd been longing for the day my mother would look at me with the same pride beaming in her eyes as she did when I was a preteen on the runway. Before the sudden weight gain. Before the *setback*, as my mother called it. Before the swell of my breasts and the roundness of my hips morphed my body into that of an Amazon. A statuesque brick house.

I was thirteen when I first graced the cover of *Vogue Italia*. Seven months later, I was swelling like an angry river, bursting out of my size zero, quickly ballooning to a size four, then six, then eight.

*"You're nothing now. You'll never be anything...At the rate you're going, you'll never make it on the runway. You'll only be good enough to shake and bounce for rap videos..."*

Those were more of her cutting words to me, on many occasions. That is how she viewed me. That is how she felt about me. And although I knew she loved me, I also knew that love, her love, came with unrelenting conditions. And most times with unbearable consequences.

No, there was no room for imperfection when you had a mother like Jade Obi Phillips, who expected nothing less than perfection. The perfect P's, according to my mother, were: Poise. Posture. Position. Then tack on the perfect image, the perfect body, the perfect skin, the perfect set of teeth, the perfect partner, and the perfect station in life. Follow this mantra, and you were guaranteed the perfect life, according to the world of Jade.

Yes, my mother loved me. But she'd always love the *perfect* me more...

"London, darling...smile..." My mother's voice drifted over toward me as the photographer tried to have me flash a toothy grin with my head slightly tilted to the right while one foot was lifted off the floor in back of me. Her tone was light and airy but laced with a tinge of attitude as she stood behind the photographer, like a backseat driver, trying to coax me, coach me, and get on my last damn nerve.

I forced a tight smile. I felt a headache pounding its way into the center of my forehead. But I had to get through this. Had to get this finished, the sooner the better. "Blow a kiss into the camera...Hold the bottle up closer to your cheek...Give me attitude...Now lick your lips and give me Pink Heat, doll..."

I cringed. *Doll?* How cheesy!

The photographer, speaking in his thick Italian-accented English, was dangerously handsome for a man in his thirties. Tanned and built like an Adonis. But he was a horny toad who winked and licked his lips on the sly every chance he got! I simply rolled my eyes. Or pretended not to notice. *Look but don't touch!*

I tried to stay focused, tried to steel myself for the dazzling whiteness of the camera's flash. But I couldn't. My mind kept swinging back and forth between Justice—the one true love of my life, whom my parents despised...to Rich—my supposed bestie, who I hadn't heard from since I'd gotten here and who had not kept one Skype date with me for whatever reason...to Anderson—my parent-approved boyfriend who was refusing to take my calls because I couldn't and wouldn't choose between him and Justice. And to think I had kissed him. That I had lifted up on my tiptoes and pulled his face down to mine in the middle of a dance floor at his fraternity's campus party and was kissing him, my tongue slipping into his wet mouth. And he was kissing me back. And everything was heating. Everything was melting. And I was caught up in the flames. God, I hated him!

I hated him for everything he was. Smart. Articulate. Handsome. Thoughtful. I hated him for being a good kisser. Hated the way his strong arms felt around me. Hated him for taking my mind off of Justice, my off-again on-again boyfriend. The only boy I'd ever loved. The only boy I'd ever given myself to. The only boy who'd ever had my heart. And I hated Anderson for making me feel messy and sexy at the same time; for making my mind replay his hands wandering all over my body when I should only be thinking of Justice.

I had cheated on my man. So, yes, I hated my faux boyfriend, Anderson, for managing, with one kiss—okay, okay, *three* kisses—to ruin my life. I was a cheater.

*And speaking of Justice, why haven't I heard from him? I have gotten not one call or text from him in almost four days.* Four days! Four fricking *loooooong* excruciating days of not hearing his voice or seeing his handsomely rugged face on FaceTime or Skype was *killlllling* me!

And I had my mother to thank for my misery.

In less than two weeks, she had managed to turn my whole world upside down, inside out, and every which way in between. She'd literally stripped me of my life. And she had no damn care in the world.

"*Londra, fare l'amore per la fotocamera*," Luke shouts in Italian, suggesting I make love to the camera. *Ohmygod! How vulgar!*

I sighed.

My mother shot me a scathing look that read *Do. Not. Try. Me. You had* better *pretend this is where you want to be.*

Before I could put on my mask and get with the program, my mother asked the photographer and his crew if she could have a moment alone with me. To motivate me, she claimed.

"What in the world is wrong with you, London?" she snapped when she thought everyone was out of earshot.

"I want to go home."

She blinked. "For the next two weeks, *this* is your home. Get used to it."

I pouted. "I miss my friends."

She scoffed. "Trust me. Those spoiled little girls back at Hollywood High aren't losing any sleep over *you*. Their worlds are going on without *you*. As a matter of fact, I bet you haven't heard from any of your so-called *friends* since you've been here. Have you?"

I folded my arms and turned away from her. I was done. However, my silence only encouraged her to continue her babbling.

"London," she hissed, grabbing me by the arm and turning me to her, "what would you rather do, huh? Hang with some loudmouth attention whore, is that it? Rich will have to buy her way out of school because she's been raised to be a mattress for the richest fool who'll have her. The only thing she'll ever be good for is performing Cirque du Soleil acrobatics in some boy's bed, having babies, and carrying razors under her slithering tongue—"

I snapped my neck in my mother's direction. "Mother, do I talk about any of your friends, huh? Oh, wait. You don't have any." I narrowed my eyes. "I don't care what Rich does with her life. That's not my concern. She's my friend."

My mother laughed in my face. "In this industry there is no room for friends, my darling daughter. Friends stab you in the back. This is a cutthroat business. You have enemies and allies. Nothing more. Do you think I made it as far as I have, being concerned about having friends? No. I made it to the top of my game by knowing the difference between friendships and alliances. Trust me. Rich doesn't know the first thing about being a friend. That girl is nobody's friend. And she's definitely not yours, darling. So the sooner you get that through that luscious head of yours, the better."

I sucked my teeth. "I don't care. I want to go home."

"And do *what*, huh? Become some double-chin piglet with ankles the size of ham hocks, wobbling off to some godforsaken factory job? You want to be some big biscuit-eating, dimpled-butt oaf with saggy air-bag breasts, like your father's side of the family? Would you rather scrub toilets for a living, is that it, London? I am trying to help you build a legacy. Not help you piss your life away on some two-dollar pipe dream of doing God knows what else other than what you were destined to do."

For a moment I had...Absolutely. No. Words. Was she effen *serious*?

She continued, "*This* is your life, London. So you had better get used to it. Now, if *you* don't want this life, then speak now so I can make arrangements to have you shipped off to England to boarding school. Because, make no mistake, my darling daughter. You will *not* be returning to Hollywood High. Now pick a door. And choose it very wisely. Because the choice you make today will be the one you will have to live with. Now, be the darling I know you can be. Make your mother proud. Give me what I want, London, or I make the next two years of your life a living hell."

I blinked. *Dear God, what have I done to deserve this? Have I sinned that bad?*

I wanted to scream. I wanted to stomp. Wanted to pound my fists. Wanted to kick. Have a full-fledged tantrum. Wanted to defy every last one of my mother's beauty rules and have a pig fest, eating up everything in sight. What I wouldn't have done to kick off my heels and flee and never look back. What I wouldn't do to be able to hide out in my suite and sit cross-legged on my king-size Baldacchino Supreme bed amid cake crumbs and smeared bowls of Chunky Monkey ice cream.

I'd do anything to be at the Saddle Ranch on Sunset Boulevard, sinking my teeth into a big, juicy T-bone steak. Better yet, what I wouldn't do to be back at Muddy Moments, a run-down hole-in-the-wall in San Diego, with

Rich and her future ex-boo, Knox, and Anderson, sucking down on a platter of their infamous honey-coated hot wings and a slab of ribs. And I didn't even eat anything off of a pig.

Yes, yes, yes! I'd kill to scarf down a family-size bag of Cool Ranch Doritos and a bag of Oreos...then I'd beg the evil fat gods to spare me from gaining an ounce. I'd boldly do all of those things then I'd post pictures of my lips slathered with chicken grease and rib sauce and dusted with doughnut powder all up on Instagram.

My mother wanted perfect. I'd show her a perfect mess! And for the grand finale, I'd give her my perfect escape.

"Well," my mother huffed impatiently. "I'm waiting. Now, what's it going to be, London, the runway or boarding school? The clock is ticking."

I swallowed, then begrudgingly replied, "The runway."

She fussed with the big curl at the end of my bang that swooped along my jawline. "I knew you'd see it my way. Now go take a moment to get your thoughts together. And when you come back out here, you had better be in the mindset to serve it to the camera. Do I make myself clear?"

I clenched my teeth. "Perfectly." I briskly walked off as she stood there saying something slick and crazy in Italian about me being a selfish, ungrateful brat. Whatever.

One of the many assistants swarming around the photo shoot rudely thrust a large white envelope at me as I made my way toward the makeshift lounge area. She said it was sent via courier. Curious, I stared for several seconds at the envelope with its typed address label, wondering who'd sent me mail. I turned it over, pulling the tab and opening it. Inside was a manila envelope with a set of large eyes elaborately drawn in black ink on the front of it. On the back in red ink the words FOR YOUR WEEPING EYES ONLY was written across the seal.

*WTH?* I reached over for a fingernail file someone left on the table and slit open the envelope, pulling out the items inside: photos.

I blinked. *OMG! What the fu...?*

I glanced at the anonymously photographed images of the nude chick in the on-all-fours pornographic poses. There was a tattoo of a colorful butterfly just above her booty crack. I blinked, blinked again. *Ohno ohno ohno...* I felt my stomach lurching as I stared at the guy's hand on the chick's naked booty cheek. Right on the webbed part between his thumb and forefinger was a tattoo of a small black dagger with red drops of blood dripping from its tip.

I screamed, crumpling the pictures tight in my fist.

It was Justice's hand!

Fiona Madison is everywhere everyone wants to be—and she knows just how to keep frenemies, haters, and admirers guessing. She keeps it cute and knows how to turn a party out no matter how tough things get at home—or how lonely she really is. The only relationship a guy can have with her is BWB (Boo-With-Benefits). Anything more is a major not-going-to-happen....Until someone Fiona never sees coming is suddenly too close, understands her all too well—and is turning this diva's life upside down...

Diva Rules
by Amir Abrams
Coming in May 2015

Turn the page for an excerpt from *Diva Rules*...

# 1

*Diva check...*
Hey, hey now! It's Diva Roll call...Are you present?
*Rude, check...*
*Bitchy, check...*
*Spoiled, check...*
*Selfish, check...*
*Overdramatic, check, check...*

Scrrrrreeeech! Hold up. That is *not* what *this* diva is about. No, *hunni!* Being a diva is all about attitude, boo. It's about bein' fierce. Fabulous. And always fly. It's about servin' it up 'n' keepin' the haters on their toes. And the rules are simple.

So, let's try this again.

Fiona's my name. Turning boys out is my game. Fashion's my life. Being fabulous is my mission. And staying fly is a must. Oh, and, trust. I serve it up lovely. Period, point blank. At five-seven, a buck-twenty-five with my creamy, smooth complexion, blonde rings of shoulder-length curls, and mesmerizing green eyes I'm that chick all the cutie-boos stay tryna see about. I'm that chick with the small waist and big, bouncy booty that all the boys love to see me shake, bounce 'n' clap. I'm that hot chick that the tricks 'n' hoes at my school—McPherson High—love to hate; yet hate that they can't ever be me.

Like I always tell 'em: "Don't be mad, boo. I know I give you life. Thank me for giving you something to live for."

Conceited?

No, hun. Never that.

Confident?

Yes, sweetie. Always that.

No, boo. I don't *think* I'm the hottest thing since Beyoncé's "Drunk In Love" video. I'm convinced I am. Big difference. *Snap, snap!* Don't get it twisted.

Now who's ready for roll call?

Always fly, check...

Always fabulous, check...

Always workin' the room, check...

Always snappin' necks, check, check...

Always poppin' the hips 'n' turnin' it up, check, check...

Wait. Wait. Wait. Let's rewind this segment *alllll* the way back for a sec. Yes, I keeps it cute, all day, every day, okay? And, yes, I know how to turn it up when I need to. I'm from the hood, boo. Born 'n' bred. But that doesn't mean I have to be hood. No, honey-boo. I'm too classy for that. Trust. But know this. If I have to let the hood out on you 'n' introduce you to the other side of me, it ain't gonna be cute. So don't bring it 'n' I won't have to sling it.

If you wanna check my credentials, just ask the last chick I had to beat *down*. She'll gladly show you the stamp I left in her forehead, *okay?*

Soooo. Moving on. As I was saying, I'm from the hood. Lived on the same block, in the same house, all my life. I know these streets like I know the back of my hands 'n' the curve of my hips. They can be mean 'n' dangerous 'n' ohhh, so exciting. And, yeah, the streets might be praising me, but they ain't raising me. So I'm not about to serve you some effed up tale about a chick being lost in the streets, eaten 'n' beaten alive. No, no. I'm a hood goddess, boo. That chick the wanna-bees bow down to 'n' the lil thug daddies worship. But, trust. This ain't no hood love story. So be clear.

No, hun. I wasn't born with a silver spoon hanging from my pouty mouth, but that doesn't mean I can't dream, either. That doesn't mean I can't want more than what I already have. And, yeah, a chick dreams about getting outta the hood. Traveling the world. Bagging a fine cutie-boo, or two, or three, who I can call my own. And being filthy rich. One day I will be. Trust. But for now, that doesn't mean I can't wear the illusion like a second skin. And, trust. I wear it well, boo.

So if you're hoping for some sob story about some broke-down, busted, lil fast-azz, boy-crazy ho tryna claw her way outta the hood, trickin' the block huggers up off'a their paper for a come up, sorry, boo-boo. Not gonna happen. If you're looking to hear about a chick going hungry or sleeping on some pissy-stained mattress, or having her hot pocket stuffed in some dirty panties going to school smelling like a sewer, then go find you another seat, boo, because you're sitting in the wrong arena. That stage-play is being run somewhere else. If you're looking to hear about some fresh-mouthed chick who got beat with fists 'n' locked in closets, that's not gonna be featured here, either. Sorry, hun. I can't tell you a thing about that. Well, I could. But that's not my story. So I'll save that for some other hood chick.

So who am I?

I'm that hot chick, boo.

I'm a diva.

I'm a boss *bish* . . . and *whaaaat?!*

# STEWARDS
## SHAPED BY
# GRACE

# To Lois

*whose giving of her own free will*
*to family, church, and community*
*indelibly marks her as*
*a steward shaped by grace.*

# STEWARDS
# SHAPED BY
# GRACE

## The Church's Gift to a Troubled World

by
**Rhodes Thompson**

**Chalice Press**
St. Louis, Missouri

Unless otherwise indicated, all scripture quotations are from the Revised Standard Version Bible, copyrighted 1946, 1952, © 1971, 1973 by the Division of Christian Education of the National Council of Churches of Christ in the United States of America.

From the *Good News* Bible—Old Testament: Copyright © American Bible Society 1976. New Testament: Copyright © American Bible Society 1966, 1971, 1976. Used by permission.

From *The New English Bible*, ©1976. The Delegates of the Oxford University Press, Inc., and The Syndics of the Cambridge University Press, 1961, 1970. Reprinted by permission.

Portions of chapter fourteen which appeared in *The Disciple*, October, 1985, © Christian Board of Publication, are reprinted by permission.

Cover design: John Robinson

Fourth Printing, 1998.

**Library of Congress Cataloging-in-Publication Data**

Thompson, Rhodes.
  Stewards shaped by grace : the church's gift to a troubled world.
  Includes bibliographical references.
  1. Stewardship, Christian. 2. Bible. N.T. Epistles of Paul—Criticism, Interpretation, etc. I. Title.
  BV772.T45                1990 248'6                90-350-44
  ISBN 0-8272-3431-7

*Printed in the United States of America*

# Table of Contents

# Introduction

# A Hostage Word

Words, like persons, are sometimes held hostage until they are robbed of their original identity. One such unhappy hostage is the word "stewardship." This book invites you to join an expedition to set this languishing captive free and to restore it to its original health and authority.[1]

Surprisingly, the church is responsible for leading the word stewardship astray. Brainwashed from pulpit and pew, stewardship has traded its vocation of serving the world for a preoccupation with saving the church. Not until it is rescued from this "edifice complex"[2] that leads the church toward death can stewardship share in God's "healing of the nations" (Rev. 22:2).

That rescue mission must begin by wresting stewardship from the clutches of guilt and gimmickry whose tactics of shaming and manipulating have made it a bad news word. When liberated, stewardship can again proclaim good news about who God is and what God has done, is doing, and will be doing in our world. By responding to God in gratitude and faith, people enter into a covenant relationship that blesses all creation.

I have a sense of mission in helping that happen. Growing up in a parsonage home in Canada and Kentucky, under parents who loved us, the church, and the world, my heart was soon widened to embrace the globe. By 1945, at a youth conference between World War II's V-E (Victory in Europe) Day and V-J (Victory in Japan) Day, those influences called forth my commitment to ministry.

Student conferences and mission service in Europe and Japan, plus work camps and seminars in Mexico, Jamaica, India and Nicaragua, have since given me five and a half years of exposure to the needs and opportunities of the world beyond national boundaries. That has energized my efforts to relate local church mission to this larger global context during two and a half decades of pastoral ministry.

The invitation to teach at Phillips Graduate Seminary in Enid, Oklahoma, included the faculty's expectation that the global and pastoral values gleaned from those years be added to the mix of ministerial education. Nine years of teaching and preaching stewardship in seminary and in church settings have facilitated that integration of the academic and the practical, the objective and the subjective, the head and the heart. Giving three addresses at the Mid-Winter Event of the Commission on Stewardship of the National Council of Churches also helped build that bridge between theory and practice.

The style of this book, drawing on *both* practical *and* academic experience, risks not being academic enough for some nor practical enough for others. Sharing personal experiences where theology has come alive for me risks going beyond what some may consider appropriate self-disclosure. But such risks must be taken if a bridge of "imaginative thinking" about stewardship is to be built between our "left brains" (using what is academic, objective, and "from the head") and our "right brains" (using what is practical, subjective, and "from the heart"). Reflecting my joyful pilgrimage, this book sets forth the broad outlines of an evolving stewardship shaped by grace.

Another matter of style is the desire to be "faithful and fair"[3] in speaking of God and humanity so as to challenge all readers with the good news of stewardship. Please understand that some quotations reflect a time when this issue had not arisen. Generally, scripture is from the Revised Standard Version of the Bible; otherwise, notations appear after selections from the New English Bible (NEB), Today's English Version (TEV) and the New Testament in Modern English by J.B. Phillips (JBP).

Although I come from the ranks of white, middle-class, North American Protestants, this book aims to celebrate the "single new humanity" (Eph. 2:14-15, NEB) of nationalities, colors, classes, denominations, and faiths into which Christ has drawn me. Like Paul, "I am under obligation" (Rom. 1:14) to God's global family that has prompted the writing of this book. Hopefully, it will call local congregations and their leaders, both lay and clergy, to participate more fully in the quest for global solidarity.

The shape of this book reflects a conversation with a student at Christian Medical College, Vellore, India, where my wife Lois and I served as volunteers for nine weeks in 1982. "What do you study during medical school?" I had asked. He responded, "During our first year we learn about the body as it's been created to function when it's healthy." Then he exclaimed, "Wow! How beautiful the body is when it works that way!"

He continued, "The next year we learn about pathology, sickness, affliction—anything that keeps the body from functioning normally. Finally, during the rest of medical school, we learn how to facilitate healing and restore health."

This approach to medical education offers a good way to teach stewardship. Our world is healthy when God's intentions are unfolding. In wonder we ponder God's "grace" at work, but faithless people, spurning God's ways in favor of their own, bring sickness upon themselves, others, and nature as well. In personal and social pathology we detect the ravages of "sin." Yet God loves us freely and wills to heal our faithlessness. Together with those who respond in faith to such grace, God enters into a "covenant" to bless all creation.

Health, sickness, healing. Grace, sin, covenant. On these themes hinge the organization of this book.

Part I, "Amazing Grace! How Sweet the Sound," shows how Pauline theology grounds stewardship in God, whose grace-full nature and activity are revealed "in Christ." We will also see how God has created us to share in the work of stewardship.

Part II, "Sin as Rebelling Against God's Grace," emphasizes our freedom to reject God's invitation. "I'll do it my own way," we boast. We must acknowledge complicity in the present state of our world, then determine whether to settle for the status quo or break free and seek a better way.

Part III, "Covenant as Context for Shaping Stewards," points to God's more excellent way which encourages some to say, "I choose to work with God." When we take this step in faith, God's means of grace in the church help shape us as steward people. We will consider how Baptism, the Lord's Prayer, the Cross, and the Lord's Table facilitate this process.

This book is written to help us on our pilgrimages as "stewards shaped by grace" and in our efforts to build up the church in love for its mission in our world. For this book, I want to express thanks to Phillips Graduate Seminary for the chance to teach stewardship; to the Commission on Stewardship of the National Council of Churches for encouraging me to write; and to Claremont School of Theology for providing me office space and library use for writing this book. Detailed responses from full readings of early drafts came from Stuart McLean, T.J. Liggett, Darwin Mann, George Tolman, John C. Bennett, John C. Long, Ronald Vallet, Jeanne Moffat, Dale Stitt, Shirley Barnum, and Pat Cameron. Further suggestions and encouragement came from Mark Thompson, John Killinger, Harold Fey, Karen Carter, and Ernest O'Donnell. Each, I hope, will note how seriously I responded to their suggestions. To all named and unnamed, who contributed to this book that has been in process across my lifetime, my deepest gratitude.

## NOTES

[1]Harold E. Fey, prominent Disciples of Christ minister, educator, author and journalist, died January 30, 1990, in Claremont, California. While writing this book on study leave at Claremont School of Theology, my wife and I had an apartment at nearby Pilgrim Place where the Feys were living in retirement. Though his poor eyesight did not permit Dr. Fey to read and critique the first draft of this book, his invaluable suggestions for shaping the first paragraph of my Introduction call forth my deepest gratitude.

[2]Colin W. Williams, *Where in the World? Changing Forms of the Church's Witness*. National Council of the Churches of Christ in the United States of America, 1963. p. 12.

[3]Keith Watkins, *Faithful and Fair: Transcending Sexist Language in Worship*. Abingdon, 1981. I recommend this book highly for study/discussion of this important issue.

# I

# Amazing Grace! How Sweet the Sound!

# 1

# *Beginning with the*
# *Benediction*

Recently I was one of a group of seminary professors from the United States who met Drs. Mabelle and Raj Arole in the village of Jamkhed, India. While Mabelle and Raj were students at Christian Medical College in Vellore, India, in the 1950s, they had discovered their common bonds of Christian faith, intelligence that made them honor graduates, and desire to do community health work among the poor in rural India.

After graduation, marriage, and five years of village work in India, they enrolled at Johns Hopkins Medical School in the United States for graduate work in public health, maternal and child care, and family planning. There, with the help of Professor Carl Taylor, they drew up a revolutionary plan for providing medical service to Indian villages.[1]

Upon returning to India the Aroles searched for four months to find a place most needing community health services. That led them to a dry and dusty area, almost denuded of trees, 300 miles southeast of Bombay. That area met their criteria: It was starkly poor, virtually without medical services, lacking a Christian presence, and populated by those really wanting medical care, no matter what the cost. If their plan would work there, it could become a model for any part of India or the Third World.

Using seed money from the Christian Church (Disciples of Christ) and the United Church of Christ, on five acres of donated land in Jamkhed the Aroles built a twenty-four-bed hospital as a center for curative medicine. When surrounding villages clamored for help, they answered with "tough love": "How can we go to you if you don't have a road?" After the people got government help and built the roads themselves, the Aroles went. They responded to requests for immunization programs when their terms had been met: "Get 90 percent of your children together for us. To have just a few children protected won't do any good." They gave an identical challenge to each village: "In five years you must assume responsibility for running your own health program, for we only have money to help you get started. Additional funds you will have to find from the Indian government and from among yourselves."[2]

Our visit that day to the village of Bavi illustrated what this empowerment of people had accomplished in seventeen years. Sitting with village women and men on blankets in their community building, we talked with the woman serving as community health worker. Though illiterate, she amazed us with the intelligent leadership she was giving in that village.

In India, whose population reached 803 million in 1987 and may top one billion by 2000; where only 39 percent of couples use birth control; where 25 million babies are born each year; and where children under four comprise 43 percent of all deaths[3] population control is working in Bavi! Prenatal supervision and basic changes in birthing procedures had resulted in no infant deaths in Bavi for the past ten years. Oral rehydration ("a fistful of sugar and a pinch of salt in a measured cup of water") had dramatically dealt with diarrhea, a major cause of children's deaths in the Third World. Consequently, families were limiting themselves to two children by using contraceptives, made available by the government through this health worker. Many people had had vasectomies and tubal ligations. Only eight village women were pregnant when we were there.

In India, where leprosy has too long been a scourge and where victims of this illness still fear diagnosis and being cast out from home and village, leprosy has been brought under control in Bavi! The twenty-one people diagnosed with this disease were kept in the village for their treatment and cure. One of those cured patients, now the proud owner of a prospering small business, shared with us another contagion: his enthusiasm!

In the Third World, where only one acre of new trees is planted for every ten acres cut down; where fully seventy percent of fuel requirements are met by wood; and where timberlands equal to forty Californias will vanish by the end of this century,[4] a massive reforestation project on communally owned lands is being carried out in Bavi! The people have carefully prepared seedbeds, nurtured the seedlings, drilled wells, devised irrigation systems, and transplanted 475,000 trees.

All this is happening with little outside economic aid because the people of Bavi have been equipped to take full responsibility for their community health program. They are being empowered by God to become stewards. The results—self-esteem and joy—were apparent on their faces as they talked with us.

Later, while we were visiting some adobe homes in Bavi, the villagers invited us to share tea. Soon water was boiled, cups of tea were given, and a tray of anise seeds was passed for us to sample their spicy taste. Suddenly, that tea and those anise seeds were transformed into sacraments of grace, our eyes opened wide, and we recognized the living Christ there among us. Afterward, akin to the first-century experience of two men at Emmaus, our group buzzed with excitement: "Did not our hearts burn within us when we sensed his living presence in that village?" (Lk. 24:32).

What were the signs of his presence among us? By "breaking down the barrier which lay between us...Christ, our living Peace, [had] made a unity of the conflicting elements" (Eph. 2:14, JBP) of Americans and Indians, Christians and Hindus, rich and poor, women and men. The risen Christ had gone ahead of us to India to live among the poor. Through loving deeds being done, and through tea and anise seeds, he invited us to become partners with him and with them in God's new creation. Through our stay in India we had received a benediction of "grace...and peace from God our Father and the Lord Jesus Christ" (Eph. 1:2).

Bavi marked for me the beginning of an eight-month study leave to write this book. Interestingly, Ephesians also begins with a "great benediction" (1:3-14) containing "a digest of the whole epistle...replete with key terms and topics that anticipate the contents of what follows."[5] For this letter succinctly summarizes the gospel of God—and the theme of stewardship. It also describes the blessing God gave me at Bavi.

My ability to receive that blessing was heightened by intensive study of Ephesians in recent years. Of that letter Francis Beare writes: "The Epistle to the Ephesians occupies a place of supreme importance in the history of Christian theology. It could almost be said that through the centuries the influence of Paul has been felt primarily through this epistle."[6] This sentiment is equally shared by scholars who completely disagree about its authorship. Some believe Paul himself wrote it, while others ascribe its writing to someone at a later date who

> ...attempted, as Paul never did, to reduce Paul's bold and brilliant ideas to a system, to correlate them one with

another, to bring them under the dominion of a single ruling theme—the eternal purpose of God to unite all things in heaven and on earth in Christ; and so to demonstrate their significance, not alone for the particular social situation which first called forth their expression, but for the life of the church in all ages.[7]

Those words enhance the value of Ephesians by revealing how its Pauline theology challenges the church to find its life by losing itself in God's mission to the world. Through some key terms and topics of that "great benediction," the living word of God spoke to me that day in Bavi.

*God's blessing comes unsolicited into people's lives.* That is why Ephesians speaks of God's amazing grace, "freely bestowed" (1:6) and "lavished upon us"(1:8) in forgiveness and redemption while we were yet sinners. We call this "prevenient grace," that is, God acting for us before we have done anything to deserve such love. Paul's marvel over "the foolishness of God" at work at Corinth fits my awe over the miracle of Bavi:

> not many of them were wise according to worldly standards, not many were powerful, not many were of noble birth; but God chose what is foolish in the world to shame the wise, God chose what is weak in the world to shame the strong, God chose what is low and despised in the world, even things that are not, to bring to nothing things that are, so that no human being might boast in the presence of God.
>
> 1 Corinthians 1:26-29

As God's grace came unsolicited to those villagers of Bavi, so it spoke surprisingly to us through them that day. "The mystery of God's will" (Eph. 1:9) cannot be understood apart from that amazing grace of God.

*God's blessing provides for the needs of all the family.* Ephesians uses the Greek word "oikonomia" to describe God's "plan for the fullness of time" (1:10) as a way for meeting the needs of all the human family. Compounded of "oikos" (house) and "nomos" (law, rule), this word signifies household management that seeks the welfare of each family member. It echoes Gandhi's belief that "the earth has enough for everybody's need, but not enough for everybody's greed." Of special interest to us, "oikonomia" is often translated "stewardship," as in Ephesians 3:2.

According to Markus Barth, this plan or stewardship of God is "not a timetable, blueprint, or program," but an "uncompleted performance,"[8] in which all are invited to participate. Thus the excitement of Bavi, a whole community acting for the common good. Watching this village meet some basic needs better than many American cities leads one to discern God choosing what is foolish, weak, low, and despised to "destroy the wisdom of the wise and the cleverness of the clever...so that no human being might boast in the presence of God" (1 Cor. 1:19, 29).

*God's blessing embraces the natural order as well.* So that people may be blessed, God is also working "to bring all creation together, everything in heaven and on earth" (Eph. 1:10, TEV). For too long we have been deaf to the groaning of the whole creation and to the plundering of our planet as we have given prominence to salvation history. But Rolf Knierim contends

> that history truly belongs to creation, and not creation to history...[for] while history cannot destroy creation and creation will not destroy history, history can destroy life and itself.... Human life is not a product of history. It is a product of creation and belongs to the continued existence of the order of creation.[9]

So we celebrated the way the people of Bavi have joined hands with God "to bring all creation together." Their massive reforestation project has provided work and income for the people, and healing for the wounded land. As we visited those people at work and wandered through new groves of trees, history and creation were embracing each other.

> For you shall go out in joy,
>     and be led forth in peace;
> the mountains and the hills before you
>     shall break forth into singing.
> and all the trees of the field
>     shall clap their hands.
>
> Instead of the thorn shall come up
>     the cypress;
> instead of the brier shall come up
>     the myrtle.
>                                   Isaiah 55:12-13

*God's blessing offers us Jesus Christ as the model for our stewardship.*
In biblical times, the steward was not an ordinary servant who
simply took orders and did the bidding of others. He was, rather,
a superior servant, a sort of supervisor or foreman expected to make
decisions, give orders, and take charge. What he managed did not
belong to him but to another, to whom he was responsible and at
whose pleasure he served.[10]

Again, according to Markus Barth, Ephesians regards Christ as
*The Steward* (the *"oikonomos"*) of God but, "while a scheme or plan
is to be carried out...Jesus Christ is not given a detailed job description. Rather he is trusted to act out freely what pleases the Father."[11]
In Bavi, Christ, that Steward, is living in those gentle people whose
leadership and gifts are blessing that village and the land. Moreover, those villagers go to New Delhi to speak before government
committees whose members, akin to us that day, are staggered at
the complete assurance of these common people (Acts 4:13, JBP).

*God's blessing incorporates us into a community of blessing.* Paul
knew Christians could not live solitary lives, because "to each is
given the manifestation of the Spirit for the common good" (1 Cor.
12:7); and because "God chose us to be his own people in union with
Christ because of his own purpose" (Eph. 1:11, TEV). Commenting
on the meaning of Paul's favorite phrase, "in Christ," James Sanders writes, "To be in Christ is to be in a believing community which
is bonded together by belief in God's work in Christ for the world
which God created and loves."[12] We are a people blessed, to be a
blessing!

Where are such a people to be found? In the closing words of
*The Company of the Committed,* Elton Trueblood wrote:

> Somewhere in the world there should be a society con-
> sciously and deliberately devoted to the task of seeing how
> love can be made real and demonstrating love in practice.
> Unfortunately, there is really only one candidate for this
> task. If God, as we believe, is truly revealed in the life of
> Christ, the most important thing to [God] is the creation of
> centers of loving fellowship, which in turn infect the world.
> Whether the world can be redeemed in this way we do not
> know. But it is at least clear that there is no other way.[13]

*God's blessing promises the believing community the Holy Spirit as
empowering presence.* "You believed in Christ, and God put his
stamp of ownership on you by giving you the Holy Spirit he had

promised" (Eph. 1:13, TEV). God's mission is too hard for stewards to achieve by their own resources. Therefore, the Holy Spirit is God's guarantee of power to the community of faith for achieving God's mission for the benefit of the whole world.

Somehow, and in ways that cannot be fully expressed nor explained, God is using Mabelle and Raj Arole and those gentle people of Bavi and the surrounding countryside to do a new thing in that poverty-stricken land. Speaking only of what I have seen and heard, the psalmist's words give voice to my praise: "This is the Lord's doing; it is marvelous in our eyes" (Ps. 118:23).

"We Rejoice! In the Hope We Share!," Jane Mook exulted as she wrote about the Aroles. In response to the question, "Is there witness in the work of the Aroles beyond the service given?" she concluded with these words of Dr. Mabelle Arole:

> It is very difficult in this day and age and place to preach the gospel openly, but the people ask us why we are here—what is our motive—and we tell them. One day the leaders of Jamkhed came to us and said, "We know now that you have come to us because of the cross. So you must put up a cross on top of your hospital building to tell everyone that you are Christians and that it is the cross that brings you here." They themselves then designed the cross—a huge one—and put it up. At night it is lighted and it is like a beacon in the sky, visible for fifteen miles around. It is a constant reminder to both them and us of the power of God in Christ, the power that brought us here.[14]

This much I know: In the village of Bavi Christ is alive and at work through that community of people and Drs. Raj and Mabelle Arole. Together they are partners in one of God's centers of loving fellowship whose power is infecting and redeeming that barren land—and the world beyond it.[15]

What a benediction with which to begin our effort to revalue stewardship as the good news of God's grace poured out in blessing on all creation, with Jesus Christ incorporating us into a community of faith entrusted to share in that saving action! So let us turn now to the ways in which this stewardship of God is spelled out more fully "in Christ."

NOTES

[1]Jane Day Mook. "We Rejoice! In the Hope We Share!" *A.D.*, October 1973.
[2]*Ibid.*
[3]Werner Fornos, *Gaining People, Losing Ground: A Blueprint for Stabilizing World Population.* Science Press, 1987, pp. 45, 12.
[4]*Ibid.*, pp. 18, 14.
[5]Markus Barth, *The Anchor Bible*, Vol. 34. Doubleday & Co., 1974, p. 97-98.
[6]Francis W. Beare, "Introduction to Ephesians," *Interpreter's Bible*, Vol. 10. Abingdon-Cokesbury, 1953, p. 605.
[7]*Ibid.*, p. 604.
[8]Barth, *Anchor Bible*, p. 87. John Reumann's monumental work on "oikonomia" in his doctoral dissertation, The *"Righteousness of God" and the "Economy of God": Two Great Doctrinal Themes Historically Compared*, makes the same case.
[9]Rolf Knierim, "Cosmos and History in Israel's Theology" (Dedicated to Claus Westermann). *Horizons in Biblical Theology* 3, 1981, p. 95. See the whole chapter, pp. 59-123.
[10]Douglas John Hall, *The Steward: A Biblical Symbol Come of Age.* Friendship Press, 1982, p. 17.
[11]Barth, *Anchor Bible*, pp. 88, 109. Also see John Reumann, "Jesus the Steward: An Overlooked Theme in Christology," from *Studia Evangelica,*Vol. V, edited by F. L. Cross. Akademie-Verlag, Berlin, 1968.
[12]James Sanders, "The Bible and the Believing Community," *Biblical Literacy Today.* Summer 1987, p. 5.
[13]Elton Trueblood, *The Company of the Committed.* Harper & Brothers, 1961, p. 113.
[14]Jane Day Mook, "We Rejoice! In the Hope We Share!"
[15]A letter from Jane Day Mook dated February 10, 1990, reported that "Raj Arole was recently granted one of the Indian Government's highest honors, the Padma Bhushan jewel in the lotus."

# 2

# God's Purpose
# Set Forth in Christ

*Where Do We Go from Here: Chaos or Community*? asks Martin Luther King, Jr., in the title of his last book. One senses the same problem in an imaginative plot a famous novelist never got around to developing: "A widely separated family inherits a house in which they have to live together."[1] In a world reduced to neighborhood dimensions, shall we invite chaos by building walls of separation? Or dare we opt for community by learning to live together in our world house?

Chaos or community? That is God's question, too! God sees our broken world, its people torn asunder by classism, racism, sexism, nationalism; its natural resources plundered, leaving creation groaning. Rich and poor, white and black, men and women, Americans and Russians live in alienation. The face of the earth, pockmarked by erosion and deforestation, seared by toxic wastes, threatened by the prospects of nuclear winter, is mirrored in the familiar lines of the nursery rhyme:

> Humpty Dumpty sat on a wall;
> Humpty Dumpty had a great fall
> All the king's horses and all the king's men
> Couldn't put Humpty together again.

Thanks be to God for opting for community, and for putting our Humpty Dumpty world together again! That is happening in Christ, God's Steward, who discerned God's way of operating and has been given "all authority in heaven and on earth" (Mt. 28:18). Yes, God's "purpose set forth in Christ" for our broken world is "to unite all things in him, things in heaven and things on earth" (Eph. 1:9-10). What all the king's horses and men could not do, we believe Christ has already done: "For [Christ] is our peace, who has made

11

us both one, and has broken down the dividing wall of hostility...that he might create in himself one new [humanity] in place of the two, so making peace, and might reconcile us both to God" (2:14-16).

In his paper, "Christ the Healer," Roland Miller sees the purpose behind God's stewardship patterning our own:

> Let us get a sense of the grand design of the God of the universe. You must see yourself and set your ministry in the cosmic context of the healing God. I heard Krister Stendahl say, "God's agenda is the mending of creation." I liked that then, and still do. As my salutation to you I could have said, I greet you, menders of creation in a broken world, in the name of the Mender![2]

My own pilgrimage has been one of discerning God, the Mender, at work "uniting all things in Christ." In 1946, at Texas Christian University, Professor C. A. Burch suggested *relationship* as the best word for describing the Christian faith. Subsequently, a triangle, with God at the apex, and with others and self at the two corners of the base, became an apt symbol of maintaining a loving relationship with God, neighbor and self.

Eight years later, at Lexington Theological Seminary, Professor George Moore added a missing link by suggesting that I write a paper on "the relationship of soil welfare to soul welfare" or "the relationship of soul welfare to soil welfare." "It doesn't matter how you state it," he said, "for you'll discover that we're inextricably related to the earth and its resources—for better or for worse!" Wrestling afresh with the idea of *relationship* yielded the circle as a more apt symbol of the round earth on which God, people and nature are interrelated in one bundle of living.

"The central vision of world history in the Bible," writes Walter Brueggemann, "is that all of creation is one, every creature in community with every other, living in harmony and security toward the joy and well-being of every other creature."[3] This vision sees all persons as "children of a single family...and bearers of a single destiny, namely, the care and management of all of God's creation." Though no word fully captures the vision, the Hebrew word "shalom" best expresses the "dream of God that resists all our tendencies to division...and misery" and that embraces "all those resources and factors which make communal harmony joyous and effective."[4]

Shalom, then, affirms that God, our Creator, has been at work from the beginning, bringing order out of chaos, community out of alienation. That is why all who are interested in the health of church and society, and of the earth itself, must never cease studying this word, for "shalom language points to what lies at the heart of the universe: the shalom-making spirit and power we call God."[5]

Why is this shalom-making purpose so important to God? The answer is close at hand. In homes where chaos prevails, physical and emotional needs go unmet; but community fosters the common good. In an economy where chaos reigns, production slows, distribution lags, people suffer; but community promotes the general welfare. In a world where chaos exists, poverty, violence and war erupt; but community facilitates the careful use of the earth's resources for "the healing of the nations." Household management in cosmic context is not possible, even for God, where chaos prevails; therefore, God made another effort at community-building, this time "in Christ."

Although this purpose of God was "to be put into effect when the time was ripe" (Eph. 1:10, NEB), how did God propose to do that? The answer that this was done "in the blood of Christ" (Eph. 2:13) and "through the cross" (Eph. 2:16) has spawned many theories of atonement trying to explain how the death of Christ made separated people into one new humanity. My seminary thesis, "Atonement in Christian Thought," exposed me to this wide range of thought, under which lies the apostle Paul's bedrock of faith: "The word of the cross is folly to those who are perishing, but to us who are being saved it is the power of God" (1 Cor. 1:18).

In three friends that "word of the cross" has become flesh for me, speaking clearly of God's mending of creation. "Called to Be One by the Cross of Our Lord" was the theme of the 1984 Week of Prayer for Christian Unity during which I was invited to preach at St. Francis Xavier Catholic Church in Enid, Oklahoma. The assigned text from Isaiah 53 included verse 5b: "upon him was the chastisement that made us whole, and with his stripes we are healed." As I meditated on those words, the first of those friends walked into my mind—and into my sermon, too.

During the summer of 1948, in between student conferences in England and Holland, I was on a solo trip to Rome. Five years of high school Latin had brought that city to life for me; but, not speaking the Italian language, I was lost. Thanks to a chance encounter, an American Catholic priest, then serving with the Passionist Order in Rome, guided me to the Forum and Coliseum, then later to the Catacombs and St. Peter's as well. Thus began a lifelong friendship with Father Malcolm LaVelle who later served as World Superior of the Passionist Order and sat with the rank of bishop at Vatican II. Annual Christmas notes, his visit to our home in Japan, our family rendezvous with him in England on our homeward way, and a final visit in St. Louis in the late 1970s kept our friendship growing for thirty-five years until his death. First in pre-Vatican II days, then afterward, it formed a bridge that made us "separated brethren"[6] one, "through the cross of our Lord!"

My second friend is Stanley Manierre who was shot down in the South Pacific during World War II.[7] The four surviving members of his crew drifted on a raft toward Saipan where they were captured by the Japanese army. Thence they were flown to Yokohama and transferred to a prison camp near Tokyo, where, but for the kindness of a single guard, he experienced close-at-hand how brutal human beings can be to one another. Hating his captors, he prayed for deliverance. "If you'll get me out of here," he promised God, "I'll go back to church when I get home!"

Though many "fox-hole believers" had very short memories, Stanley Manierre was as good as his prayer when he returned safely home. One day while teaching a Sunday School class of junior high boys about the love of God and love for neighbors, he realized he was still harboring hatred for the Japanese two years after returning from prison camp. He simply was not able to understand how Jesus could have cried out "forgive them" for the very people pounding nails through his flesh.

Happily, the teacher himself finally learned the lesson that Jesus looked upon all people as precious children of God needing forgiveness to be reconciled to God and one another. One day light shined into his darkness: "Here I was mouthing love and harboring hatred. I knew I needed God's forgiveness. I confessed my sin, and through God's amazing grace I was forgiven."[8]

At that very moment a new life began for Stanley Manierre. Set free from hating and free for loving, he soon found himself in seminary. Subsequently, he served as pastor of a Baptist church in Hanson, Massachusetts. "But the Lord had more plans for me," he writes. "I felt God's call to return to Japan: this time not with bombs, but with the Bread of Life, to build bridges of peace and reconciliation."[9]

Yes, Stanley Manierre and I served together as missionaries with the United Church of Christ in Japan! Though we may never fathom the mystery of how the cross frees people from sin, in Stanley Manierre I experienced the atoning purpose of God in Christ, uniting erstwhile enemies to one another and to God.

My third friend, Tweedy Evelene Sombrero, a young Navajo woman and 1988 graduate of Iliff Seminary in Denver, now serves as minister of a United Methodist congregation for Native Americans in Phoenix, Arizona. While she was a student at Phillips Graduate Seminary in the early 1980s, I was assigned to be her advisor. Instead, I became her advisee as she marshalled her Native American wisdom and culture in defense of our endangered planet. Ponder these eloquent excerpts from her final paper for my class on "Stewardship in Global and Congregational Context":

> In discussing the relationship of humankind to the Earth, we must understand the basic difference between the Navajo view of Mother Earth and what the Western European or Contemporary American mind means when it tosses around poetic metaphors like "mother nature" or "mother earth." The Contemporary American means that the earth and all of nature is like one's natural mother, but the Navajos and all other American Indians mean that one's natural mother is the closest thing we will ever know to one's real mother, the Earth .... Our real mother IS the Earth. Our natural mothers are just pale imitations of the Earth-force....

> Modern technology is moving Anglos rapidly toward a different kind of life. But as technology grows, people forget where it all came from. It all came from the Earth and the Sky.... People are becoming over-progressed and over-mechanized...removed from both the Earth and the Sky. People are using all of the Earth's power without thought. They are pumping power out of the Earth — the oil, the gas, the water. It's like taking blood from a human being. You take too much, it can't survive. It gets weak....

> When you take something from the Earth, or from nature, you must give something back. It is important that the relationship between you remain equal.... We take from all of the elements—Earth, Air, Fire, Water—whatever each one has to give us. In return, we offer thanks and respect.... During mining and drilling, plants are destroyed, so it would be right to offer the Earth seeds, and seedlings to replace what we remove. There has to be an awareness that we cannot always take, but must give in return. And we must give in proportion to what we remove from our Mother, the Earth.[10]

16

God is speaking powerfully to us through the words of these "gentlers" of the earth, the Navajos. For God's purpose set forth in Christ is "to bring all creation together, everything in heaven and on earth" (Eph. 1:9-10, TEV). Without a doubt, they bear witness "to what lies at the heart of the universe: the shalom-making spirit and power we call God."[11]

Leo Tolstoy's words, "where love is, there God is also," were never more true than at the cross of Christ, which reveals how far God's amazing grace goes in reconciling us to God's self and to one another. Wherever alienation and brokenness are, God is already busy with the work of reconciliation. For, as Roland Miller says, "Mending is an expression for God's total movement of creative love toward suffering humanity" and a call to us as well to share that purpose as "menders of creation in a broken world, in the name of the Mender!"[12] As the first essential component in God's stewardship of our world house, what glad good news this brings to our Humpty Dumpty lives and world!


NOTES

[1]Martin Luther King, Jr., *Where Do We Go from Here: Chaos or Community?* Harper & Row, Publishers, 1967, p. 167.
[2]Roland E. Miller, "Christ the Healer," from *Health and Healing: Ministry of the Church* ed. by Henry L. Letterman. Wheat Ridge Foundation, 1980, p. 16.
[3]Walter Brueggemann, *Living Toward a Vision.* United Church Press, 1976, p. 15.
[4]*Ibid.*, p. 16.
[5]Paul L. Hammer, *The Gift of Shalom.* United Church Press, 1976, p. 11.
[6]It may be apocryphal that when Pope John XXIII used the phrase "separated brethren" to describe Roman Catholics and Protestants, he is said to have placed the accent not on "separated" (as had been the custom) but on "brethren." But whether he said it this way or not, he lived it; and the church ecumenical owes him a great debt of gratitude for convening Vatican II and for the new spirit of openness that now characterizes so many relationships between Catholics and Protestants.
[7]Details of the following story are contained in an article by L. Stanley Manierre, "He Laid His Life on the Line for Us," in *The American Baptist,* September 1975, p. 11.
[8]*Ibid.*
[9]*Ibid.*
[10]Tweedy Evelene Sombrero, final paper on "Stewardship in Global and Congregational Context," pp. 13, 15-16. Written at Phillips Graduate Seminary, fall semester, 1982.
[11]Hammer, *The Gift of Shalom,* p. 11.
[12]Miller, "Christ the Healer," p. 16.

# 3

# God's Power
# Accomplished in Christ

Without power to carry it out, even the most compelling purpose counts for naught. How many committees plan their work, then fail to work their plan? What is needed is "the ability to achieve purpose,"[1] and the good news is that this is the kind of power God possesses.

Although beyond measuring, God's power has already been "accomplished in Christ when [God] raised him from the dead...made him sit at his right hand...put all things under his feet and...made him the head over all things for the church" (Eph. 1:19-22). This is "the foundation of the glorious work of grace which God is accomplishing in the created universe" by "the infinite power which alone could accomplish so great a design."[2] The resurrection validates the cross, by providing the power to "unite all things in Christ."

Ephesians 1:19 uses four Greek words to speak of this mighty power of God. Literally translated, the verse reads: "the immeasurable greatness of his power (*dynamis*) in us who believe, according to the working (*energeia*) of the power (*kratos*) of his might (*ischys*)." In turn, those words suggest: ability to accomplish what one has taken in hand; activity, or power at work; power over others that subdues or rules; inherent strength or might.[3] Yet, having used them all, this writer knows they cannot fully describe God's power.

However, far from discerning such power at work, many people live as if God were dead. Some old churches in changed inner-city neighborhoods repeat tired litanies of a golden past when "God gave the growth," as if to suggest that God has now retired or else joined the "white fright flight" or "black middle-class

17

exodus" to the suburbs. Though they have eyes, they do not see God still working in the inner city. Though they have ears, they do not hear God calling servants to share in that work.

God's resurrection power is available now for achieving God's purpose in the world, but many want it for their purposes. That is precisely what James and John wanted from Jesus: "Grant us to sit, one at your right hand and one at your left, in your glory" (Mk. 10:37). Still expecting the Messiah to come in kingly power, they coveted sharing that glory with the one they believed to be the Messiah. Not yet willing to let Jesus use them for his purposes, they wanted to use him for theirs.

James and John shared a common desire with Gentile rulers in their day—yes, even with ordinary folks like you and me in our day —"to lord it over others." That is power, to be sure, but not the power of which Jesus spoke. He minced no words in warning his self-seeking disciples: "But it shall not be so among you" (Mk. 10:43). Thereby he informed them that God will not be used by those seeking their own purposes.

Many modern-day disciples of Christ have yet to learn this lesson. Congregations dream dreams, make plans, draw up budgets, organize financial campaigns—then ask God for power to achieve their purposes. But God does not bless programs that subvert God's purpose, nor does God bless doctrines that belie God's Word made flesh. When we wrap our plans in God talk, we should not be surprised to hear rumblings from Mt. Sinai: "You shall not take the name of the Lord your God in vain; for the Lord will not hold him guiltless who takes his name in vain" (Ex. 20:7).

On the other hand, "the working of God's great might" lies behind "God's purpose set forth in Christ." Jesus tried to help his disciples grasp this truth by offering them a new image of power in God's world: "whoever would be great among you must be your servant, and whoever would be first among you must be slave of all. For the Son of man also came not to be served but to serve, and to give his life as a ransom for many" (Mk. 10:43-45). What is to be coveted is not power to lord it over, but to serve people. In his coming, Jesus made God's purpose clear: "I came not to be served but to serve, and to give my life as a ransom for many" (Mk. 10:45). Rosemary Radford Ruether declares:

> In God's kingdom the corrupting principles of domination and subjugation will be overcome. People will no longer model social or religious relationships, or even relation-

ships to God, after the sort of power that reduces others to servility. Rather they will discover a new kind of power, a power exercised through service, which empowers the disinherited and brings all to a new relationship of mutual enhancement. Jesus' image of God and Christ as Servant transforms all relations, including relations to God.[4]

Significantly, the 1980 Conference of the Commission on World Mission and Evangelism of the World Council of Churches at Melbourne, Australia, chose as its theme, "The Crucified Christ Challenges Human Power." Reflecting on that theme, Thomas Wieser noted that the Gospels clearly testify that the coming of Jesus and the proclamation of the kingdom of God involve "the setting forth of a radically other power constellation in this world... [for] Jesus preaches and practices [the power of love] as a wholly new option for the exercise of power."[5]

How true! In contrast to lording it over people, serving people is "a radically other power constellation in this world" and "a wholly new option for the exercise of [the power of love]." Serving people is the stewardship God authorized Jesus to carry out in our world house.

Furthermore, God's purpose (the end) determines the nature of God's power (the means). For in God's way of operating, these two must be consistent with each other. Since power is the ability to achieve purpose, only loving means can achieve God's loving end. Dorothy Sayers wondered why God chose the cross as a way to redeem the world instead of lifting the right hand of power and striking the world perfect. Her answer: God had set that kind of power aside, in favor of a new understanding of power. Lording-it-over-people power destroys people, while servant power, to which "that cross, that thorn and those five wounds bear witness,"[6] unites and builds up.

"Peace Through Power" has been a favored motto of those who since World War II have spent trillions of dollars turning plowshares into swords while labeling missiles "peacekeepers" and terrorists "freedom fighters." Although these power-brokers even now claim credit for the dramatic developments in Eastern Europe during 1989-90, those who discern God at work in history delight that the principal change agent has not been "swords' loud clashing nor roll of stirring drums," but the moral power of non-violent direct action. A. J. Muste's motto better captures the truth: There Is No Way To Peace; Peace Is The Way!

The life and writings of Martin Luther King, Jr., reveal his search for God's kind of power for achieving God's purpose. That was his dream: to break down the dividing wall of hostility between blacks and whites in order to make one new humanity. During his first year of leadership of the Montgomery bus boycott, hostility and threats against him and his family brought him to his wits' end. Exhausted, sleepless, courage almost gone, he determined to take his problem to God. Head in hands, he bowed over the kitchen table and prayed aloud to God.

> I am here taking a stand for what I believe is right. But now I am afraid. The people are looking to me for leadership, and if I stand before them without strength and courage, they too will falter. I am at the end of my powers. I have nothing left. I've come to the point where I can't face it alone.[7]

In that moment of extremity God assured Martin Luther King he was not alone. An inner voice bid him to stand up for righteousness and truth. Almost at once his fears waned and his uncertainty started to disappear.[8] During the next twelve turbulent years that led to his assassination, he found "strength to love" by trusting in that "great benign Power in the universe whose name is God" and who "is able to make a way out of no way, and transform dark yesterdays into bright tomorrows."[9]

In the early 1960s when King gave a commencement address at Bethune Cookman College in Daytona Beach, Florida, I was a minister in that community and fortunately had the chance to meet and to hear him. That increased my appreciation for his leadership of the civil rights movement, as well as my distress over the events in Selma, Alabama, on Sunday, March 7, 1965, as six hundred blacks set out on a march to the state capitol in Montgomery to present their grievances to Governor George Wallace. They did not get far that day, for they were clubbed, bull-whipped and teargassed by state troopers in an orgy of violence that sent shock waves across our nation.

That set thousands of others marching across the land. The next day I am thankful God's nudges compelled me to join my first picket line at the Marion Hotel in Little Rock, Arkansas, where I was then serving as pastor of Pulaski Heights Christian Church.[10] The Southern Attorneys General were meeting there at that very time, so it seemed appropriate for a small group of concerned blacks and whites to protest such police brutality to them.

In March 1985 a commemorative march from Selma to Montgomery was held, at which time Associated Press correspondent Jules Loh wrote about the striking changes in Selma since 1965:

> Population is the same, about 26,000. Back then, only about half the streets were paved—guess which half. Outhouses were prevalent in the black sections. Today, all Selma's streets are paved and lit, all homes connected to sewer lines. Blacks now serve on the city council and all city departments.[11]

In the march's opening ceremony at Brown Chapel AME Church, the civil rights movement's foremost shrine in Selma, Joe Smitherman, Selma's mayor in 1985 as he was in 1965, occupied the pulpit—and this is what he said:

> "My hands are as dirty as the others'. I ordered the arrest of Dr. King. We were wrong, but we did it. And I'm sorry."

> Then...Mayor Smitherman stood and shared a hymnal with Jesse Jackson and joined in singing "The Battle Hymn of the Republic." If that symbolism was lost on the current generation, older cheeks were wet with tears.[12]

And wonder of wonders, when the marchers reached Montgomery on that commemorative march, the same man who had refused to see them twenty years earlier was there as governor again, thanks to black votes that had helped elect him—but this time George Wallace welcomed the marchers warmly![13]

Despite all that remains to be done in achieving racial justice, even in Selma as the events of March, 1990, remind us,[14] what startling evidence of God's resurrection power at work in modern-day disciples of Christ, breaking down the wall of hostility that separates people and making one new humanity! What a promise that "the immeasurable greatness of God's power" is still available for the achievement of God's shalom-making purpose "in us who believe!"


NOTES

[1]Leslie D. Weatherhead, *When the Lamp Flickers*. Abingdon-Cokesbury, 1948, p. 141.
[2]Francis W. Beare, Exegesis on Ephesians, *The Interpreter's Bible*, Vol. 10. Abingdon-Cokesbury, 1953, p. 632.

[3]*Ibid.*

[4]Rosemary Radford Ruether, *Sexism and God-Talk*. Beacon Press, 1983, p. 30.

[5]Thomas Wieser, Editorial, from *The International Review of Mission*, Volume LXIX. No. 273, January 1980, p. 3.

[6]Dorothy L. Sayers, "The Choice of the Cross" (from "The Devil to Pay"), *Masterpieces of Religious Verse*, edited by James Dalton Morrison. Harper & Brothers, 1948, #592, p. 189.

[7]Martin Luther King, Jr., *Strength to Love*. Fortress Press, copyright 1963; first Fortress Press edition, 1981, p. 113.

[8]*Ibid.*

[9]*Ibid.*, p. 114.

[10]"Arkansans Picket Alabama Official," *Arkansas Gazette*, Tues., March 9, 1965, p. 4A.

[11]Jules Loh, Associated Press special correspondent, Enid *Morning News* (Enid, Oklahoma), Sunday, March 10, 1985, p. A1.

[12]*Ibid.*

[13]Jesse Jackson, "The New, Redeemed South Still Needs a New Deal," *Los Angeles Times*, Sunday, March 18, 1990. In this syndicated column from Washington D.C., Jesse Jackson wrote: "The measure of the change we made can be taken in the person of George Wallace himself. I went back to Selma and Montgomery recently to reflect on our past and to rejuvenate for the future. With a contrite heart, Wallace told me that he regrets the role he played during those years and wants instead to be remembered for the civil-rights position he came to later in his career. In his last term as governor, Wallace appointed African Americans to his cabinet and an African American as a press aide. He also appointed numerous African American lawyers to the bench, giving him a record, he said, better than any other governor in the South."

[14]Jesse Jackson had returned for the 25th anniversary march from Selma to Montgomery in March, 1990. The title of his article mentioned above calls attention to the unfinished work of human relations yet to be done in the South. In fact, Selma itself was experiencing social unrest at the very time of this 1990 march, related to the dismissal of a black principal from one of the city schools.

# 4

# God's People
# Created in Christ

But someone asks, "If God has the power to accomplish purpose, why doesn't 'shalom' prevail across the earth? Why is ours such a broken world?" Some homespun wisdom comes from a farmer who bought a rocky, bramble-covered piece of ground and, after several years of toil and sweat, turned it into a garden. Hard at work one day, he heard his preacher shouting over the fence, "Brother Brown, you and the Lord have surely made a beautiful garden here." "Yes, sir," he quickly replied, "but you should have seen it when the Lord had it all alone!"

That farmer had hold of one of life's important truths: God does not make gardens "all alone" but only in cooperation with people. Oh yes, God has the power to make gardens all alone, but has set that kind of power aside in favor of a better way of exercising power, namely, making gardens together with us.

What a risk God took in making that choice! By making people in the divine image, God should have had partners aplenty to help manage the world house and meet the global family's needs. But by doing their own thing, "following the course of the world," and winding up dead in their sins, human beings caused hell to break loose on earth (Eph. 2:1-3). Then, surprisingly,

God, who is rich in mercy, out of the great love with which he loved us, even when we were dead through our trespasses, made us alive together with Christ.... For by grace you have been saved through faith; and this is not your own doing, it is the gift of God—not because of works, lest any man should boast. For we are his workmanship, cre-

ated in Christ Jesus for good works, which God prepared beforehand that we should walk in them.
Ephesians 2:4-5, 8-10

"Created in Christ Jesus for good works." That is welcome news for people at cross purposes with God and one another. While we were in Japan, missionary friend Lew Lancaster helped us "feel" that in a devotional exercise. Directing us to stretch hands forward, palms up, he asked us to make tight fists, fingers gouging into our palms. Next, he bid us tense all muscles of our arms, faces, torsos, legs, then draw our arms about ourselves, squeezing ourselves as hard as we could. Despite our discomfort, we were asked to remain in this tense posture for a few seconds before extending our hands forward, fists still tightly clenched. Then, what relief to relax first our legs, torsos, faces, arms; and at long last to open our fists, wiggle our fingers and feel the blood once again coursing through our veins. In delightful liberation we were encouraged to reach our hands out to touch and bless our neighbors. Soon the room was awash with laughter, as handshakes, pats and hugs became the order of the day.

"For which stance did God make you?" I ask, after leading this exercise. While awaiting answers, I give mine. "God didn't make me to clutch and grasp to myself, but to reach out with hands and feelings, touching and blessing those around me. Down, then, with the heresy that giving hurts, and on with the truth that giving really feels good!" For, speaking biblically, "We are God's handiwork, created in Christ Jesus to devote ourselves to the good deeds for which God has designed us" (Eph. 2:10, NEB). Crafted by God, our designer lives are made for giving!

In the biblical story God calls people to be servants, ones like Abraham whom God promised to "bless...so that you will be a blessing...and by you all the families of the earth shall bless themselves" (Gen. 12:1-3). But watching people turn instead to live for themselves, God entered the re-creation business:

Therefore, if anyone is in Christ, he is a new creation; the old has passed away, behold, the new has come.... In Christ God was reconciling the world to himself, not counting their trespasses against them, and entrusting to us the message of reconciliation. So we are ambassadors for Christ, God making his appeal through us.
2 Corinthians 5:17,19-20a

No longer are we "foreigners or strangers," but "fellow citizens with God's people and members of the family of God" (Eph. 2:19, TEV). In short, we are a servant people called church.

Fr. Aloysius Pieris discerns a "christic factor" dynamically at work in this process: "in Jesus, God and the poor have formed an alliance against their common enemy, mammon."[1] By mammon Jesus meant more than money but what we do with money and what it does with us. Jesus modeled a spirituality that was both a *struggle to be poor* (discerning how to decrease the wastefulness of the affluent) and a *struggle for the poor* (discerning how to eliminate want).[2] Therefore, true disciples opt to live in *voluntary poverty* by giving up mammon in such ways that those born into *forced poverty* will benefit by their renunciation. "In other words, the affluent are called to be poor so that there be no poor."[3]

Thus Pieris sees the church as God's new people comprised of two categories of the poor: the poor by "option" who are the *followers of Jesus* (Mt. 19:21), and the poor by "birth" who are the *proxies of Christ* (Mt. 25:31-46).[4] Their Christian spirituality is inspired by these two motives: "to *follow Jesus* who *was* poor then, and to *serve Christ* who *is* in the poor now."[5] Viewing these communities of converts as "a personal and a visible guarantee of the new order," Pieris pays them a high compliment: "This incipient 'structural revolution' is known as the church—which is good news to the poor, because the poor by birth and the poor by option constitute it."[6]

It was within such a faith community that Paul received his "stewardship [*oikonomia*] of God's grace that was given to me for you" (Eph. 3:2). As God's steward he felt himself charged "to make all men see what is the plan [*oikonomia*] of the mystery hidden for ages in God who created all things; that through the church the manifold wisdom of God might now be made known" (3:9-10).

Ephesians makes this clear: The church has a central role in God's scheme of things! So now, to "the stewardship of God"[7] must be added "the stewardship of the church," a task in which all who answer God's gracious call are invited to participate—and for the accomplishment of which God's great power is made available, through faith, to all who believe.

In the summer of 1953 I saw God's people, the church, engaged in God's shalom-making purpose set forth in Christ. Representing the Admissions Office of Transylvania College, I went to visit a prospective student at a Presbyterian home mission center at Morris Fork, deep in the Kentucky mountains. Turning off the asphalt highway, I went as far as the gravel road took me, then hiked the remaining distance to the center. Imagine my dismay when the young man was not at home that day!

Happily, something better awaited me. I met Sam VanderMeer, the Presbyterian missionary who had gone there by horseback in 1923 when no roads led into that isolated region. Unbeknownst to Sam, a circuit riding mountain preacher, Ike Gabbard, had long been concerned about the Morris Fork area. "O Lord, please send us someone to come to help, to teach these people about Thee, and a better way of life," had long been his heartfelt prayer. In their first meeting, Ike Gabbard threw his arms around Sam, rejoicing, "You are the answer to my prayer! The Lord sent you here. God bless us as we work together for him." [8]

Together, Sam and those uneducated, poverty-stricken people set to work. Utilizing nature's abundant supply of wood and stone, they built a church, school, and community center as ways of addressing human needs. Acquiring agricultural training from the University of Kentucky, Sam shared that knowledge with farmers eager to use it in turning eroded hillsides into fertile fields.

One day Sam penned a note to the Presbyterian mission center at Wooten's Creek thirty miles away. "I have heard of your clinics," he wrote. "I have some children here who need medical help. I can't get it here and wonder if I may bring three or four of them to your next clinic?" Quickly came the reply. "Of course, we can certainly make room for a few more children."

While the children got treated, Sam fell in love with Nola Pease, the lovely nurse caring for them. The long journey by horseback across many "creeks 'n' hollers" did not deter their courtship, so in the summer of 1927 Sam and Nola were married. As Sam's partner for the next forty-two years, Nola served as midwife in welcoming a thousand babies to Morris Fork. [9]

But, best of all, "Saminola" empowered those mountain people to accept their stewardship of life. J. Garber Drushal, after retiring as President of the College of Wooster, gratefully recalled his legacy from Sam VanderMeer: "Always try to get young people to do more than they thought they could and do it better than they expected. In working with college students for over forty years, I tried to apply that principle." [10]

Judy Luddy put it this way:

Sam's ideas didn't disrupt their lives, beat them down, inflame them to anger, or promise them Utopia—here or hereafter. He just helped them to see what could be done with what they had before their eyes and inside their heads, so that they observed everything around and about with a sharp new sense of potential.[11]

Visiting with Sam VanderMeer on that July day, I began to understand why his face glowed. I shall never forget his parting words, "Some day I'd like to write a book about my experiences here. If I do, it will have two parts. The first part will tell what I found here, and I'll call that 'The Tired Land.' And the second part"—with that he gestured toward the surrounding hills and valley—"will tell what's happened here across these thirty years, and I'll call that 'The Tired Land Smiles!'"[12]

As he spoke, my eyes feasted on a pleasant valley and con-toured hillsides where "the corn was as high as an elephant's eye," and the ears of my heart confirmed that "the hills were alive with the sound of music!" I saw and heard the celestial harmony of shalom that day, for all creation was one, every creature in commu-nity with every other, living in harmony and security toward the joy and well-being of every other creature.[13]

Yet that had happened because thirty years earlier Sam VanderMeer, opting for *voluntary poverty*, had heard—and an-swered—God's call to join hands with those simple mountain folks at Morris Fork, born into *forced poverty*. Together, as the incipient "structural revolution" called church, they had been living toward the vision of God's purpose set forth in Christ. That day I was witness to the mighty work that God had empowered that man, his wife, and those people to do. Working together with God, they had turned that rocky, bramble-covered place into a beautiful garden and put a smile on the frowning countenance of that mountain countryside.

Morris Fork had experienced the church's stewardship at its best, honoring God, blessing people, and cherishing nature. The joy of it all overflows in these words of Frederick Luddy:

No one ever "joshed" more people into tasting the inner and outer goodness of life, "joshed" them into reverence, than did Sam VanderMeer. Without his smiles, and those of his tireless helpmate, the tired country would not have smiled. Its transformation from a place of frequent vio-lence and constant isolation to a community of peace and new horizons was their conscious translation of Jn. 10:10, "I came that they may have life, and have it abundantly"[14]

Purpose set forth, power accomplished, people created—"in Christ"! Ephesians responds with worship and praise to this "plan [stewardship] of the mystery hidden for ages in God who created all things," whose "manifold wisdom" is to "be made known...through the church" to all people (3:9-10). Surely there is no better way to ponder the meaning of stewardship than to fall on our knees before the Creator, Redeemer, and Sustainer of the world (Eph. 3:14-19) who invites us of the church to help put a smile on the countenance of our broken world. God will not do that all alone, but only together with us!

## NOTES

[1]Aloysius Pieris, *An Asian Theology of Liberation*. Orbis Books, 1988, p. 15.

[2]*Ibid.*, p. 15, 20.

[3]*Ibid.*, p. 20.

[4]*Ibid.*, p. 21.

[5]*Ibid.*

[6]*Ibid.*, p. 110.

[7]*"Oikonomia"* appears for a third time in Ephesians 3:9, translated as "plan" (as in 1:10), although I again suggest "stewardship" as a better way of helping us grasp this great mystery of God.

[8]Nola Pease VanderMeer, with Frederick L. Luddy, *The Tired Country Smiles*. Harlo Press, 1983, p. 75.

[9]*Ibid.*, pp. 42-45.

[10]*Ibid.*, p. 220.

[11]*Ibid.*, p. 218.

[12]Sam VanderMeer never got around to writing that book, so Nola undertook that labor of love after his death. Although it bears the title, *The Tired Country Smiles*, I vividly recall Sam VanderMeer saying "the tired land" when he talked to me that day. Although her book is not divided into the two parts of which he spoke, my heart was strangely warmed by its story of God's grace shaping some of those people at Morris Fork into an unforgettable community of servant people called church.

[13]Walter Brueggemann, *Living Toward a Vision*. United Church Press, 1976, p. 15.

[14]VanderMeer, *The Tired Country Smiles*, p. 236.

# 5

## *Responding with the Doxology*

Even as J. B. Phillips' book, *Your God Is Too Small*, enlarged people's theologies, so the first three chapters of Ephesians give birth to a vision of the grace-shaped stewardship of God. Now it is time to consider some of the "stretch-marks" this new-born vision leaves upon our consciousness.

Douglas John Hall's *The Steward: A Biblical Symbol Come of Age* accelerated that process by convincing me that my theology of stewardship was too small. In turn, this illuminated for me the word of God in Ephesians which expands our ways of thinking about God's stewardship.

*Such stewardship begins, not with what we do, but with who we are.* "Deeds of stewardship arise out of the being of the steward....the act is an expression and consequence of the life that enacts it."[1] Thus we must learn whose and who we are, lest Biff's epitaph for his salesman father, Willie Loman, describe us as well: "He had the wrong dreams, all, all wrong. He never knew who he was."[2] Our heritage of faith will never let us forget that we are God's, made in God's image to be God's stewards, co-managing resources and affairs in our world house.

*It follows that stewardship points first to God's doing, not to ours.* Faithful response to God is our first step toward understanding God's gracious and consistent ways of blessing all creation. "The authority [we] bear is wholly bound up with the One whose creation [we] tend; and...is valid only when it is an adequate representation of the Creator's love for what He will have tended."[3]

How, then, can we discern what "an adequate representation of the Creator's love" for all creation really is? Fortunately, faith enables us to perceive God's "decisive engagement" in creation and history as a "consistent, compassionate demand for justice and righteousness."[4] Precisely that kind of prophetic imagination is present in these now familiar words of Ephesians: "For [God] has made known to us in all wisdom and insight the mystery of his will, according to his purpose which he set forth in Christ, as a plan for the fulness of time, to unite all things in him, things in heaven and things on earth" (1:9-10).

George Webber reports the trauma of graduating from Union Theological Seminary and "being dropped" into the East Side slums of New York City for a ministry at East Harlem Protestant Parish. That multiracial and economically poor neighborhood immediately confronted him with urgent issues that had not even been discussed during his seminary years. Although overwhelmed, he tackled the challenge of taking the Lord of the church to pagan streets where the name of Jesus was only a swear word.

However, beginning with an assumption that "the church possesses its Lord as though in an ark of salvation to be carried around on our shoulders," he learned instead that "in East Harlem there were many signs of his presence for us to discover. If Jesus Christ is truly Lord, then we are called to point to signs of his presence, to join in his continuing ministry rather than to bring him as a stranger to a world from which until the Christian clergy arrive he is otherwise absent."[5]

How much we have to learn from George Webber's experience! It can teach us that stewardship is also God's call, not to take Christ to some place from which he is absent, but to discern where God in Christ is already decisively engaged in our world and then to ponder how we can adequately respond to God's love that is already there.

*Therefore, this kind of stewardship has primarily to do, not with the church, but with the world.* Stewardship is not "only the means" to the end of mission but is itself "the church's mission"; or, to reverse the phrase, "the mission of the church *is* its stewardship."[6] God gives us stewardship, not as a mere means for supporting the church, but as the church's mission for serving the world. Furthermore, God promises all the support needed by servant people for that mission.

Gustavo Gutierrez believes that, when we recognize our identity and vocation as God's people, church renewal will happen:

> For this renewal cannot be achieved in any deep sense except on the basis of an effective awareness of the world and a real commitment to it. The changes in the Church will

be made on the basis of such awareness and commitment. To seek anxiously after the changes themselves is to pose the question in terms of survival. But this is not the question. The point is not to survive, but to serve. The rest will be given.[7]

*When stewardship is shaped by grace, it evokes faith and love, rooted in the worship of God.* This worship, or liturgy ("the work of the people"), is not confined to holy places, but happens wherever people are engaged with God and humankind in creation and history. Contemplating God's great design for the world, and eager that the readers fully comprehend its meaning for the church's mission, the writer of Ephesians bursts into praise to God:

> For this reason I bow my knees before the Father, from whom every family in heaven and on earth is named, that according to the riches of his glory he may grant you to be strengthened with might through his Spirit in the inner man, and that Christ may dwell in your hearts through faith; that you, being rooted and grounded in love, may have power to comprehend with all the saints what is the breadth and length and height and depth, and to know the love of Christ which surpasses knowledge, that you may be filled with all the fulness of God (3:14-19).

In singing the praise of "the love of Christ which surpasses knowledge," Ephesians adds to the conventional three dimensions of height, depth and breadth a fourth dimension of length. It is a way of pointing to the impossibility of fully grasping the manifold wisdom of God.[8] It is akin to the psalmist's way of celebrating God's grace that embraces the whole universe:

> Whither shall I go from thy Spirit?
>     Or whither shall I flee from thy presence?
> If I ascend to heaven, thou art there!
>     If I make my bed in Sheol, thou art there!
> If I take the wings of the morning
>     and dwell in the uttermost parts of the sea,
> even there thy hand shall lead me,
>     and thy right hand shall hold me.
>                                 Psalm 139:7-10

These four expansive dimensions of breadth, depth, height and length shatter the cage of words that has held stewardship hostage.

They free stewardship from telling bad news about us—and for proclaiming good news about God. They free it from resorting to gimmickry—and for helping us discern how to be part of God's doing! They free it from losing its life in "saving" the church—and for finding its life in "serving" the world. In short, these dimensions of the love of Christ free stewardship from groans—and for gratitude. At long last, thank God Almighty, stewardship is freed from its captivity!

Although Ephesians does not fully define these four dimensions of God's love revealed "in Christ," it does pray for "power to comprehend" what they are. To assist with that task God offers us the gift of the indwelling Christ. Our responsive faith and love become "the manner in which, and the means by which, Christ inhabits the heart."[9] When God's gift is thus received, Ephesians believes we will know Christ's love which surpasses knowledge and be filled with all the fullness of God.

W. M. Clow, in *The Cross in Christian Experience*, links these four dimensions of Ephesians 3:18 with John 3:16.[10] Not only does that help with comprehending divine love that surpasses knowledge, but it also prompts the wonder and gratitude that so often find their best expression in that "work of the people" called worship.

*"For God so loved the world"*: When Christ dwells in our hearts through faith and love, we experience God's love as that of "the Father from whom every family in heaven and on earth is named" (3:14-16), in whom all things are united "in heaven and...on earth" (1:10), so that all humanity may "have access in one Spirit to the Father" (2:18). That comes alike to Jews and Arabs, Americans and Russians, Sandinistas and Contras; to Jane Fonda and Phyllis Schafley, Fidel Castro and Ronald Reagan, Madalyn Murray O'Hair and Jerry Falwell, to you and to me. The love of God puts its arms around the whole world—and expects the church to do the same. This is the *breadth* of stewardship!

"For God so loved the world *that he gave his only Son*": When Christ dwells in our hearts through faith and love, we experience "the immeasurable riches of [God's] grace in kindness toward us" (2:7), "even when we were dead through our trespasses" (2:5), so that we have been "made alive" (2:1) and "are no longer strangers and sojourners, but...fellow citizens with the saints and members of the household of God" (2:19). Yes, Mary Magdalene, Zaccheus, Saul of Tarsus, Augustine, John Newton, and others like you and me have been turned from lust, greed, hatred, fanaticism, and selfishness toward social usefulness that has blessed, and is blessing, the human family. The love of God reaches into the depths of sin to redeem people for such purposes and expects the church to do the same. This is the *depth* of stewardship!

"For God so loved the world that he gave his only Son *that whoever believes in him*": When Christ dwells in our hearts through faith and love, we are lifted up by "the immeasurable greatness of the power of God in us who believe, according to the working of his great might" (1:19), and find ourselves "strengthened with might through his Spirit in the inner [person]" (3:16). In 1948 at a conference in Europe, I heard Chinese Christian K.H. Ting say, "It's never a matter of the church being too weak to be missionary, but rather of the church not being missionary enough to be strong!" Still strong and standing tall in the Lord, he serves today as a bishop in the vigorously growing church in China. We can count on it: The love of God empowers servant people, through faith, to surmount their problems and to fulfill their mission. This is the *height* of stewardship!

"For God so loved the world that he gave his only Son, that whoever believes in him *should not perish but have eternal life*." When Christ dwells in our hearts through faith and love, we experience God's resurrection power which "raised Christ from the dead" (1:20) and which has also "raised us up with him, and made us sit with him in the heavenly places" (2:6), thereby filling us "with all the fulness of God" (3:19). Our God whose steadfast love endures for ever is in the world blessing us and all generations to come— and expecting the church to be a blessing also. This is the *length* of stewardship!

Shattering our small theologies, Ephesians dares us to view stewardship in four dimensions, remembering that "the love of Christ surpasses knowledge." Our task is like that of the Mother Superior in "The Sound of Music" who tried to deal with Maria, a girl whose expansive spirit could no more be contained in a convent than a cloud, a wave, or a moonbeam could be captured in a human hand.

Though we cannot catch stewardship and pin it down, we venture this modest risk, taking care not to imprison it again in a cage of words:

Stewardship is
God's grace working God's purpose out in the world,
in, with and through us, who,
in grateful response to God and through faith in Jesus Christ,

34

enter into a covenant relationship
with the empowering Spirit of God
that blesses all of creation.

With that working definition in mind, Eph. 3:20-21 offers us a doxology with which to respond to God. It also increases our expectancy of just what might happen in the church and in the world if we dare to respond fully to God's amazing grace in gratitude and faith:

Now to [God] who by the power at work within us is able to do far more abundantly than all that we ask or think, to [God] be glory in the church and in Christ Jesus to all generations, for ever and ever. Amen.

## NOTES

[1]Douglas John Hall, *The Steward: A Biblical Symbol Come of Age.* Friendship Press, 1982, p. 129.
[2]Arthur Miller, "The Death of a Salesman," *Best American Plays—Third Series 1945-1951,* edited by John Gassner. Crown Publishers, 1952, p. 47.
[3]Hall, *The Steward,* p. 128.
[4]Davie Napier, *Song of the Vineyard: A Guide Through the Old Testament.* Revised Edition, Fortress Press, 1981, p. 149. Personal conversation with Davie Napier confirmed that essential prophetism as he defines it sees God's "decisive engagement," not only in history and all interhuman relationships, but in creation as well.
[5]George W. Webber, *Today's Church: A Community of Exiles and Pilgrims.* Abingdon, 1979, pp. 23, 27-30.
[6]Hall, *The Steward,* p. 130-131.
[7]Gustavo Gutierrez, *A Theology of Liberation.* Orbis Books, Maryknoll, 1973, p. 262.
[8]Markus Barth, *The Anchor Bible,* Vol. 34. Doubleday & Co., 1974, pp. 395-397.
[9]*Ibid.,* pp. 370-371.
[10]W. M. Clow, *The Cross in Christian Experience.* Hodder & Stoughton, 1908, pp. 52-64. Subsequent references in the text are to verses in Ephesians.

# II

# Sin as Rebelling Against God's Grace

# 6

## *Worshiping the Creature, and Descending into Hell*

While some people respond to God's "plan for the fulness of time" with praise, others endorse Omar Khayyam's proposal:

> To grasp this sorry Scheme of Things entire...
> shatter it to bits—and then
> Re-mould it nearer to the Heart's desire![1]

Following that script Adam and Eve strove to "be like God, knowing good and evil" (Gen. 3:5). Their defiance of God and God's way in favor of themselves and their own way began a trail of broken relationships, alienating people from God, from one another, and from the created order. In their story is mirrored the story of all people. Although what could be known about God was plain to them, Paul charged that they had foolishly "exchanged the truth about God for a lie and worshiped and served the creature rather than the Creator" (Rom. 1:19, 25).

Of course, Paul was describing the problem of sin, or, perhaps more properly, of people as the responsible authors but also the poor victims of sin, the ones who are blinded by it and closed to the truth.[2] Calling sin the "No which opposes the divine Yes," Karl Barth detects its presence wherever people turn aside from the grace of their Creator, thereby destroying the possibilities of their creaturely beings and radically compromising their own destinies.[3]

This sin that clings so closely to us visits us in many guises. Medieval theologians named Seven Deadly Sins, with Pride as Queen, and with Envy, Wrath, Gluttony, Sloth, Sensuality, and Greed as members of her court. Karl Barth believed three forms of sin—pride, sloth, and falsehood—made the atonement of Jesus Christ necessary.[4] This chapter focuses on pride, not because it is the key to every human situation, as feminist theologians tell us,[5] but because of its role in shaping western culture, the context in which we are called to be stewards of God.

Within self-centered people, Karl Barth suggests, pride prompts "the mad desire to be as God," leading them to rob God of that which is only God's. When this "mad exchange takes place," the obviously outstanding feature of world history stands revealed, namely, the all-conquering monotony of the pride in which people have always lived to their own detriment and to that of their neighbors.[6]

The play, "The House by the Stable," imaginatively portrays Queen Pride tempting Man, her lover, to make this "mad exchange." Man's response to Pride mirrors our own sinful natures:

MAN:
You are my worshipful, sweet Pride; will you be so arrogant always to others and humble to me? Will you always make me believe in myself? I am Man, but before you came, Pride, I was half-afraid that someone or something had been before me, and made me and my house, and could ruin or cast aside. But when I look in your dove's eyes, Pride, and see myself there, I know I am quite alone in my greatness, and all that I have is quite my own.[7]

"I am Man...I know I am quite alone in my greatness, and all that I have is quite my own!" Such is the essence of an *imago hominis* (image of humanity) that Douglas John Hall calls the formative image of modern western culture since the fourteenth century. This image contains an idea "at best questionable to Christian belief, and at worst the essence of sinful presumption: the idea of man's mastery of nature and history.... The concept of mastery implies that it lies within the power of the one who claims mastery to do what he wills."[8]

Valerie Saiving agrees. She believes the "modern era"— stretching from the Renaissance and Reformation up to very recent times, and reaching the peak of its expression in the rise of capitalism, the industrial revolution, imperialism, and the triumphs of science and technology—can be called the "masculine age par excellence" because it "emphasized, encouraged, and set free precisely those aspects of human nature which are peculiarly significant to men."[9]

So, with "man as master" over the past six centuries, how fares our modern world? Despite Paul Tillich's prophetic judgment that this tutelage was leading our civilization inexorably toward destruction and sounding its death knell with the "guns of August" on August 1, 1914,[10] World War I merely added exuberance to the refrain: "I am man…I know I am quite alone in my greatness, and all that I have is quite my own."

When World War II ended, and as the Cold War escalated in 1950, Kermit Eby offered an "Invocation to the Hydrogen Era" at a Conference on the Church and Economic Life at Detroit. As he began, his words prompted critical reflection on developments fraught with life-and-death consequences for the human family:

> We meet today in the potential glare of the hydrogen
>     bomb.
> We may see more clearly by it or be blinded.
> History will judge us.
> The hydrogen bomb is the culminating accomplishment of
>     a civilization that has professed Christianity.
> Out of Christian Russia came Bolshevism and the
>     Communist State.
> Out of Christian Italy came Mussolini and the Fascist State.
> Out of Christian Germany came Hitler and the Nazi State.
> Out of Christian United States came Hiroshima.[11]

As he continued, his words framed a call to confession for ministers—and churches—more infatuated with success than with faithful witness to God's claim upon their lives:

> We have accepted the coca-cola concept of religion.
> We produce an effervescent, scintillating, sparkling
>     sermon,
> attractively bottled in pseudo-psychological
>     terminology,
> pleasing to the consumer, even if it causes a few
> spiritual hiccups, and available for all customers
> at the fairly standard rate of the
> weekly contribution.
> Every Sunday on the pulpit:
> the pause that refreshes.
>
> After nineteen hundred and fifty years we have
>     arrived
> at the hydrogen bomb and the coca-cola concept of
>     religion.[12]

But alas! Many chose to greet the hydrogen era, not with penitence, "God, be merciful to me a sinner!" (Lk. 18:13); but with arrogance, "I am Man...I know I am quite alone in my greatness, and all that I have is quite my own."

More recently, James Douglass, a contemporary prophet, warned that "we live alongside the steady preparation for nuclear holocaust as unseeing as were the onlookers of Nazi genocide." He went on to ask:

What is Trident?
Trident is the end of the world.
What do you mean?
Trident is a nuclear submarine being built now which will be able to destroy 408 cities or areas at one time, each with a blast five times more powerful than the Hiroshima bomb. Trident is 2,040 Hiroshimas. One Trident submarine can destroy any country on earth. A fleet of Trident submarines (thirty are planned) can end life on earth.[13]

Yet even the 1981 launching of a nuclear submarine christened "Corpus Christi" (Body of Christ) aroused only enough protest to cause President Reagan to change its name to "City of Corpus Christi!" Despite that, we can still hear the refrain: "I am Man...I know I am quite alone in my greatness, and all that I have is quite my own."

"Man as master"—and nuclear Armageddon waiting in the wings! But even if nuclear holocaust does not happen, Dorothee Soelle warns: *The Arms Race Kills Even Without War.*[14] Military expenditures usurp funds needed for social and economic programs and babies die of malnutrition. Or we can recite a litany of ecological disasters like Appalachia...Love Canal...Agent Orange...Times Beach...Acid Rain...Chernobyl. And, with "man as master," a half billion people are starving, 1.2 billion are without pure water, 1.3 billion are inadequately housed, and one-third to one-half are without access to health services of any kind. All this, yet still no widespread demand for a change in the way "Spaceship Earth" is presently being administered!

Worshiping and serving the creature rather than the Creator has indeed gotten us a remolded "Scheme of Things." Furthermore, it has gotten us a new religion as well, for, in pursuit of fame, wealth, security, or whatever,

people sooner or later create gods. But gods never leave their makers alone. Because people put themselves in a position of dependence on their gods, invariably the moment comes when those things or forces gain the upper hand. The things or forces control their creators as idols, as gods who can betray their makers. It is conceivable then that the means to progress which our own hands have made—the economy, technology, science and the state—have become such forces today, imposing their will on us as gods.[15]

The psalmist warned people who thought to free themselves from God of the subtle enslavement awaiting them: "Their idols are silver and gold, the work of men's hands.... Those who make them are like them; so are all who trust in them" (Ps. 115:4, 8). Lest we think we are talking about mere objects, J. C. Massee warns that "an idol is anything which has a greater formative influence in the life of men than has the spirit of the living God."[16] Before we can be God's instruments "for the healing of the nations" (Rev. 22:2), we must identify those idols and the ways they squeeze us—their makers—into their molds. Without such painful diagnosis, there is no healing for us and our world.

While idolatry never leaves its makers alone, its consequences inevitably play havoc also in the wider human family. Sin never stays at home. It is a social gadabout whose vocation is to curse. The Genesis stories of garden, brothers, flood, and tower are "progressive variations on a theme" of pride: People willfully sin against God, and the ensuing alienation ripples forth to engulf the earth and all who dwell therein.[17] Paul's analysis of idolatry's social effects in Romans 1:26-32 is a stark commentary on the progressive degeneration of evil: "There is nothing static in evil; it cannot be arrested at any given point...those who abandon God lack the power to check the spread of corruption in every part of their experience."[18]

From among the idols competing with God for our loyalties today, greed, growth, and security demand our closest scrutiny. Having insinuated themselves into our way of living, it is difficult to distinguish their service from what we are called to offer God. When the Israelites were tempted to worship both God and idols, God spoke, "You shall have no other gods before me" (Ex. 20:3). When the Colossians faced similar temptation, Paul wrote, "Christ is all, and in all" (Col. 3:11). Why? Because idols shape us for their service, not God's; and because our obeisance to them curses ourselves and others. Preoccupation with their service keeps us from being God's stewards.

42

By discerning the difference between serving God and serving idols, we may yet restore the faded beauty of stewardship, rediscovering it as the best way of honoring God and blessing the earth and all who dwell therein. But the brightness of God's way will never be fully appreciated until we confront the utter darkness of worshiping idols; so, for now, we are about to take a journey into hell!

NOTES

[1]Omar Khayyam, *Rubaiyat*, tr. by Edward Fitzgerald. Grosset & Dunlap Publishers, 1946, p. 117.

[2]Karl Barth, *Church Dogmatics*, Vol. 4, Pt. 1. T. & T. Clark, 1956, p.138.

[3]*Ibid.*, pp. 144, 140.

[4]*Ibid.*, pp. 142-144.

[5]Susan Nelson Dunfee, "Christianity and the Liberation of Women." Ph.D. dissertation, Claremont Graduate School, 1986.

[6]Barth, *Church Dogmatics*, Vol. 4, Pt. 1, pp. 421-22, 507.

[7]"The House by the Stable," a Christmas play, quotation from a class sermon for which the student could supply no footnote, nor have I been able to find the source.

[8]Douglas John Hall, *Lighten Our Darkness: Toward an Indigenous Theology of the Cross*. Westminster Press, 1976, p. 46-47. Also see pp. 43-50.

[9]Valerie Saiving, "The Human Situation: A Feminine View," from *Womanspirit Rising: A Feminine View*, ed. by Carol P. Christ and Judith Plaskow. Harper & Row, 1979, p. 35.

[10]Hall, *Lighten Our Darkness*, p. 43. Hall writes, "Paul Tillich frequently said that the nineteenth century ended on August 1, 1914. He meant that that image of man was shattered by the 'guns of August.'"

[11]Kermit Eby, "Invocation to the Hydrogen Era," an address delivered at the Conference on the Church and Economic Life at Detroit, 1960; first produced in *The New Populist* and reprinted by permission of the author in a leaflet published by Disciples Peace Fellowship, Indianapolis, Indiana.

[12]*Ibid.*

[13]James W. Douglass, "Living at the End of the World," a portion of which article is printed in Douglas John Hall, *The Steward: A Biblical Symbol Come of Age*. Friendship Press, 1982, p. 118.

[14]Dorothee Soelle, *The Arms Race Kills Even Without War*. Fortress Press, 1983.

[15]Bob Goudswaard, *Idols of Our Time*, (originally published as *Genoodzaakt goed te wezen*, 1981; translated by Mark Vander Vennen) Inter-Varsity Press, 1984, p.13.

[16]J. C. Massee, *The Gospel and the Ten Commandments*. Fleming H. Revell Co., 1923), pp. 44-45.

[17]Davie Napier, *Song of the Vineyard: A Guide Through the Old Testament*. Revised Edition, Fortress Press, 1981, p. 48.

[18]Gerald R. Cragg, Exposition on Romans, *Interpreter's Bible*, Vol. 9. Abingdon, 1954, p. 401.

# 7

# An Idol Named Greed

"Why do so many middle and upper middle class North American Christians feel poor?" Ellis Cowling posed an answer in his book, *Let's Think About Money*.[1] Later, in a chalk illustration, he brought his diagnosis to life for me.

Let us visualize a circle containing a figure representing our annual income. Then let us draw an arrow from the center to the outer rim, indicating that, whatever that figure may be, most of us spend it all! Few imagine getting by on anything less, for already we are having trouble making ends meet.

While we are struggling with the problems of life, enter modern advertising, suggesting ways to end our "woes." This or that new product, we are promised, will soon have us as satisfied as those people featured in the ads. Their not-so-hidden methods persuade us that those "goods" will bring us ease and happiness.

Whence the money to purchase these things? Luckily, an unexpected salary increase enlarges the circle, and soon we own those coveted products. The arrow now reaches to the outer rim of the second circle. Then, all too quickly—"I'll give you six months, no more!" Ellis Cowling warned—an aftershock comes. The new wears off those gadgets, but without delivering the promised happiness. Life has surely played a trick on us!

Once again we are at the end of our means, dismayed not at the seller's promises but at our wrong buying. Dragging our new boat to the lake every weekend no longer affords the same keen pleasure, so we begin coveting a backyard swimming pool to save us that long trek. Never questioning whether happiness can be bought, we set sights on other gadgets for which other raises will be spent.

43

44

Enlarging circles represent our new income, with that arrow soon pressing against their outer rims. How sad this "same song, third (fourth, fifth...) verse, little bit louder, little bit worse," accompanied by the crescendo of its one-word lyric: more, More, MORE, MORE!

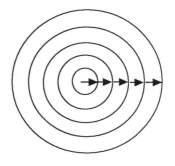

In this process lies the reason most middle and upper middle class North American Christians *feel poor*, and *talk poor*.[2] Adoring and wanting things we do not have, we can never acquire enough to satisfy all our desires. Ellis Cowling believed this attitude characterizes modern materialists who worship not their present possessions but what they do not own. In practice, this "adoration of the unpossessed" is a kind of idolatry that "flourishes along with our devotion to the Christian faith."[3]

For many, this idolatry has more formative influence on their lives than the living God. Its gods of the marketplace are too easily worshipped. Its scriptures—modern advertising—are unthinkingly heeded. Its promised rewards—happiness, security, and the good life—are blindly trusted. Its consequences—loving things and using people—sneak up on us. Its name is GREED.

But let us be clear. Material things are part of God's good creation. Jesus prayed for daily bread, knowing that we must *have* some things if we are to *be*. However, after meeting life's basic necessities, if continuing accumulation of things becomes the end for which we live, greed enters and stewardship exits.

Two classical Greek words delineate this contrast. *Oikonomia* describes household management that blesses the whole family; *chrematistike* "expresses the pursuit of self-enrichment, for ever greater monetary possessions, if need be at the expense of others."[4] Thus Bob Goudswaard's warning that in western civilization "economics" is increasingly shaped, not by the stewardly concern of *oikonomia*, from which the word is derived, but by the greedy selfishness of *chrematistike*.

This is clearly mirrored in our patriarch, Jacob, whose name meant "he supplants," or "he supersedes by treachery." In their mother's womb he struggled with his twin brother Esau, trying to supplant him even at birth. As he came forth "his hand had taken hold of Esau's heel" (Gen. 25:26).

Jacob continued to covet Esau's station in life as they grew to manhood. Craftily he studied his brother, bided time, then answered quickly when opportunity knocked. Knowing Esau better than Esau knew himself, Jacob caught him hungry, played to his weakness, then walked away with a birthright bought for some bread and pottage (Gen. 25:27-34).

Still Jacob was not satisfied; he wanted more. Conniving with his mother, he tricked his blind father Isaac out of the blessing due to Esau. When Isaac expected Esau, Jacob came, announcing, "I am Esau your first-born." It sounded like Jacob's voice, but Isaac was fooled by the smell of Esau's clothing that Jacob wore and by the touch of what felt like Esau's hairy hands, but was instead goatskins covering Jacob's hands. So Jacob got Isaac's blessing, but Esau's curse, "Is he not rightly named Jacob? For he has supplanted me these two times. He took away my birthright; and behold, now he has taken away my blessing" (Gen. 27:36).

Fearing Esau's anger, Jacob fled to Haran where Laban, his uncle, welcomed him with room, board, and a job. During the next twenty years first one, then the other, outwitted each other. Jacob lived up to his name, creating not "shalom" but dissension that finally set him fleeing home to Canaan:

> Thus [Jacob] grew exceedingly rich, and had large flocks, maidservants and menservants, and camels and asses. Now Jacob heard that the sons of Laban were saying, "Jacob has taken all that was our father's; and from what was our father's he has gained all this wealth." And Jacob saw that Laban did not regard him with favor as before.
>
> Genesis 30:43—31:1-2

So Jacob returned from abroad, very successful in his "pursuit of self-enrichment, for ever greater monetary possessions, if need be at the expense of others."[5] Though God continued to be at work upon his life, presently he was still beholden to the service of the idol, GREED.

How much we can learn from Ellis Cowling and from Jacob! (1) When things become our center of value and the ends of our striving; (2) when self-interest is the primary norm for determining how things are to be acquired and used; and (3) when people are used as mere means or tools for serving our ends; then, whatever our other professions of faith in God, GREED is the lord or idol of our lives.

1. Jacob made "status" and "things" (birthright, blessing, and fortune) his center of value and the ends of his striving. Since the Renaissance, "man as master" has followed suit. Edging God out of the world (Bonhoeffer), the industrial revolution made "goods" our center of value, ascribing to them the power to usher in "the good life." As industries in affluent societies caught up with meeting basic human needs, productive capacities shifted toward satisfying wants. Then, as producers and advertisers joined hands to create and develop desires not previously existing, wants, not needs, governed the economic scene.[6]

John Kavanaugh sees this as a major challenge to faith for those *Following Christ in a Consumer Society*. As idols shape those who make them, so economics shape us. Based on expanding consumption, blessed with a superabundance of goods and services, guided by the values of consumption, marketing, and producing, our economic system well knows the kind of person most suitable for its purposes. "When people...have most of their needs fulfilled, how are you going to get them to continually want and buy more? Is it possible that it would be more financially rewarding if people were conditioned to be dissatisfied cravers rather than appreciators of the goods of the earth?"[7]

Each year more than fifty billion advertising dollars are spent to make us cravers of what we do not own. In 1957 Vance Packard sounded the alarm about the "hidden persuasion" shaping us. Psychological studies of subsurface desires and drives lay bare our vulnerable points, enabling advertisers to fashion, bait, and drop their hooks in the sea of prospective customers. So, Packard warned, "Let the buyer beware!"[8] In many Christians the adoration of the unpossessed comfortably flourishes alongside our professed devotion to God, and few have enough insight or courage to give this idol its rightful name, GREED.

2. In coveting things, Jacob let self-interest chart his course, much like that rich fool in Jesus' parable:

> "What shall I do, for I have nowhere to store my crops?" And he said, I will do this: "I will pull down my barns, and build larger ones; and there I will store all my grain and my goods. And I will say to my soul, Soul, you have ample goods laid up for many years; take your ease, eat, drink, be merry."
>
> Luke 12:17-19

Jacob listened to the counsel of GREED: "Pursue goods without concern for God's will and your neighbor's welfare. Live the sin with an 'I' in the middle lifestyle,[9] and you can't go wrong. That's norm enough for guiding your behavior."

Since this has been one of the marks of the image of humanity that has formatively influenced western civilization during the past six centuries, we should not be surprised by its shaping influences on our culture, economics, and politics.

In 1776, as if it were an unwitting birthday present to the new nation, Adam Smith published *The Wealth of Nations.* There he contended that the individual acting in his or her own self-interest would do that which in the aggregate would also be in the best interest of all. The Invisible Hand would orchestrate socioeconomic life in such a way that the common good would best be served by an economic morality of principled self-interest. *The Wealth of Nations* became the capitalist text and America the home of capitalist individualism.[10]

Fifty years later, after an extensive visit to the United States, Alexis de Toqueville published *Democracy in America.* Contrary to Adam Smith, he saw individualistic self-interest seeking its own rather than the common good. Of those who had gained or kept enough to look after their own needs, he wrote:

Such folk owe no man anything and hardly expect anything from anybody. They form the habit of thinking of themselves in isolation and imagine that their whole destiny is in their hands.... Each man is forever thrown back on himself alone, and there is danger that he may be shut up in the solitude of his own heart.[11]

In 1974 that danger loomed large in an article on "Lifeboat Ethics: The Case Against Helping the Poor," by Garrett Hardin. He advised each rich nation, viewed metaphorically as a lifeboat of limited capacity, to resist the temptation of trying to live by the Judeo-Christian ideal of being "our brother's keeper" (Gen. 4:9). That sort of conscience, intent upon bringing complete justice to poor nations, would guarantee complete catastrophe, not only for the richer nations, but for all. Therefore, Garrett contended, survival for the rich nations requires constant surveillance to keep the poor out of their lifeboats![12]

3. Poor Jacob! The ethics of greed slowly squeezed him into its mold: The more he loved things, the more he used people. In his obsessive quest for self-enrichment, Jacob increasingly perceived

Esau and Laban as "tools" to gain his own ends rather than as "brother" and "uncle." No wonder the sons of Laban murmured, "Jacob has taken all that was our father's; and from what was our father's he has gained all this wealth" (Gen. 31:1).

That game plan is still popular, as *USA Today* made clear in a cover story entitled, "Foreigners flood Mexico with plants." That article estimated that the 588 foreign-owned production plants in Mexico at the end of 1982 would increase to 1,500 by the end of 1988! And why that "flood"? The sub-headline answered, "The reasons: cheap labor, drop in peso, tax breaks."

> (1) Cheap labor: Mexico's hourly wages ($1.02) are 27% lower than Korea's ($1.39) and 39% lower than Taiwan's ($1.67).
> (2) Low capital costs: The peso has plummeted in value, from 700 pesos to the dollar in 1986 to 2,290, so land and equipment are cheap.
> (3) Tax breaks: Under USA law, companies can ship USA-made components to [these production plants] for assembly. No duty is levied on the USA-made content when the finished goods come back.[13]

With new eyes to see GREED, how disquieting is that article's information! Aware of how business shapes us to be dissatisfied cravers for more, encourages us to make self-interest the norm of our striving, and tempts us to use people as the means for achieving our ends, we shudder.

But GREED does not stand alone, for it gives birth to another idol named GROWTH. So let us continue our descent into hell to meet the second member of this trinity of Evil which proposes its "still more excellent way" for ordering the life of our world.

## NOTES

[1]Ellis Cowling, *Let's Think About Money: How to Live and Give on What You Earn.* Abingdon, 1957, p. 15.

[2]Thomas E. Ludwig, Herold Westphal, Robin J. Klay, and David G. Myers, *Inflation, Poortalk, and the Gospel.* Judson Press, 1981. "Is there a bright side to the gloom and doom of sky-high inflation and the ever shrinking dollar? For Christians the answer is an optimistic 'yes!' Utilizing insights from economics, psychology, philosophy, and biblical theology, the

49

authors "analyze how 'poortalk' keeps men and women constantly dissatisfied and always driving for more.the discussion of how greed has infected the American dream underlines the need to be free from consumerism and the insidious borrow-and-buy syndrome" (quoted from back cover).

Cowling, *Let's Think About Money*, p. 23.

Bob Goudswaard, *Capitalism and Progress: A Diagnosis of Western Society.* Eerdmans, 1979, pp. 211-212.

*Ibid.*

John Kenneth Galbraith, *The Affluent Society.* Houghton Mifflin Co., 1958, p. 156.

John Francis Kavanaugh, *Following Christ in a Consumer Society.* Orbis Books, 1981, p. 46.

Vance Packard, *The Hidden Persuaders.* Pocket Books, 1957, p. 30.

Karl Menninger, *Whatever Became of Sin?* Hawthorn Books Inc., 1973, p. 13.

Bruce C. Birch and Larry L. Rasmussen, *The Predicament of the Prosperous.* Westminster Press, 1978, pp. 51-52.

As quoted in Robert Bellah, Richard Madsen, William M. Sullivan, Ann Swidler, and Steven M. Tipton, *Habits of the Heart: Individualism and Commitment in American Life.* Harper & Row, 1985, pp. 37-38.

Garrett Hardin, "Lifeboat Ethics: The Case Against Helping the Poor," *Psychology Today,* Vol. 8, No. 4, September 1974, pp. 38 ff.

"Foreigners Flood Mexico with Plants," Section B Cover Story, *USA Today,* Friday, March 11, 1988. Also see "Pressures on Industrialized Societies," in Werner Fornos, *Gaining People, Losing Ground: A Blueprint for Stabilizing World Population.* Science Press, 1987, pp. 22-23. The 1983 law enticing corporations into Mexico (nine hundred U.S. companies alone in the first four years) also exempts them from having to pay health benefits, unemployment compensation, and the like, thereby depriving Mexican workers of what U.S. social justice standards consider to be just compensation. Furthermore, U.S. workers are losing their jobs. Does this stampede across the border by corporations from "free-world" nations, and do their practices in employing and compensating Mexican people, bear witness to "economics as if people mattered"? (E.F. Schumacher).

# 8

# *An Idol Named Growth*

Yes, thanks to the idol named GREED, "adoration of the unpossessed" helps give birth to another idol named GROWTH. Avid pursuit of goods generates the powerful "thrust for growth" pervading the industrialized societies of our world. Robert Stivers believes "the gradual acceptance by the vast majority of American citizens of...values and life-styles...supportive of economic growth...has become virtually a religion."[1]

Nobel Prize winner and physicist Dennis Gabor echoes a similar concern: "'growth addiction' is the unwritten and unconfessed religion of our times."[2] Bob Goudswaard warns that economic growth becomes an idol when we put unconditional *trust* in economic and technological progress as guides to the good life and mediators of happiness, thereby treating something of *some* worth as if it were of *ultimate* worth.[3]

Again, let us be clear. Some economic growth has brought much good and is essential to human well-being. However, when this means becomes an end that edges God out by investing human systems and structures with godlike qualities, such growth becomes cancerous. Those who worship GREED soon fall on their knees before GROWTH as it panders to their insatiable craving for more. Thus Nicholas Wolterstorff contends that "what we find of fundamental worth in our modern world-system is less accurately described as *increased production* than as *increased mastery of nature and society so as to satisfy our desires.*"[4]

Paul warned that those who worship and serve the creature, not seeing fit to acknowledge the Creator, are soon filled with all manner of wickedness (Rom. 1:24-32). Their idolatry spawns wrath and fury, tribulation and distress, until every part of life is infected by the spreading corruption and subjected to God's righteous judgment (Rom. 2:1-11). Five manifestations of the idol named GROWTH will show how *systemic sin* is fueled by *personal sin* lurking in lifestyles harmful to the human family. Even without detailed diagnosis, they illustrate how dissatisfied craving (worshiping the idol named GREED) is tied to the structures of economic growth (worshiping the idol named GROWTH).

*Economic Imperialism.* Imperialism signifies a nation's policies and practices to extend power and dominion over the political and economic life of other areas. Interestingly, even the death throes of colonialism after World War II served as birth pangs for a new form of economic imperialism, as former overlords (and others) opportunistically put colonialism to new service. Today, that resurrected system still locks poor countries into what Arthur Simon calls "a losing arrangement":[5]

1. Political independence has not prevented the economic system of colonialism from continuing to be used to enrich the First World at the Third World's expense.

2. Lacking the capital to industrialize, Third World export earnings come primarily from raw materials whose commercial values are purposely kept low by First World buyers.

3. Worsening terms of trade follow, due to the widening price gap between Third World exports (raw materials) and First World imports (manufactured goods).

4. Heavily dependent on income from single crops (coffee, cocoa, bananas, etc.), the Third World produces luxuries for First World export rather than food for itself.[6] These crops are also highly vulnerable to wildly fluctuating commodity prices.

5. Tariffs and quotas are often imposed on Third World nations that turn their raw materials into manufactured goods. First World "free market" beliefs quickly waver when faced with competition from labor-intensively produced goods.

Proponents of fairness should not rest comfortably with these structures that guarantee "our" winning and "their" losing. But we devotees of the GROWTH idol are too busy enjoying "the good life" to change the game rules that work so well for us.

*Profit Maximization.* In 1891, as the neo-Calvinist movement began in the Netherlands, Abraham Kuyper charged "laissez-faire" mercantilism with foreshadowing deep trouble.

The thirst and the chase for money, the holy apostle taught us, is the *root of all evil;* and as soon as this angry demon was unchained...no deliberation was sharp enough, no cunning sly enough, no deceit shameful enough in order, through superiority in knowledge, position, and basic capital, to acquire money and ever more money at the expense of the socially weaker.[7]

A century later, wherever profits matter more than people, that demon is still unchained. It roams freely in all industrialized nations. For example, when multinational corporations watched infant formula sales drop due to declining birth rates in developed nations, booming birth rates in developing countries caught their eyes. Marshalling capital and technology, they baited and cast the hooks of hidden persuasion into the Third World sea. Just how good the fishing was in Brazil came to light in a 1977 supermarket sales print-out reporting a profit rate of 72 percent for infant formulas as compared to one between 15 percent and 25 percent for all other supermarket products.[8]

But as profits soared, so did the Third World infant death rate[9]—and the alarm of those for whom people mattered more than profits. A global boycott was organized against Nestle, the world's largest multinational food corporation and the major manufacturer of infant formula. In 1977 Nestle's $10 billion of sales was larger than the gross national product of 108 countries![10] In 1978 Nestle had 140,000 employees and 294 plants in 52 countries, and did about 20 percent of its business in the Third World. Nestle's was boycotted because, of all the infant formula multinationals, it was least responsive to cries for change in its destructive marketing practices in the Third World.

Though the Davids of the world seemed poorly matched against this Goliath, they won! Of Nestle's 1984 decision to abide by the World Health Organization Code regulating infant formula marketing procedures, a February 1988 United Church of Christ newsletter reported, "Finally it agreed that the lives of infants must come before corporate profits." But then, these sad words:

> Now, some evidence indicates that Nestle is giving, encouraging and even pressuring hospitals to take large quantities of infant formula supplies in violation of the Code. In 1986, the World Health Assembly resolved that Nestle and others in the industry must stop violating the Code....

What is next? Clearly, Nestle and the other multinational

companies must be made to live up to their promises and know that our concerns will not fade. Nestle is being told they must stop this practice that is endangering the lives of the newborn and infants by October 4, 1988, or the boycott will be reinstated.[11]

That was no idle threat. Nestle having chosen not to live up to its promises, the Davids of the world again resumed their boycott against this corporate Goliath and its policies of profit maximization, that angry demon, still unchained.

*De-capitalization.* Another evidence of the idol of GROWTH in the United States is the aura of holiness surrounding talk of "capitalism." Indeed, many have richly benefited from the capitalist way of conducting economic life. Marxist predictions of class warfare between a burgeoning proletariat of exploited workers and a narrowing elite of rich owners and managers have not come true. Some profit shared in fair wages has helped create a middle class. Other profit reinvested in capital expansion has provided more jobs and products essential to the good life. When capitalism works this way, we call it "good."

Sad to say, capitalism presents another face to the very poor in the United States. In 1988, 32.4 million people, or 13.6 percent of the U. S. population, lived below the official poverty level of $9,300 for a family of three and $11,200 for a family of four. Nearly 40 percent of these people try to survive on  incomes of less than half of the poverty line. Numbered among these poor are 11 percent of the White population, 27 percent of all Hispanic and 31 percent of all Blacks.[12]

Unfortunately, poor people in the United States are the ones most seriously impacted by unemployment. Many of them have also been underemployed, earning the national minimum wage of $3.35 an hour, enacted by Congress in 1982. Although Congress regularly grants generous salary increases to its own members, its first minimum wage increase in eight years became effective only in April, 1990, when the "working poor" began earning $3.80 an hour.

Sadder still, capitalism has also failed to present "a kinder and gentler" face to most of the people of the Third World. Already we have noted the industrial rush into Mexico these days, lured by the chance to maximize profits because of cheap labor, low capital costs and tax breaks. Those suppressed wages will not transform poor workers into a middle class.

The motto now is to work for the world market rather than for the internal market. Effective demand on the national market is not, and is not intended to be, the source of demand for national production; demand on the world market is, and is intended to be, the source of market demand. Therefore there is no reason to raise the wages of the direct producers, because they are not destined to purchase the goods that they produce. Instead the goods are supposed to be purchased on the world market far away.... Thus, there is a polarization of income, not only between developed and undeveloped countries on the global level, but also on the national level, with the poor getting poorer and the rich getting richer.[13]

Regrettably, most profits from these operations will not be invested in the host countries to raise their miserable standards of living, but whisked elsewhere on the globe for further maximization. Consequently, such businesses give credence to Marxist predictions of class warfare, thereby sowing the seeds of "inevitable revolutions."[14] Rather than blessing the Third World with a rising middle class and decent standards of living, they de-capitalize it instead:

Europe did not "discover" the underdeveloped countries; on the contrary, she created them.... Some of the people with whom the Europeans came into contact were, of course, relatively primitive. But nearly all of the people encountered in today's underdeveloped areas were members of viable societies which could satisfy the economic needs of the community. Yet these societies were shattered when they came into contact with an expanding Europe.[15]

The consequences of our worship of the idols of GREED and GROWTH have gone abroad to curse. But industry's "outward bound" trek curses us as well, for we badly need these corporations to help deal with our endemic unemployment/underemployment problems and to reinvest their profits in hurting areas of our own economy. In other words, by their foreign junkets our nation, too, is being de-capitalized!

*Ecocide.* On "Earth Day" in 1970, smoldering private concern about "ecology" broke into public blaze. By 1989 *Time* departed from its annual Man of the Year designation by naming the "endangered Earth" its Planet of the Year. Citing natural and human-caused disasters from earthquakes to overpopulation to pollution of the world's beaches, and calling for "a universal crusade to save the planet," *Time* warned: "This year the Earth spoke, like God warning Noah of the deluge."[16]

My concern about ecology, the totality of relations between organisms and their environment, followed my study of "The Relationship of Soil Welfare to Soul Welfare" in the mid-1950s. That brought new reverence for "Mother Earth," and growing alarm about fatal wounds being dealt to an average of eight inches of topsoil that spells the difference between global life and death. Later, my reverence embraced "Brother Water" as I read of the near demise of Lake Erie, and even now "Sister Air" as I shudder over reports showing ozone loss over the northern hemisphere about three times greater than scientists had expected.[17]

Roger Shinn identifies three kinds of ecological hazards being created by the technologies of growth:

1. catastrophic accidents, of which the Soviet nuclear disaster at Chernobyl is a dramatic example;

2. the exhaustion of non-renewable natural resources, due partly to increasing population and more to rising consumption;

3. the saturation of the atmosphere, the earth's waters, and sometimes the soil with pollutants.[18]

Sometimes, flagrant abuse has drawn sharp rebuke; for example, the asbestos industry is no more, although our society is still dismantling its lethal legacy. Nevertheless, industries whose thrusts of growth-at-any-cost cause ecological disasters try to deflect the finger of blame. Even unions become defensive when jobs are threatened by concerns about ecology; thus the union bumper sticker charging a growing lobby of "friends of the earth" with POLLUTING THE ECONOMY!

Some environmentalists wither before such pressure from the advocates of growth, for the idol of GROWTH exercises great power in our society. Yet Richard Grossman argues that

far from being side effects or impacts, today's inequities and ecological messes are the societal arrangements for control and quantity....the purpose of growth politics is control and the purpose of finances and technologies which serve growth politics is M-0-R-E. The purveyors get their control by destroying people's ability to decide where money goes; they get their M-0-R-E by destroying the earth. And they masquerade their purposes and their mayhem within the metaphors of growth.[19]

*Unholy Alliances.* Gunnar Myrdal analyzes the parties to this masquerade, as well as the mayhem that follows in its wake. He begins with colonialism's built-in mechanism that led colonial powers to ally themselves with privileged groups in the colonies who shared their interest in maintaining the economic status quo. After political independence, neo-colonialism perpetuated those alliances for self-serving purposes. First World business people winked at upper-class regimes, no matter how repressive, if they supported a business climate.

Many enterprises also carry a historical load of reckless exploitation, corruption, and even plain fraud from earlier times.... There are many...such potential scandals that must be prevented from exploding by keeping close to the oligarchy and often by bribing them.[20]

In examining "The Economic Dimension" of *Nicaragua: The Land of Sandino*, Thomas Walker offers a classic illustration of such masquerade and mayhem.[21] In three centuries, Spanish colonialists took the relatively advanced agrarian society they found in Nicaragua and set it firmly on the *road to underdevelopment*. They extracted all the wealth they could, oriented the economy toward external rather than internal markets, and created a wealthy elite with a solid stake in the status quo.

Then, just before the Spanish left in the 1820s, coffee was introduced to Nicaragua and by the 1870s had prompted a strong global market. That encouraged the ruling elite to monopolize and redirect the country's productive capacity toward cultivating that one export product. Using trickery, violence, and self-serving legislation, they got the fertile lands and cheap labor needed for such production. While the profits enriched them and their foreign partners, the poor suffered.

During the following century so few benefits "trickled down" to the poor that, by the late 1970s, 20 percent of the population received 60 percent of the national income, while 80 percent made do with the other 40 percent. Worse still, the poorest 50 percent had access to only 15 percent of the national income, for an average of about $200 per person per year.

Atop this pyramid of human misery from 1937 to 1979 perched the Somoza family. As father Anastasio and his two sons, Luis and Anastasio, used dictatorial power to amass a financial empire, the United States was a loyal ally, even as "inevitable revolution" toppled them on July 19, 1979.

> By the time the dynasty was overthrown the family had accrued a portfolio worth well in excess of $500 million (U.S.)—perhaps as much as one or one-and-a-half billion dollars. The Somozas owned about one-fifth of the nation's arable land and produced export products such as cotton, sugar, coffee, cattle, and bananas. They were involved in the processing of agricultural products. They held vital export-import franchises and had extensive investments in urban real estate. They owned or had controlling interests in two seaports, a maritime line, the national airline, the concrete industry, a paving-block company, construction firms, a metal extruding plant, and various other businesses including Plasmaferesis de Nicaragua, which exported plasmas extracted from whole blood purchased from impoverished Nicaraguans. Finally, the Somozas had huge investments outside Nicaragua ranging from real estate and other interests in the United States to agricultural enterprises throughout Central America to textiles in Colombia. Shortly before their overthrow, they even bought controlling interests in *Vision*, the Latin American equivalent of *Newsweek* or *Time* magazines.[22]

"It seems to me I've heard that song before!" Same tragic ballad, with but a change of names: Somoza...the Shah...Duvalier... Marcos...Noriega. But alas! in that ballad one name stays the same, namely, the United States. Nor will that change until GREED and GROWTH quit convincing U.S. policymakers that these unholy alliances are in the national self-interest.

But we must not delay, for our tour of hell moves deeper into the darkness where we will meet the final member of a trinity of Evil. What GREED causes us to crave and GROWTH enables us to grasp, an idol named SECURITY promises to help us keep.

58

NOTES

[1]Robert L. Stivers, *The Sustainable Society, Ethics and Economic Growth.* Westminster Press, 1976, p. 34.

[2] *Ibid.*

[3]Bob Goudswaard, *Capitalism and Progress: A Diagnosis of Western Society.* Eerdmans, 1979, p. 152.

[4] Nicholas Wolterstorff, *Until Justice and Peace Embrace.* Eerdmans, 1983, p. 65.

[5]Arthur Simon, *Bread for the World.* Paulist Press, Revised Edition 1984, pp. 104-105.

[6]Frances Moore Lappe & Joseph Collins, *Food First: Beyond the Myth of Scarcity.* Houghton Mifflin Co., 1977. This book reveals that the Third World has enough arable land and resources to meet its own basic needs if "food first" were its priority; however, so much of its arable land has been co-opted for raising cash crops for export to the First World that its own people go unfed.

[7] Abraham Kuyper, *Christianity and the Class Struggle,* trans. Dirk Jellema. Piet Hein, 1950, p. 35.

[8] This print-out, *Supermercado Moderno,* February 1977, was discovered by the Interfaith Center for Corporate Responsibility (425 Riverside Drive, New York, NY 10027) and cited in Leah Margulies, "A Critical Essay on the Role of Promotion in Bottle Feeding," PAG Bulletin, Vol. VII, No. 3-4. September-December, 1977, p. 77.

[9]James B. McGinnis, *Bread and Justice: Toward a New International Economic Order.* Paulist Press, 1979, p. 214. See Chapter 12, "Nestle: A Case Study of a Multinational Corporation," for indepth background of this boycott in progress at that time. This chapter also touches on many difficulties encountered in formula feeding: scarcity of pure water; problems in getting fuel for fires to boil water and to sterilize bottles; lack of sanitation and of sewage and garbage disposal; swarms of flies in and outside of homes; no refrigeration; illiteracy as a barrier to reading and following instructions; minimum wages and insufficient money to buy an adequate amount of formula. While I worked for nine weeks as a volunteer at Christian Medical College and Hospital in Vellore, India, in 1982, a pediatrician told me that a can of Nestle's Lactogen (infant formula) cost 35 rupees and contained an eight-day supply of milk for an infant; four cans a month would cost 140 rupees. Daily wages for unskilled workers at that time were 5-7 rupees daily for men and 4-5 rupees daily for women. A father would have to work 20 full days at the highest daily wage simply to pay for those four cans of Lactogen! One can easily see why bottle feeding is a major cause in the deaths of babies in the Third World. In contrast, mothers' breast milk is very economical, nutritious, easy to digest, always at hand. It needs no preparation and has no microbes that can make a baby ill.

[10] On KFWB Radio Station, Los Angeles, on April 27, 1988, news item reported that Nestle, still the world's largest food company, had reached the $28 billion annual sales level.

[11]"Nestle: Will the Boycott Resume?," *Courage in the Struggle.* February, 1988,

Vol. 3, No. 2, published monthly by the Office for Church in Society for the United Church of Christ, 105 Madison Avenue, New York, NY 10016.

[12] Barbara Howell, "U.S. Hunger: The Problem Grows," Background Paper No. 106, June 1988, *Bread for the World* (802 Rhode Island Avenue N.E., Wahington, D.C. 20018).

[13] Andre Gunder Frank, *Reflections on the World Economic Crisis*. Hutchinson, 1981, p. 131.

[14] Walter LaFeber, *Inevitable Revolutions: The United States in Central America*. W. W. Norton & Co., 1983. In his Introduction (p. 14), LaFeber cites the "Jekyll and Hyde personality" of North American capitalism. "U.S. citizens see it as having given them the highest standard of living and most open society in the world. Many Central Americans have increasingly associated capitalism with a brutal oligarchy-military complex that has been supported by U.S. policies—and armies. Capitalism, as they see it, has too often threatened the survival of the many for the sake of freedom for a few." Henry Cabot Lodge, U.S. Ambassador to the United Nations, offered this advice during an Eisenhower Administration cabinet meeting that was discussing ways of responding to the threat that the new Castro government posed to the hemisphere: "We should focus on the Declaration of Independence rather than the Communist Manifesto where [the focus] has been, and in doing so we should not endeavor to sell the specific word 'Capitalism' which is beyond rehabilitation in the minds of the non-white world."

[15] Keith Griffin, "Underdevelopment in History," in *The Political Economy of Development and Underdevelopment*, ed. Charles K. Wilber. Random House, 1973, pp. 72, 74-75.

[16] "Earth: 'Planet of Year,'" *Enid Morning News* (Enid, Oklahoma). Sunday, December 25, 1988, p. A-14.

[17] Donnella H. Meadows, "The Hole Story," in the *Los Angeles Times*, Sunday, April 3, 1988, Section V, p. 1.

[18] Roger L. Shinn, "Technology: Opportunity and Peril" in *The Egg*. Summer 1986, Vol. 6, No. 2, p. 4. This is a quarterly journal of the Eco-Justice Project and Network of the Center for Religion, Ethics, and Social Policy and Genesee Area Campus Ministries and of the Eco-justice Working Group of the National Council of Churches of Christ in the U.S.A. and the Joint Strategy and Action Committee.

[19] Richard Grossman. "Growth as Metaphor, Growth as Politics," in *The Egg*. December 1985, Vol. 5, No. 4, p. 4.

[20] Gunnar Myrdal, *The Challenge of World Poverty: A World Anti-Poverty Program in Outline*. Random House-Vintage, 1970, pp. 72-73, 264-65.

[21] Thomas W. Walker, *Nicaragua: The Land of Sandino*. Westview Press, Second Edition, Revised and Updated, 1986, see Chapter 4, pp. 55-74.

[22] *Ibid.*, pp. 65-66.

# 9

# An Idol Named Security

"But there's nothing wrong with wanting to feel secure," you say. Abraham Maslow would quickly agree. In his theory on the hierarchy of human development,[1] Maslow stated that realization of human potential required the meeting of (1) *basic* needs and (2) *meta* needs. One's basic physical and psychological needs had to be reasonably met before meta—or spiritual—needs for meaning and being could be satisfied. Accomplishing this involved a lifelong process of becoming or self-actualization.

Failure to meet these basic physical and/or higher spiritual needs results in "illness" or, more aptly, in a state of deprivation. Being deprived of basic physical needs almost always precludes actualization of the higher levels of potential, while reasonable satisfaction of basic needs provides a "cure" and permits a resumption of growth.

Now the plot thickens, for the first two stages of Maslow's human development model involve basic survival and security needs. Viewed superficially, our whole globe appears to face a crisis of deprivation: developing nations preoccupied with meeting basic survival needs, and developed nations obsessed with basic security needs. But that view will not hold, for we are haunted by the First World poor, penniless and powerless, fighting daily for survival, and by the Third World rich, surfeited with ill-gotten wealth and power, worrying daily about security. However, since the rich and powerful so often make policy, this much is clear: For most of them, their security needs, not the survival needs of the poor at home or abroad, have priority in shaping life in today's world.

So what are we doing to meet our security needs? As individuals and families we are arming ourselves to the teeth and adopting fortress mentalities. First, pistols under our pillows, then double and triple locks on the doors, then iron grills on the windows, then electronic burglar alarms, then a Doberman on the prowl in a yard encircled by a chain-link fence, then....

As United States citizens, we have turned ourselves into a National Security State mobilized for global competition over armaments, monetary balances and scarce resources.[2] First, we grant the state absolute sovereignty to pursue the goal of guaranteed security, then pay taxes to acquire weapons of mass destruction, then employ morality to rationalize our national self-interests, then persuade people to support wars, both hot and cold, against the "enemy" of the moment, then....

All the while we have been caught up in what Bob Goudswaard calls "the role reversal of idol and idol worshiper":

Though initially we thought ourselves able to use and control weapons technology, the reality is that increasingly it controls us. We surrender to the further testing and expansion of the arsenal of destruction, an arsenal which years ago went over our heads. A god has arisen, and fear and hypnosis are its tools of terror. We trust it for our security. It requires unbearable financial sacrifice and perhaps even human sacrifice.... We must realize that gods never loosen their grip on people. If nations choose gods, they become slaves to their gods.[3]

Why have we done this? Frankly, being frightened, we have increasingly trusted the idol of SECURITY to free us from fear.

1. We have been frightened by the Soviet Union, charged by our policymakers with being the superhuman enemy responsible for the international communist conspiracy. "But the death knell of that conspiracy has been sounded and a dismantled Berlin Wall has given Europe—and our world—a face-lift!" you rejoin. Yet, our fear still lives, as a March, 1990, headline reminded: "Security: How much is enough?" The article began:

Defense Secretary Dick Cheney warned Friday that the United States would become "a second-class power" if the military budget was cut in half this decade, as some defense experts are urging. "There is no question that changes in the world do justify long-term budgetary savings, but there is a point below which we cannot go if we want to remain a superpower," Cheney said in a speech to the National Newspaper Association.[4]

Therefore, as in therapy, we must identify and understand the roots of our fear if we are to be set free from it. Typical of the Cold War rhetoric motivating United States foreign policy since World War II are these words of General Matthew D. Ridgway:

> Grave as are the domestic issues which confront us—inflation, the poverty level, drug abuse, crime and the erosion of moral principles—they are of lesser importance than the potential menace of a foreign state which sees us as the only major barrier to the expansion of its power, and once this barrier is demolished or neutralized, a clear open path to the seizure of the riches of this, the most affluent people on earth.

> In this savage, brutal, amoral world we must, if we value our independent national existence and our fundamental principles, insure that our armed forces are adequate for our security against the most dangerous challenge any foreign power is today capable of presenting.[5]

Even granting that the Soviet Union and the United States have had reasons to fear each other, does that justify our U.S. nuclear arsenal now capable of "overkilling" that enemy thirty times? Or the national debt expended to acquire it, tripled since 1980, and surpassing three trillion dollars by April, 1990? Fear for our security has anesthetized us from thinking about what this legacy will mean to generations unborn. Yet, still frightened, we keep building three new nuclear weapons every day, adding more billions to that debt.

On the Eve of Thanksgiving, 1989, president George Bush hailed the dramatic changes sweeping Europe as "a joyful end to one of history's saddest chapters" and as a golden opportunity for East and West to "once and for all end the Cold War."[6] However, still paralyzed by fear, we are incapable of cashing in on this incredible "peace dividend."

2. We are also frightened by the little people of the Earth who, angered by the "long train of abuses"[7] visited on them by the unholy alliances of First and Third World elites, resort to revolution to change their status quo. Forgetting from whence we came and the idealism that gave us birth as a nation, we do to them today as we were done to by King George in 1776.

Since World War II our leaders have been adept at blaming Third World discontent on the international communist conspiracy. Third World elites have eagerly agreed, thereby justifying the harsh repression they have employed to preserve their profits and the status quo. Since that explanation no longer suffices, what they fear the most now stands revealed, namely, the reordering of those societies according to the norms of social justice. Nicholas Wolterstorff contends:

there ought in fact to be revolutions there—profound restructurings of these inequitable and oppressive social orders. The injustices suffered are vastly greater than those that were experienced by American colonists at the hands of the British when they fought their own revolution. It is sheer cynicism to label every move for reform a communist plot. The lesson to be learned from restlessness of oppressed people is that injustice must be rectified, not that oppression must be instituted.... The mighty wind of security legislation and armament buildups sweeping across the world today produces only more insecurity.... Uneasy sleeps the tyrant. One cannot preserve privilege and at the same time enjoy security. The path to security is justice.[8]

On December 17, 1989, Brazilian voters celebrated their first free presidential election since a U.S.-inspired military coup overturned Joao Goulart and his democratically elected government in 1964. Focusing on the upwelling of democratic spirit in Europe at that time, the U.S. media virtually ignored events in Brazil, the world's sixth most populous nation, whose population of 160 million exceeds that of all the countries of Eastern Europe combined.

Questioning such outrageous oversight, Lawrence Weschler offered some clues. Candidate Luis Inacio da Silva, although losing by a razor-thin percentage, was raising the question of what the First World was doing to the Third. Refuting the military generals' national security doctrine that a third world war had already started between the forces of godless communism and those of Christian liberty, da Silva declared:

I will tell you that the third world war has already started, a silent war, not for that reason any less sinister. This war is tearing down Brazil, Latin America, and practically all the third world. Instead of soldiers dying, there are chil-

64

dren; instead of millions wounded there are millions of
unemployed; instead of the destruction of bridges there is
the tearing down of factories, schools, hospitals, and entire
economies…. It is a war over foreign debt, one which has
as its main weapon interest, a weapon more deadly than
the atom bomb.[9]

Small wonder our leaders fear that kind of talk, for it puts at risk
our lucrative investments in the Third World. So, not their survival,
but our security dictates our foreign policy.

3. We are frightened by the very weapons our leaders promise
will make us safe and secure. In 1886 Alfred Nobel discovered
dynamite and promptly called it "security powder!" Earlier he had
written, "I hope to discover a weapon so terrible that it would make
war eternally impossible."[10] Was similar naiveté at work among
those who developed the atom bomb that fell on Hiroshima? Or
among those working still on ever more lethal weaponry? Instead,
they are setting loose upon the earth a Frankenstein that chills us
with forebodings of nuclear winter.

What prompted Alfred Nobel to give vast sums of money from
his weapons factory to the Nobel Peace Prize? Could it have been
remorse over naively expecting weapons to create peace? If that did
not motivate him then, might it now? "Consider the history of
NATO (North Atlantic Treaty Organization) strategy: We first
considered the use of nuclear weapons *impossible* (1948), later *im-
probable* (1970), still later *probable* (with the rise of the concept of a
limited nuclear war in 1979), and now some experts say that their
use is *inevitable.*"[11] Happily, other experts have turned the
"Doomsday Clock" a few minutes backwards from midnight due
to recent world events. Nevertheless, until we begin in earnest to
dismantle not only the Berlin Wall but nuclear weaponry, we have
every right to be frightened.

Is the national security state—or the idol named SECURITY
making good on its promises? The talk of many politicians is not
reassuring. John F. Kennedy's "missile gap" in 1960 and Ronald
Reagan's "window of vulnerability" in 1980 may have contributed
to victory in their presidential campaigns, but both statements were
based on "fright" more than "fact." Lack of security was their
common theme song.

Behind our feelings of insecurity lies idolatry's inability to calm
human restlessness. St. Augustine calls us to pray: "O God, you
have made us for yourself, and our hearts are restless till they find

their rest in you." Instead, we exchange the truth about God for a lie and worship and serve the creature rather than the Creator (Rom. 1:25).

*Our idolatrous quest for national security subverts our values.* Early in his presidency (April 1953), Dwight Eisenhower called the arms race a theft from our world's poor and a pursuit of security that was not a way of life but "humanity hanging from a cross of iron."[12] In his farewell message (January 1961), he warned that unwarranted influence by the military-industrial complex would endanger our liberties and democratic processes. Across his career he learned that "there is no way in which a country can satisfy the craving for absolute security—but it can easily bankrupt itself, morally and economically, in attempting to reach that illusory goal through arms alone."[13]

Unfortunately, not Eisenhower's quotations but George Orwell's book has provided the script for our national drama. In that book, *1984*, written in 1948, Orwell foresaw the emergence of national security states, perpetually mobilized against each other, stockpiling weapons and fighting over global resources. Truth and traditional values would be transformed into "national security values" by "Big Brother." Dissidents would be eliminated as threats to national security. Others would be immobilized by the silence of fear.

> But in the very failure to respond and speak out against human injustices, true religious values are successfully subverted by the values of national self-interest. To condone, or silently abide, lying, stealing, false pride, hate, murder, violence or injustice on the part of the state (regardless of the national security rationale being used), while condemning it in individuals, is to feed a cancer that will cut away at the flesh and soul of spiritual life till there are but dead bones and emptiness—a spiritual vacuum impotent to inspire faith in God or to motivate human behavior on the side of life and humanization.[14]

These 1977 words of the Misches, along with Orwell's book and Eisenhower's speeches, provided an eerie backdrop for the Iran-Contra Scandal which began unraveling in 1986. In testimony before a congressional committee investigating that scandal (July 1987), Lt. Col. Oliver North admitted lying to Congress, planning to sell arms to a terrorist state, violating a law passed by Congress, destroying evidence, and considering the president and everyone on his staff above any law, including the Constitution. Afterward, many called him "a national hero"; but the *Lexington* (KY) *Herald-Leader* dissented:

> Let's be clear about the issue here. The issue is not the wisdom of supporting the Nicaraguan rebels, or Congress' on-again, off-again support for them. The issue is the rule of law in a democratic society.

> Judged in that context, Oliver North is not a hero. He is a dangerous zealot who feels no remorse over breaking any law in the pursuit of his own vision of patriotism.

> If North were truly patriotic, his allegiance would be to the Constitution, the democratic process it established and the laws passed under that process. Instead, he has sought at every turn to undermine these foundations of American democracy.[15]

Meanwhile, increasingly insecure, we grow more frightened. As Maslow tells us, our fixation at this stage of growth blocks the actualization of higher levels of spiritual development, both as individuals and as a nation. The idol of SECURITY is not capable of effecting our "cure" so that we may pursue growth toward a human world order.

*Our idolatrous quest for national security destroys the lives of our world's poor.* The greater our insecurity, the more we see the world in terms of our fears rather than the needs of others. German theologian Dorothee Soelle challenges us to wake up to the consequences of our quest for security.

> How about us? Can we see, hear, touch? We live and obey and carry on in a state of apathy, of anesthesia, as if life had not changed in our ever more self-militarized country, as if the bomb could not touch us because it is meant only for others, only for later, only for a real emergency.

> No, it is here, it is inside of us and has anesthetized us. It rules over us. *The bombs are falling now* as the American peace movement puts it. For me this has a double meaning: the bombs are falling on the poorest of the poor. Every minute a child under two years of age dies of starvation. Another one is dying as I speak this sentence. The bombs are falling now on those we allow to die of hunger and other curable diseases....

The bombs are also falling on us. The death machine which we service, for which we think, carry on politics, go vote, invest, and train, this MIC (military-industrial complex) machine in which we are but a cog, determines our life. That is what is killing us! The arms race kills, even without war! Those who still think, who still feel, feel insecure in the security state. [16]

But "the bombs are falling now" has a triple meaning, for "low intensity war" rages in many lands. Low-intensity conflict is an effort "to defend threatened United States interests in conflict environments short of conventional war."[17] Toward that end three billion dollars in U.S. aid has been invested in El Salvador across the past decade; in recent years that has amounted to $1.5 million dollars daily.[18] Our return: seventy thousand people killed in an unabated civil war, and thousands of refugees seeking sanctuary in the United States. This low-intensity conflict

> integrates economic, psychological, diplomatic, and military aspects of warfare into a comprehensive strategy to protect "U.S. valuables" against the needs and demands of the poor…. It uses terror and repression to intimidate or punish, cosmetic reforms to pacify or disguise real intent, and disinformation to cover its bloody tracks. It defines the poor as enemy, consciously employs other peoples to die while defending "U.S. interests," and makes use of flexible military tactics.[19]

Sadly, U.S. foreign policy is playing by the same script in lands like Angola, Afghanistan, the Philippines. Clearly, our fears, not their needs, are shaping U.S. foreign policy around the globe.

How very true: The arms race is killing, with—and even without—war. Overkill and underfeed are walking together across the surface of our earth:[20]

> U.S. spending for defense exceeds the total annual income of the poorest billion people on earth.

> UNICEF estimates that for every $100 it spends, one child's life is saved. Using this basis, $1 billion from the arms race would save 10 million children.

> The price of one jet fighter could set up about 40,000 village pharmacies. The cost of a tank could provide storage facilities for enough rice to feed 20,000 people for a year or provide classroom space for 30,000 children.[21]

68

More tragically, developed nations, through arms merchants, have lured more than thirty developing countries to spend more on their military budgets than on health and education combined. Between 1970 and 1980 these countries' arms purchases grew almost 500 percent, from $3.9 billion to $19.5 billion. In fifty-four such lands a United Nations study found that each dollar spent on arms appeared to reduce agricultural output by twenty cents, thereby literally turning plowshares into swords—or jets.[22]

Overkill and underfeed! Those words may bother some, but not the merchants of death who have never had it "so good" and who praise the idol of SECURITY for the blessing of such lucrative markets. Indeed, as our short tour of hell ends, they are having a party with that trinity of Evil, GREED, GROWTH, and SECURITY, and lustily singing together, "Eat, drink, and be merry; for tomorrow we may die!"

NOTES

[1]Gerald and Patricia Mische, *Toward a Human World Order: Beyond the National Security Straitjacket.* Paulist Press, 1977, pp. 24-30. The Misches make imaginative use of Abraham Maslow's theory of human development in assessing the human crisis of the final quarter of the twentieth century and the viability of a human future.
[2]*Ibid.*, p. 53. See Chapter 3, "The National Security State," pp. 44-66, for a fuller elaboration of this post-World War II phenomenon which shapes and defines most of the nations of our world today.
[3]Bob Goudswaard, *Idols of Our Time.* Originally published in 1981; translated into English by Mark Vander Vennen and published by Inter-Varsity Press, 1984, pp. 72-75. See the entire sub-section, "A Complete Ideology," on these pages.
[4]*The Wichita* (KS) *Eagle*, March 17,1990, p. 1.
[5]Matthew B. Ridgway,"Leadership," Op Ed. Page, New York Times, November 14, 1972.
[6]"End to Cold War Sought by Bush," *Enid* (OK) *News and Eagle*, Nov. 23,1989, p. 1.
[7]*The Declaration of Independence*, July 4, 1776.
[8]Nicholas Wolterstorff, *Until Justice and Peace Embrace.* Eerdmans, 1983, pp. 122-123.
[9]Lawrence Weschler, "The Media's One and Only Freedom Story," Columbia Journalism Review, Vol. XXVIII, No. 6, March/April 1990.
[10]Goudswaard, *Idols of Our Time*, p. 65.
[11]*Ibid.*, p. 75.
[12]Dwight D. Eisenhower,"The Chance for Peace," address before the American Society of Newspaper Editors, April 16, 1953.

[13] As quoted in Richard Barnet, *The Economy of Death*. Antheneum, 1969, p. 21.

[14] Mische, *Toward a Human World Order*, p. 230.

[15] "Can a man who undermines the rule of democratic law really be a national hero?", an editorial, *Lexington* (KY) *Herald-Leader*, July 16, 1987, p. A-16.

[16] Dorothee Soelle, *The Arms Race Kills Even Without War*. Fortress Press, translated from the German, copyright 1982, by Kreus Verlag, English translation copyright,1983, pp. 101-102. Emphasis added.

[17] Joint Low-intensity Conflict Project, United States Army Training and Doctrine Command, "Joint Low-Intensity Conflict Project Final Report, Executive Summary," Fort Monroe, Virginia, August 1, 1986, p. 1.

[18] Jack Nelson-Palmeyer, *War against the Poor: Low-intensity Conflict and Christian Faith*. Orbis Books, 1989, p. 17.

[19] *Ibid.*, p. 42.

[20] Arthur Simon, *Bread for the World*. Paulist Press, Revised Edition 1984, p. 154.

[21] *Ibid.*, pp. 143-144.

[22] *Ibid.*, p. 151.

# 10

## *Turning from Hell's Gloom Toward the Noonday*

Indeed the Idols I have loved so long
Have done my credit in this World much wrong:
Have drown'd my Glory in a shallow Cup,
And sold my reputation for a Song.

Omar Khayyam[1]

"Abandon hope, all ye who enter here!"[2] These words over the gate of hell in Dante's "Inferno" also belong over the gangplank of the luxury liner that a variety of writers have portrayed as an image of our planet:

> This ocean liner is in danger of sinking, but not so much because of the hordes of hungry passengers clinging to the rail and massed together in its dirty and dangerous holds as because of the deportment of the first-class passengers. These passengers...have insisted on bringing along their automobiles, their freezers, their television sets, their kitchen disposal units, and their pets.... On the deck of the ship are amassed assorted tanks, airplanes, explosives, and a small army of guards, which the first-class passengers have brought along in order to assure themselves of a safe and undisturbed voyage.[3]

These 1977 words of Adam Daniel Finnerty were no doubt prompted by Garrett Hardin's 1974 proposal of "lifeboat ethics" and E.F. Schumacher's 1972 conclusion that

> The earth cannot afford, say, 15% of its inhabitants—the rich who are using all the marvellous achievements of

science and technology—to indulge in a crude, materialistic way of life which ravages the earth. The poor don't do
much damage; the modest people don't do much damage.... The problem passengers on Space-ship Earth are the
first-class passengers and no one else.[4]

If we Christians who are economically privileged cannot see
ourselves in this imagery, we will miss the impact of our worship
of GREED, GROWTH and SECURITY, and the import of Nathan's
words to David, "You are the man!" (2 Sam. 12:7). When will we
quit blaming the victims; admit that major changes in the political,
economic, and social structures of the world's life are long overdue;
and realize that the fate of other people's lives—and ours as well—
await basic changes in those structures as well as in our lifestyles?

Our difficulty in accepting a part of the responsibility for the
state of the world is that "Christianity itself" is "an integral part of
the problem!"[5] After describing North American society's aversion
to admitting negatives, Douglas John Hall contends that "Christianity is nothing more nor less than the official religion of the
officially optimistic society."[6]

The church pays a high cost for this "chaplaincy to the status
quo." "Sin" could not be made positive, hence Christians have
adjusted their doctrines to fit the mastering of the world.[7] The "whole
person" (body and spirit) was the Bible's concern, but Christians
have tended to "spiritualize" their faith, avoiding issues with a
"material" component, such as hunger, peace, and justice. The
"whole world" is under the Lordship of Jesus Christ, but Christians
have privatized their faith to avoid social-public action.[8] Forfeiting
a prophetic critique, Christians have retreated into their "comfort-
able worlds" of privilege and possessions, diminishing God's
sovereign rule of the "whole world."

The words of 1 Peter 4:17 counter these narrow perceptions of
ours and understand judgment as beginning with the church: "For
the time has come for judgment to begin with the household of
God." If we are still inclined to point the finger of blame elsewhere,
Reinhold Neibuhr warns: "A spiritual leader...who has lost his
illusions about mankind and retains his illusions about himself is
insufferable. Let the process of disillusionment continue until the
self is included."[9]

There are dangers in acknowledging our complicity in the sin
of the world and of the church. The unaccustomed sensitivity of a
bad conscience can spawn "a certain confusion and helplessness as

to future strategy"; nevertheless, Catholic theologian Johann Baptist Metz urgently counsels:

> Do not be afraid of the powerlessness of this bad conscience of yours. It is with this experience, in fact, that many things begin to happen. And in this situation of far-reaching radical change, it is the courage to have a bad conscience, and the perseverance not to allow oneself to be talked out of it, that may be the only way today to have a conscience at all.[10]

But amidst the bad news, there is good news to proclaim. "Judgment does not call for guilt but repentance, and hope is experienced as the forgiveness that frees us from guilt to make a new and creative response. The church cannot afford to be paralyzed by guilt when it should be witnessing to God's forgiveness."[11]

This reminds us that Dante's literary journey ended, not in hell, but in heaven, evoking Dorothy Sayers' comments:

> It is the deliberate choosing to remain in illusion and to see God and the universe as hostile to one's ego that is of the very essence of Hell. The dreadful moods when we hug our hatred and misery and are too proud to let them go are foretastes in time of what Hell eternally is. So long as we are in time and space, we can still, by God's grace and our own wills assenting, repent of Hell and come out of it....

> There is no power in this world or the next that can keep a soul from God if God is what it really desires. But if, seeing God, the soul rejects Him in hatred and horror, then there is nothing more that God can do for it.[12]

Dante's vigorous notion of free-will makes clear that persons must choose life with God or life without God.

William McElvaney, commenting on Jesus' encounter with the Gerasene demoniac (Mk. 5:1-20), sees that story as "a microcosm of the world as it is today": isolated, alienated, living among the tombs, and crying out for identity and meaning. This demoniac "is a collective and yet individualized picture of us all. He is in us. We are in him. We are fractured, bruised, and frenetic humanity."[13] Yet, that broken, demon-filled man first experienced Jesus as torment, then discovered that he had been healed and given a new identity and vocation.

> No picture of Jesus is biblically complete unless it includes Jesus the Tormenter, the bearer of God's disturbing love.

He torments our torment, both realized and unrealized. He disturbs our illusions with the truth in order to make us free. He torments our greed with the gospel of solidarity with others. He challenges our lovelessness with a life of risk and outreach. He calls into question our idolatry of despair with a message of hope. To neglect this dimension of our biblical heritage is to render the gospel trivial and insipid.[14]

Quickened by the disturbing grace of God, free will helps restore us to relationship with God who has made us for God's own self. The New Testament Greek word *metanoia*, translated repentance, means a radical change *(meta)* of mind *(nous)* that affects one's whole self. One turns away from that which leads to death and turns toward that which leads to life.

While in Nicaragua in 1986, our Witness for Peace group helped 115 members of the Christian farming cooperative at El Largartillo dedicate a school replacing one the Contras had previously burned down. It was named in honor of a young Swiss Catholic layworker, Maurice Demierre, who was helping with the rebuilding when the Contras killed him. Members of his family and of the family of his widow, Chantal, had also come from Switzerland to share in that dedication.

That fall I heard Chantal speak in Wichita, Kansas. After telling how profoundly her mother had been affected by her visit to Nicaragua, she said, "My mother left Nicaragua, crying, because her whole reference system had been broken!" A radical change of mind and heart had opened her up to a whole new life as a responsible citizen of the world.

On his way back home, repentance also happened to Jacob, full of anxiety about how his aggrieved brother Esau would receive him. During a sleepless night before their reunion, Jacob wrestled with God who gave him the new name Israel ("he who strives with God"). As he limped away from that encounter, he had a new identity. No longer wanting to enrich himself at others' expense, he desired to live out of a new covenant relationship with God and others. A new day—a future of promise—had dawned for that erstwhile supplanter! (Gen. 32:22-31.)

In summary: The first section of this book has set forth God's plan for the fullness of time and how God proposes to effect that plan. God will not do this alone, but only in cooperation with those who respond in faith. The second section has set forth humanity's alternative plan for ordering life on earth. It is not working. It is programmed not for life but for death.

The stage is set for the third and final section of this book. God has a plan, but will not carry it out alone; nor can humanity carry out that plan without God's help. Covenant relationship and stewardship affirm that God and humanity, working together, can do what neither can do alone.

Believing that ours is a time of transition from an old civilization that is dying to a new human order that is emerging, Gerald and Patricia Mische challenge us to look for signs not only of decay but of expectant birth.

> The birth image is apt. The healthy delivery of our shared future is not automatic. Nor will it be without pain. New birth seldom comes without pain....

> In the birth process, if the birth passage remains rigid and does not widen, the pain intensifies. The unborn life is in peril and the mother's life is endangered.

> This birth image provides insights into the pain being experienced in the human community today. Existing socio-political structures are too rigid and narrow to give healthy delivery to new stages of human growth and development struggling to be born....

> Our task now is not to fight against our pains and crises, reacting against the symptoms.... It is rather to recognize the positive pregnancy of our times, to work with the birth spasms, giving our energies to a widening of the birth passage, *making ready the way for the birth of a new stage in human development.*[15]

As partners with God in that birthing process, Jurgen Moltmann urges us to spurn "*re*volution," whose preoccupation with destroying past wrongs often keeps it from shaping a new future, and to embrace "*pro*volution," whose thrust is to create that which has not yet been present in history. "In provolution the human 'dream turned forward' is combined with the new possibility of the future and begins consciously to direct the course of human history."[16]

The "dream turned forward!" What fitting words to guide us toward a rediscovery of stewardship as God's grace working through our faith!

NOTES

[1]Omar Khayyam, *Rubaiyat*, tr. by Edward Fitzgerald. Grosset & Dunlap Publishers, 1946, p. 93.

[2]Dante Alighieri, *The Divine Comedy: The Inferno, Purgatorio, and Paradiso,* translated by Lawrence Grant White. Pantheon Books,1948, p. 5.

[3]Adam Daniel Finnerty, *No More Plastic Jesus.* Orbis Books, 1977, pp. 2-3.

[4]E.F. Schumacher, "Implications of the Limits to Growth Debate—Small is Beautiful," *Anticipation No. 13.* World Council of Churches, 1972.

[5]Douglas John Hall, *Lighten Our Darkness: Toward an Indigenous Theology of the Cross.* Westminister Press, 1976, p. 74.

[6]*Ibid.*

[7]*Ibid.*, pp. 98-103.

[8]Bruce C. Birch and Larry L. Rasmussen, *The Predicament of the Prosperous.* Westminister Press, 1978, pp. 48-54.

[9]Reinhold Niebuhr, *Leaves from the Notebook of a Tamed Cynic.* Willett, Clark & Colby, 1929, p. 91.

[10]Johann Baptist Metz, *The Emergent Church.* Crossroad Publishing Co.,1981, p.94.

[11]Birch and Rasmussen, *The Predicament of the Prosperous,* p. 143.

[12]Dorothy L. Sayers, *Introductory Papers on Dante.* Harper & Brothers, 1954, pp. 66-67.

[13]William K. McElvaney, *Good News Is Bad News Is Good News....* Orbis Books, 1980, p. 37.

[14]*Ibid.*, p. 38.

[15]Gerald and Patricia Mische, *Toward a Human World Order: Beyond the National Security Straitjacket.* Paulist Press, 1977, pp. 351-353.

[16]Jurgen Moltmann, "Religion, Revolution and the Future," an essay in *The Future of Hope,* ed. by Walter H. Capps. Fortress Press, 1970, p. 116.

# III

# Covenant as Context for Shaping Stewards

# 11

## *By Water God Claims Us for Service*

God plans to use the church to bless the world. After sharing the good news of God's Yes to all creation, the writer of Ephesians promises power to get that work done: "Now to [God] who by the power at work within us is able to do far more abundantly than all that we ask or think, to [God] be glory in the church and in Christ Jesus to all generations, for ever and ever. Amen" (3:20-21).

In every age God's Yes evokes two responses. While sin can only say No, faith says Yes to God by gratefully offering the "grace...given to each of us according to the measure of Christ's gift...for building up the Body of Christ" (Eph. 4:7, 12), thereby helping the church fulfill its mission in the world. Midway in many of his letters Paul used "therefore" as a signal to begin telling of faith's response to divine grace. Let me suggest that "therefore" is a perfect hinge between Ephesians 1—3 and 2 Corinthians 8:1-5, where Paul tells how God's power and grace, working through faith, brought glory to the church.

> We want you to know, brethren, about the grace of God which has been shown in the churches of Macedonia, for in a severe test of affliction, their abundance of joy and their extreme poverty have overflowed in a wealth of liberality on their part. For they gave according to their means, as I can testify, and beyond their means, of their own free will, begging us earnestly for the favor of taking part in the relief of the saints and this not as we expected, but first they gave themselves to the Lord and to us by the will of God.
>
> 2 Corinthians 8:1-5

That passage tells of an unheralded miracle, for out of severe affliction and extreme poverty came an abundance of joy and a wealth of liberality! Paul credited that mighty work not to the churches but to "the grace of God...shown in the churches." Behind the churches' action was the prevenient grace of God who had acted for them before they had done anything to deserve such love. That grace prompted their response.

As Ephesians 1—3 celebrates that amazing grace of God, it also reminds us of our "glorious inheritance in the saints" (Eph. 1:18), part of which was the new covenant God made with the house of Israel: "I will put my law within them, and I will write it upon their hearts; and I will be their God, and they shall be my people...for I will forgive their iniquity, and I will remember their sin no more" (Jer. 31:33-34).

Thus brought into covenant relationship by God's initiative, the people called church are commissioned to call forth others' faith, then to help shape them as stewards. In partnership with these stewards God intends to care for the world and everybody in it. That is what God's plan (*oikonomia*) is all about.

For this task of steward-making God has equipped the church with means of grace, often called sacraments. "Through both shaping and reflecting attitudes and assumptions about the value of persons, the sacraments play a profound role in forming Christians to act in their daily lives."[1] They point to God's way of self giving to us through a kind of love the New Testament called "'agape,' the unselfish pouring out of self for the benefit of another, without thought of return."[2] God makes this love known to us "definitively in the underlying sacrament, Christ," whose living presence becomes "audible and visible" again and again in the church's sacraments and means of grace.[3]

The faith that marked the Macedonian churches' response to God's self giving astounded Paul. The anatomy of their miracle best unfolds by heeding the internal clues in 2 Corinthians 8:3-5, which suggest that these three verses be studied in reverse order. Taking slight literary license to make each verse a complete sentence, this revised order reads:

vs. 5 - First, they gave themselves to the Lord and to us by the will of God—and this, not as we expected.
vs. 4 - Then, they began begging us earnestly for the favor of taking part in the relief of the saints.
vs. 3 - Finally, they gave according to their means, as I can

testify, and beyond their means, of their own free
will.

The movement and substance of these verses provide the frame-
work in Part III for examining faith's response to grace and for
revealing how covenant provides the context for making stewards.

The Macedonians' story began in idolatry (1 Thess. 1:9), but
God used churches Paul had planted in Macedonia to offer them
new life in Christ. The new covenant which Jeremiah had promised
was now theirs for the receiving. Liberation from their past, forgiveness for their sins, the abiding presence of God with them, the
fellowship of a community of faith, and a new future: These
gracious gifts of God awaited their response.

The Macedonians answered Yes: "first they gave themselves
to the Lord [being united with Christ] and to us [being united with
the church] by the will of God." According to the *Baptism, Eucharist
and Ministry* document of the World Council of Churches' Faith and
Order Commission, that is the meaning of baptism: "the sign of new
life through Jesus Christ [that]unites the one baptized with Christ
and with his people."[4] Representing unprecedented convergence
in the modern ecumenical movement, this document sees five
principal New Testament images illuminating God's self giving in
baptism. Taken together, they reveal more fully "how [the
Macedonians] turned to God from idols, to serve a living and true
God" (1 Thess. 1:9).

As the Macedonians turned from idols to God, their experience
was beautifully described by Paul: "You were buried with [Christ]
in baptism, in which you were also raised with him through faith
in the working of God, who raised him from the dead" (Col. 2:12).
Baptism initiated them into an ongoing process of *participation in
Christ's death and resurrection,* and of continually turning from the
ways of death to the ways of life, not by their own working, but by
the working of God.

Through that, they learned that "baptism...now saves you, not
as a removal of dirt from the body but as an appeal to God for a clear
conscience, through the resurrection of Jesus Christ" (1 Pet. 3:21).
Thus the Macedonians were no longer immobilized by sin and
guilt. *Conversion, pardoning and cleansing* had liberated them from
their past and opened for them a new future. Into the Macedonians'
cleansed lives from which sin had been cast out, baptism also brought
a wonderful gift: "Repent, and be baptized every one of you in the
name of Jesus Christ for the forgiveness of your sins; and you shall

receive the *gift of the Holy Spirit*" (Acts 2:38). The good news was that God had called them not to work alone but in Spirit-empowered partnership.

Baptism further expanded this partnership of the Macedonians and God through their *incorporation into the body of Christ*. How well Paul said that: "For by one Spirit we were all baptized into one body—Jews or Greeks, slaves or free—and all were made to drink of one Spirit" (1 Cor. 12:13). As they were drawn into a global community of support and service to the world, their provincialism was drowned in the waters of baptism.

This new covenant relationship between the Macedonians and God was to be not the sign of their privileged claim on God's love but rather *the sign of the kingdom* whose coming God intended as a blessing to all creation. They had literally been born again to be the people of God. Baptism, a sign of the service to which God was calling them, was a lifelong reminder that, "unless one is born of water and the Spirit, he cannot enter the kingdom of God" (Jn. 3:5).

Although not mentioned in this report of God's grace shown in the churches of Macedonia, baptism was assuredly the sign of God's self giving that shaped them for their service in the world. Not one but all five of these vivid images lifted up in the *Baptism, Eucharist and Ministry* document describe their spiritual formation. They were clearly "living into their baptisms"[5] that "once-in-a-lifetime experience that takes your whole life to complete."[6] No wonder the Macedonians first gave not their money but themselves to the Lord, for they had learned well this truth: "By baptism, God makes us Christians; because of our baptism we try each day to become disciples. But all hinges on what God has done for us through the Church."[7]

When the Macedonians had thus put on Christ in their baptisms, Paul surely reminded them: "And if you are Christ's, then you are Abraham's offspring, heirs according to promise" (Gal. 3:29). Even as their identities were to be henceforth shaped by their association with Christ, so were their vocations to be shaped by the promise God had given to Abraham: "I will bless you...so that you will be a blessing ...and by you all the families of the earth shall bless themselves" (Gen. 12:1-3).

By water God claimed those Macedonians for service—and in the covenant community of faith God still does the same today.

Baptism tells us who and whose we are. Baptism calls us to a life of stewardship. As believers in Jesus Christ and members of his church, God has made a covenant with us to be stewards of God's spiritual grace, God's unearned and unmerited love through visible material signs. God has called us to be God's sacrament, God's presence and activity in human history so that the world when it looks at how we live our lives within the church will see a sign of God's purpose for human life, and when it looks at how the church acts in society will see a sign of God's will for human life being manifested in history.

Our baptism provides us with a picture of who we really are and a picture of the world as God intends it to be. Throughout our lives we are to strive to live into that baptism.[8]

Stewardship without the steward is bare, as the Macedonian experience teaches us. It causes us to revalue baptism as a sacrament of God's self giving for shaping stewards in the context of the covenant community. What if the church made more of these rich meanings of baptism all year round? Would gimmickry still be needed to make people give money for the church's mission? Are we worrying about people's stewardship before we have helped them, by God's grace, to become stewards?

Dynamically conceived, baptism is a sign-act of God's constant self giving to us in the church. By reminding us of our covenant with God, it keeps us growing, as Ellis Cowling learned. We left him, back in Chapter 7, caught in the idolatry of adoring the unpossessed and mired in perpetual discontent symbolized by a maze of concentric circles. As time passed, he realized that the illusion gripping him could never relieve his dissatisfied craving. Even new salary raises could not long keep him happy.

With that thought God's grace was given new operating room in his life; and in faith Ellis Cowling did an about-face. His repentance (*metanoia*) is symbolized by the turn of that arrow on the diagram. Turning from perpetual misery about what he did not have, he began thanking God daily for what he did have. Trading idolatrous "pursuit of goods" for God's "pursuit of the Good," he began to find rest for his soul. Soon, God and he were doing things that nei-

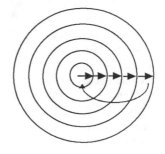

ther could have done alone, and a future bright with new possibilities lay ahead.

The person who best exemplified living into his baptism for me was Kirby Page. Gripped by a picture of the world as God intends it to be, he spoke, wrote, and acted out of the picture of who he really was. He traveled and spoke in all states of the U.S.A. and in forty-three nations, from World War I days until he died in 1957.[9] Better than anyone I have known, Kirby Page blended personal faith and social witness. Following seminary, he interspersed two decades of sustained study and writing and two decades of travel and itinerant preaching. A vital prayer life was the wellspring of boundless energy and joy that marked his activity. As he spent ten thousand of the nearly fifteen thousand mornings across those four busy decades in prayer, God blessed him...to be a blessing.[10]

His personal faith and social concern were rooted in deep convictions about God, people, and Jesus Christ as the supreme revelation of who God is and what we may become. For him there was no conflict between evangelism and social action. He believed God had called him to be a "social evangelist."

> An evangelist must bring about a conviction of personal sin, and a social evangelist must produce a consciousness of corporate iniquity. We sin as individuals and we sin as employers and as workers, as Caucasians and as Negroes, as Americans and as Russians. Salvation must be individual, and redemption must be corporate as well. The personal gospel is one side and the social gospel is the other side of the good news of God in Jesus Christ, our Lord.[11]

In Senator Joseph McCarthy's heyday I heard Kirby Page speak truth in loving ways that opened dialogue with hostile listeners. In him, prophet and pastor blended, for he cared enough for people to confront them with God's truth, which alone could bring peace of mind and peace on earth. When subjected to opposition and called objectionable names, he took comfort in Jesus' promise: "Blessed are you when men revile you and persecute you and utter all kinds of evil against you falsely on my account. Rejoice and be glad, for your reward is great in heaven, for so men persecuted the prophets who were before you" (Mt. 5:11-12).

Living into our baptism means being immersed day by day into covenant relationship with God who, in Christ and in the church, is shaping stewards to help bless this earth and all its people. The church is not a "being in itself," but the servant Body of Christ "for the sake of the world."[12]

Knowing that, the Macedonian Christians, Ellis Cowling, and Kirby Page gave themselves to the Lord to be such stewards. Baptism is a sign-act reminding us that God's amazing grace and self giving demand our souls, our lives, our all. Earlier we said stewardship has first to do with God, not us; but now we say it has everything to do with us as well. Christian stewardship requires nothing less than ALL that we are and have!

## NOTES

[1]James F. White, *Sacraments as God's Self Giving* . Abingdon, 1983, p. 93.

[2]*Ibid.*, p. 14.

[3]*Ibid.*, pp. 27, 13.

[4]*Baptism, Eucharist and Ministry*, Faith and Order Paper No. 111. World Council of Churches,1982, pp. 2-3. The emphasized phrases in the following paragraphs are from this document.

[5]John H. Westerhoff III, *Building God's People in a Materialistic Society*. Seabury Press, 1983, p. 37.

[6]Martin Luther, as paraphrased by William H. Willimon, *Worship as Pastoral Care*. Abingdon Press, p. 159.

[7]White, *Sacraments as God's Self Giving*, p. 43.

[8]Westerhoff, *Building God's People in a Materialistic Society*, p. 37.

[9]Living into his baptism through which God gave him his identity and vocation, Kirby Page left an indelible mark on me and our family. In 1951, while working with the Quakers, I accompanied him on a three-week speaking tour of his native Texas. In 1958, we named our youngest daughter, Jody Page Thompson.

[10]Kirby Page, *Kirby Page, Social Evangelist: The Autobiography of a 20thCentury Prophet for Peace*, ed. by Harold E. Fey. Fellowship Press, 1975, p. 73, 80.

[11]*Ibid.*, p. 56.

[12]Alexander Schmemann, *Sacraments and Orthodoxy*. Herder and Herder, 1965, p. 82.

# 12

## Through Prayer God Makes Us Part of the Global Family

What fun to see the musical, "Oliver," on Broadway! Quickly gripped by that little orphan's plight, we watched with mixed emotions as a man named Fagin befriended him. Though saddened by Fagin's designs to enrich himself at the expense of Oliver and the ragtag band of urchins he was training to be pickpockets, we were gladdened that they were being provided with "food, glorious food" and with the camaraderie of Fagin and of one another. Suddenly, before we knew it, we were caught up in the rollicking song inviting Oliver to "consider yourself one of the family." In global terms those lyrics echo in Karl Barth's words:

> What took place on Golgotha took place *pro me*, not exclusively but inclusively. It is *pro me* only because—first of all—it is *pro nobis*, for the whole world. I cannot think of it as having taken place *pro me*, except as I address God as "Our Father which art in heaven" and make the requests "Give us this day our daily bread, And forgive us our trespasses, Lead us not into temptation, But deliver us from evil." And now that Israel and the Gentiles have become one people in the death of Jesus Christ no limit can be set to this "us." Of myself I cannot be an object of the mercy of God except as I am one of the "us" to whom God has shown it without restriction.[1]

So does the word of God's grace come to us through the Lord's Prayer, helping us consider ourselves part of God's global family. No wonder Augustine included the Lord's Prayer in his list of the sacraments,[2] thereby affirming it as one of the principal ways in which he had experienced God's self giving.

That prayer assuredly became a means of grace in the disciples' lives. Coveting God's presence as Jesus experienced it in his life, one of the disciples asked him, "Lord, teach us to pray" (Lk. 11:1). In response, Jesus gave them the prayer whose most familiar form is found in Matthew 6:9-13:

Our Father who art in heaven,
Hallowed be thy name.
Thy kingdom come,
Thy will be done,
    On earth as it is in heaven.
Give us this day our daily bread;
And forgive us our debts
    As we also have forgiven our debtors;
And lead us not into temptation,
    But deliver us from evil.

The Matthean context makes it clear that, for Jesus, praying was not a matter of heaping up empty phrases. Jesus gave us not a prayer to say but a way of praying whose "axioms, elementary rules, and first principles" we must make "part and parcel of ourselves."[3] We do that by following the example of Paul who urged us to "pray constantly" (1 Thess. 5:17) and of brother Lawrence for whom praying meant "practicing the presence of God."[4] Since we live, move and have our being in God (Acts 17:28), prayer sensitizes us to "God with us" everywhere and all the time, whether at church or in the world. As the principles of this prayer permeate our attitudes and actions, the more we know God's self giving in our daily lives and the more we consider ourselves part of God's global family.

In the Lord's Prayer "the fundamental principles of the religion on which the gospel of Christ rests... [are] given to us, not in the cold and formal theology of a carefully considered creed, but in the warm and devotional terms of spontaneous prayer."[5] Clearly identifying to whom we pray, "Our Father who art in heaven," this prayer binds us to our Creator's global family. "Of myself I cannot be an object of the mercy of God except as I am one of the 'us' to whom God has shown it without restriction."[6] It also brings awareness that God's grace surpasses knowledge: "Jesus taught us to compare God with our best, and then to acknowledge a Mystery beyond the best which no words can hint."[7]

Furthermore, this prayer helps us see all of life in the light of God's nature, purpose, and will: "Hallowed be thy name. Thy kingdom come, Thy will be done, On earth as it is in heaven." In Jesus' day, a name signified essential nature. As revealed in Christ, God's name signifies "that kind of love known as 'agape,' the unselfish pouring out of self for the benefit of another, without thought of return."[8] We revere that name by living harmoniously in that network of interrelationships that reflects God's loving nature. Jesus called that the kingdom of God, a term that appears ninety-five times in the first three gospels. For those who accept God's rule, God's will is not something to be borne, but something to be done to expand God's gracious sovereignty into every realm of life on earth.

Finally, this prayer guides us in asking for those things needful for the doing of God's will: "Give us this day our daily bread; And forgive us our debts, as we forgive our debtors; And lead us not into temptation, but deliver us from evil." To live for God we need bread to sustain our bodies. To love for God we need forgiveness so that we may be instruments of peace. To achieve for God we need strength to persevere in our times of testing. Bread, forgiveness, strength: For these needs we must learn to pray, not only *pro me*, but *pro nobis*, for the whole world. Remember, from start to finish in this way of praying, "no limit can be set to this 'us.'"[9] That is why the Lord's Prayer is another crucial means of God's self giving within the covenant community of faith where God is busy shaping stewards.

With some new clues about "the grace of God...shown in the churches of Macedonia," we return to those newly baptized members of a covenant community where the walls of hostility between Jew and Greek, slave and free, male and female, had come tumbling down. As the community took seriously its task of nurturing these babes in Christ, the Lord's Prayer increasingly sensitized them to that larger world of "us." With new ears those Greek Christians heard about the famine-caused suffering of their Jewish Christian family in Jerusalem. With caring hearts they came to Paul "begging...earnestly for the favor of taking part in the relief of the saints" (2 Cor. 8:4). Imagine: Christians begging their leaders for the privilege of giving! A strange alchemy was at work, for water and prayer were creating global Christians eager to build a bridge of reconciliation over the troubled waters of their world.

Frank Laubach was that kind of Christian. When I heard him speak in Austin, Texas, in 1951, I was stirred by his advocacy of "the little people of our world." In the early 1960s, still on fire with those concerns, he was sharing in a prayer circle with a small group of us in Boca Raton, Florida. As he talked, he bobbled in his hands a beach ball on which had been painted a globe of the world. Suddenly, he tossed the ball across the circle where a surprised woman caught it, then heard his strange request. "Sister, please lead us in prayer and, when you have finished, pass the world on to the next person, and so on around the circle until everyone has prayed."

Stranger than the request, we heard no self-centered prayers that day. No one prayed, "God, bless me and my wife, my son John and his wife, us four and no more." Nor, "God, bless us two and that will do." Nor, "God, bless only me. That's as far as I can see." Those fabled prayers of a family, a couple, and a bachelor too often become ours when we settle for "a sweet little nest, somewhere out in the west, and let the rest of the world go by."

We often sing about "the whole world in *God*'s hands." However, that day Frank Laubach bid us pray with "the whole world in *our* hands." What a difference that made in our prayers! What a difference it would make in our prayers, our life-styles, our church budgets today! For when God's concerns become ours, our hearts will be widened to embrace the globe; no longer will they be restricted by our own affections.

That kind of praying and concern influenced Elizabeth Barrett Browning to pen these words:

> The human race
> To you, means such a child or such a man
> You saw one morning waiting in the cold
> beside that gate, perhaps...
>     [But] I call you hard
> To general suffering...


> Does one of you
> Stand still from dancing, stop from stringing pearls
> And pine and die because of the great sum
> Of universal anguish?...You cannot count
> That you should weep for this account; not you.
> You weep for what you know. A red-haired child,
> Sick in a fever, if you touch him once,
> Though but so little as with a finger-tip,
> Will set you weeping; but a million sick...?
> You could as soon weep for the rule of three
> Or compound fractions. Therefore, this same world,
> Uncomprehended by you, must remain

Uninfluenced by you...
We get no Christ from you.[10]

"You weep for what you know." How true! If we of the church are to feel the pain of our world and, behind that, the agony of God, we must get to know the world and its people. Otherwise, not comprehending our world, we will not influence it. The world will get no Christ from us; but worse, we will not discern those points of human pain where God in Christ is already at work, calling for stewards to share that work.

Some of my pilgrimage will help you understand why I weep and why I believe God uses "those who weep" to help others understand. My world really began growing during attendance at three Student Christian Movement conferences in Europe in 1948. All were steeped in prayer and Bible study, but the last one in the Swiss Alps was the most memorable. Of the forty-five in attendance, perhaps a dozen were from the United States. Christoph Hinz from East Germany became my best friend. We had much in common: both theological students; both twenty years of age and approximately the same height and build.

However, between American and European conferees there were differences, like our too many clothes, and their too few, reminding us how World War II was still limiting their access to life's basic necessities. The night before the conference ended, some of us Americans slipped into the common room after hours, and dumped our suitcases of clothes in a large pile. On top we left a note, hoping for anonymity: "Help yourselves to any of these clothes you can use."

The next morning at breakfast, Christoph came directly to me. "I want to thank you for the clothes," he began, only to be interrupted by my embarrassment at not having been able to remain anonymous. "Oh, Christoph, it was nothing!" That was true. My best clothes I had left at home lest I feel too much out of place in postwar Europe. But then his response, "To you it is nothing; but to me it was just like Christmas!"

The first time I told that story, at a student conference at Green Lake, Wisconsin, I cried, weeping for what I knew. Already that experience was beginning to change my life!

Since then my world has kept growing. With the Quakers, whose praying—long on silence and devoid of empty phrases— had long bonded them to the global family, I had my introduction to the Third World during a six-week work camp at Nativitas,

Mexico, in 1950. My principal work: helping villagers dig latrines in cooperation with the Mexican Health Agency as a first step toward improving community health. Again, as a Quaker work-camper at Gaimersheim, Germany, in 1951, I worked alongside World War II refugees from Eastern Europe helping build homes. *Our* praying and *my* bonding to the global family were inextricably linked.

More praying and bonding characterized four and a half years of global service and residence across the next three decades. Most of that was in Jamaica and Japan, including a return from Japan via southeastern Asia, the Middle East, the Soviet Union, and Europe. But let me focus on the experiences that the decade of the 1980s provided in India and Nicaragua.

Christian Medical College and Hospital stands today as "God's sacrament" in Vellore, India. Conceived and nurtured in prayer, it has been shaping thousands of stewards since 1900, among them Drs. Mabelle and Raj Arole (see Chapter 1). Its story begins with Ida S. Scudder, one of a remarkable family, forty-two members of which through four generations gave a total of nearly eleven hundred years to missionary service in India.

Born in India in 1870 to Sophia and John Scudder, Ida returned with her family to the United States in 1878. In 1882, the board appealed to her doctor father to return alone to India, leaving his family in the care of relatives. Two years later his wife joined him. Embittered by losing both parents to India by the time she was fourteen, Ida knew one thing for sure: She would never be one of "those missionary Scudders."

Nevertheless, in 1890 Ida went to India, in answer to her father's cable, "Come immediately. Your mother ill and needs you." While there, many experiences played upon the heart of that Scudder rebel, climaxing one evening when three husbands came seeking her assistance for their wives, two facing death in child-birth, the other from critical illness. "But it's my father you want, not I," she had replied. "He's the doctor. I'm not even a nurse. I can't help you." Because their religious traditions would permit no man to care for their wives, each spurned her offer and walked off into the night.

That night two Idas struggled with each other, one rebelling with every fiber of her body, the other tremulously aware. One considered it nonsense that God should speak to people; the other's heart agonized over so much human need. One felt there was nothing one person could do; the other wondered about the three women dying less than a mile away for want of a woman doctor. One was certain she could not fill that need even if God were to ask her; the other was certain it was God who was asking.

The next morning three women had died. Ida wept the morning hours away, but by noontime she got up, washed her face, and walked briskly to her mother's and father's room. "I'm going to America and study to be a doctor," she announced steadily, "so I can come back here and help the women of India."[11]

Now begging earnestly for the favor of relieving suffering in her global family, Ida went back to India as a doctor in 1900. Six months later her father was dead, and she was in charge of his work. Today her one-bed hospital has 1250 beds, and is the greatest medical center in all Asia. Although financial support and encouragement come from forty Protestant denominations in ten countries, only about a dozen of the three thousand members of the staff come from abroad. A school of nursing, a medical college, and programs for therapists and paramedics are now training twelve hundred students. Beyond Vellore, a leprosy hospital and rural health and development programs flourish.

Amidst such growth, whence the commitment to healing ministry? Dorothy Clarke Wilson answers: "Only the white dome of the chapel remained as it had been in the beginning, the heart through which all the energy of this vast organism was poured."[12] Nine weeks as volunteers there in 1982 enabled my wife Lois and me to experience firsthand the powerful role of prayer in the life of that great medical college and hospital.

Leaving India that summer, Lois and I spent an intensive weekend with the Missionaries of Charity in Calcutta. That included visiting four centers of their work, doling out soya milk powder, and helping feed some too weak to feed themselves at the Home for the Dying. Where does one find resources to keep ministering there? Although Mother Teresa was not there, I remembered her answer in the film, "Everyone, Everywhere": "I take Jesus into my body every morning at the Mass, and it is he who serves through me!" Theologically, Protestants say it differently, but what a testimony to grace sufficient for her daily needs!

In August 1986 I visited Nicaragua with Witness for Peace and Habitat for Humanity, two groups earnestly seeking ways to relieve suffering that has been going on for a long time. U.S. Marines were involved there from 1912 to 1933, and U.S. diplomats from 1935 to 1979 while the Somozas made themselves the wealthiest family in Central America. Who was concerned about Nicaragua during all that time when most people existed on rice, beans and tortillas day-in, day-out; drank disease-laden water; and died for lack of medical care?

How those Nicaraguans have suffered since 1972! That year's earthquake killed 10,000; the 1978-79 insurrection that ousted the Somoza regime killed another 50,000; and the U.S.-sponsored contra war killed 30,000 more. A comparable percentage of the U.S. population would see more than six million dead! That figure has numbing symbolism to us of the twentieth century.

Before going to Nicaragua I had learned that 95 percent of the people were Christian. But I had not anticipated being welcomed as a Protestant to share in five Roman Catholic Masses at Achuapa, Chicopipe, Lagartillo, and Managua. I prayed with Presbyterians in Jinotega, representatives of the Evangelical Committee for Aid to Development in Leon, and Habitat volunteers at German Pomares. There, in February 1986, Presidents Jimmy Carter and Daniel Ortega had prayed together as they dedicated Habitat houses. Surely you understand how God's self giving through prayer has made me more aware than ever that I am one of the "us" that comprises God's global family.

However, all the poor are not "out there" in other lands. Growing numbers are in our own land as I learned firsthand during ten years as pastor of Memorial Boulevard Christian Church in inner-city St. Louis, Missouri. On a hot July day in the late 1970s, a man came to our church seeking food. Since our food bank was empty, I asked if he could make it till tomorrow when supplies would be replenished. He assured me that he could.

Then he asked, "Anything I can do to help around the church? I was once a church custodian. I really loved that job because I love the Lord." What a nice surprise! Our custodian was sick. The trash needed moving to the curb for Tuesday pickup. Off he went to tackle that job.

Sometime later it struck me that I had failed to tell him on which street the trash would be picked up. I went to a window to see where he was carrying it. Just at that moment one of those bags ripped open, emptying its garbage from a church barbecue. Suddenly I saw a hungry man gorging himself on bits of meat, bread and slaw. I wanted to cry out, "Stop!," yet I could not, for this proud man had assured me he could make it till tomorrow.

I wept as I watched. When he finished and started toward the wrong street with the bag, I rushed out, calling, "Oh sir. I'm so sorry I failed to tell you where to carry the trash. Let me help you carry it to the other street." "No problem," he replied. "I'll do that myself." Before I got back, the job had been finished and he was gone.

That night I went shopping and had three bags of groceries for him when he returned the next day. While driving him to his home, he once more offered help. Again I accepted, welcoming help in restocking our food bank and, even more, wanting to know more about him. After helping carry the food into his home, I saw him plug in his refrigerator. As he opened the door, the light illuminated a pan of wilted weeds.

On our way to pick up the supplies, he told again about his days as a church custodian and then, these words: "The Lord's really been good to me. Yesterday, when I was really desperate, he brought me to your church and to a kind man!" What he did not know was that I had seen him eating garbage less than twenty-four hours before.

I shall never forget that man and his words, for they penetrate the consciences of us who so often major in poortalk even as we live in luxury. Sensing that God's self giving had helped him and me, too, to consider ourselves part of the global family, the warm thought occurs that God had arranged a family reunion for the two of us! He felt himself blessed, as he said; but I am certain the greater blessing was mine.

My experiences lead me to weep for what I know. They help me identify with those Macedonians who came to Paul "begging earnestly for the favor of taking part in the relief of the saints." In Christ they had been given a new identity and a new global family. When they learned about the suffering of their sisters and brothers in Jerusalem, they wept!

In his letter to the Romans (9:1-3) Paul shared his own weeping for what he knew. The following paraphrase based on the J.B. Phillips translation provides an appropriate testimony to ways the Lord's Prayer has helped sensitize me to our global family:

Before Christ and my own conscience in the Holy Spirit I assure you that I am speaking the plain truth when I say that there is something that makes me feel very depressed, like a pain that never leaves me. It is the condition of my sisters and brothers in the global family of God.

# NOTES

[1]Karl Barth, "The Doctrine of Reconciliation," *Church Dogmatics*, Vol. IV, Pt. I. T. & T. Clark, 1956, p. 504.

[2]James F. White, *Sacraments as God's Self Giving*. Abingdon, 1983, p. 70.

[3]Alexander Whyte, *Lord, Teach Us to Pray*. George H. Doran Co., 1923, p. 257.

[4]Brother Lawrence of the Resurrection, *The Practice of the Presence of God*. Newman Press, 1957.

[5]John F. Scott, *The Religion of the Lord's Prayer*. Abingdon-Cokesbury, 1946, pp. 7-8.

[6]Barth, *Church Dogmatics*, Vol. IV, Pt. I, p. 504.

[7]George Buttrick, Exposition on Matthew, *The Interpreters Bible*, Vol. 7. Abingdon-Cokesbury, p. 309.

[8]White, *Sacraments as God's Self Giving*, p. 14.

[9]Barth, *Chuch Dogmatics*, Vol. IV, Pt. I, p. 504.

[10]Elizabeth Barrett Browning, "Where There Is No Vision—," from "Aurora Leigh," Second Book, *Masterpieces of Religious Verse*, ed. by James Dalton Morrison. Harper & Brothers, 1948, #1561, pp. 472-473.

[11]Dorothy Clarke Wilson, *Dr. Ida: Passing on the Torch of Life*. Friendship Press, 1976, pp. 3-43. Eleven earlier printings under the title of *Dr. Ida*, copyright 1959.

[12]*Ibid.*, pp. 2-3.

# 13

## By the Cross God Challenges Us to Deny Ourselves

"I decided to know nothing among you except Jesus Christ and him crucified" (1 Cor. 2:2). In those words Paul commends to us the cross of Christ as a sign "par excellence" of God's self giving.

The cross reveals what God has done for us in Christ. "God shows his love for us in that while we were yet sinners Christ died for us" (Rom. 5:8). Even while convicting us of sin, God's amazing grace offers forgiveness as well, as John Newton knew: "'Twas grace that taught my heart to fear, and grace my fears relieved."[1]

The cross also reveals what God desires to do through us in Christ. "[Christ] died for all, that those who live might live no longer for themselves but for him who for their sake died and was raised" (2 Cor. 5:15). By dying "pro nobis," for the whole world, Christ makes each person "one of the 'us' to whom God has shown (mercy) without restriction."[2]

With that in mind, the New Testament expands the idea of the cross from the wood on which Jesus died, to the principle by which he called *all* to live: "If any man would come after me, let him deny himself and take up his cross daily and follow me. For whoever would save his life will lose it; and whoever loses his life for my sake, he will save it" (Lk. 9:23-24). Self-denial and losing one's life for Christ's sake are clearly ways we are called to live within the global family.

However, before discussing self-denial, we must talk about self-affirmation. Jesus called for that by teaching, "You shall love your neighbor as yourself" (Mt. 22:39). To be sure, self-love can easily be distorted. Some people love themselves too much, as their pride, arrogance, and exploitation of others reveal. But others love themselves not enough, as their poor self-esteem makes clear.

Virginia Satir was convinced that "the crucial factor in what happens both *inside* people and *between* people is the picture of individual worth that each person carries around" and that "the family is the 'factory' where this kind of person is made.... Feelings of worth can flourish in an atmosphere where individual differences are appreciated, mistakes are tolerated, communication is open, and rules are flexible—the kind of atmosphere that is found in a nurturing family."[3]

Jesus called all people to discover their worth and identity as children of God and as members of the global family. Only then can they celebrate their God-given gifts and decide freely how to use them for the common good. Jesus believed that God is the one who makes it possible for a person to say "I" and for all the powers that lie imprisoned within to be unchained.[4] For those locked in pride, community and caring are God's way out. For those locked in self-negation, responsible selfhood within community and caring is God's gift. God's self giving for men and women, young and old, enables fulfillment in community.

Among those who experience such God-intended fulfillment the virtue of imagination, or better yet, phantasy, always flourishes, in Dorothee Soelle's opinion. Its best illustration is found in that one whose life was an expression of true fulfillment: Jesus of Nazareth.[5]

> The phantasy of Christ is the phantasy of hope, which never gives up anything or anyone and allows concrete reversals to provoke nothing but new discoveries. The phantasy of faith holds fast the picture of a just society and never allows itself to be talked out of the kingdom of righteousness. Phantasy is...the "know how" of love. It never retires before it has achieved some new insights. It is inexhaustible in the discovery of new and better ways. It is ceaselessly at work improving the welfare of others.[6]

Dorothee Soelle further believes that the strength of Jesus arose out of his keen sense of identity and his joyous self-realization.

> Phantasy has always been in love with fulfillment. It conceives of some new possibility and repeatedly bursts the boundaries which limit people, setting free those who have submitted themselves to these boundaries which thereby have been endlessly maintained. In the portrayal of the Gospels Jesus appears as a man who infected his surroundings with happiness and hope, who passed on his power, who gave away everything that was his....

And it is this that we can learn from Christ. The more fully one is aware of one's own identity, the easier it is for him to let go of himself. His hands do not grasp vice-like that portion of existence which has come his way. Since he has experienced and can call the fullness of life eternal his own, he is not out to hold fast. He can open his hands.[7]

Proud, walled-off, empty selves grasp everything for themselves. Caring selves open their hands to pass their power and everything they have to others. Jesus calls his disciples to deny control of their lives to their proud selves so that their caring selves can take up crosses of loving concern for others, thereby infecting their surroundings with happiness and hope. Self-denial like that is the forerunner of joyous giving!

That contagious spirit of Jesus had surely infected Hiley Ward when he wrote. "The starting point in creative giving is in asking questions, and primarily one question: 'How can I give everything?'" Then, after giving assurance that he was not calling people to divorce themselves, hermit-like, from all material things, Hiley Ward rephrased the question: "How can I use everything for God?"[8]

That question really set my imagination spinning, for life is full of opportunities for giving away/using everything for God as we touch and bless others. Taking people somewhere in our cars offers possibilities to give our cars away to those persons during those journeys. Sharing family hospitality with guests provides chances to give our homes away to them while they visit within our walls. Smiling and listening are ways to give ourselves away to friends and strangers every day.

Take note that we are here talking about stewardship: giving away, imaginatively using, all we are and have in ways that honor God and bless people. Suddenly, stewardship—so limited by legalism, percentages, and careful calculations—breaks free at the ten-yard line and runs for a ninety-yard touchdown! God invites us to play the game of stewardship on all one hundred yards of the field of life—and to play it with nothing less than all our hearts, minds, souls and strength.

Hiley Ward next suggests how to maximize the joys of giving and using everything for God and others. At first, he startles us with the challenge to "be stingy for Christ's sake!"[9] Not miserly, for the world is overpopulated with unconverted Ebeneezer Scrooges, but stingy for Christ's sake! Those words call us to ask not "How much shall I give?" but "How little do I need for myself?" By economizing on ourselves, we multiply the opportunities for sharing with others. We live simply that others may simply live. Self-denial is not for one's own sake, but for Christ's sake. That is the spirit of the cross.

Albert Schweitzer knew the satisfaction of such creative self-denial. Visiting his native Alsace in 1957, he did not come on the first class section of the train. That prompted the question, "Why did you come second class?" "Because there was no third class," came his quick reply.[10] Albert Schweitzer had learned that by denying himself that little bit of comfort, he could save money that could then be used to save lives at his hospital in Lambarene, Africa. Therein lay his joy.

But stinginess for Christ's sake requires distinguishing our needs from our wants. Wrestling for three decades with this matter has led me to conclude that we human beings have three basic needs: (1) to exist; (2) to be fully human; and (3) to be uniquely ourselves. We must be careful stewards of resources to satisfy these needs.

First, the need to exist. According to Ellis Cowling, physical survival depends on eight necessities: air, water, food, clothing, shelter, fuel, fire, and medical care. Without these, we die. The world has enough of these things for everybody's need, but not enough for everybody's greed (Gandhi). Despite God's concern about human greed, few of us make it our concern. While many die for lack of food, others eat themselves to death. While many shiver, lacking clothes, others' closets are crammed with unused clothes. While many are homeless, others have multiple homes. Prayer and Cross, as means of grace, help us distinguish the difference between need and greed.

Second, the need to be fully human. Human beings are more than animals; therefore, we have needs for more than physical existence. Scripture says, and Jesus reaffirms, that we cannot live by bread alone; we live on every word that God utters (Mt. 4:4, NEB). To be fully human is to live for God and for others, not for ourselves, and to nurture the image of God within us and others. For example, we can exist without education, but "the mind is a terrible thing to waste," as United Negro College Fund ads tell us. Nations invest heavily in education to draw out their people's potentialities that are so important for national health and welfare. Resources must be allocated for educational purposes, as well as for other aspects of human development.

Third, the need to be uniquely ourselves. Paul marveled at the gifts of grace he saw, believing that "to each is given the manifestation of the Spirit for the common good" (1Cor.12:7). 1 Peter 4:10 rejoins with a fitting exhortation, "As each has received a gift, employ it for one another, as good stewards of God's varied grace." Having blessed us with gifts, God trusts us to use them as a blessing to others. Identifying, developing, and using our gifts is not only important for our own sakes, but, especially, for the common good.

Thank God, resources became available to develop the unique gifts of Anne Sullivan, a nearly blind resident of a state poor house in Massachusetts. Later, she became "the miracle worker" who helped Helen Keller burst the boundaries of her lost sight, hearing and speech. What inspiration that story has contributed to the common good of the human family![12] In each of us as well, something unique wants to be developed. Whatever it is, once released, it can be used to honor God and bless people. Stinginess for Christ's sake will also free some of our resources to help others develop and release their unique potential so that it, too, can be used for the common good.

Beyond these human *needs*—to exist, to be human, and to be uniquely ourselves—lie human *wants*. Hungry people do not have to be told that they need food. That is obvious to those involved in feeding the poor. Only when physical needs are consistently met are people free to think about other needs. Often, however, even before tending to their physical needs, they are caught up with satisfying wants, like the rest of us. In the opinion of John Kenneth Galbraith, wants are constructed by our imagination, influenced by an affluent society. Our productive economy employs advertising to "create" the wants it must satisfy in order to sell its products and in order to grow. Thus Galbraith writes, "If production is to increase, the wants must be effectively contrived."[13]

If we are to be God's stewards praying for "daily bread" *for all*, then we are called to resist temptations to live for "daily cake" *for me*. We will refuse to play out the script of the hidden persuaders which lures us to "spend [our] money for that which is not bread, and [our] labor for that which does not satisfy" (Isa. 55:2). That will not threaten the stability of our economy as some allege; for what we refuse to spend on "contrived wants" can be invested in "basic needs" that help others to live.

To be sure, this form of self-denial, if widely practiced, would require a realignment of the economy geared toward meeting human needs rather than satisfying created wants. Toward that kind of systemic change of the international economic order our Christian faith surely calls us to work. Meanwhile, instead of buying so much junk food for over-feeding ourselves, we could buy food and milk for malnourished children. Instead of buying foolish gifts for those who have everything, we could honor them by sharing necessary things with those who have almost nothing. In that process, we will discover the grace and joy hidden in self-denial. What we refuse to waste on "our" wants, that do not satisfy, can help meet others' needs, bringing them life and joy, and equipping them to contribute to the common good.

The cross by which Jesus calls us to live demands choice. In *The Cross in Christian Experience*, W. M. Clow makes that clear by distinguishing between burdens and crosses.[14] Burdens describe things that happen to us, often bringing misery and suffering. They are universal, coming unbidden to all of us at one time or another; and they are inescapable, offering us no alternative but to carry them. The good news about them is that God will supply us grace sufficient for that task.

But crosses are things we choose to carry. They are neither universal nor inescapable; some people do not have them, because they have chosen not to carry them. We can always say "no" to carrying a cross; but if we have one, it is because our grateful response to God's grace and our love for sisters and brothers in the global family constrained us to say "yes" when we took it up.

Clow's distinction has revolutionized my way of thinking about the cross by which Jesus calls us to live. No longer can I say of those coping with life's common tragedies and afflictions, "My, what terrible crosses they are carrying!" My father's early bout with polio left him with a badly crippled leg. That was not a cross, but his burden—and God gave him grace to bear it. When he chose to be a minister of the gospel, that became the cross he took up daily — and God gave him grace to carry it joyfully. We take up our crosses because the love in our hearts for God and for others will let us do nothing less.

One day a man ran up to Jesus, asking, "Good teacher, what must I do to inherit eternal life?" When Jesus reminded him of keeping the moral commandments, he replied. "Teacher, all these I have observed from my youth." Jesus looking upon him, loved him, then gave him an alternative vision of life. "You lack one thing; go, sell what you have, and give to the poor, and you will have treasure in heaven; and come, follow me." But "at that saying his countenance fell, and he went away sorrowful, for he had great possessions" (Mk. 10:17-22). "The Great Refusal" that story has been aptly called, for that man said "no" to carrying his daily cross.

How strange that our memory of that encounter so often ends there, focused on that man's sorrow, oblivious to the joyful import of "the rest of the story." As Jesus mused about "how hard it will be for those who have riches to enter the kingdom of God," his dismayed disciples cried, "Then who can be saved?" Jesus' reply, "With men it is impossible, but not with God; for all things are possible with God," prompted Peter's words, "Lo, we have left everything and followed you" (Mk. 10:23-28). "The Great Refusal" was countered by "The Great Acceptance."

Accepting Jesus' invitation involves daily cross-bearing, but it also includes amazing words of promise:

> Truly, I say to you, there is no one who has left house or brothers or sisters or mother or father or children or lands, for my sake and for the gospel, who will not receive a hundredfold now in this time, houses and brothers and sisters and mothers and children and lands with persecutions, and in the age to come eternal life.
>
> Mark 10:29-30

That biblical story still happens, as Millard Fuller's life bears witness. From his youth he was grounded in the Christian faith. However, by the time he married, graduated from the University of Alabama Law School, and entered law practice and business in Montgomery, "making money" became his obsession.

Within five years he was a millionaire, living in a gorgeous home built on twenty acres in an exclusive area, enough room for a swimming pool, barn, and pasture for saddle horses. He owned three cattle farms, totalling two thousand acres, and a cabin and two speedboats at nearby Lake Jordan. A full-time maid helped with their two children. He drove a Lincoln Continental for commuting to his office, home, farms, and cabin.

That all of this was threatening his relationship to the church, his moral standards, his health, and his marriage did not occur to Millard until his wife, Linda, left to seek counseling from a pastor in New York City. Suddenly, he began thinking about more than making money. When Linda called and asked him to come pick her up, he was overjoyed. As their time of reconciliation began, Millard writes:

> My momentous decision was already beginning to be made. And when Linda agreed wholeheartedly, I knew it was absolutely right.

We would sell our land and houses and boats and cars and cattle and horses. We would also sell the business to my partner if he wanted it, and to someone else if he didn't. And we would give all the money away.

We had gone too far down the wrong road to be able to correct our direction with a slight detour. We simply had to go back and start all over again, but this time we would let God choose the road for us.

As we began to do this, the love of Christ restored honesty to all our relationships. And our love for each other, which had nearly been lost, began gradually to return and to grow steadily stronger.

Together, Linda and I embarked on a tremendous journey of faith.[15]

How God's grace has worked through their faith since those days in 1965! Out of their struggle, Habitat for Humanity was born in 1976, committed to the vision of building decent houses in decent communities for God's people in need. These houses are then sold to the poor who return the principal invested in their houses (without interest and profit), usually on twenty-year repayment plans. Upon receipt, that returned principal is immediately reinvested in building more houses. By April 1990, Habitat had four hundred fifty-five affiliated chapters in the United States, six in Canada, three in Australia, and one in South Africa, as well as seventy-two sponsored projects in twenty-five Third World nations. Since 1976, with "all of us working together, and God at work in our work,"[16] Habitat volunteers have witnessed a modern miracle, the housing of more than five thousand families—and are busily on their way toward doubling that number!

The self-denial that made that sowing possible has brought an overflowing harvest. God has not only kept but exceeded that promise to the Fullers. Centuries before, the grace of that bountiful God had done far more than could be asked or imagined in those churches of Macedonia.

Today, the same happens wherever people give themselves to the Lord and to the Lord's purpose through the church, then begin begging earnestly for the favor of taking part in the relief of their sisters and brothers in the global family. Thank God for Water, Prayer, and Cross as means of grace that keep drawing us into covenant relationship with the empowering spirit of God and shaping us into stewards who are blessed to be a blessing.

104

NOTES

[1]John Newton, "Amazing Grace."

[2]Karl Barth, "The Doctrine of Reconciliation." *Church Dogmatics*, Vol. IV, Pt. I. I. & T. Clark, 1956, p. 504.

[3]Virginia Satir, *Peoplemaking*. Science and Behavior Books, Inc., 1972, pp. 21, 3, 26.

[4]Dorothee Soelle, *Beyond Mere Obedience*. Pilgrim Press, 1982, p. 64.

[5]*Ibid.,*p. 49.

[6]*Ibid.*, pp. 63-64.

[7]*Ibid.*, pp. 56, 58-59.

[8]Hiley H. Ward,*Creative Giving*. Macmillan, 1958, p. 147.

[9]*Ibid.*, p. 156.

[10]*Ibid.*, p. 158.

[11]Ellis Cowling, *Let's Think About Money*. Abingdon, 1957, p. 15.

[12]Robert M. Bartlett, *They Dared to Live*. Association Press, 1938, pp. 76-80.

[13]John Kenneth Galbraith, *The Affluent Society*. Houghton Mifflin Co., 1958, pp. 156, 160. Chapter 11, "The Dependence Effect," deals with modern want creation in our society, a sign that our production is geared, not toward meeting spontaneous consumer demand, but toward satisfying wants the productive process has itself created.

[14]W.M. Clow, *The Cross in Christian Experience*. Hodder & Stoughton, 1908, pp. 232-234.

[15]Millard Fuller, *Love in the Mortar Joints: The Story of Habitat for Humanity*. Association Press, 1980, pp. 52-53. See Chapter 4, "Making Money in Montgomery."

[16]From a speech by David Rowe, former chairman, Board of Directors, and now Director of Operations, Habitat for Humanity International.

# 14

## At the Table God Teaches Us Global Etiquette

After the Macedonians turned from idols to God, then made God's concerns theirs, they gave. They illustrate Waldo Beach's thesis that "all behavior is faithful, in that it is done in allegiance to and out of a trust in some object of love depended on, usually without conscious thought, to give meaning to living." This reveals a three-leveled analysis of people-in-action: "We do as we are, and we are as we love—meaning by love: ultimate attachment."[1] Understanding their new object of love to be the God revealed in Jesus Christ, we can now perceive the anatomy of the Macedonian miracle: trusting, being, doing.

Studying the verses of 2 Corinthians 8:3-5 in reverse order has revealed those Macedonians-in-action. They did not start by giving money; instead, "*first, they* gave themselves to the Lord and to us by the will of God" (vs. 5). How true: Stewardship without the steward is bare. God gets our stewardship by first claiming us and our loyalty; therefore, baptism is the means of grace that initiates us into a lifelong covenant relationship with Christ and the Body of Christ.

Upon giving ourselves to the Lord and to the church, God shapes our thinking, feeling, and being through other means of grace. The Lord's Prayer bonds us to the global family, and the Cross helps us deny ourselves in order to be a blessing to our wider family. When God's concerns become ours, we soon find ourselves, like the Macedonians, "begging ...earnestly for the favor of taking part in the relief of the saints" (vs. 4).

Then, in allegiance to and trust in the living God, we give, like the Macedonians, "according to (our) means...and beyond (our) means, of (our) own free will." Therein we truly see the Pauline ethics of response: our faith answering God's grace!

105

God provides yet another means of grace to keep us from stumbling as we participate in the outworking of God's grace in our giving. Knowing how easily we forget whose and who we are, God spreads the Lord's Table at the heart of the church's public worship. At this feast of joy we remember and re-experience God's mighty acts in creation, in history, and "in Christ," thereby recovering our identity. No wonder many Christians since the end of the first century have preferred to call the Lord's Supper the "eucharist" (thanksgiving).[2]

To assist in understanding how the Lord's Table shapes us as steward people, William Willimon suggests that we recall how some common human experiences at table have influenced us.[3] For me, very warm memories cluster around the walnut table in the dining room of my childhood home in Kentucky. I remember mom, dad, my brother, my sisters, and me sharing prayer, food, and fun there, all the while learning the manners that made our eating together more enjoyable, even as they prepared us for relating courteously to people around other tables across a lifetime.

Would that our world might learn such manners; instead, our world faces a crisis in courtesy! In 1981, the richest fourth of the world feasted on 78 percent of its gross national product, while the other three-fourths struggled to get by on the remaining 22 percent.[4] We stand in need of George Buttrick's reminder that the petition, "Our Father...give *us* this day *our* daily bread," teaches that "social righteousness is really a matter of table manners: We ought not to glut ourselves while others hunger.... This prayer asks Christ to preside at the world-table."[5]

Here is what Christ as host would see if the global family were reduced proportionately to a party of twenty at a table laden with enough food for all:

> one child, decidedly overweight, yet still eating heartily, totally unaware of others at the table with eyes riveted on him/her, watching;

> four others, well-fed and healthy, animatedly conversing as they enjoy their meal, equally oblivious to eyes focused on them, watching;

> nine others, now finished with their eating, but quite obviously wishing they might have a second helping;

> three children, gaunt, hollow-eyed, one gazing dejectedly at her empty bowl, another crying, the third watching

hungrily as others eat;

three children, listless, uncomprehending, and in the throes of dying of starvation at the very table where others are feasting.[6]

Some stuffing themselves, others starving: Such an absence of manners would turn mothers and fathers into instant teachers of courtesy. Significantly, the Lord's Table, at the center of the church's life and worship, is God's sacrament of grace "par excellence" for teaching us global table manners. Thank God the disciples remembered so much Jesus said and did at that table.

*At the Lord's Table we gain understanding of ourselves as steward people and as the body of Christ.* Properly discerning that body is essential to observing the Lord's Supper in a worthy manner, as Paul warned: "For any one who eats and drinks without discerning the body eats and drinks judgment upon himself" (1 Cor. 11:29). For me, discerning the body long meant seeing the bread as symbol of the broken body of the crucified Jesus, but deeper study convinced me that Paul also saw the bread as symbol of our participation in the living body of Christ, the Church.

Is not this Paul's clear message in 1 Corinthians? In 10:16b-17 he assigned this new meaning to the body: "The bread which we break, is it not a participation in the body of Christ? Because there is one bread, we who are many are one body, for we all partake of the one bread." In 11:20-22 he castigated those who carelessly participated in this one body: "When you meet together, it is not the Lord's supper that you eat. For in eating, each one goes ahead with his own meal, and one is hungry and another is drunk." Thereby Paul charged them with despising the church of God and humiliating those who had nothing. Then, after emphasizing in 11:29 the importance of "discerning the body," he declared in 12:27: "Now you are the body of Christ and individually members of it." Paul's focus here was not on the dead body of Jesus, but on the living body of Christ, the church, of which we are members.

"Discerning the body" therefore calls us to the steward task of "re-membering" the broken body of Christ, the church, thereby equipping ourselves for "the healing of the nations" (Rev. 22:2).

As one of my students wrestled with a book, *The Eucharist and Human Liberation,* by Tissa Balasuriya, a Roman Catholic priest from Sri Lanka, he resisted this call to help put together the "dismembered" body of the church. In the midst of his struggle I asked, "Is the Lord's Table bigger for you now than before you read that book?" After a quiet moment he replied, "Yes, it is." Later, in a term paper he wrote: "I didn't agree with everything Fr. Balasuriya wrote; but, after reading his book, I confess that I've had to put some new leaves into the Lord's Table—and I have some people sitting there who weren't there before."[7]

What an apt image for the church, the steward people of God! That "table" is an image of God's messianic banquet to which "people will come from the east and the west, and from the north and the south, and take their seats in the kingdom of God" (Lk. 13:29, JBP). God has prepared a bountiful table, wanting none to perish and all to have eternal life. That "one bread" helps us discern the one body of Christ and unites us so that together we may get the banquet hall ready and welcome all who come. That task calls us to add new leaves to our Lord's Table, re-membering the broken body of Christ, and welcoming all who accept God's invitation to come and eat.

*At the Lord's Table we learn how to nurture and equip ourselves for work as stewards.* Based on long years of character research Ernest Ligon contended that the single most important influence upon the developing character of a child was a father's conversation at the dinner table.[8] Both my father and mother figured prominently in that influence at our table. But if parents have such formative influence upon us at our family tables, how much more the conversation around the Lord's Table ought to be shaping us as Christian stewards. That table talk centers in scripture, sermon, and prayer, all testifying to the mighty acts of God as Creator, Redeemer, Judge, and Parent of our Lord Jesus Christ. At the heart of that table talk are "the words of institution": "And [Jesus]took bread, and when he had given thanks he broke it and gave it to [his disciples]" (Lk. 22:19). These four verbs describe the central actions of the Lord's Supper: take, give thanks, break, give.

These four verbs describe how life is to be lived wherever Christians go. As stewards we begin our vertical relationship with God from whom we first "take" or, better yet, "receive"; and to whom we then "give thanks." John Taylor calls this "'the eucharistic life,' the life that is built on ...an intense awareness of [God] who is to be thanked."[9] Living out of gratitude we enter our horizontal relationship with God's global family before whom we "break" bread and to whom we then "give" it. Taking and breaking bread, oblivious to God and others, perpetuates the global crisis in courtesy; but learning at the Table to be joyful stewards thanking God for what we've received, then sharing it with others, is to live eucharistically.

*At the Lord's Table we are empowered to carry out our mission as steward people in the world.* The element of the miraculous has long been associated with the eucharist, but permit me to offer a modern understanding of the miracle of the Table. After discerning the body and learning what stewards are called to do, table talk is transformed into the body language of the church and of us! Over time, God's grace changes the spoken words of institution into visible actions that shape the church's mission in the world and our participation in it. Voicelessly dramatized, they become the acted signs that bequeath new life to us and "healing to the nations" (Rev. 22:2). We lift our hands upward to God, palms open, to "take"/"receive" the divine grace and gifts that sustain life. We lower our hands, folded in prayer, to "give thanks" to God from whom all blessings flow. We then use our hands to "break" that bread and to reach out in blessing as we "give" it to others. These actions, practiced as we gather at the table, delineate the ways in which we are to live, move, and have our being as we scatter into the world.

That miracle changes table talk into body language, and Sunday ritual into weekday etiquette, in global context. Suddenly we stop going ahead with our own meals: "So then, my brethren, when you come together to eat, wait for one another...lest you come together to be condemned" (1 Cor. 11:33-34). Most families do that when unexpected company drops in at mealtime, a practice knowingly called "FHB" (Family Hold Back). How your family communicates that message I do not know, but my wife Lois occasionally does it by pressing her foot on mine under the table when she sees me reaching for two biscuits, knowing there are no more in the kitchen! That signals me to stop with one—yes, and to enjoy doing so—so that our guests might be fed.

When we share like that at church, we *stop taking communion*— and *start giving communion* instead! That happens at All People's Christian Church in Los Angeles where we were members while I was writing this book. Every Sunday the Lord's Table is spread, the words of institution shared, and God thanked for the bread and the cup. Then, row by row, the people come around the Table, break a piece of bread from the loaf, dip it in the cup, and give it to each other. We do not "take communion" for ourselves; instead, we "give communion" to one another. That kind of sharing with others beside us at the table or in the pew keeps us from thinking of communion as being "just between me and God." In this way Sunday practice at the Lord's Table will profoundly affect—and pattern—weekday performance as God's servant people in the world.

All of this gives insight into how those Macedonians gave not only according to but beyond their means. Usually that phrase enters our conversation when we talk about living or spending beyond our means. But seldom, if ever, do we speak of giving beyond our means, even though that is not altogether alien to our experience.

What parent has not foregone a coveted "want" in order to supply an urgent "need" for a child? That kind of giving does not hurt; it feels good. Or, to use table analogy, who among us has not eaten less so as to share food with friends unexpectedly arriving at mealtime? But after eating less, we left the table feeling full—and why? Because we are more than appetites with skins stretched over them, but whole persons with minds, hearts, and souls as well—and all of us got filled by breaking and sharing food with beloved friends! The common denominator of these experiences is not deprivation but exhilaration, not grief but joy. The miracle of giving always happens where love of God and others is present. Again, let it be said: That kind of giving does not hurt; it feels good.

Significantly, the stories of Jesus' feeding of the five thousand and the four thousand in the gospels are full of this spirit of love and joy. In them the early church found the kind of blessings that came through the Lord's Supper, so they couched their telling of them in the eucharistic language of taking, giving thanks, breaking, and giving. By them they were encouraged to rediscover again and again that "five loaves and two fish are never enough until you start to give them away."[10] As they gave beyond their means, mysteriously their deepest needs were met and they were satisfied.

Even greedy Jacob got caught up in this new-found joy of giving. Fearing the worst from Esau, his aggrieved brother whom he had cheated twenty years earlier, he sought to appease his anticipated wrath with a mighty gift of flocks and herds. But with a surprising "I have enough, my brother; keep what you have for yourself," Esau declined the gift, simply satisfied at being reconciled with his long-lost brother, Jacob. In response, we can scarcely believe our ears when Jacob says, "Accept, I pray you, my gift that is brought to you, because God has dealt graciously with me, and because I have enough" (Gen. 33:11). Just imagine it: Greedy, grasping Jacob freed from dissatisfied craving—and freed for thankful and generous sharing with his estranged brother Esau!

Jacob had enough—and to spare. Where the love of God and others is present, miracles really do happen!

Today, the economic miracle of Habitat for Humanity is based upon the gospel accounts of the feeding of the multitudes.

> The economic lessons we must learn from these great miracles of our Lord are, first, to take whatever is available in a given situation of need (all of it!); second, to thank God and ask for His blessing; third, to get ourselves organized; and finally, to launch an effort to meet the need with those available resources. When we move out in faith, God moves, too, and our small supplies are miraculously multiplied to fill the need.[11]

In October 1985, Enid Habitat for Humanity was born. Since then, we have experienced the "economics of Jesus" firsthand by helping six families in Enid and about eight others in the Third World move into decent houses (U.S. affiliates tithe their income to support these overseas projects). Despite an oil boom going "bust," wheat prices plunging, businesses closing or moving away, and banks failing, we have taken the available resources the people of Enid have given us, thanked God for them, then used them all in our construction work. AND GOD HAS ALWAYS PROVIDED US WITH MORE! Today, more than $100,000 invested in these properties is returning to us in monthly payments, without interest and profit, from our new homeowners. As we invest that recycled money and new gifts in more houses, we exchange knowing looks and warm smiles, much like those Macedonians must have done as they marveled over the "grace of God shown in their churches" in an "abundance of joy" and a "wealth of liberality."

When we stay close to the Lord's Table, God's grace transforms its table talk into our body language, enabling us to give, not only according to our means, but beyond our means for the sake of the world God loves so much. And then the age of miracles begins!

## NOTES

[1]Waldo Beach, *The Christian Life*. Covenant Life Curriculum Press, 1966, pp. 36-39.
[2]James F. White, *Introduction to Christian Worship*. Abingdon, 1980, p. 203.
[3]William Willimon, from my class notes at Claremont (CA) School of Theology, where he was a visiting professor in June, 1984.

[4]Arthur Simon, *Bread for the World*. Paulist Press, Copyright 1975, Revised Edition, 1984, p. 49.

[5]George Buttrick, Exposition on Matthew, *Interpreter's Bible*, Vol. 7. Abingdon-Cokesbury, 1951, p. 313.

[6]My scenario for a world-table party of twenty is based on current world population of 5 billion, 1.25 billion (25%) from the More Developed Countries (MDCs) and 3.75 billion (75%) from the Less Developed Countries (LDCs). (See Arthur Simon's 1984 statistics above; also Werner Fornos, *Gaining People, Losing Ground: A Blueprint for Stabilizing World Population*. Science Press, 1987, p. 61.) Although the first child symbolizes the United States (250 million or 5% of world total), note that 30 million U.S. citizens falling under federal poverty guidelines are undernourished. The next four symbolize the remaining 1 billion (20%) of MDC population. Lacking access to the latest LDC population, I used figures from the 1970s, allowing for higher LDC population growth and worsening conditions: Nine symbolize the "poor" (2.25 billion or 45%), three the "poorer" (750 million or 15%), and three the "poorest" (750 million or 15%).

[7]Gary W. Johnson, quoted from a term paper submitted for a class on the Theology and Practice of Public Worship at the Phillips Graduate Seminary, Enid, Oklahoma, Spring, 1982.

[8]Ernest Ligon, from an address I heard him give at the Florida Pastor's Conference in Gainesville, Florida, in the early 1960s.

[9]John V. Taylor, *Enough Is Enough*, Augsburg Publishing House, 1975, p. 62.

[10]Source unknown.

[11]Millard Fuller, *Love in the Mortar Joints*, New Century Publishers, 1980, p. 90.

# 15

## *Grace's Calling Card: Giving of Our Own Free Will*

2 Corinthians 8:1-5 contains Paul's anatomy of a miracle. Paul shows how God's grace (vs. 1) prompted some poverty-stricken churches (vs. 2), first, to give themselves to the Lord (vs. 5); to make God's concerns theirs (vs. 4); and to give liberally and freely (vs. 3). When studied in this order, as we have seen, much new meaning tumbles forth from this passage.

Another discovery is now revealed: God's grace shown in those churches was complemented by people's voluntary response. "For they gave according to their means, as I can testify, and beyond their means, *of their own free will*" (vs. 3).

Precisely! No legalistic response to the amazing grace of God is appropriate. That is why Paul wrote: "Each one must do as he has made up his mind, not reluctantly or under compulsion, for God loves a cheerful giver" (2 Cor. 9:7). God's grace obviously encourages, but does not force, that decision to be made. However, when faith responds to grace, God's power at work within that life—or within the churches—is able to do far more abundantly than all that people can ask or think (Eph. 3:20). What we cannot do, or cannot even imagine being done, God's grace working through our faith does.

That was Paul's experience. By works of the law he failed to earn God's love; but, when God got his attention and response on the Damascus Road, in that conversion he was "justified by faith in Christ, and not by works of the law" (Gal. 2:16). With other Christians in the early church he discovered that "salvation comes not through works of the law by way of what we *achieve* but through faith by way of what we *receive* from God."[1] Suddenly freed from anxious striving, he rejoiced, "For freedom Christ has set us free;

113

stand fast therefore, and do not submit again to a yoke of slavery" (Gal. 5:1).

Moreover, he knew that involved responsible stewardship. "For you were called to freedom, brethren; only do not use your freedom as an opportunity for the flesh, but through love be servants of one another. For the whole law is fulfilled in one word, 'You shall love your neighbor as yourself'" (Gal. 5:13-14).

Having been justified by grace through faith in Jesus Christ, Paul thereafter expressed gratitude for the law as a custodian that had guided and disciplined him, but only "until Christ came, that we might be justified by faith. But now that faith has come, we are no longer under a custodian" (Gal 3:24-25). Courageously, Paul replaced his trust in the law with faith in Christ and encouraged others to do the same.

In that regard Paul ventured into "stewardship education and promotion" relying solely on faith in God's grace, not in law. Many preach a theology of grace up to the Pauline "therefore" point in their proclamation; beyond that, their exhortation smacks of law. Not so with Paul, who did not rely on the money-raising methods of the community of faith in earlier centuries. Nor did he resort to gimmickry in the effort to manipulate reluctant people to give.

Instead, desiring "to be justified by faith in Christ, and not by works of the law, because by works of the law shall no one be justified" (Gal. 2:16), Paul urged the churches to use God's "means of grace" for shaping steward people. These were not seasonal emphases for annual financial campaigns but year-round ways in which the church blessed God's people as they gathered, so that they might be a blessing to the world as they scattered. Paul celebrated God's grace shown in the Macedonian churches not only in the joyful liberality of their giving but also in the shaping of the stewards who did that giving. A review of the previous four chapters reveals how God's self giving brought those Macedonians up in the Spirit so they would know the meaning of justification through faith in Jesus Christ.

God used baptism to initiate the Macedonians into covenant relationship with Christ and the church. They first responded by giving not an offering but themselves to the Lord and to the church and its mission. "Themselves" included not part but all they were and had. Baptism by immersion aptly signified their total commitment, giving them a new identity and vocation. Their new way of being in the world made them part of "the stewardship of all believers."[2] Living into that baptism and exercising that stewardship involved them in a lifelong covenant to love the Lord their God with all their hearts, with all their souls, with all their minds, and with all their strength (Mk. 12:30).

God used the Lord's Prayer to raise their consciousness of and their love for the wider global family. Learning of God's purpose to unite all things in Christ, they yearned to bridge the chasm between Jewish and Gentile Christians by sharing in the relief of the saints in Jerusalem. Their covenant to love God expanded to love their neighbors as themselves (Mk. 12:31).

God used the Cross to call them to self-denial, enabling them to live no longer for themselves but for Christ and for others (2 Cor. 5:15). The magnificent obsession of organizing life so as to help satisfy their neighbors' needs gripped them. Life's meaning shifted from "being served" toward "serving" and "giving their lives for others" (Mk. 10:45).

God used the Lord's Table to help them bring all these learnings together in courtesy befitting the global family: praising God from whom all their blessings flowed, and living out of that gratitude; being aware of the other family members at the table so everybody received enough to eat; and seeing themselves as stewards who shared the table's bounty with others and took no more for themselves and their families than they needed.

Finally, God used those steward people, shaped by grace, to give joyfully, liberally, and of their own free will! As Kahlil Gibran would say, they had let God speak through their hands and smile through their eyes upon the earth.[3] Those Macedonian Christians had themselves become another means of grace, a visible word "about the grace of God...shown in the churches" (2 Cor. 8:1) and an audible "word of the Lord sounded forth from you in Macedonia and Achaia" (1 Thess.1:8). God is expecting the same of us, writes John Westerhoff:

> God has called us to be God's sacrament, God's presence and activity in human history so that the world when it looks at how we live our lives within the church will see a sign of God's purpose for human life, and when it looks at how the church acts in society will see a sign of God's will for human life being manifested in history.[4]

The experience of the Macedonian churches has profoundly influenced my developing theology of stewardship and the writing of this book. Their experience must become ours if the church today is to be the instrumentality through which God's eternal purpose, already realized in Christ Jesus our Lord, is to be made known to our world. This requires that we, like Paul and the early church, pay our due respects to the law, then dare to trust solely in the grace of God through faith in Jesus Christ. That means setting stewardship free from its captivity to law and self-serving institutional survival ends and free for God's mission of serving this world. Although that will be no easy task, let us examine more carefully some of the characteristics of stewardship shaped by grace.

A few comments about my early stewardship education are in order. Born in 1928, one of five children, my first memories are from the years of the Great Depression. Since my mother never held a job outside our home, it required wizardry to help my preacher father's salary meet all our family needs. But during those years ten percent—a tithe—came off the top of their salary every month and was given back to the church for its witness and mission. I noted that this was done, not reluctantly nor under compulsion, but joyfully. From those two practitioners of tithing, I caught that experience. Since my wife Lois and I had similar family backgrounds, we began our married life in 1952 as tithers. But we did not long remain tithers, for soon we moved far beyond that ten-percent figure in giving to the church and charities, a practice we continue to this day.

So, I am indebted to the experience of tithing in my own pilgrimage. Nevertheless, as time has passed, I have said less and less about tithing and more and more about joyful and faithful stewardship of all that we are and have. It is unfortunate that tithing and stewardship are so often regarded as synonymous. A familiar story will serve to highlight some of my deepening concerns about these matters.

Zacchaeus was a chief tax collector, and rich. His wealth, gained dishonestly in a despised job, had not made him happy; instead, his townspeople scornfully called him sinner. Perhaps he had heard that a teacher named Jesus was saying some interesting things about wealth and about happiness. Maybe that is why he climbed up into a tree to see him as he passed through town. Surprisingly, Jesus came, saw him, called him down from the tree, and invited himself to his home! There Zacchaeus received him joyfully for a visit that changed his life.

There is no record of their table talk, but three sentences tell of its happy consequences: "And Zacchaeus stood and said to the Lord, 'Behold, Lord, the half of my goods I give to the poor; and if I have defrauded any one of anything, I restore it fourfold.' And

Jesus said to him, 'Today salvation has come to this house, since he also is a son of Abraham. For the Son of man came to seek and to save the lost'" (Lk. 19:8-10).

Late in 1986 this familiar story came alive for me with this happy thought: Thank God Jesus did not challenge Zacchaeus to tithe! That quickly prompted the question: Why? In search of an answer, I take comfort in Paul's exhortation, "Have this mind among yourselves, which is yours in Christ Jesus" (Phil. 2:5). It is my hope that my reverent speculation about this story's meaning may stimulate yours so that it may speak the word of God afresh to the church today.

*Jesus did not challenge Zacchaeus to tithe, because Zacchaeus needed first to mend his broken covenant with God; and, until he decided to do that, nothing else could make him whole.* God's primary concern was not Zacchaeus' money, but Zacchaeus. His ill-gotten gain was a symptom of his crisis of loyalty. After falling in love with the idol, mammon (material wealth and possessions), and being shaped by its debasing influence, he had acted in violation of the common norms of justice and compassion. So Jesus may have talked with Zacchaeus about getting his priorities straight by trusting in God alone, knowing that "no servant can serve two masters, for either he will hate the one and love the other, or he will be devoted to the one and despise the other. You cannot serve God and mammon" (Lk. 16:13). Surely Jesus challenged Zacchaeus to exercise his own free will to turn from that idol to serve a living and true God.

*Jesus did not challenge Zacchaeus to tithe, because he really believed God's grace at work in Zacchaeus could do far more than all that Jesus himself could ask or imagine.* Preveniently, God had already been at work in Zacchaeus before Jesus came to town, troubling his conscience about his ill-gotten gain, haunting his memory with almost forgotten scriptures about justice and compassion, tormenting his mind with the forlorn faces of the poor, and nudging him to climb that tree. Then, while he was wrestling with God, Jesus came into his life. That joyful visit helped him see redemptive possibilities in himself. More than a sinner, he was a son of Abraham and an heir of God's promises. Even his wealth, dishonestly earned, selfishly spent, and cruelly invested at heavy interest, might still be redeemed by being given away to the poor and oppressed. More than filthy lucre, it could be a means of grace to heal and bless. Suddenly, the amazing grace of God gave that wretched man a new identity and vocation as a son of Abraham, blessed by God to be a blessing.

*Jesus did not challenge Zacchaeus to tithe, because children of Abraham are called to live by faith, not law* (Gal. 3:6-14). He knew Zacchaeus needed time with God to work out more fully the implications of his new identity and vocation. Later, when Christ came into Paul's life, Paul was converted from slavishly following prepackaged laws guaranteed to fit all situations to living and walking by the Spirit (Gal. 5:25). Afterward he had gone into Arabia to confer not with flesh and blood but with God who had called him through grace (Gal. 1:15-17). Having tasted the freedom of life in the Spirit, Paul could never again submit to a yoke of slavery. As God had blessed Abraham so that he would be a blessing, Jesus knew God would also bless Zacchaeus and Paul, both of whom were sons of Abraham. Having been blessed during forty days in the wilderness after his baptism, Jesus also wanted Zacchaeus to have time with God, understanding more fully his new identity and vocation. Jesus, not about to upstage God by offering Zacchaeus a prewritten script for his life, encouraged him to receive in faith God's guidance.

*Jesus did not challenge Zacchaeus to tithe, because, given his great wealth and people's great need, he could do so much more.* Whatever that might be, Jesus left to God's grace and Zacchaeus' own free will. But of the Zacchaeus who responded, it can aptly be said: "For if a man is in Christ he becomes a new person altogether—the past is finished and gone, everything has become fresh and new. All this is God's doing" (2 Cor. 5:17-18a, JBP). This despised tax collector, scorned as a sinner, had experienced the love of God while he was yet a sinner. Though small of stature, he now stood tall, warmed by acceptance, forgiveness, and the chance to begin life all over again.

Watch out for people who have been forgiven much! Not always, but more than sometimes, they see other lost, lonely and despicable ones through new eyes, looking for ways to bless them as they themselves have been blessed. So Zacchaeus, having been forgiven much, loved much. "Behold, Lord, the half of my goods I give to the poor; and if I have defrauded any one of anything, I restore it fourfold" (Lk. 19:8). The old wineskins of the law could not contain the new wine of his joy and generosity. That being true, thank God Jesus didn't challenge Zacchaeus to tithe!

The experiences of Paul and the Macedonians and of Jesus and Zacchaeus challenge churches clinging to law in their practice of stewardship to take the leap of faith toward stewardship shaped by grace. That leap, no easier for us than for Paul and the early Christians, requires proclaiming salvation by grace through faith in Jesus Christ rather than by works of the law. That means trusting

God's grace that we *do not* control rather than programs and formulas that we *do*. As we do that, through faith, God's power at work within us will do far more abundantly than all that we ask or think. Not by legalistic prescriptions, but by God's Spirit, glory will come to the church, not from what we *achieve* but from what we *receive* from God.

This leap of faith makes all of life the arena of our stewardship and starts us singing: "The earth is the Lord's and the fulness thereof, the world and those who dwell therein" (Ps. 24:1). Unfortunately, tithing often spawns talk about "the Lord's part" and limiting giving to only ten percent of one's money. But the Lord of all holds us responsible for the whole "money game." *Money earned* by exploiting the poor or from industries whose pollution and products curse life displeases the Lord who requires us "to do justice, and to love kindness, and to walk humbly with [our]God" (Mic. 6:8). *Money spent* on revelry and luxurious life-styles (Am. 6:4-7) while the poor are trampled upon and brought to an end (Am. 8:4-6) is offensive to God. *Money invested* in corrupt business enterprise may gain wealth, but it also incurs guilt in the sight of our righteous God (Hos. 12:7-8). *Money given*, if it be the symbol of life lived in ways that honor God and bless people, causes light to rise in the darkness (Isa. 58:6-12). No wonder Jesus talked so much about money, for it is a crystallized expression of the use we make of our time, talent, and interest. *Stewardship means using all we are and have to honor God and bless people.* Salvation came to Zacchaeus on the day he began that happy pilgrimage.

This leap of faith toward a stewardship shaped by grace requires heavy dependence on the Lord for guidance in church program and budget planning. Too often those plans are based on the conventional wisdom that "charity begins at home"; on last year's precedents; on next year's anticipated membership growth and the estimated additional pledge support that will bring; and the state of the economy. Then our praying really begins, asking God's blessing on *our* work and *our* budgeted goals. I wish that were a parody, but I know it is not.

John Pritchard found a better way to chart his future course. Nearing retirement in the late 1970s, he seemed to "have it made": graduate of both Princeton and Harvard, successful contractor, proud husband and father. But happy he was not, and soon he was wondering out loud to his minister what he could do to bring more meaning into his life. Surprisingly, his minister advised a prayer retreat at the Church of the Savior in Washington, D.C., from which this would-be activist returned, committed to spending two hours a day meditating and journaling.

Then, about a year later, his preacher made another suggestion that took him to Americus, Georgia, for a visit with Millard Fuller. The previous year had slowed the pace of his life enough so that he saw God at work there with Habitat for Humanity and heard God's call to join the work party. "There's no more burn-out for me now," John has told me as he directs Habitat/Kansas City. Elsewhere he has said, "I've spent much of my life building second homes for the rich. I intend to spend the remainder of my life building first homes for the poor."[5]

That suggests another thing about this leap of faith toward stewardship shaped by grace. Recognizing that our lives and resources are not our possessions but a trust from God, we, too, will seek God's guidance in clarifying our vocations, and increasingly Jesus' "job description" will become ours as well:

> The Spirit of the Lord is upon me,
>> because he has anointed me to preach good news to
>> the poor.
> He has sent me to proclaim release to the captives
>> and recovering of sight to the blind,
>> to set at liberty those who are oppressed,
>> to proclaim the acceptable year of the Lord.
>>> Luke 4:18-19

But are our churches channels through which the "Zacchaeus" in you and me can share resources with our world's poor? Even "outreach" dollars are more geared to serving us on regional and national levels than to serving the poor at home and abroad. James Stewart warns, "If our congregational life ever becomes an end in itself, if we become introverted ecclesiastically and satisfied in our introversion, if our horizon is this society of ours, this building, this minister and people, this particular spiritual family circle, we are on the road to perdition."[6]

Twenty-six years as a pastor convince me that church budgets enabling the "Zacchaeus" in us to reach out in blessing to the poor are crucially important in helping people give liberally and freely. And Charlie Shedd agrees:

> "Verse after verse, passage on passage, wisdom sayings, stories, the words of Jesus himself. And all delivering the

same message: God is looking for channels through which he can pour his blessings to a needy world.... The basic principle is the same—big church, little church. When the outlets are right, the Lord provides plenty at the inlets."[7]

Hopefully, it is becoming apparent why Jesus, Paul, and all the Apostles never made tithing the basis for Christian giving. Richard Foster says it this way: "The tithe simply is not a sufficiently radical concept to embody the carefree unconcern for possessions that marks life in the Kingdom of God.... It can never bring the freedom and liberality which is to characterize economic relationships among the children of the Kingdom."[8]

Ronald Sider sees the economic life of the early church being shaped not by law but by grace, not by tithing but by "koinonia." That Greek word, "koinonia," is variously translated to describe *fellowship* with the Lord Jesus (1 Cor. 1:9), *participation* in the blood and body of Christ (1 Cor. 10:16), and the *contribution* from the poverty-stricken churches of Macedonia for the poor among the saints at Jerusalem (Rom. 15:26). Consequently, "oneness in Christ for the earliest Christian community meant unlimited economic liability for, and total economic availability to, the other members of Christ's body."[9] Perhaps John Wesley said it best of all:

"I do not say, be a good Jew; giving a tenth of all you possess. I do not say, be a good Pharisee; giving a fifth of all your substance. I dare not advise you, to give half of what you have; no, nor three quarters; but all! Lift up your hearts, and you will see clearly, in what sense this is to be done...."[10]

Suddenly, a heartening insight dawns: Although many among us in our society and all across our world are too poor to tithe, all of us, poor and rich alike, can give/use all we are and have in ways that honor God and bless people. Paul's "grace-full" principle of equality challenges—and fits—all people:

For if the readiness is there, it is acceptable according to what a man has, not according to what he has not. I do not mean that others should be eased and you burdened, but that as a matter of equality your abundance at the present time should supply their want, so that their abundance may supply your want, that there may be equality.

2 Corinthians 8:12-14

122

Some disagree that people are ever too poor to tithe. But my experience in the Third World and inner-city St. Louis exposed me to people whose poverty I had wittingly or unwittingly helped to create and whose liberation from it still receives too little of my time and resources. Luke's biting words to first-century scribes and Pharisees jump across the centuries: Woe to you twentieth-century religious leaders! For you load people with burdens hard to bear, and you yourselves do not touch the burdens with one of your fingers (Lk. 11:46). Watching poor folks in St. Louis facing the winter choice between "meat" and "heat," I could not lay on them the burden of tithing that would have forced them to forego both at risk of health and life.

When the stewardship of abundance through programs of our church supplied the needs of the poor, we were always doing more than feeding the hungry and clothing the naked. We were using that which God had entrusted us to break and share with others to help them exist, thereby making possible the stewardship of their gifts for the common good of their families and of our community and world. The poor are always more than poor; they are God's children, designed by God to play a special role in the life of our world. Literally, we were being stewards together, working in solidarity and sharing in a mutual partnership of both giving and receiving.

In such moments of sharing and of grace we experience love as the fulfillment of the law, love as an exhilarating sense of equality and of being one in the global family of God. But we also confront a kind of paradox, according to John Knox; for, in asking for love, Christ asks more than any legal code asks. Yet, while love is more demanding and costly,

> at the same time it is less irritating and burdensome. This last is true because love, as Jesus taught it, *is* God making himself known *in our hearts:* when we feel the demands of love, we feel them *from within....* One who merely obeys rules is trying to save himself; one who loves is trying to serve God. The one obedience is slavery; the other 'perfect freedom.' And this is true because what we call 'freedom' is really our experience of belonging with *heart, soul, strength,* and *mind* to what we know is worthy to possess us; and what can that be but the God who made us and made us for himself?[11]

So praise God from whom all blessings flow!

Praise God for those Macedonian churches who "gave according to their means...and beyond their means, of their own free will" (2 Cor. 8:3).

Praise God for Zacchaeus and his happy words, "Behold, Lord, the half of my goods I give to the poor; and if I have defrauded any one of anything, I restore it fourfold" (Lk. 19:8).

Praise God for the promise of Ephesians 3:20-21: "Now to [God] who by the power at work within *us* is able to do far more abundantly than all that we ask or think, to [God] be glory in the church and in Christ Jesus to all generations, for ever and ever. Amen."

## NOTES

[1]Dwight E. Stevenson, *Preaching on the Books of the New Testament*. Harper & Brothers, 1956, p. 103.

[2]Douglas John Hall,*The Steward: A Biblical Symbol Come of Age*. Friendship Press, 1982, pp. 126-129.

[3]Kahlil Gibran, *The Prophet*. Alfred A. Knopf, 1923, pp. 20-21.

[4]John H. Westerhoff III, *Building God's People in a Materialistic Society*. Seabury Press, 1983, p. 37.

[5]Millard Fuller, with Diane Scott, *No More Shacks: The Daring Vision of Habitat for Humanity*. Word Books, 1986, pp. 111-112.

[6]James S. Stewart, *Thine Is the Kingdom*. Charles Scribners, 1956, p. 53.

[7]Charlie W. Shedd, *The Exciting Church Where They Give Their Money Away*. Word Books, 1975, pp. 13, 16.

[8]Richard J. Foster, *Freedom of Simplicity*. Harper & Row, 1981, p. 50.

[9]Ronald J. Sider, *Rich Christians in an Age of Hunger: A Biblical Study*. Inter-Varsity Press, 1977, p. 101-107.

[10]John Wesley, from "The Danger of Riches," *Arminian Magazine*,1781, quoted by Hiley H. Ward, *Creative Giving*. McMillan Co., 1958, pp. 54-55.

[11]John Knox, Exposition on Luke, *Interpreter's Bible*, Vol. 8. Abingdon-Cokesbury, 1952, pp. 217-218, 193.

# Conclusion

# Needed: Stewards to Set "A Hostage Word" Free

"Is there anything on the native ground of my own experience my biography, my history—which testifies to the reality of the holy?" asks Sam Keen in his book, *To a Dancing God*. Then he continues, "If we can discover such a principle at the foundation of personal identity, we have every right to use the ancient language of the holy, and therefore, to mark out a domain for theological exploration."[1]

This book proposes that being "stewards shaped by grace" is a principle of identity and vocation meriting such theological exploration. How do we go about being "good stewards of God's varied grace?"(1 Pet. 4:10). "My biography, my history" cannot be told without bearing witness to the grace of God at work in my life as person and ours as family; in my service to the church as pastor, missionary, and seminary professor; and in ecumenical social witness as a concerned citizen of our nation and world. Some of that has been shared throughout this book; more had been intended in a hoped-for Part IV. However, space constraints suggest that that might better be done in another book.

Therefore, perhaps it is enough for this book to set forth a theology of stewardship that urges the church to turn from annual four-week crash efforts at money-raising based on the imported gimmickry of Madison Avenue. Instead, it challenges the church to make more intentional year-round use of water, prayer, cross, and table, the means of grace by which God shapes stewards. When stewards shaped by grace are the church's gift to our troubled, broken world, they will bless everyone and everything they touch. That is this book's main message, offered as a contribution for serious dialogue in the churches.

Ultimately, that is the only way "hostage stewardship" can be set free: through the lives of stewards shaped by the grace of God. Those believers in life and the bounty of life respond to "that word," not with groans, but with gratitude, knowing full well that

stewardship is
God's grace working God's purpose out in the world
in, with and through us, who,
in grateful response to God and through faith in Jesus Christ,
enter into a covenant relationship
with the empowering Spirit of God
that blesses all of creation.


NOTE

[1]Sam Keen, *To a Dancing God*. Harper & Row,1970, pp. 99-100.